Adam returned and handed her a blue T-shirt. "Get some sleep."

"Thanks, I'll..." Her voice trailed off as their fingers touched. She took a reflexive half step back.

What was wrong with her? She'd kissed this man—really kissed him. Why did this feel so much more intimate? Because she was alone with him in a big isolated house, she decided. Not only were they alone, she was going to be sleeping in a shirt he'd worn dozens of times. The fabric felt soft in her hand and she imagined it against his skin. Unexpectedly, her heart was racing.

His eyes gleamed at her, the pupils dilating as he spoke. "I wish I had something better, but—"

"No, no. It's fine, really." An anticipatory shiver tiptoed up her spine. She could feel the air between them almost sizzle.

He gazed down at her, his eyes dark, restless with the same desire she felt. Their bodies were just inches apart. She could feel the warmth seeping from his rock-hard body to hers. It wouldn't take much, she realized. All she would have to do was make a forward move....

MERYL SAWYER

KISS of DEATH

HQN™

ISBN-13: 978-0-373-77175-2
ISBN-10:   0-373-77175-4

KISS OF DEATH

www.HQNBooks.com

Printed in U.S.A.

*The best way to love anything
is as if it might be lost.*
                    —G. K. Chesterton

This book is dedicated to my "girls":

Debbie
Marcy
Susan
And our mascot, Redd

Also By Meryl Sawyer

Half Past Dead
Better Off Dead
Lady Killer
Tempting Fate
Every Waking Moment
Unforgettable
Closer Than She Thinks
Trust No One
Thunder Island
Half Moon Bay
The Hideaway

PROLOGUE

ADAM HUNTER, YOU'RE DEAD.

Adam knew he was at death's door and his gut cramped. In less than a split second he realized his life was over.

Finished.

The other guys hadn't sensed the danger, didn't know death was a heartbeat away. Adam watched—his breath suspended in his lungs—unable to utter a word.

His body didn't seem to belong to him. It was almost as if he were seeing a film, as if this must be happening to someone else—not him. He wasn't meant to die—not now, not here.

Some distant part of his mind still functioned, warning him. Blood coursed through his veins and reality arced through him like a jolt of electricity, spurring him to action. Move! Run! But there wasn't any time to run—nowhere to run—no place to hide.

A garbled sound clawed its way out of his throat. *Duck!* In an instant his world exploded in all-consuming pain and the bleak darkness of hell.

SHREDS OF BLOODY IMAGES dissolved into the present. His uncle's chauffeur was driving Adam to Calvin Hunter's Greek villa. Adam was still too engulfed in a tide of memories to notice much as the limousine sped along the narrow road. The panicky, trapped feeling returned and surged through his body with vivid reality, then subsided as he realized the danger had passed. By some strange miracle, Adam had survived.

He'd cheated death.

The others had not been so lucky. A half ton of steel surrounding them and seven pounds of reinforced Kevlar per man hadn't protected them.

Adam hadn't managed a good night's sleep since escaping death. He thought if he could go home, he would be able to finally get some rest. Adam longed to put his head down on his own pillow and stretch out on his own bed—safe at last.

Home.

What a concept. He didn't have a home. All his so-called worldly possessions were in a storage unit, gathering dust.

He was still alive and traipsing around in paradise. He was a long way from the hellhole in Iraq where he'd come within inches of dying. Thanks to an inexplicable twist of fate, Adam had now arrived at his uncle's villa in the Greek Isles. His uncle had sent his private jet to Turkey, where Adam was supposed to be recuperating at the U.S. Air Force base.

Calvin Hunter greeted him with a smile some might have mistaken for the real deal. "Adam, how was the flight?"

Adam shrugged dismissively. He realized it was a rhetorical question. Hell, Calvin knew the flight to Siros Island on his jet had been spectacular. His uncle would expect Adam to be impressed, but once you've looked death in the eye, it's hard to be impressed. Damn near impossible.

"How are you feeling? Are you okay now?" his uncle asked, touching his arm in a way that was meant to show concern. Adam doubted his uncle was worried about him. If anything, Calvin seemed a bit nervous. He kept looking around as if he was expecting someone.

"Never better." This was a bald-faced lie, but Adam didn't know his uncle well enough to discuss how he was feeling. Maybe if Tyler were here, Adam could tell his best friend how he really felt, but Tyler was halfway around the world in California.

"Nice place," Adam said because he felt it was expected. *Nice* was an understatement—like saying Versailles was "nice." The villa must contain as much loot as Versailles, too. Security guards manned the front gate and ringed the perimeter of the walled estate. The limo that had brought him here had been armor-plated and had bulletproof glass. The man riding up front with the driver had been armed.

His uncle gazed at him for a moment with shrewd eyes. Adam tried to gauge what the older man was thinking, but didn't really give a rat's ass.

"Let me show you—" Calvin gestured with a strong hand that sported a pinkie ring with a large canary-yellow diamond "—your suite."

Adam looked down a hallway he could have driven a Hummer through with room to spare. The villa on Siros was over the top, just like the Citation jet. His uncle had always been larger than life and an enigma.

He trudged behind his uncle, still wondering why Calvin had sent for him now. His uncle had always distanced himself from their small family. Even though Calvin Hunter's primary residence was in San Diego, he hadn't bothered to return when his half brother had died four years earlier. Adam had handled his father's funeral arrangements alone. Of course his father's friends had offered to help, but there had been no other relatives at his side. He was still pissed with his uncle. Calvin had sent a floral arrangement and a condolence telegram. That was it.

He supposed that cheating death had somehow gotten his uncle's attention. That must be why he'd stepped back into Adam's life and sent the jet to pick him up.

Calvin Hunter was in his early fifties but looked a decade younger. He retained a military stride from his years in the navy as an arms specialist in naval intelligence. The hell of it was, Calvin Hunter was a dead ringer for Adam's father. Adam hadn't been able to feel much since "the incident" last month but now—seeing his uncle—memories of Adam's father resurfaced. And he hated Calvin for resurrecting the past with all its sadness.

"This is it," his uncle said as he gestured toward the open door of a suite with a sweeping view of the harbor.

Without a hint of enthusiasm, Adam muttered, "That's a killer view."

Calvin studied him with cool blue eyes, as if he were an egg about to crack. "Why don't you change into fresh clothes and join me on the terrace for a drink?" Without waiting for a response, Calvin pivoted in place, then walked away.

Adam sauntered through the room and tossed his well-worn duffel on the brocade bedspread. Fresh clothes? Yeah, right.

He crossed the marble-tiled room again and went out onto the balcony. The majestic sweep of ocean and rolling hills beyond captured his attention. The timelessness of Greece and its long history awed Adam. He was the center of his own world, but being here reminded him that the earth was bigger than one man.

Others had died needless, bloody deaths. And countless men had cheated violent ends to their lives. He wasn't unique. In the long history of this planet, Adam was merely another man who had been granted a second chance. He should be grateful, but somehow, the shock hadn't worn off yet.

Adam stood silently and gazed at the boats bobbing at anchor and the crescent-shaped stretch of cafés lining the quay until he lost track of time. The sharp, frantic barks of a dog sent him back into the suite, which consisted of a sitting area that opened through a vaulted archway into the huge bedroom where Adam had carelessly tossed his duffel.

He rummaged through his things and found a pair of jeans and a *Coldplay Rules* T-shirt. Neither were what his mother— God rest her soul—would have called clean, but he didn't possess anything better. One of the guys in his unit must have thrown a few things in a duffel as he was being Medvaced to one of the field hospitals set up in Iraq.

He scrounged around and came up with his dop kit. If his clothes weren't pristine, at least he could shave. He wandered into the bathroom and spotted the claw-foot bathtub with a handheld shower.

"When was the last time you showered?" he said out loud. His mind was playing tricks again. He couldn't remember, but he must have bathed in Turkey.

The words echoed in the high-ceilinged room. He shucked his jeans and shirt, then peeled off his shorts. They dropped to the floor beside the tub.

He turned on the taps but didn't wait for warm water before stepping into the tub. It had been over two years since his last real hot shower. The field units had cold showers, which the guys actually liked since the desert was hotter than hell. A fine spray misted over his still-bruised body. Unexpectedly, needles of scalding water pummeled his skin. He stared at the showerhead for a moment before the thought—hot water—registered. He adjusted the taps.

Using the bar of soap from the wall-mounted wire rack and a washcloth, he scrubbed his entire body twice. The shampoo on the rack smelled like peaches, but he used it anyway. His fingers told him how long his hair had gotten without him quite realizing it. He'd been overdue for another military buzz cut when he'd almost died. After that, no one bothered with his hair.

He dried himself, then found his comb in the dop kit and slicked his hair back behind his ears. It hung down to the nape of his neck. He found a throwaway razor in his kit, but there wasn't any shaving cream. He used the bar of soap to lather up.

Adam caught his reflection in the gold-rimmed mirror.

Beneath brown brows a shade darker than his hair, Calvin
Hunter's emotionless blue eyes stared back at him. Well, shit,
what did he expect? He and his father, as well as Calvin, had
all inherited Grandpa Hunter's eyes. But his father's and grandfather's blue eyes had sparkled with life and good humor. He'd
had those eyes once, too.

Dressed in the black T-shirt and jeans, he wandered down
the hall in search of the terrace. The villa was obviously old
but immaculately maintained. Potted palms with ivy cascading from their bases were dramatically placed among what had
to be authentic antiques. He spotted armed men moving
about—not quite out of sight. More guards?

"Thees way, meester," called a small man who must be one
of the servants. He pointed to a double set of French doors that
were opened onto a terrace overlooking the magnificent
harbor. The setting sun bled into the night and washed the sea
with a peaceful amber glow that reminded Adam of his childhood years in California.

His uncle, attired in white slacks and a navy sports jacket, rose
from a round garden table. He looked over his shoulder at the
house, and Adam saw the curtains move, then caught a man's
profile. One of the guards must be watching to make certain
Adam didn't harm his uncle or something. Weird. Friggin' weird.

In his uncle's arms was a small dog that had no fur on his
body except for tufts of hair on his paws and tail. His head had
some hair, and long hanks of fur sprouted from his ears. The
poor mutt was a genetic disaster.

"Feeling better?" his uncle asked in a deep baritone that
matched his military bearing.

"Ask me after I've had a drink."

Uncle Calvin gestured to a chair facing the view. "Have a
seat. What would you like?"

His automatic response would have been "beer," but he
stopped himself. "Got a good pinot noir?"

"Of course." His uncle turned to the servant and said something in Greek. The little man scuttled away.

Calvin proudly explained the goofy-looking canine was an international show champion. Not only had the dog taken Westminster "by storm," the pampered mutt had won the Frankfurt International.

Adam decided his father would have hooted at how taken Calvin acted with a dog. When Calvin had retired from the navy, Adam's father had expected him to spend time in San Diego, golfing and hanging out at the officers' club. Instead, Calvin had gone into dog shows with baffling enthusiasm.

Who'da thunk? Calvin had taken to the show circuit. He became a judge and had flown around the country to dog shows. Soon he'd gained quite a reputation and had become an international judge, sought by dog shows worldwide.

Was the freaky little dog worth a lot of money? Was that the reason for the guards? Nah, he decided. There was too much security around to be guarding one small dog. Something else had to be going on.

The servant arrived with a glass of pinot noir. Adam took a sip. He couldn't remember the last time he'd relaxed with a glass of wine.

"You're probably wondering why I brought you here."

"Didn't give it much thought."

Two beats of silence. When his uncle spoke there was a slight tremor in his voice that vanished after the first few words. "Adam, what was it like to be in the crosshairs of death?"

"I don't want to talk about it."

His uncle gazed into the distance for a moment. "I need to know—"

"What in hell for?" Adam realized he'd shouted. "Sorry. It's hard for me to talk about. My good buddies died—yet I was lucky enough to live. It's not cocktail conversation."

His uncle's gaze softened. "I didn't mean for you to think I was taking this lightly. I know it must have been…more horrible than I could possibly imagine."

Adam almost said: *Got that right.* He stopped himself in time. He wasn't firing on all cylinders here, but he could tell his uncle was anxious about something. "It was unreal. It happened so fast. I hardly had time to think."

"Yet you escaped serious injury."

"Lucky me. I can't explain it. By some miracle, I survived."

Calvin studied him for a moment, then spoke. "I think someone is going to try to kill me."

Adam wasn't certain he'd understood his uncle. He'd been pretty screwed up since the explosion. He didn't respond for a moment as he let the idea settle in his brain. Who would want to kill a man who showed dogs? He thought about the guards and the armor-plated limo. Obviously, his uncle was more than just a little concerned.

"Who? Why?"

"Telling you would only put your life in danger." He fed the dog sitting in his lap a bit of cheese from the platter of appetizers on the table. "As my only living relative, if anything happens to me…I'm asking you to investigate."

The words detonated on impact. Adam jumped to his feet, sloshing the wine over his hand. "You're serious, aren't you?"

His uncle slowly nodded. "I wouldn't ask this of you if I didn't believe there's a real—"

"You've got to tell me more. I can't help—"

"Too much is at stake. I won't put you in danger. You've suffered enough."

Adam decided not to press his uncle right now. He'd always been an insular man. Calvin would tell him when he was ready. "If anything happens, I won't give up until I learn the truth. You have my word on that."

CHAPTER ONE

"THIS IS MY least favorite stop," Miranda told Whitney with a sigh. The cousins pulled up to a mansion overlooking the Pacific on Old La Jolla Farms Road. They hopped out of the Grand Cherokee and unloaded Whitney's Golden retriever from the back. Lexi at their heels, they walked up to a dazzling limestone estate with statuesque palms accenting the motor court in front of the home.

"Don't you have enough dogs to service without a problem one?" Whitney asked.

"Brandy's a love. It's his owner who's the pill. Trish Bow-rather owns a swank gallery on Prospect Street in downtown La Jolla. She insisted on meeting you before she'll allow you to take care of Brandy. My other clients know you're my cousin and trust my judgment. Unless you screw up big-time, they'll keep you."

Miranda rang the bell and a few moments later, a patrician looking blonde in her mid-forties greeted them with a withering expression.

"Your dog's only pet quality," she told Whitney before Miranda could open her mouth to introduce them.

Without looking down, Trish dropped a long-nailed hand to the shiny head of a Golden retriever the color of warm cognac. "Brandy could have been a champion, but I just didn't have the time."

Whitney tried for a smile that didn't quite work. She knew

many show dogs had professional handlers. If Trish Bowrather had really wanted to show her Golden, she could have hired a pro.

Ever bubbly, Miranda exclaimed in her cheeriest voice, "This is my cousin, Whitney Marshall. She'll be taking over my route."

"Come in. Let's discuss Brandy's schedule."

At the mention of his name, Brandy swished his tail through the air. Lexi wagged her tail in response. Fortunately, Lexi was a lady. She made no move to sniff Brandy the way most dogs would have. Whitney had no doubt Trish wouldn't tolerate a dog who "misbehaved."

With a stiff nod, Trish showed them inside. Whitney decided the home reflected the woman. Sleek, impressive, cold.

"Just a second," Trish said. "I hope your dog is on flea medication."

"Absolutely," Miranda assured the woman before Whitney could. "Lexi's on the Program."

Whitney gave her dog a pill on the first day of every month. It protected Lexi against fleas and ticks for thirty days.

"Good." Trish studied Whitney for a moment. "Do you intend to bring your dog—"

"Her name's Lexi. I find dogs walk better and enjoy themselves more if they have a companion."

Trish considered this information, then nodded thoughtfully. They followed her inside to a living room with a floating stairway that led to the second level. A sweeping expanse of glass showcased a mesmerizing view of the ocean. Through the doors that opened onto the deck, Whitney could smell the briny scent of the sea and hear the thunderous crash of the surf on the rocks just beyond the house. The water shimmered in the midday sun, but in the distance a band of dark, ominous clouds sulked along the horizon.

In the center of the living-room ceiling, a mammoth chandelier of glass orbs tinkled in the breeze drifting in from the ocean. They sat on a pearl-gray leather sofa with accent pillows of dark charcoal in a nubby material that was scratchy to the touch. Perfectly behaved, the dogs settled at their feet. Automatically, Whitney reached down and stroked Lexi's smooth head.

"I understand you're divorced," Trish said, as if Whitney had a contagious disease.

"Yes. It was final two months ago."

Trish offered her a thin-lipped smile. "Trust me. You're better off without the bastard. I dumped mine seventeen years ago."

Whitney nodded and wished her heart was as hard as Trish's seemed to be. The serrated blade of pain went through her despite her best efforts to brace herself. Would she ever recover from Ryan's betrayal?

"I hope you took the jerk to the cleaners," Trish continued.

Actually, all Whitney had to show for nine years of marriage was an aging SUV and Lexi. Ryan had given up the Grand Cherokee easily but he'd fought hard to keep their house and a worthless piece of property out in the boonies.

"Whitney plans to open a dog spa in a year or so, when she's saved enough money," Miranda said. It was obvious to Whitney that her cousin wanted to steer the conversation away from Whitney's divorce. She knew how touchy Whitney was when it came to Ryan Fordham.

"Really?" Trish was clearly astonished. "There are already several in the area. Competition will be stiff."

"Mine will be different," Whitney replied. Why did Miranda have to mention it? She wasn't positive just what she was going to do. She'd worked for a software firm until a month ago, when they'd outsourced her job to India. With so many changes hitting her all at once, Whitney wasn't certain exactly what plans to make. She'd mentioned the spa as a *possibility*—not a sure thing.

"She's going to be using organic products to groom animals and feature holistic treatments like acupuncture," Miranda volunteered in her upbeat voice.

"I see," Trish replied with an undertone of indifference.

"Whitney's great with animals," Miranda said, filling the awkward silence.

"You're living locally?" Trish asked Whitney.

"I've moved into Miranda's place in Torrey Pines. She won't be needing it now that—"

"I'm getting married," Miranda interrupted, every syllable charged with excitement.

"Really?" Trish cocked one eyebrow. "You never mentioned being engaged."

"We've been together a long time. We just decided to make it official."

"This is what I have for Brandy's schedule." Whitney wanted to move the topic to a more professional level. There was something in Trish Bowrather's expression that said she disapproved of Miranda's plans. What business was it of hers? Clearly, she'd had a miserable experience, but that didn't mean Miranda couldn't have a successful marriage.

Whitney went through a list of activities that Miranda had given her, which included a walk each morning, a weekly visit to the Dog Spaw for grooming and a massage, a biweekly trip to the Bark Park where he could "socialize" with other dogs, a standing appointment each month with the vet for a checkup whether Brandy was ill or not and a monthly appointment with a canine dentist.

No question about it. Brandy was a gold mine. Miranda charged per visit and tacked on a mileage fee. It would be like taking care of three dogs. From what she could see, Brandy wouldn't give her any problems.

"That is correct," Trish said when she'd finished going over the schedule. "Just remember to check his paws when you pick him up at the Dog Spaw. Sometimes they forget to lacquer his claws. We want Brandy to look his best." She petted the dog's head. "Don't we, boy?"

The dog thumped his tail. It seemed obvious that no matter how snippy Trish Bowrather was, she genuinely cared about her dog. And she'd been through a divorce. Whitney wouldn't go so far as to say she liked her, but Trish wasn't as bad as she'd first thought.

"Brandy has standing appointments. They don't mind if you're a few minutes late, but for his morning walk, I need you here at nine sharp. He must be back by nine-thirty. I take Brandy to the gallery with me. We open at ten."

"I understand. I won't be late," Whitney assured her.

"If you are, I'll find someone else."

Trish gave her a few more instructions before walking them to the front door. "Tomorrow, promptly at nine," Trish again reminded Whitney as they left.

Miranda waited until they were in Whitney's SUV before saying, "See what I mean? The woman's a bitch, but Brandy is a love and Trish pays on the minute."

"I think I can handle it." Whitney thought for a moment. "Did you see all that expensive art and stuff? It makes me nervous to have a key and the code for her alarm system."

Miranda patted her arm reassuringly. "That's why I'm bonded. The insurer has transferred the policy to your name. Since I started Marshall's Pet Concierge, I've only had one problem. A woman's ring was missing after I'd spent the weekend at her home dogsitting."

Whitney groaned inwardly. Picking up animals at so many expensive homes when the owners were gone made her wary. Her cousin's company—now hers—was insured, but still…

"My insurance company paid the woman for her missing emerald ring," Miranda said. "Know what happened then?"

Whitney regretted not knowing the story. She wished they'd

been closer after Miranda had unexpectedly come to live with her family, but their personalities had been too different. Then Whitney had married Ryan. He hadn't cared for Miranda. Whitney had been stupid enough to allow her husband to drive her away from her only living relative.

"She found the ring?"

"No," Miranda replied with the smile Whitney remembered fondly from childhood, when she'd thought her older cousin hung the moon and envied the string of broken hearts that trailed behind Miranda like a comet. "A year later she reported another robbery. She claimed some expensive paintings had been stolen from her home. The insurance company became suspicious, and their investigator proved she'd never purchased them. During the investigation, he discovered she'd never owned an emerald ring, either."

Whitney shuddered. "Wow. Did your insurer get the money back?"

Miranda waved her hand. "Are you kidding? She'd long since spent it, but my rates had gone up because I had a claim against me. They refunded my overpayments and reduced my rate back to where it had been."

"We live in a litigious society. People love to sue and file insurance claims." Whitney thought a minute. "What about Jasper's house? Is that covered?"

Not only was Whitney taking over her cousin's pet concierge business, she had moved into Miranda's tiny caretaker's cottage behind a mansion in Torrey Pines, an upscale suburb just north of San Diego. Her cousin had been receiving free rent in exchange for taking care of a small dog and watching the main house. The owner had died, but his dog was still there. The executor had agreed to pay for the animal's care until a relative came for the dog later this month.

"You're covered by their home owner's insurance. Why are you so worried?"

"I wander around a lot in that big old house because I can never find Jasper and he doesn't come when I call."

"Forget calling for him," Miranda advised. "Look for him in the dog run on the side yard or under the coffee table in the living room."

"Yesterday I bumped into a credenza, searching for him. I nearly knocked over some antique that's probably worth more than I'll make in a year."

"Don't worry about it. Jasper will get used to you. He hid from me in the beginning. He's lonely and confused. He's probably waiting for his master to come home."

How sad, Whitney thought. She remembered the first days after she and Ryan had split up. She'd wandered around their tomb of a house, waiting for the door to open and her husband to return.

It had been frighteningly lonely. She could only imagine how a poor animal must feel. He wouldn't understand that his owner had died and was never going to walk him, play with him or pet him again.

"You might try bringing Jasper to the cottage to stay at night," Miranda said. "I didn't because I was over at Rick's so much, and he doesn't like dogs."

Never trust a man who doesn't like dogs, Whitney thought. She wanted to warn Miranda about Rick, but considering the mess she'd made of her marriage, how could she criticize?

"ALL SET TO LEAVE?" Whitney asked when they'd completed their pet rounds and had returned to the cottage Whitney was taking over from Miranda. They'd brought Da Vinci, a Chihuahua, with them to stay while the dog's owners were in Las Vegas. The little dog was accustomed to being carried everywhere. Whitney had him in one arm and a tote with his food and toys in her free hand.

The wind had kicked up and voluminous clouds with leaden

underbellies hovered overhead. Rain had been predicted for several days, but the fronts had blown over, leaving the ground dry during a drought that could lead to another drastic fire season.

"I have a few more things to store in the garage, then everything else will be at Rick's. Our flight to Fiji isn't until ten." Miranda's laugh sounded a little giddy. "When I come back, I'll be Mrs. Broderick Babcock."

Whitney mustered a smile. She wished she were comfortable cautioning her cousin about this man. She'd never met the attorney, but his reputation as a legal shark was well known. They were keeping the wedding a secret so his clients wouldn't panic because he wasn't ten minutes away.

The whole situation seemed a little odd to Whitney, but she told herself that this was another man—like Ryan—who put his career first. And like her ex-husband, the man Miranda was so anxious to marry didn't seem to care to meet Miranda's closest relative.

It was after dark by the time Whitney helped Miranda move the last of her things into the single-car garage behind the cottage. It was small and narrow compared to modern garages. The estate had been built in the 1920s when caretakers were lucky to have a car. Miranda's older-model Volvo was parked in the carport, which had been constructed sometime after the small garage had been built. It was time to send her cousin off, but Whitney needed to find the words to express her feelings first.

"Thanks for all you've done. I really appreciate it. I don't know what—"

"Don't be silly. You would have done the same for me." Miranda hugged her tight and held on for so long that it embarrassed Whitney a bit. She hadn't realized how much Miranda cared about her. Finally Miranda released her and opened the door to her car.

"I still want to repay you the money you spent on Mom."

"I told you before. I don't need it. Besides," Miranda added with a smile that seemed a bit melancholy, "I owed it to your mother. She took me in when no one else would. It's the least I can do." Miranda kissed Whitney's cheek and hugged her again. "Take care."

"Be happy," she called to the trail of exhaust Miranda's car left in the moist air that held the promise of rain. For some reason the silence sent a chill through her. It was probably just the oncoming storm, but a vague sense of dread kept her from moving.

You're just upset about all the changes in your life, she told herself. No, it was more than her husband's betrayal and the loss of her job that bothered Whitney. Despite the way Miranda made light of the situation, there was a lot unsaid and unsettled between them. And it was Whitney's fault.

She slowly returned to the small cottage with Lexi and Da Vinci. Boxes of her things were piled everywhere. Even though she'd spent several nights here, Whitney had unpacked only what was absolutely necessary.

The cottage consisted of a small sitting room with a kitchenette off to one side and a tiny bedroom with a bath. It wasn't much compared to the large home she'd shared with Ryan but she didn't mind. She changed out of her clothes and into a filmy Victoria's Secret nightie. She preferred their cotton nightshirts and had several. She couldn't remember where she'd packed them, so she'd put on the sexy nightgown Ryan had given her last Valentine's Day. When she found her nightshirts, she'd throw the darn thing away.

The telephone rang, startling Whitney. It must be a client needing a dog walked or something. She wended her way through the stacks of boxes just as the answering machine clicked on.

"Whitney?"

It couldn't be Ryan's voice, could it? She must be imagining this, the way she'd dreamed he'd come back to her—begging forgiveness. Saying he still loved her. In her dream, she would let him dangle before reluctantly agreeing to give him a second chance. Then she would wake up and realize nothing had changed. Her husband had left her for another woman.

"Are you there? Pick up."

She'd once loved the man behind the voice too, too well. Her throat became as taut as a bowstring, making it difficult to swallow. *Never give up so much of your heart—ever again.*

"Listen, babe. I need to talk to you." The last voice she ever wanted to hear continued to come through the small black box. "It's *really* important. Call me. You know the number."

His demanding tone irritated Whitney. Whatever was "really" important probably wouldn't mean anything to her. No doubt it was something trivial, like Ryan's lost college yearbook. He'd accused her of taking it, then he'd found it but hadn't bothered to call. She'd rummaged through dozens of boxes for nothing. Whatever he wanted this time could wait until morning.

CHAPTER TWO

ADAM JERKED UPRIGHT in bed, his hand reaching for a gun that wasn't there. Another explosion rocked the room.

Run. Take cover.

Heart battering his ribs like a fighter's punches, he lurched to his feet, then remembered where he was. Home. Well, not home exactly but close enough for government work. He had just returned to the United States and was staying in his uncle's house. His life wasn't in danger. A thunderstorm had blown in—that's all.

He groped in the darkness for the lamp he remembered seeing on the nightstand. He turned the switch. Nothing. Aw, hell. The power must be out.

Adam stood there, recalling his promise to his uncle. Should Calvin Hunter die, Adam would thoroughly investigate the circumstances, though his uncle had refused to give him any details. Now, just over two months later, Uncle Calvin was dead. The coroner's report stated a massive coronary was the cause of death.

Someone will try to kill me.

His uncle's words echoed through his head. Since being notified of his death, Adam had wondered if uncle Calvin had really died of natural causes. Heart problems did run in the family. Adam's father and grandfather had both died of heart attacks.

A jagged blast of lightning lanced through the bedroom, revealing the small dog cowering under the covers beside him.

The rain pelted the windows—fast, loud and explosive—like machine gunfire. A sharp sense of danger racked his body. He sucked in a stabilizing breath and tried to get his bearings.

What was that?

It sounded like breaking glass downstairs. Was his imagination running wild? Since nearly being killed, Adam hadn't been able to conquer this jumpy feeling. Trauma—mental and physical—did crazy things to your head. He could come undone in a heartbeat, he realized.

Had he gone over some unseen edge?

Adam fumbled in the dark until he found the jeans he'd slung over the foot of the bed and scrambled into them. He strained to catch another sound, but all he heard was the rat-a-tat of the rain pummeling the roof. Something like a cat's whisker brushed the back of his neck. He felt the top of his bare spine, but nothing was there.

The house had been broken into once already during his uncle's funeral. According to the police, all that had been taken had been his uncle's computer. The theft had fueled Adam's suspicions. The house was full of valuables. Why had a laptop computer been taken while other things had been left behind? It was possible something had scared off the burglar, and now he had returned.

Adam plunged into the darkness with a bone-chilling dread that must be a form of post traumatic stress. This was nothing. He'd been through worse and had lived to see another day.

Don't go down there! Are you nuts?

Adam refused to listen to the voice in his head. Some unseen force propelled him forward. He groped his way in the dark, tiptoeing along the corridor and venturing down the sweeping staircase to the first floor. If a burglar had broken in, he intended to surprise him. This time he would be ready. He wouldn't be trapped again.

Adam halted at the bottom of the stairs and squinted into the darkness. He'd been so jet-lagged when he'd arrived that he'd hardly noticed the layout of the lower floor. He'd headed directly upstairs and settled into one of what appeared to be several guest bedrooms. He seemed to recall a large living room with a dining room opening through an archway off to one side.

Breath suspended in his lungs, he listened to the shadows. He thought he heard something. Or maybe it was nothing. The storm was just unleashing its full fury, making it difficult to tell. He opened his mouth to call "who's there," but the words stalled in his throat. The muscles in his neck quivered. What was he thinking? Only an idiot would give away his position.

Although the area was as dark as a dungeon, he detected movement—little more than a darker shape in a pitch-black room. The burglar must have broken one of the small panes on the French doors to get into the house. He thought he saw a shadow shift and heard what might have been a muffled thump.

Adam flattened himself against the wall, anticipating being exposed by another flash of lightning. He watched the intruder, but it was impossible to tell much. Shapes were discernible only by varying degrees of darkness. The short man seemed to be wearing a raincoat and some type of cap.

The intruder had something that glinted in his hand, probably a flashlight. No. The guy would have a flashlight turned on. He must be armed with a gun or a knife. Knowing he himself was unarmed, it took Adam only a split second to decide what to do.

Legs pumping like pistons, he charged across the room and leveled the guy with a flying tackle. Thrown off balance by the powerful thrust of Adam's body weight, they went down in a bone-crushing jumble of limbs. With a whoosh, the air shot out of the prick's lungs. Thunk! The weapon hit the tile floor. He scrambled to grab the man's arms, intending to pull them behind his back and haul him to his feet. The wiry little guy contorted like a pretzel and emitted a pitiful-sounding wail, but Adam kept him pinned down.

Still trying to control the man's arms and get them behind his back, Adam's hands encountered something surprisingly soft. His fingers dug in, clutching a soft mound of flesh beneath sheer fabric.

What in hell?

His breath lurched painfully and his heart stutter-stepped. A female. No way! The two years he'd spent without a woman in his life must have backfired on him. He really *was* losing it.

Adam reached up and yanked a wet knit cap off the intruder's head. Out spilled a tangle of blond hair, bringing with it a whiff of spring-fresh shampoo. The scent distracted him for a second. The body shifted beneath him, soft—undeniably feminine. Aw, crap.

Couldn't be.

He double-checked, his fingers finding smooth skin beneath the open front of her raincoat. His thumb accidentally plunged into the hollow between her breasts. Man oh man, was she built. Not centerfold breasts, but tantalizing just the same.

The feminine smell. The soft skin. His brain reminded him that she was a thief, but his body didn't give a damn. After months upon months of seeing women covered from head to toe or clad in baggy military uniforms, his one-track mind excluded everything except the erotic signals her body was sending.

A flicker of lightning in the distance illuminated the room for a split second. He had the fleeting impression of blazing green eyes. Her mane of wild blond hair tumbling alluringly across the floor. An open raincoat revealed half-exposed bare breasts. Heat spiraled through him, pooling in his groin.

He had to steel himself to keep from running his hands all over her. She twisted beneath him, arching her hips, struggling to free herself. His body tingled from the erotic sensation. In a heartbeat the iron bulge of his sex jutted against her.

"Help! Help!" She ripped out a screech that lashed through him like a razor-sharp blade. Reality returned. This was a thief, not a woman to be seduced. What *was* he thinking? Women could be every bit as dangerous as men—a lesson he'd learned the hard way. But what were the odds of encountering two deadly women within a few months?

She shrieked again. He jerked his hands off her breasts but kept her pinned to the floor with his body. She might be a woman, wearing a weird outfit, but she'd broken into the house.

"Lemme go!"

She bucked violently and rammed her head into his chest while she unleashed a frenzy of beating fists and kicking legs in a futile attempt to dislodge him. He held fast, trying to decide how to handle this situation. Women usually didn't break into places on their own. A man must be lurking somewhere nearby. She cut loose with another scream that could have been heard on the far side of hell.

"Shut up!"

She clawed his face and speared at his eyes, but he ducked in the nick of time. Her fingers caught the base of his neck, raking down the tender flesh.

"Cut it out!" His nose was just inches from hers, and he had the impression of an oval face and a trembling lower lip.

"Get off me!"

She thrashed and tried to knee him in the groin but he held her down. He needed to tie her up with something while he called the police. She grabbed a fistful of his hair and yanked. "Lemme go!"

With one hand, Adam twisted her wrist and broke her hold. "Don't make me hurt you."

She bit his arm, sinking her teeth into his flesh, but he
didn't relent. "I've got you outweighed by a hundred pounds,"
he told her from between clenched teeth. She wasn't very big,
but she was a hellcat. "This is a fight you can't win."

She bit his arm again, clamping down for all she was worth.
Pain shot up to his shoulder and he bent double, certain she'd
drawn blood. Her teeth were still attached to his arm. With both
hands he grabbed her neck to frighten her and make her let go.
Suddenly her body went slack.

He hadn't choked her too hard—had he? The bile rose up
in his throat. He hadn't meant to hurt her—just stop the
vicious biting. He released the woman and jumped up, dis-
gusted with himself.

She shot to her feet and torpedoed away. The little faker
wasn't escaping from him. He rushed after her, caught her in
two long strides and grabbed her by the shoulders, then locked
his arms around her. For a moment they moved together like
dancers. She kicked backward, slamming her heel into his
shin and shrieking like a demon. Undoubtedly she was attempting to alert her companion and get his help. He must be
outside, where the storm masked the ruckus.

"Goddammit," Adam roared. He hauled her backward, accidentally stumbling into the sofa and losing his balance. They
landed on the cushions, but this time she was on top, still
braying like a pissed-off mule.

"Don't you dare hurt me."

"I'm not going to hurt you." He pushed her off him. They
were side by side, breathing like marathon runners. It took him
a second to tell her, "Just shut up and stay put while I call the
cops."

"*You're* calling the police?"

"Hey, I don't care if you are a woman. You broke into this
house—"

"No, I didn't." Darkness obscured her face but he felt her

long hair whipping across his nose as she turned on him. "You're the one who shouldn't be here."

"What?" Adam was dead certain she was going to scream again. He put his hand over her mouth and anchored her sexy bod in place with the weight of his leg. "Listen. I'm Adam Hunter. I inherited this house from my uncle. I have every right to be here. Who the hell are you?"

He felt her soft lips moving beneath his palm. He slowly lifted his hand. And waited for another bone-rattling shriek.

"I'm Whitney Marshall. I live in the caretaker's cottage. I just came in to get Jasper."

Jasper, the butt-ugly show dog he'd first seen at his uncle's villa in Siros. The little mutt who'd crawled in bed with him the moment Adam had turned down the covers. Could she be telling the truth? Was she taking care of the dog? "I heard breaking glass."

Two beats of silence. "I know. I knocked over something with my umbrella while I was looking for Jasper so I could feed him."

"You weren't calling Jasper."

"It doesn't do any good. Jasper won't come. He usually hides under the coffee table."

"What about the weapon in your hand?"

"Weapon?" Hostile silence, then, "That was my umbrella."

Umbrella? Shit. He lifted his leg off her, reluctantly admitting, "I guess I made a mistake."

"Do you always act like a raving lunatic when you make a mistake?"

She attempted to climb over him, and his sex-starved body again kicked into overdrive. She was caught up in the raincoat and what little she was wearing beneath. Her soft, full breasts brushed his bare chest. She jerked back and he expected her to hit him…or bite him again. She scuttled sideways and crashed to the floor, then scrambled to her feet and charged off into the darkness.

Adam slowly rose, scalp prickling, arm throbbing, blood trickling down from the base of his neck onto his chest. He could still smell her perfume and feel her sexy body beneath his. Of all the freaking luck.

CHAPTER THREE

SWEATING AND PANTING, her heart thundering painfully against her ribs, Whitney raced out into the downpour. She managed to reach the cottage, slam the door shut behind her and quickly lock it. She could still feel the brute's weight crushing her, his huge hands locking around her neck in a death grip. She'd never been forced to physically defend herself until tonight.

Squeezing her eyes shut and leaning back against the door, she willed her body to stop shaking. She hadn't been able to get a good look at the creep, but even now she could see his fiendish eyes glittering as if he were on some controlled substance. His features had been obscured by the darkness but she had the impression of white teeth the size of tombstones.

Just when she thought her life was turning around this had to happen. She'd counted on living here, but with that monster in the main house, it would be impossible. She could understand him mistaking her for a burglar—after all, the house had been hit during Calvin Hunter's funeral—but the creep's marauding hands…inexcusable.

The big goon probably had a felony record for sexual assault. She heaved a sigh, attempting to catch her breath, and assured herself the man was nothing more than a letch. Still, how could she live here with him so close? She would never get a good night's sleep.

Where could she go? Her bank account was down to less than a hundred dollars. Her only alternative was to hang in there until Miranda returned, then borrow money from her cousin to rent another place.

Whitney gingerly touched the throbbing lump forming on the back of her head from when he'd knocked her down on the hard tile. The bump was so tender that her eyes watered. The salty tang of his blood was still on her lips from biting him. She'd been dead certain he intended to rape and kill her. So what if she'd drawn blood?

"Serves the creep right," she muttered out loud.

Lexi and Da Vinci were hovering at her feet, tails swishing in the darkness. She slipped out of the lightweight raincoat and let it drop to the floor. All she had on beneath was the sheer nightie. When she'd thrown on her raincoat to get Jasper, she'd never dreamed she would run into anyone.

"Okay, okay, out of the way," she told the dogs, her voice shaky.

She bumped into a box and stubbed her toe on the way to the chair beside the sofa, which was loaded with clothes and things she'd heaped there while unpacking. She dropped into the welcoming cushions, feeling slightly nauseous. A panicky feeling returned in a wave of fear that surged upward from the depths of her queasy stomach.

The electric power returned with a blinding flash and the cottage lit up. Not being alone in the dark calmed Whitney a little. She checked the locks on the front and back doors. She was safe.

Briiing-briiing. The telephone rang, and Whitney tensed. She let the machine Miranda had left behind pick up the message.

"It's me again." Ryan's disembodied voice filtered across the room. "Call me no matter how late you get in. It's really important."

Naturally, Ryan presumed she would do as he told her. Let him rot in hell along with the beauty queen. They'd married two days after his divorce from Whitney became final. She removed the receiver from the hook. If he called back, he wouldn't wake her. Let the jerk wait.

Whitney sent the dogs out the back door to do their business before going to bed. Clouds tumbled across the moon as the wind herded them inland. The rain had slackened to a mist, but it dripped off the trees and bushes, plopping onto the small used brick patio behind the cottage.

Whitney wiped off Lexi's paws with one of Miranda's old towels. "Good girl. Ready for bed?"

Lexi scampered off for her doggie bed at the foot of Whitney's bed. Da Vinci was still sniffing around and trying to decide which bush to bless by lifting his leg on it. She allowed him to take his time, remembering Miranda's warning. They're called *Chiwee-wees for a good reason.* Da Vinci was evidently prone to boo-boos and often left suspicious stains on the rug. She waited until the Chihuahua finally selected a spot and hoisted one little leg. She dried him off, then put him on the floor.

Whitney knew she'd locked the front door, but she double-checked anyway. Peering through the small panes of glass, she saw the light upstairs in the main house was still shining. Just knowing the pervert was there creeped her out.

Now the rain had stopped, leaving a somnolent dripping from the eaves. The storm had passed, thunder only a distant rumble, lightning a flicker to the east. A lone coyote howled. Its bleak call struck her as overwhelmingly lonely.

Something about the emptiness of the night disturbed her, which was silly. She wasn't alone. Granted, the place was a good distance from the next house, but this was suburbia, for God's sake. She flicked off the porch light, unable to shake the feeling her world was no longer familiar. Or friendly.

She went into the bathroom to get ready for bed. As she brushed her teeth, she thought about Ryan's call. What could he possibly want? They hadn't spoken in months. Rather than hire expensive attorneys to split what little they had, she'd agreed to arbitration. She'd allowed him to keep the house with the huge mortgage.

Whitney had taken the Grand Cherokee. Although the SUV wasn't new, it was paid for, and she needed transportation. They'd had little else except a full service of china and a worthless piece of property that Ryan—who didn't have a head for business—had insisted they purchase as an investment. The land turned out to have toxic waste in the soil and couldn't be sold without going through an expensive decontamination process. She'd quitclaimed the land to Ryan along with the house in order to keep Lexi.

And to get Ryan Fordham out of her life forever.

WHITNEY AWOKE THE NEXT MORNING with Da Vinci licking her face and wagging his tail. The spoiled little dog had slept on the bed with her.

"No," she groaned, looking at the alarm and realizing she'd failed to set it properly. She'd overslept. "You have to go out, don't you?" At the sound of her voice Lexi popped up from her bed and shook her head. The movement made her ears flap, Lexi's signal that she had to relieve herself.

"Let's hit it." Whitney shrugged into a robe and escorted them to the back door. The small fenced patio and patch of grass were still wet from the rain. When they'd finished, she quickly fed them, showered and threw on some clothes. She did *not* want to be late to Trish Bowrather's on the first day.

She walked to the carport attached to the single-car garage that was so crammed full of Miranda's stuff, there wasn't room for the SUV. Whitney glanced up at the main house. All the curtains were drawn. If she didn't know better, she would think no one was home. The jerk must still be asleep.

She loaded the dogs and was backing out when she realized a car had pulled in behind her, blocking her exit. She didn't know anyone who drove a silver Porsche. It might be Adam

Hunter, she thought, then wondered why he would be using the back driveway when a four-car garage was located on the other side of the house. Of course, after last night, there was no telling what that maniac might pull. But a man in a suit stepped out of the sleek sports car.

Ryan.

In a heartbeat, her world shifted and became out of focus. Just the slightest patina of sweat sheened her forehead. She could have blamed it on the bright morning sun and the humidity in the air from the storm, but she knew better. How could he have this effect on her? Hadn't the pain of his betrayal made her a stronger person?

Lexi immediately stuck her head out the window and barked a happy greeting. *Why me?* Whitney asked herself as she slid out of the SUV. Whatever Ryan wanted had to be really important for him to drive out to Torrey Pines from San Diego when patients would be waiting in his office at nine.

"You didn't call me back." Ryan sounded genuinely shocked, but then, he always was when he didn't get his way.

"What do you want?"

His mouth quirked into a smile, but she knew him too well. He was merely flashing his chemically whitened teeth. The man could turn on the charm like a searchlight, when it suited him.

Tall and imposing, with surfer blond hair and a golden tan, Dr. Ryan Fordham made women's hearts pound just by walking into a room. He was a shade shy of pretty, Whitney told herself, something mean curdling inside her. A tide of heartbreak rushed in, sweeping away rational thought.

"There's a little problem." He reached into the open window of the Jeep and stroked Lexi's head. The little turncoat couldn't wag her tail fast enough.

"What's the matter?" She battled the urge to tell him to get his hand off her dog. Although Lexi adored Whitney, the retriever had always been very fond of Ryan. Why not? He'd never had a cross word for the dog.

He stopped petting Lexi and turned to Whitney. "I'm joining a new practice. I need to sign a lease for an office building and finance some equipment. The credit check showed your name is still on the house and the property in Temecula."

"I thought the settlement agreement handled the transfer of title on both places. The judge accepted the documents."

Ryan studied the tips of his highly buffed shoes. "Apparently the judge was in a hurry and didn't notice it wasn't notarized. So it couldn't be recorded. I have the papers in the car. All you have to do is sign in front of a notary. I'll take them right to the county recorder's office to be legally registered."

Whitney was amazed that Ryan could get *any* credit. He was up to his ears in debt with a huge mortgage. He also had the lease on the office he'd used before switching from general surgery to the more lucrative field of cosmetic surgery. On top of everything was an astronomical malpractice premium that had to be paid quarterly. He walked over to the Porsche and she added expensive car leases to the list of her ex-husband's debts. No telling what Ashley—his girlfriend, now wife—was driving.

Ryan returned with a bound sheaf of papers in his hand. He flipped it open in front of her to a page with a red Post-it flagging a space for her signature. "All you have to do is sign here." He zipped to another page. "And here." He paged to the end of the document. "And here. But you must do it in front of a notary."

A warning bell sounded in a distant part of her brain. Why were there so many pages? The original document from the arbitrator had been much smaller, hadn't it?

"Come with me now," Ryan continued in his smoothest voice. "There's a notary at American Title who'll take care of everything. They open at nine."

"I can't today. I'm already running late. Besides, I want an attorney to look over everything before I sign."

"What?" Ryan slapped the side of the Jeep with the document. "Why let a lawyer pad his bill by reading something you've already agreed to? Besides, you don't have the money for a lawyer."

Whitney realized she was dealing not with the charming Ryan Fordham but the imperious Ryan Fordham. Once she'd thought this persona was authoritative. Now he merely sounded arrogant. She manufactured a smile and bluffed. "Miranda is marrying Broderick Babcock. He'll read the papers for nothing."

That stopped him. Ryan stared at her slack-jawed. Broderick Babcock was a legend in San Diego, in the state. He'd successfully defended several high-profile clients that most people believed were guilty and didn't have a prayer of avoiding prison.

"Why bother Babcock?" Ryan asked, his voice smooth again. "This isn't any big deal."

"I still want him to review the document. But it'll have to wait. He took Miranda to Fiji for a two-week honeymoon."

"What?" The word exploded out of Ryan. "Wait two weeks? No fucking way! You come with me right now. We'll be at American Title when they open."

He was shouting now, the way he occasionally did when things didn't go his way. Ryan had a hair-trigger temper that rarely surfaced. Between his charm, good looks and assertive attitude, people usually gave in to him. Whitney always had—but not anymore.

"I'm not signing anything until Rick has read and approved the document." She said this as if she knew the attorney, even though she'd never met the man. "Now move your car. I'm late for work."

Ryan grabbed her by the shoulders and shook her hard. "You bitch. You're doing this to get back at me for falling in love with Ashley."

She told herself this wasn't true. It was only prudent to have an attorney read what appeared to be a complicated document—a different document than she'd originally signed. But she had to admit Ryan had put her through hell. His betrayal had been acute, devastating. She'd sacrificed her dream of becoming a veterinarian to put Ryan through medical school. Now she was penniless and forced to start over.

"Let go of me." She tried to wrench away, but he only tightened his grip and began to shake her with even more force.

"I want you out of my life forever. This has to be settled today."

"Leave me alone," she snapped as she struggled to control the quaver in her voice. A bolt of fear shot up her spine. She'd seen Ryan upset many times, but never like this. Something else was wrong besides the improper transfer of property.

"Come with me now or else—"

"Don't threaten me. Let me go this instant."

Ryan shook her so hard that her head snapped back, wrenching her neck and shoulders. Pain lanced down her neck into her upper arm.

"You heard the lady. Let her go." The order sounded like the crack of a whip.

Ryan instantly released her, and they both whirled around to see who was speaking. A tall, powerfully built man stood in the trellised opening of the bridal wreath hedge that separated the main house from the caretaker's cottage. He must be Adam Hunter. The air whooshed out of Whitney's lungs as if the brute had tackled her again.

Head cocked slightly to one side, Adam Hunter gazed directly at Whitney. His arresting eyes were marine blue. If he was on something—the way she'd thought last night—it was an overload of testosterone. His eyes weren't fiendish at all; they were alert, predator's eyes. There was nothing more exciting to a natural-born hunter than vulnerable prey. Last night, clad in little more than a nylon raincoat, she'd been an easy mark.

In the utter darkness, she'd assumed him ugly. He was far from it, but she wouldn't call him handsome, either. He was attractive in an edgy, masculine way that said he was world-weary but aching to throw a punch if given any excuse. She imagined him clobbering Ryan and smiled inwardly.

Adam was dressed in well-worn navy Dockers and a gray polo shirt, but she had the impression he played the hand life dealt him. He would be at home in a boardroom, wearing Armani or dressed as a hit man in black, brandishing a gun fitted with a silencer. She would bet her life that the hit-man mode would be his choice.

His straight nose was slightly long, his square jaw was stubbled with hair the same shade as the black mop that was long overdue for a haircut. He had a well-toned body that she doubted came from hours at a gym. Somehow she couldn't see him on a treadmill or pumping iron beside a bunch of other guys.

"Look," Ryan began in his most placating tone. "My wife—"

"Ex-wife," she corrected, then didn't know what else to say. How could she expect the guy who'd manhandled her to be much help? The endless moment stopped when she managed to say, "He's trying to force me to sign papers that I want my attorney to review first."

Adam's take-no-prisoners glare said this was more than he needed—or wanted—to know. He shifted his weight from one foot to another, but his stance remained just as defiant.

"She's just being stubborn." Ryan gave Adam a man-to-man look.

"You were *way* too rough with the lady," Adam replied in a tone that could have frozen vodka. "Leave—now."

Ryan opened his mouth, set to argue, thought better of it and stomped off to his car. His wimpy exit showed Ryan for what he was—a pretty boy who relied on charm. When that failed he turned into a bully. With a screech of tires, the Porsche shot out of the driveway.

Whitney turned, but Adam Hunter had vanished as stealthily as he'd appeared.

CHAPTER FOUR

TRISH BOWRATHER WAS backing her midnight-blue Jaguar out of her garage when Whitney arrived. Brandy was in the passenger seat, his head out the window. Trish slammed on the brakes and rolled down her window, yelling, "You're late."

Whitney jumped out of the Jeep and ran over. "I'm sorry. My ex-husband showed up unexpectedly. He wouldn't let me out of the driveway until a neighbor helped get rid of him."

She hated bringing up personal issues, but she had no idea what else to say. She'd never had Miranda's aptitude for shading the truth.

Trish's eyes became distracted for a second, as if she was recalling something from long, long ago. "I thought your divorce was final."

"It is. He claims there was some mix-up in the paperwork involving the property settlement. I think I should have an attorney look over these new documents before I sign."

"Absolutely!" Trish stepped out of the car, dressed in a chic black suit accented with sterling-silver jewelry. "You need a lawyer to check. It sounds highly unusual."

"That's what I thought."

Trish studied her a moment, an understanding expression softening her features. "Was he physical with you?"

Whitney realized she must still appear shaken from the incident. "Well...a little, I guess. Ryan didn't hit me or anything but he grabbed my shoulders—"

"File a police report. Then get a restraining order," Trish shot back, conviction underscoring every word. "That'll keep that bastard away from you."

Whitney managed a weak nod. She didn't want to antagonize Ryan any more than she already had. There probably wasn't a valid reason not to sign the documents, but a little voice kept insisting she consult an attorney.

Trish put her hand on Whitney's arm. "Look. Take Brandy for his walk. Stop by the Daily Grind for a latte. Relax a little bit, then drop Brandy off at the gallery. There's a police station nearby. File a report. If the jerk threatens you again, get a restraining order."

An unconvincing "Good idea" was the best Whitney could muster.

"Here, Brandy," Trish called, and the dog scrambled out of the open driver's door, his leash in his mouth.

"Take your time," Trish advised as she walked back to the Jag. "Calm down. Don't let that creep ruin your day."

"Don't worry. I won't," Whitney said to appease her.

Whitney watched Trish speed away. She couldn't help being shocked at the change in the woman since yesterday. Evidently, Trish had suffered through a very rough divorce. She understood how unreasonable ex-husbands could be.

Get a restraining order?

She reluctantly admitted to herself that Trish had struck a nervous chord. Today Whitney had seen a side of Ryan that he hadn't revealed in nine years of marriage. Ryan had been cold and verbally abusive at times, but he'd never been rough with her.

Was he cracking up?

Surely not. Ryan was just stressed out, she assured herself as she hooked Brandy to his leash and opened the door for Lexi. Her ex's switch to cosmetic surgery had meant leaving his old partners and finding a new practice. Cosmetic surgeons needed to maintain a certain image. Sophisticated offices and the latest in equipment attracted the kind of clientele who gladly parted with stratospheric sums of money in order to appear more youthful. That consumed cash at a rapid rate.

Most people believed doctors made boodles of money, but that was no longer as true as it once had been. Malpractice insurance and the cost of equipment had eroded doctors' earning power. Ryan had compounded his problems by making several bad investments, like the property with the toxic chemicals in the soil.

Well, he'd gotten what he deserved, she assured herself. During the last year of their marriage, Ryan had behaved unforgivably. Always moody and temperamental, he'd become more so. She'd asked him dozens and dozens of times if she could do anything to help. He'd denied anything was wrong, claiming it was just the pressure of his first year in practice. His long hours became longer and more erratic, his fuse shorter. Still, Whitney hadn't suspected anything until she'd discovered the receipt from La Valencia, an expensive hotel in La Jolla.

He could have leveled with her and said he'd fallen for another woman, but he hadn't. Even when she confronted him, Ryan continued to deny it until she'd told him that she'd called the hotel and found out he'd registered with his "wife." When she'd had him dead to rights, Ryan had walked out the door "to find himself."

She was halfway down the street, with Brandy and Lexi on their leashes and Da Vinci snuggled into his custom-built sling harnessed to her chest, when her cell phone rang. She switched the leashes to one hand and grabbed the phone clipped to her waist.

"I hope you've had time to come to your senses."

She was tempted to hang up on Ryan, but that wouldn't deliver the message she really wanted to send. She'd had all she was ever going to take from this man.

"Well, Ryan," she replied in the sweetest tone she could manage. "You were unforgivably physical with me and I have a witness. I'm filing a police report and if you come near me again, I'll get a restraining order. You may recall that I have a friend who works for the *Tribune*. I'll make sure this appears in the paper. Should do worlds of good for your business, don't you think?"

There was nothing but dead air on the other end of the phone. No doubt Ryan was in shock. She'd never talked back to him like this when they'd been married. He'd presumed she was going to do just what he wanted.

"You wouldn't." He didn't sound as sure of himself as he usually did.

"I mean every word," she bluffed. "Just mail me what you want signed. As soon as Rick and Miranda return, I'll have him look over the documents. If he approves, I will, and I'll get them back to you immediately."

He grunted something that might have been "okay" and hung up. Whitney knew he was pissed. She told herself she was being prudent to wait until a lawyer could look over the papers, but a small part of her conceded she wanted to make things difficult for Ryan. What he'd done still hurt more than she cared to admit and she deserved a bit of revenge.

She'd first bumped into Ryan Fordham while rushing to a class at UCLA. He appeared to be another surfer being forced by his parents to study, but the opposite proved to be true. Ryan was brilliant—a fact not lost on the man—and he was attending college on an academic scholarship, studying premed.

He didn't have time or money to date but he carved out a place for Whitney. Before she knew it, she'd moved in with him. When she'd been accepted to UC Davis to study veterinary medicine, she'd been faced with a choice. It was much harder to get into vet school than medical school. Still, she'd allowed Ryan to persuade her to put her plans on hold until he received his medical degree.

They'd married just after graduation. Ryan's mother and Miranda, Whitney's only living relative, accompanied them to the Santa Monica courthouse, where they were wed. For reasons Whitney still didn't understand, Ryan hadn't liked Miranda.

True, her cousin could be a bit of a wild child at times, but who could blame her? Miranda had been orphaned at fifteen when her parents died in a car crash. She'd appeared at their door with a social worker the day before the funeral. While the older woman met with Whitney's mother, a single parent, Whitney had consoled Miranda.

"I don't have anywhere to go," her cousin had whispered, tears in her eyes.

Now it was Whitney who had nowhere to go—thanks to Ryan Fordham. She honestly didn't know what she would have done without Miranda. Her cousin had taken her in without asking any questions.

Ryan could rot in hell until she had someone look over the papers. It wasn't much, but she had to admit it gave her satisfaction to see him squirm.

ASHLEY FORDHAM HEARD THE opening bars of "Proud Mary" and knew she had a call on her cell phone. Whenever she heard the song, she fondly remembered her father. She could see him smiling, his slight overbite making him appear happier than he really was.

"Just a minute," she told Preston Block, her personal trainer. "I'm expecting a call from Ryan." She yanked her phone off the waistband of her yoga pants.

"It's me, babe." Ryan sounded discouraged.

"Did Whitney sign?"

A long beat of silence. "No. She wants to show the papers to an attorney."

"Why? She signed them after arbitration."

"Whitney's just being difficult to get back at me," Ryan said wearily.

Ashley caught Preston's eye and smiled even though she wanted to scream. Why couldn't Ryan have convinced the bitch to sign? How hard could it be?

Ashley tried for a teary voice. "We'll lose the house."

She had her heart set on a spectacular home with a dock for a yacht in Coronado Keys, just south of Ryan's offices in downtown San Diego. In order to buy it, they needed to sell the monstrosity of a house Ryan and Whitney had owned.

"It's not just the house," Ryan replied, his voice charged with anger. "It's…everything."

Ashley used an encouraging tone. "You'll think of something. You always do."

He told her he loved her and they hung up. She loved him, too, and had from the first day she'd met him. She knew Ryan was under a lot of pressure right now. The expense of buying in to a new practice. Skyrocketing malpractice insurance. The house she wanted. She would do anything to help him.

Preston was still watching her, and she hoped her frustration and anger didn't show on her face. No sense in getting frown lines over this. Too much was at stake. If Ryan couldn't handle his ex, she would. Ryan didn't have to know a thing. Like many men she'd encountered since childhood, Ryan needed to believe he was in charge.

"A problem?" Preston asked.

Ashley had been working out with Preston at Dr. Jox Fitness Center for the last three years. He had the hots for her. She could see it in his eyes as he put her through the workout he'd custom designed for her.

Ashley had known she was beautiful since her mother had entered her at age five in the Little Miss Idaho contest and she'd won. But years of countless contests hadn't led to a first in the Miss USA or Miss America pageants. Worse, she hadn't received the lucrative modeling contract that her mother expected. A ruptured appendix that she didn't seek treatment for until it was too late unexpectedly cut her mother's life short, leaving Ashley alone in San Diego to prepare for the Miss San Diego contest.

Ashley had decided she was sick of beauty pageants—something she'd never had the courage to tell her mother. At twenty-four, she was getting too old to compete. She had to find a job, but she just had a high-school diploma and no marketable skills except her looks.

She'd landed a position as a receptionist with a group of cosmetic surgeons. It didn't take her long to see how much money the doctors made from nips and tucks. She allowed one of the doctors to enhance her naturally pouty lips with a touch of Restalyne and had a chemical peel that made her flawless skin look perfect even without a bit of makeup.

When she could claim she'd been "enhanced" by the cosmetic group, she moved up the food chain from the entry-level receptionist's position to "spokeswoman" for the group. She met with patients in "preliminary sessions" to show what could be achieved with their services. Ashley was living proof of how skilled the surgeons were.

Prospective clients assumed her breasts were silicone and her naturally high cheekbones a result of implants. Liposuction must account for her trim tummy and slim thighs. Ashley merely smiled and never mentioned Mother Nature's gifts. Instead, she encouraged the women—and a growing number of men—to use the doctors' services.

She was good—invaluable really—a natural-born salesperson who could persuade anyone to go under the knife without them realizing they'd been conned. After years of automatically turning on the charm in her quest for a beauty title, this was a no-brainer. Within a year her salary quadrupled based upon the number of patients who mentioned her when they signed up for cosmetic "enhancements."

Kah-ching!

Ashley knew what she wanted—a husband with a successful cosmetic surgery practice. Then she could give up the parading around and convincing ugly women that surgery could improve them. She didn't want to pitch plastic surgery all her life. She wanted her own home; she'd been on the road since childhood. She planned to take courses in interior design and decorate her own home herself. Eventually she might open a design studio, but she wasn't sure she wanted the headaches owning a business might bring.

Ryan Fordham had appeared at the cosmetic group—an answer to her prayers. She'd been contemplating starting an affair with an older member of the group who had a wife who could haunt a house and charge by the room. But Ryan had immediately changed her mind. He could have had his pick of beautiful women, but he was genuinely interested in her.

They'd gone for coffee—to discuss a "spokesperson's role" in promoting a cosmetic surgeon's practice. After their short conversation, for reasons Ashley could never explain, she was totally in love with Ryan Fordham. She'd never been in love before, but now she knew how her mother had felt when she'd met Ashley's father. Ashley thanked her lucky stars that Ryan was a doctor, not an electrician. If he had been, Ashley still would have loved him just the way Ashley's mother had loved her father. Even after her father left them, her mother never looked at another man.

She'd known when Ryan first gazed at her that he was interested. Men were so transparent. They tried to hide what they were thinking, but she could always detect their lust. It was a skill her mother had taught her before she was eight. Judges, even those evaluating little girls, had that telltale glaze in their eyes. You smiled, batted your lashes, twitched your fanny and played them to your advantage.

The more time she spent with Ryan, the more she loved him. He was driven to be successful, which was second only to his valiant attempts to make her happy. She'd assured him she was happy; he was the man of her dreams. Still, Ashley wanted more—for him and for herself.

If he had any drawbacks, Ryan was weak with his ex-wife. Ashley understood. It was guilt—plain and simple. The woman had sacrificed to put him through medical school. Whitney had played the martyr to the hilt, exiting the marriage, asking for nothing except a beat-up SUV and a dog. Ashley had to be careful not to appear conniving while handling this for Ryan.

"I do have a bit of a problem," she confessed to Preston. Even though he wanted her just like countless other men had over the years, she needed Preston as a friend. The problem with being so beautiful was that other women were jealous. Preston was her only friend and sleeping with him would ruin their relationship. More important, she would never cheat on Ryan. Still, she realized she could use sex to manipulate Preston.

"Enough for today," she told him. "Let's hit the juice bar."

Dr. Jox had a pricey juice bar that served fresh squeezed juices and made healthy smoothies. Ashley ordered pomegranate juice because its antioxidant properties would keep her skin flawless, while Preston asked for a wheatgrass smoothie. She signed the tab for both drinks and they went outside to one of the small tables under the canopy of a towering ficus tree.

"What's the problem, Ashley?"

She told him part of the story and kept the emphasis on the ex-wife who was so jealous that she was refusing to sign papers she'd already signed once. She laid it on thick about never having had a home and always being on the road. Just when she'd found her dream home, the conniving ex was determined to ruin everything.

"There might be a way," Preston said when she'd finished

with tears studding her long eyelashes. "What does the ex value the most?"

Ashley hadn't a clue. Whitney was an attractive blonde with innocent green eyes, but she was nowhere near Ashley's league. They'd never met, but Ashley had seen photographs of Whitney in an album she'd found in the trash.

Then it hit her. The mutt. Ryan's ex had demanded the dog. "She's crazy about her Golden retriever."

"That's the key," Preston assured her with a confident smile. "Use the dog as leverage."

CHAPTER FIVE

ADAM SAT ACROSS THE DESK from Jerold "Jerry" Tobin, his uncle's attorney and executor of Calvin Hunter's estate. The portly, balding lawyer leaned back in his swivel chair, steepled his fingers across his chest and shook his head.

"I'm afraid Calvin's left us with a mess. Probate could take a year at least—maybe longer."

How convenient. Tobin would rack up a huge bill. Judging by the pictures lining the wall, the lawyer spent countless hours on the golf course. What better way to pay for expensive greens fees than a complicated probate?

"There may not be a lot left for you to inherit," the lawyer told him. "It's hard to tell at this point just what Calvin had and what he owes. I've brought in a forensic accountant to go over your uncle's files."

"Is there any problem with me staying in the house?"

"No. We're paying the woman in the caretaker's cottage to look after the place and take care of the dog. I forget her name—"

"Whitney Marshall." Adam wasn't about to forget her name—or the way she'd felt beneath him last night when he'd mistaken her for a burglar. Honest to God. What *had* he been thinking? He'd pawed her like some horny teenager in the back of a car.

This morning, when her ex-husband had been shaking her, Whitney had seemed vulnerable—nothing like the spitfire who'd kicked and bitten him. What kind of a prick got rough like that? It was none of his business, he reminded himself. But his mind kept drifting to her all morning.

"I could terminate the woman—"

"No. Don't do that." He didn't want to add to Whitney's problems. It appeared that she had enough to deal with right now. Besides, he owed her big-time for the way he'd behaved last night. "I'll just be there until I can find a place of my own."

"All right. We'll leave the arrangement as is."

"Did my uncle have any business partners?" Adam asked. He didn't add that one of them might have wanted Calvin Hunter dead.

"No. Not that I knew about." The lawyer studied him a moment, a calculating gleam in his eyes. "I don't suppose there's any reason why you can't see your uncle's file. You're going to inherit all his assets and liabilities."

"Liabilities?"

"I just warned you about Calvin's finances," the attorney reminded him. "Since your uncle held several properties in joint tenancy with you—"

"Wait a minute. What are you talking about? I don't own anything with my uncle."

Tobin leaned back in his chair and stared wordlessly at him for a moment. "Didn't your father or uncle tell you?"

"Tell me what?"

"When you were a minor, your uncle signed over half the house in Torrey Pines as well as two buildings in San Diego to you. They're held in rather complicated corporations. Your father came to this office when I prepared the documents and signed them for you since you were underage."

"He never told me a thing."

For a moment Adam was shocked, then he realized what his father had been thinking. He hadn't wanted Adam to rely on someone else's money. He'd always pointed out how rich kids got into trouble and never made anything of themselves.

Uncle Calvin had tried to pay for his education when Adam had transferred from the University of San Diego to the John Jay College of Criminal Justice in New York City. Adam had refused the offer. It wasn't just his pride; his uncle hadn't been around much. He barely knew the man.

Now that he thought about it, Calvin Hunter had been proud of Adam in his own way. He'd flown to New York from God-only-knew-where in Europe when Adam graduated at the top of his class at John Jay. He'd taken them out to dinner at some swank restaurant in Manhattan. Then, as usual, Calvin Hunter had flown out of their lives.

It had been another five years before he'd heard from Calvin again. When Adam was promoted to detective, Uncle Calvin called to congratulate him. His swift promotion had been the result of hard work, but the degree from one of the most prestigious criminal justice colleges hadn't hurt. Uncle Calvin had reminded him of this fact when he'd called. It was almost as if going to John Jay had been his uncle's idea.

"I can't say for sure how bad things are until the forensic accountant conducts an audit, but you may be responsible for any outstanding debts against the property you owned jointly with your uncle."

Great. Just what he needed—more bills. Being deployed overseas didn't stop car payments or the bills he'd inherited from his father. "What about the villa on Siros and the Citation?"

"Both were leased and your uncle was behind in the payments. Same with his house here. When he died, I brought the house payments up to date. It's a valuable asset. I didn't want to risk foreclosure."

"I was under the impression my uncle was wealthy." Adam didn't really know or care about his uncle's money, but his

father had always said Calvin had made numerous investments, and they'd brought him a lot of money.

"That's what I thought, too. I worked with your uncle for
years. He had a great many valuable assets." The attorney
spread his pudgy hands wide, palms up. "This…cash flow
problem seems to be a recent development."

"What did he do with all his money?"

"Hard to say. We'll know more when the accountant goes
over everything." The attorney shuffled through some papers
on his desk before adding, "Do you know anyone that your
uncle would have given three thousand dollars in cash on the
fifth of every month?"

"No. I have no idea." Adam thought a moment. "Maybe he
used the cash himself."

"I don't think so. He withdrew cash periodically from ATMs
during the month, and he charged a lot to his American Express
card. This monthly withdrawal has been going on for over a
year."

"There are plenty of people—gardeners, pool cleaners, car-
detailing services—who want cash so they don't have to report
it to the government."

"True, but I've accounted for those employees. I'm thinking
he was giving out a lump sum each month…for some reason."

Adam shifted in his chair. "Are you thinking blackmail?"

"No, no, no," the attorney responded just a bit too quickly.
"I'm sure there's a reasonable explanation. The forensic accountant may turn up the answer."

ADAM'S NEXT STOP WAS the coroner's office. He knew the assistant coroner, Samantha Waterson, from his time on the San
Diego police force. The woman didn't miss much. She handled
most of the autopsies for the coroner even though he signed
all the death certificates.

"Hey, Adam. It's great to see you," Samantha greeted him.

The redhead had a smile that dominated her face and almost made you overlook the spray of freckles across her nose and the smallish brown eyes magnified by round tortoiseshell glasses. "How long's it been?"

"Over two years." He'd last seen Samantha at his farewell party the night before he shipped out.

"So how was Iraq?"

He shrugged. No sense depressing people with the truth. His National Guard unit had been sent over for what was supposed to be two years. Their stay was extended for another eight months. Even after he'd nearly been killed, Adam had been stuck at a desk job until his tour was over.

"I stopped in to discuss the autopsy you did on my uncle."

"I received your message from Iraq about Calvin Hunter. I made sure I performed the autopsy myself."

"The cause of death is listed as a massive coronary."

"That's right. His heart was in really bad shape. Don't worry, though. He didn't suffer. He died instantly."

"Is there a medication or a poison or something that could cause such a heart attack?"

"Is that why your e-mail requested a full toxicology report?"

He decided to level with Samantha. When he'd been on the force, she'd always helped him. Aw, hell. She'd autopsied his cases first whenever he'd asked. "I saw my uncle in Greece about two months ago. He was worried that someone might kill him."

"Wow! Why?"

"He refused to say. He thought I'd be in danger if I knew too much. Then seven weeks later he keels over of a heart attack. It makes me suspicious."

The more he thought about his uncle's warning, the more sense it made. In his own way Calvin Hunter had cared about him. Maybe as he aged, he missed having children and had tried to make up for it by giving Adam part of his holdings. And warning him about the danger.

Samantha swiveled in her chair and studied the plaques and awards lining her office wall for a moment. "I assume you read the police report."

"I did." He didn't add that a buddy on the force had faxed him the info while he was still in Iraq.

Samantha nodded thoughtfully. "An unidentified female phoned 911 and said your uncle was having a heart attack. Paramedics arrived within minutes but no one was around. They assumed someone had been passing by."

Adam took a deep breath. "My uncle was dead."

"The 911 record says the call came from your uncle's telephone."

Adam nodded, wondering who the mysterious woman could have been. "Someone was in the house with him—then disappeared. He keeled over in his office upstairs. It's impossible for a passerby to see into that room. The whole place is set too far back from the street for someone to merely be passing by and notice anything."

"Your uncle definitely died of a massive coronary," Samantha assured him. "But was it induced or natural? From what I could tell, it appeared to be natural. It'll take four to six weeks to get the tox screens back, so I won't be positive until then. They went out two weeks ago, so it'll be at least another two weeks before I have anything to tell you."

He knew toxicology reports were processed at the Fulmer Center in Santa Barbara. They performed toxicology reports for most of Southern California's municipalities except Los Angeles, which was large enough to have its own lab.

Adam thanked her and left, his mind on his uncle. Calvin Hunter hadn't outwardly shown how much he'd cared—at least not in a way a growing boy would notice—but his uncle had tried to help. Now it was his turn.

He had no intention of sitting on his ass and waiting. His gut instinct said Calvin Hunter had been murdered—just as his uncle had feared. Adam had given his word he would investigate. Nothing was stopping him. He planned to see just what his uncle had been involved in financially. That might lead him to the killer.

"THIS IS YOUR OFFICE," Tyler Foley told Adam.

"Great view," Adam responded, still in shock. Just before he'd left for Iraq, he and Tyler had barely scraped together enough money for a rat hole of an office in a run-down warehouse that had been converted to a warren of bleak little cubes.

Tyler grinned, the same ingratiating smile that had assured him the "good cop" role when he'd worked homicide with Adam. "I guess you didn't believe my e-mails. I told you HiTech Security was going gangbusters."

"I received your messages." Adam could have said the e-mails had been the highlight of his existence, but one thing he'd already learned was that people didn't have a clue about how bad things were in Iraq. Death or boredom were constant companions, depending on where you were at any given moment. A message from home was heaven-sent. Tyler's brief accounts of the progress of their fledgling company had sent his spirits soaring. It propelled him out of the hellish confines of the present into the limitless possibilities of the future.

"Why don't I review our accounts' files so that I get up to speed," suggested Adam.

A beat of silence, then Tyler said, "I'll have Sherry teach you how to access the accounts on the computer."

Adam glanced down at the chrome-and-glass desk that was pushed up against the window of his new office. A large flat-screen monitor dominated the space. Beside it was a keyboard and a telephone with buttons for several extensions.

"You've gone paperless?" he asked Tyler.

"Just about. It's the wave of the future. Everything's on a disc these days. You'll learn—"

"Not a problem," he assured Tyler. "I had a lot of downtime in Baghdad. One of the guys was a computer guru in his real life. He taught me a lot."

Tyler cracked a laugh that might have sounded a bit forced; Adam wasn't sure. "You're probably ahead of me. Sherry handles everything. She knows where all the bodies are buried around here."

Tyler left Adam to "make himself at home" in his new office. Adam sat at the desk and gazed out at the Pacific. The water was calm now and appeared to be a glistening sheet of stainless steel. He felt like a third wheel. Obviously, Tyler had done exceedingly well without him.

Where did he fit in now?

Did he fit in at all? Anywhere?

Well, he might be able to help grow the business even more. A receptionist, two women in the office. They could hire more people and expand, once they decided which direction to go in.

When Adam and Tyler had both tired of detective work that was usually drug-related, they'd decided to launch their own private-investigation company. They'd set up shop, seeing corporate security as an emerging field.

Then Adam's unit had been called to duty. Obviously, the company had taken off in another direction. Adam had been able to tell a little about this from Tyler's e-mails.

Adam surfed through the account files for the better part of an hour. The company seemed to be very successful. The receivables were up to date, showing how financially healthy the company was, but it wasn't involved in corporate security, the way they'd intended when they'd formed HiTech.

Adam rose and walked out of his office, heading down the hall to Tyler's office.

"Mr. Foley's with a client," called Sherry.

"Please let Tyler know I need to speak with him."

Adam nodded to the brunette and returned to his office. He had the vague impression she didn't approve of him. Who could blame her? His hair was in desperate need of a cut and his clothes were barely passable. He'd spent the earlier part of the morning, after his encounter with Whitney's ex, sorting through the stuff he'd hastily put into a storage unit before shipping out. Most of it had mildewed during this overseas deployment and wasn't even fit for Goodwill.

When it came right down to it, nothing much was left of his previous life. He needed to start over—with a fresh attitude. After all, by some miracle, his life had been spared. He should make the most of this second chance. As soon as he spoke with Tyler about the company's direction, Adam was going shopping.

With nothing better to do, he Googled the articles written about his uncle's death. The few lines recounting Calvin Hunter's career in the navy were eclipsed by his win at the Frankfurt International Dog Show with Jasper. Not one of the articles mentioned a 911 call made from Calvin's home by a woman who'd fled the scene before help arrived.

That mystery followed by a robbery during which the thieves had ignored priceless antiques, but had stolen his uncle's computer and discs, disturbed Adam. What could be on his uncle's computer? Expense reports, no doubt. His uncle must have claimed judging shows was his business and probably wrote off many questionable expenses, like a Citation and a villa in the Greek Isles.

Calvin Hunter had been in financial trouble, according to his attorney. Adam needed to find out just what caused the problem and the extent of the difficulty. If his uncle had been murdered as Adam suspected, the trail might begin with his finances. From his work as a homicide detective, Adam knew most murders were crimes of passion or the result of disputes over money. Judging from what Adam had seen of his uncle's home, no woman had been sharing it with him. The money trail was the place to start.

Adam stood in his office, his fists rammed into the back pockets of his well-worn Dockers, staring out at the sea in the distance. He was just as glad his uncle hadn't left him a lot of money—just buildings with debts. When all was said and done, he wanted to know he'd built his own business. It was all about pride, he decided.

His father had been the same way. Matthew Hunter had been a building contractor. When he'd unexpectedly keeled over from a heart attack, the small savings Adam had accumulated had gone toward finishing his father's last job. It hadn't been enough, and Adam had been forced to take out a loan to complete the project and protect his father's good name.

Adam's thoughts strayed from memories of his father to Whitney Marshall. He'd been dating a woman when he'd left for Iraq. He'd told Holly that it was over before he went, and she'd quickly replaced him. He'd thought returning might trigger old feelings, but it hadn't. Instead he kept seeing Whitney's deep green eyes and tousled blond hair. He pushed brain Pause and rewound his thoughts to last night. He could feel Whitney beneath him. So soft. So sexy.

So…right.

Whitney was gorgeous, and he'd wanted to tell her so, but thought better of it. How could any man in his right mind be so attracted to someone he'd thought was a burglar? Of course, Adam might not be in his right mind. He'd been changed in ways he was still discovering.

"Hey, Adam." Tyler interrupted his thoughts. "You wanted to see me."

Adam slowly turned away from the view and tried for a smile. "Yeah, I was looking over the accounts. Seems like we're into private guard services big-time."

"Look, you've been out of touch. There's been an explosion of gated communities around here. Providing gate ambassadors—"

"Ambassadors?"

"It's a fancy term everyone uses for guards. No one wants to say guards. That implies crime. So everyone goes with ambassadors." Tyler chuckled. "It's a no-brainer, and it's our bread and butter."

Adam detected more than a hint of defensiveness in his friend's tone. He hadn't intended to make him anxious. "You've really built the business while I was gone." Adam didn't remind Tyler that most of the money to start HiTech had been his. Tyler had put up very little cash, but he had done all the work when Adam's unit was sent to Iraq. "I just thought we'd agreed to go into corporate security."

"I know, but that's a tough nut to crack." His tone was accommodating, more like the Tyler that Adam had known before leaving. "Corporate security takes a lot of computer geeks and expensive equipment. I don't think we should head in that direction yet."

"I'm not second-guessing you," Adam assured him. "I'm just getting a feel for what's happening. You've done a helluva job."

Tyler rewarded him with one of his trademark smiles, but Adam couldn't help wondering what his friend was thinking. Adam knew he'd changed a lot in the last two and a half years. Apparently, Tyler was different as well. Were they going to be close friends again? Would they be able to work together?

Hell, he hoped so. During his time overseas, Tyler had been like a lifeline. He'd e-mailed Adam at least once a week. True, most of his messages had been about the company—very little personal stuff—but they'd meant a lot to Adam. Without many relatives and not having many close friends, Adam had counted on Tyler's moral support.

"Look…" Tyler shuffled over to the window, looked out at

the view for a moment, then continued, "About Holly. We didn't mean…for anything to happen. It just did."

"No problem," Adam replied, and he meant it. Okay, maybe some small part of him had wanted Holly to wait and give their relationship a chance. But almost three years was a long time, especially since he'd given her the big kiss-off just before he'd left. Hell, most of the married guys in Iraq had problems making their marriages work long-distance. He'd been right to end the relationship when he had.

"You'll hook up with someone new," Tyler assured him. "You always were the one the women went after."

Adam couldn't help thinking about Whitney. He knew damn well she wouldn't agree with Tyler. He'd frightened the wits out of her. Worse, she had an ex who was still in the picture.

Aw, hell. No one had ever accused him of being sensible. Something about Whitney sent his brain into a tailspin. He found her really sexy. And he'd spent so much time without a woman that he needed sex in the worst way—yet something inside him was desperate for so much more than a quickie.

What did he want? Seeing death so often—so close—made him value life. He wanted a family, and that meant kids…and a wife. He needed a woman, someone special to share things with, someone to discuss important things with—someone special. He kept thinking about Whitney. She might not be that person, but it wouldn't hurt to investigate.

He smiled inwardly. Hell, he was good at investigating.

CHAPTER SIX

RYAN FORDHAM STARED out at the bay just beyond Peohe's restaurant. A Coast Guard cutter slogged its way out to sea while yachts whizzed by, their sails amber in the light of the setting sun. Beside him, Ashley chatted about the house she longed to possess. He didn't have the heart to tell her that he'd already contacted the broker and had withdrawn their bid. What choice did he have? Until Whitney signed the documents and he had full control of their property, he was precariously low on funds.

Almost totally broke, he grudgingly admitted to himself.

What money he had managed to raise must go into his new practice and toward paying off Domenic Coriz. Just the thought of the big Native American sent a bead of sweat crawling like a centipede down the back of his neck.

Why can't you stop gambling? he asked himself for the hundredth time.

You can, responded the logical part of his brain, the way it had countless times during the last three years. Over and over, he'd told himself he would never step into a casino again. Each time he broke his promise.

Gambling was an addiction, he reminded himself, and it was just as powerful as being hooked on cocaine or alcohol. Maybe more so. Winning gave him a high that he couldn't achieve even with the hottest, kinkiest sex. Losing was a total downer, but the high's promise was enough to lure him back to the tables again and again.

"What?" he asked, realizing Ashley had said something. "My mind wandered."

Ashley studied him for a moment, then repeated, "I said I picked up papers to file for my resale license. I need to put down the name of my business. I can't decide between Ashley's Interiors or Ashley's Designs."

"'Designs,'" he said emphatically. "'Interiors' limits you to decorating. With 'designs' you can branch off into other things, like art or clothing. With your talent, you can do almost anything."

Ashley rewarded him with her winning smile. It was accompanied by an adorable mischievous glint that fired her blue eyes. That captivating expression had instantly won his heart the minute he'd introduced himself to her on his first visit to the cosmetic surgery group he'd later joined. Until he'd met Ashley, Ryan hadn't believed in love at first sight. Now he was convinced.

Ryan had thought he'd loved Whitney, but he'd been mistaken. What he'd felt for his ex-wife had been a certain fondness magnified by sexual attraction. But it was so much…less than the heartfelt emotion Ashley evoked.

"You're right," Ashley told him. "Ashley's Designs it is. I'm going to start with a small office in the house."

"Good." He didn't mention that he didn't have the capital to bankroll even the most modest business. Damn Whitney. The bitch had already agreed to the settlement. Why did she have to pick now—of all times—to become uncharacteristically stubborn?

"Dr. Fordham?" Their waiter interrupted his thoughts. "A man in the bar needs to see you."

"Have him join us," Ashley responded.

"Don't bother." Ryan stood, a little unnerved. Who knew they were here? It had been a spur-of-the-moment decision to enjoy the sunset over the bay. "We don't want our romantic dinner interrupted. Do we?"

Without waiting for an answer, Ryan followed the waiter,

his apprehensive feeling intensifying. Had someone been following him? Was that how he knew they were here?

What now? His new partners were pressing him to line up financing for his portion of the long-term lease on the state-of-the-art cosmetic surgery facility. He was several payments behind on his first and second mortgage and on the home equity line of credit he'd taken out when real estate skyrocketed last year. Home sales had since flattened, yet bills kept marching across his desk with frightening regularity. But nothing could beat the pressure he was getting from Coriz.

The waiter led him into the bar area. It was jammed with twenty-something Gen-Xers trying to hook up. Ryan spotted a lone man in the far corner. He looked like a guy from the wrestling channel attempting to pass for normal in street clothes.

One of Coriz's men. Christ! They *had* been following him. The goon stepped forward as Ryan shouldered his way toward him, and the waiter melded into the crowd.

"Fordham."

The single word was low, gruff and wouldn't be noticed by the people standing around like cigars jammed into a box. Still, the menacing tone cut right through Ryan like one of the lasers he used on his patients.

He forced himself to employ his most arrogant voice. "Do I know you?"

"Naw." The creep shrugged and emphasized powerful shoulders beneath his Tommy Bahama shirt. "I'm one of Dom's guys."

Dom. Only Domenic Coriz's closest associates called him "Dom."

"Dom wants a progress report. Did your ex sign the papers?"

"Not yet, but she will," Ryan assured him, though he had his doubts about how soon he could expect to see signed documents.

"Dom don't want no fuckin' lawyers involved."

For a second Ryan's knees wobbled. How could they know Whitney planned to consult Broderick Babcock? They must be eavesdropping on him with some sophisticated device as well as following him. Those cocksuckers!

Ryan drew himself up to take full advantage of his height. Dom's man might be muscle-bound but Ryan had a good six inches on him at least. "You tell Dom that I'll take care of my ex."

The goon studied Ryan with dark eyes as if he were inspecting some alien species, then his lips curled into a smirk. "Remember this is time…s-sensitive."

The way he'd stumbled over the word told Ryan the man had never used it before. Dom must have told him what to say. Not that "time sensitive" had appeared to be in the Native American's vocabulary either. He'd probably heard the term from his fish-faced attorney.

"I'm well aware of the time factor involved."

Dom's man edged forward and for an instant Ryan thought he didn't understand what *factor* meant. Quick as a snake, a meat hook of a hand whipped out and grabbed Ryan by the balls. One deft twist of the man's wrist and Ryan had to bite the inside of his cheek to control a scream of unimaginable pain. Despite his efforts, a choked grunt escaped his lips. No one in the noisy bar noticed.

The man released Ryan's gonads, saying, "Dom always gets what he wants."

Without waiting for a reply, the cocky prick muscled his way through the crowd and vanished. Ryan didn't need the threat spelled out. *Deliver or you're dead.*

It took several minutes for the pain in his groin to ease enough to move. Both hands in front of him to protect his balls, Ryan wended his way out of the crush of kids hustling each other. He walked haltingly, each step bringing another stab of pain. He stopped and stood at the edge of the crowd for a moment, waiting until the ache subsided. He didn't want to hobble back to the table and face Ashley's questions.

He'd managed to keep his gambling a secret from Whitney. She'd thought his late night forays had been to the hospital. It had worked during his two residencies, but that excuse no longer held water. Cosmetic surgeons didn't go to the hospital at night unless there was an emergency. And having worked for a group of cosmetic surgeons, Ashley would know this.

He couldn't fool her. Just as well, he decided. He'd sworn off gambling. Still, the pull was there. A sense of inevitability seeped through him like a powerful narcotic. If only he could score big—the way he had in the past—his problems would be solved.

Remember. Dom always gets what he wants. Ryan knew he had no choice but to deliver.

IT WAS ALREADY DARK WHEN Whitney returned to the cottage. After her confrontation with Ryan, she'd been playing catch-up all day. In addition to Da Vinci, Whitney now had Maddie, a fluffy white bichon frise, while her owner traveled to a gala in New York City.

She hoisted Da Vinci out of the carrier strapped to her back. "You're spoiled silly. I'm going to have a bad back from carrying you around all day."

Da Vinci scampered after Maddie, intent on chasing her and not caring one bit about Whitney's aching back. Oh, well. Being a pet concierge brought in the money she needed, but who promised it would be easy?

Lexi licked her hand and Whitney took time to pet her retriever. The dog seemed eerily in tune with her. When Whitney had been despondent over Ryan's betrayal, Lexi had never left her side. Whitney could see what a help Lexi was going to be in her new venture. She had a calming effect on other dogs because she obeyed and didn't get excited over little things like unexpected noises or other pets.

A sharp knock on the front door stopped Whitney halfway to the kitchen to prepare two special diets and scoop a bowl of kibble for Lexi. Da Vinci went into a frenzy of sharp yips and Maddie joined in, dancing a jig on her hind legs.

"No. Bad," she scolded them. "Quiet."

It must be Ryan, she decided. The man just never knew when to give up. Once she'd thought it was an admirable quality. Now she'd been exposed to the dark side of his behavior. Trish might be right about needing a restraining order. Her anger at Ryan put steel in her spine, and she swung open the front door, saying, "Get out of here or I'll call the police."

The dark figure was backlit by the dim porch light. All she could make out for a moment was a tall, broad-shouldered silhouette. Too tall, too big for Ryan.

"I hope I'm not interrupting your dinner, Whitney."

She instantly recognized Adam Hunter's voice. He unnerved her in a way no other man ever had, but then, she'd never been attacked before. She reminded herself that he'd helped her this morning. Stay calm; the guy wasn't all bad. "No, I just came home."

He took a step forward, and the light from inside the cottage washed over him. Their brief encounter this morning hadn't prepared her for this clean-shaven man with a fresh haircut. Now he was dressed in crisp tan slacks and a light blue polo shirt that emphasized his dark hair.

His crystalline blue eyes lacked warmth or spark. They seemed vacant, almost haunted. And they bore into her with unwavering intensity. She suddenly remembered Adam had lost his uncle. The death must have upset him the way her mother's death had stricken Whitney.

She took a deep breath and forced a smile. "Thanks for helping me this morning."

"Your ex-husband seemed…unreasonably angry."

"He'll get over it."

He gazed at her for a moment in his direct way, and she knew he saw through the lie. Ryan held a grudge like an ayatollah, but she didn't give a hoot. Let him stew.

"I went to see the executor of my uncle's estate. It still isn't settled, but I'm going to stay here until I find an apartment. We want you to continue taking care of Jasper." He snapped his fingers and Jasper appeared out of the shadows. The Chinese crested gazed up at Adam as if he'd hung the moon.

Oh, well. The little dog was an international champion who'd made countless transatlantic flights. Obviously, the altitude had addled what brains the champ had once possessed. Jasper didn't come when she called his name, but he responded to a snap of Adam's fingers.

"What about the relatives who are supposed to take Jasper?"

"That's me. I'm the only relative Uncle Calvin had."

Whitney tried for a sympathetic smile, but it was difficult after last night. She again reminded herself of the incident with Ryan. Adam Hunter wasn't as bad as she'd first believed, but a gentleman would apologize.

"You'll be taking Jasper with you when you find an apartment."

"It depends." He studied the dog at his side for a moment. Jasper had no hair on his body except for his head and feet. Brown and white fur sprouted from his paws and shot out from his ears like a patch of crabgrass. Whitney had always considered the nearly hairless dogs to be a little goofy. Jasper had done nothing to change her mind.

"Depends," she prompted.

"Some apartments don't allow pets," Adam replied, a hollow tone in his voice.

There were plenty that did, she thought. Obviously, Adam didn't care enough about his uncle to give the orphaned dog a good home. It took him down another notch in her estimation.

"Jasper's a champion. Maybe I can locate a breeder who would like to show him or use him as a stud."

"He's due to be bred in a few days. That breeder might want Jasper, but I promised my uncle that I would look after his dog."

This did *not* make sense. How did he plan to take care of the dog if he rented an apartment that didn't accept pets?

"I'll feed Jasper in the morning," he told Whitney, oblivious to her concern. "If you could walk him once during the day, it'll help. Most nights I won't be home until late. Give me your number and I'll let you know if I'm not going to make it home in time to feed him dinner."

Whitney walked over to the small nook that Miranda had set up as her office and took a business card out of the box that she'd had printed at Speedy Press. She turned to give it to Adam and discovered he'd moved into the center of the room without making a sound. The dogs were hovering around his feet, sniffing.

"This has my cell number and the number here. Try the cell first. I'm usually out taking care of animals."

"Right." He reached into the cluster of dogs and plucked out Jasper. He headed for the door, the little pill of a dog tucked under one arm, then stopped. "I'm sorry about last night. I overreacted."

She couldn't help herself. "Do you always try to rape intruders?"

"Rape?" He snorted. "Is that what you thought?"

"Pardon me if I'm wrong, but when a man tackles me, then has his hands all over my body…well, rape does come to mind."

"I don't usually find naked women prowling around in the dark in my house."

"I wasn't naked. I had on my jammies."

"Jammies? Well, call me a dog, but my idea of jammies and yours are worlds apart. You were nearly nude."

"Stop it! I'm tired of people blaming me—" The astonished look on his face stopped her short. She knew she hadn't meant "people." Ryan had been the one she had in mind. He'd always managed to find a way to make anything that went wrong seem like her fault. She expelled an exasperated breath. "Okay, it was a Victoria's Secret nightgown."

They stared at each other for a moment like gunslingers waiting to draw. Whitney reminded herself that she needed a place to live until Miranda returned. *The man* might *have made an honest mistake. Smile. Show that you can forgive and forget.*

At Whitney's attempt at a smile, he said, "The house was robbed right after my uncle died. I thought you were a burglar."

"Did they get much?" Whitney had been in the house several times before Miranda left and hadn't noticed any signs of a robbery.

"They cut the burglar alarm wires and took my uncle's computer but left a lot of valuable antiques. When I heard you downstairs, I assumed they'd returned."

"I understand," she said, trying to convince herself that she did. *Remember, he's not Ryan. Adam did help you this morning.*

"I didn't mean to paw you. I was…trying to confirm you were a woman. Most robbers are men."

She nodded slowly, not mentioning the erection evident during "his pawing to confirm" maneuvers.

"Anyway, you're perfectly capable of defending yourself," he told her with the suggestion of a smile.

"I am?"

He cocked his head to one side and pointed to the livid red scratch at the base of his neck. It had been hidden by the collar of his shirt. He then showed her the large bandage on his forearm. "You bit me and drew blood."

She stared at the flesh-colored bandage, clearly remembering the metallic taste of blood. The edges around the bandage were purplish-blue. Evidently a deep bruise surrounded the bite. "You had me outweighed. All I could do was bite."

"And scream," he added with an attempt at a chuckle. "I'm sure the devil heard you all the way down in hell."

She wasn't about to apologize for defending herself, but the adorable way he had of tilting his head slightly while he was talking muted her anger. The whole incident had been a mistake. Not taking it too seriously or making more out of it than necessary seemed to be the best course.

Whitney looked up into his blue eyes—about to say something—then forgot what it was. An electrical current arced between them, and her breathing became uneven. She had the disturbing feeling that Adam was about to kiss her. For a moment, she was almost dizzy with anticipation.

"When my uncle had the fatal heart attack, a woman called 911. Was that you?"

Her brain scrambled to get a grip on the question. All she could think about was what it would be like to be held in his powerful arms. "Me? No. I wasn't living here. My cousin, Miranda Marshall, had this cottage until two days ago."

"Did she mention calling the paramedics?"

Whitney shook her head, still trying to keep her emotions from showing. "No. Miranda told me about it, but she wasn't home. She stayed with her boyfriend at night. They're off in Fiji now on a honeymoon."

He reached out and lightly touched her cheek with one finger. Their eyes held and she forced herself to remain steady even though a swarm of butterflies was fluttering through her tummy.

"Sorry about last night. Friends?"

She mustered the strength to nod, but it was difficult. Heat seemed to suffuse her entire body.

He left without another word. For a long moment she stood there, then remembered to lock the door.

CHAPTER SEVEN

TYLER GUIDED HOLLY out of Croce's. Even though it was half past two and the club had announced the last call over thirty minutes ago, people were still hanging around. The club was dedicated to the memory of the creator of "Bad, Bad Leroy Brown," Jim Croce. It was located in one of the renovated Victorian-style commercial buildings in the historic Gaslamp Quarter. There were hundreds of clubs, restaurants and galleries in the area. Croce's had been among the first to open in the seventies when the city began pumping life back into the decaying area. It was still one of the most popular clubs.

"Adam came into the office today," Tyler said as they walked back to his condo along streets lit by authentic gas lamps.

"Really?" Holly responded, in a tone he couldn't quite read. "How is he?"

Someone who didn't know Holly might not realize she had been crazy about Adam Hunter. Tyler had always assumed he was Adam's best friend, but Adam hadn't confided his reason for splitting with Holly.

Tyler had waited two agonizingly long months after Adam had left for Iraq before asking Holly out. He'd taken it slow and easy, giving her plenty of space to get over Adam. Tyler's strategy had worked. Holly was practically living with him now. She kept a small walk-up on Coronado Island near her boutique, but she spent most nights at the condo Tyler had purchased in the Marina District that bordered the Gaslamp Quarter.

"Adam seems okay physically, but he's…different."

"Different?"

Now Holly sounded interested. He glanced at her, but the wavering shadows from the gas lamps and her long brown hair concealed her face. Maybe it was just his imagination. Anyone would be concerned about a friend who'd nearly been killed.

"Adam's quieter. Doesn't joke anymore." Tyler thought about the way Adam had behaved during lunch. "He's pretty intense."

"Are you going to be able to work with him?" she asked.

Now her concern seemed to be for him, and Tyler kept his smile to himself. "Good question. Adam's still hot to go into corporate security."

Holly didn't comment. They walked in silence to the end of the block, where the historical area merged with the Marina District. Here eye-catching skyscrapers and luxurious condos captured the view of the bay. The area had a number of hotels, but it was also the trendy place to live downtown.

Tyler had sunk all the money he'd made from HiTech Security into his new place. After years on the police force, when he'd been barely able to make his monthly rent payment, it felt awesome to have a brand-new home overlooking the harbor. He'd let Holly decorate it, and she'd done an amazing job.

It was sleek and modern, furnished in stainless steel and beige leather several shades darker than the walls. It was masculine yet had enough touches of softness for a woman to be comfortable. After all, he planned to live here once he and Holly were married. Later, when they had children, he supposed they would buy a home in the suburbs. Their kids would need space to play. By then HiTech would be going great guns—even more stable and successful than it already was—and he would be able to afford anyplace Holly wanted.

"Did you explain to Adam that it's too expensive to go into corporate security?" Holly asked.

"Yeah. We talked about it." Their discussion over lunch had been strained. Tyler wasn't sure if it was the direction the company had taken or Adam himself that had made their conversation tense. "Adam's going to check into it and see exactly what it'll take."

"Then he'll realize, the way you did, that HiTech will be more profitable providing guard services."

"Probably," Tyler said, although he didn't necessarily agree. "Adam's pretty hung up about his uncle's death."

"I didn't think they were close."

Adam must have told her, Tyler decided, the back of his neck tightening. "They weren't really close, but—"

"Adam feels responsible. That's the kind of guy he is."

"I guess."

Like most women, Holly had a lot of emotional insight. Adam had probably cut off his relationship with her in case he was killed in Iraq. Holly must have figured this out. When he'd been with Adam today, Tyler had glossed over his relationship with Holly. A year and a half ago, he'd e-mailed Adam that he was seeing Holly. He'd never mentioned her again even though he e-mailed Adam on a weekly basis. Today, he might have made a mistake by not letting Adam know how much Holly meant to him. He wondered if Adam would contact her.

The phone on his hip vibrated, and he stopped. At this hour it could only be the watch commander at his guard service. "Yeah?"

"It's Butch. We've got a no-show at Ocean Heights and the backup isn't answering his phone."

"Christ!" Ocean Heights was a ritzy subdevelopment and one of his most lucrative accounts. Their board insisted on a twenty-four-hour guard at their gate. After midnight residents could have used a remote control to open the gate, the way residents in many other gated communities did—but no, Ocean Heights needed a "gate ambassador" all night long.

Weeknights it was easy to have college kids man the gate because they liked to study when things were slow, but on the weekend, they suddenly became "ill." Problem was he didn't have enough backups. If someone didn't show, he was in trouble.

He was forced to tell Butch, "I'll take it." He flipped the phone shut and turned to Holly. "I've gotta go, babe. One of the guards didn't come in, and we can't leave the gate at Ocean Heights uncovered."

"Can't you hire more backup guys?"

She sounded a little peeved. He couldn't blame her. This was the third Saturday night that he'd skipped out on her. "It's hard to find guys willing to be on standby all weekend, not knowing if they're going to get called."

"What if you paid them to wait around?"

Sometimes Holly was *way* too insightful. To make more money, Tyler kept guys on standby, but didn't pay them unless they worked. "I may have to do that or go to a sub-par list."

"What's that?"

"Hire guys who can't pass a background check." If a man had an arrest record for even a minor crime like petty theft or a DUI, he couldn't pass the check. Gated communities were suspicious of anyone with any type of a criminal record. "Wait at my place until I get off."

Holly shook her head. "I'm going home. The boutique's big sale starts tomorrow."

"Okay." He'd be dead tired anyway. The shift wouldn't be over until seven. He'd need to crash for a few hours, then head into the office. "I'll call you tomorrow afternoon and see how the sale is going."

She was silent while he walked her to her Passat. Sometimes it was hard to tell what Holly was thinking. She wasn't as open with him as his previous girlfriends. The slight air of mystery added to her appeal.

She drove off, and he stood there for a moment, thinking. He hadn't asked Holly to marry him, but they discussed the future as if they intended to spend it together. Now Tyler had the vague feeling that he knew too little about Holly's actual plans.

He drove to Ocean Heights and called Butch on his cell phone. Butch was a beefy Irishman who would develop a Sumo stomach if he didn't spend his days in the gym.

"I'm sick of this shit," Tyler told him.

"I hear you, man."

"Know of any guys who might be a little shaky on a background check but are actually okay to work standby for us? I'll pay them to be on call."

Butch said he would check at his gym. Tyler hung up and drove around the bend to the mammoth wrought-iron gate at the entrance to Ocean Heights. Beyond the guard kiosk that would have been home to several families in a third world country were brand-new Tuscan-style mansions built on lots the size of a cocktail napkin. The guard on duty was pissed because he'd had to work over an hour beyond his shift.

Tyler settled in, put his feet up and wished he had thought to pick up a magazine. Nothing was more boring than the graveyard shift. His cell phone buzzed. "What the hell," he said out loud. It was almost three-thirty in the morning. He checked the caller ID. Oh, fuck! His father.

Quinten Foley had been a commander in the navy. They'd lived all over the world until his father retired. His father had prodded Tyler to enlist, but Tyler joined the police force instead. He was a major disappointment to his father. Quinten Foley never mentioned it, but Tyler couldn't shake the feeling.

He hadn't heard from the old man in months. A call now must mean bad news—his father only checked in a few times a year and never in the middle of the night. This wouldn't be about his family. Tyler was an only child. His mother had committed suicide when Tyler was in high school. There wasn't anyone else except distant relatives somewhere in New England.

Tyler forced himself to keep his voice upbeat. "You're back in town."

"No. I'm on the Gulfstream, heading in."

His father worked as a consultant for weapons manufacturers and helped smaller countries decide what to buy, then expedited those purchases. He often supplied soldiers of fortune with the latest weaponry. His clients had to be extremely wealthy to afford his services. He never failed to let Tyler know he was in a limo or on a fancy jet. It was just another way of reminding Tyler that his own father was out of his league.

"Did I wake you?"

"Nah. Holly and I were out late hitting the clubs." No way was he going to confess to his father he was sitting on his ass in a guard shack.

"Meet me for breakfast at eight at the Outpost." It wasn't a request. It was an order to appear at a trendy restaurant frequented by retired naval officers on their way to the golf course.

"What's going on?"

"We need to discuss something."

Tyler knew that was all he was going to get out of his father until they were face-to-face. Years of working in naval intelligence and weapons had made him frickin' paranoid about what he said over a cell phone. Tyler seriously doubted any spies were monitoring his father's calls but the old man always acted as if his every word, every move was being scrutinized by "foreign operatives."

Tyler hung up and stared out into the darkness. Quinten Foley was rarely interested in his opinion. Could his father want to talk about his will? The old man was in his early fifties, an appropriate time to consider discussing his future with his only child.

TYLER CONVINCED THE MORNING-shift guard to come in an hour early so he could get home, shower and shave before meeting his father. His old man treated him with a little more respect now that he'd been able to purchase a condo.

His father probably wanted to discuss his wishes should he become ill as well as his finances. Tyler couldn't bank a smile. Quinten Foley seemed immortal, but, of course, no one was. Tyler had no idea how much his father was worth. It didn't matter. He'd suffered enough to deserve every penny he'd inherit.

He drove into the lot of the Shelter Island restaurant. As usual there were several rows of late-model American cars. Buying American had been an unwritten rule for the naval officers of his father's generation. Tyler parked his Beamer next to his father's black Hummer—not an H2 or H3 model but the original Hummer the military had used.

The Outpost was some decorator's attempt at a hunting lodge. Animal skins were nailed to the log walls in the entry, where a hostess in a safari outfit seated people. One wall of the huge room was a fieldstone fireplace bracketed by tree trunks twenty feet tall. Opposite it a soaring glass wall faced the bay. In the distance the Naval Air Station on Coronado Island glistened in the too-bright morning sun.

This was a great vantage point for the retirees to watch the Navy SEALs train while they ate. His father was already seated at the prime booth by the window. When Quinten gave you a time, he arrived at least ten minutes early himself.

"How was your trip?" Tyler asked as he slid into the booth opposite his father.

"Same old, same old."

Tall and erect, Quinten Foley had a military bearing that was impossible to miss even in golf clothes. His square jaw told the world he was accustomed to his orders being obeyed. His slate-blue eyes could level a man at fifty paces. His full head of black hair had turned silver, but it only added to his commanding presence.

"I ordered huevos rancheros for you. I know how much you like them."

Tyler didn't even attempt a smile. He'd been an eggs Benedict man—until Holly reformed him. He'd never cared for huevos rancheros.

"I have to be on the course at eight-thirty." His father smiled. "Hope all my traveling hasn't screwed up my handicap."

Tyler nodded as if he gave a shit.

"I hear Calvin Hunter died while I was away."

Adam's uncle and his father had both been navy commanders. Calvin had skippered a nuclear sub before moving to some top-secret naval intelligence position on land. The men had been golfing buddies when they both were in San Diego at the same time.

"He died of a heart attack."

"Too bad. Wish I could have returned for the funeral, but I was in Zimbabwe negotiating a deal for a client."

"Adam couldn't get back either," Tyler commented as their waitress poured him a cup of coffee. "He just returned. His uncle left him everything, including a mountain of debt."

His father's ice-blue eyes narrowed. "Calvin didn't have any debt to speak of. He made a lot of money."

"Showing dogs?"

A beat of silence. "No, in real estate."

Tyler thought a moment. "Maybe. They're just sorting through the estate. Adam doesn't know much. He wasn't close to his uncle. In fact, he was blown away that he left him everything."

"Everything?" His father actually looked stunned. The only

other time Tyler could remember seeing that expression was when his father had come home to find the MPs, and his wife dead. Tyler had been huddled in the corner with the chaplain, but his father never saw him.

The waitress arrived with a heaping plate of huevos rancheros for Tyler and put scrambled eggs, tomatoes instead of potatoes, in front of his father. To the side was a single slice of toast. The old man wouldn't butter it.

"I was wondering if you could do something for me."

"Sure." Tyler ran his fork through the gooey mess and waited for the "if I should become ill" bit.

"I was in Istanbul last year and ran into Calvin. My laptop was on the fritz. Damn things aren't reliable. I stored some info on Calvin's machine. Now that he's gone, I need to retrieve that file. Could you ask Adam to let me into Calvin's office? I'd call him myself but I only met him the one time."

How well Tyler remembered that day. They'd graduated from the police academy together. Adam's father was there— so, so proud. He'd been with Adam's uncle Calvin, who'd also been very proud of Adam. Quinten Foley had grudgingly attended, then left before the group went to celebrate at a nearby Mexican restaurant.

"No need to bother Adam," Tyler said, recalling his conversation at lunch with Adam yesterday. "Right after Calvin Hunter died, thieves broke into the house. All they took was his computer and some discs."

"You're lying."

Tyler slammed down his fork, anger building in his gut. His father had insulted him many times over the years but he'd never called him a liar. He shot back, "Why would I lie about a robbery?"

Quinten Foley flinched at Tyler's unexpected outburst. He'd never raised his voice to his father. "Sorry, son. I just can't believe…"

"As an ex–police officer, I can tell you that robberies after a death are quite common, especially if the newspapers give the time of the funeral. Criminals know everyone will be at the cemetery and not at the house."

"I see," his father replied, his tone preoccupied.

"The thieves left behind lots of valuable antiques and other things. That means they were after stuff they could sell quickly for drug money. Newer model computers can be sold in minutes on the street."

All the color leached from his father's face. His voice faltered. "R-really?"

"Swear to God." He could have added "hope to die," but he didn't allow himself the pleasure. Until last night he hadn't thought about his father's death. But one day—in the not too distant future—his father would die. Then, like Adam, Tyler would inherit a bundle.

CHAPTER EIGHT

WHITNEY WALKED INTO Trish Bowrather's Ravissant Gallery, Lexi at her side. This morning when she'd picked up Brandy for his walk, Trish had invited Whitney to stop by after her morning rounds to have coffee with her. Trish wanted to chat, and Whitney had a feeling she knew what was on the older woman's mind.

Ryan Fordham.

Whitney hadn't heard from her ex last night. She'd been half expecting another call, but it hadn't come. While she'd been out, FedEx had delivered an express envelope. In it she found the papers Ryan wanted her to sign but no note from him. She read the document; it seemed to be a longer, more legalese version of what she'd signed after arbitration, but she couldn't find the original document. It was probably in one of the boxes she'd yet to unpack.

"Hi," Trish called to Whitney, her hand over the mouthpiece of the telephone. She gestured toward a black lacquer chest that had to be an expensive Chinese antique. On top was a coffee machine and porcelain cups. Cream, sugar and artificial sweetener were beside the coffeemaker.

Whitney unhooked Lexi from her leash. The retriever bounced over to join Brandy, who was perched on a bronze silk harem pillow. It served as his dog bed while matching the studied elegance and sophistication of the gallery. She helped herself to a cup of coffee and added a splash of milk.

The gallery was a commercial version of Trish's own home. Whitney wondered if the same architect had designed both. The matte-white walls displayed enormous abstract oils. One drew Whitney nearer. Whitney shuddered, but couldn't help walking closer and closer.

"Thought provoking, don't you think?" Trish asked.

Whitney practiced her smile. The mammoth painting was mesmerizing. The oil canvas could have doubled as a wall in her small cottage. It was streaked with globs of red and neon-green paint. Off to one side was a large cobalt blue eye that seemed to follow Whitney as she moved. "Who's the artist?"

"Vladimir. He has some long, unpronounceable Russian last name, so he just goes by Vladimir. He's one of the most successful artists in the area."

The eye gave Whitney the willies, but she didn't mention it. This morning when she was loading the dogs in the SUV, she'd looked up to the second-floor window of the main house. For a moment she'd thought the curtains had shifted. Now she imagined Adam Hunter, his intense blue eyes becoming one, staring down at her from behind a razor-wide gap in the drapes. Just like the haunting eye in the painting.

"Aren't you exhausted?" Trish said. "How many dogs have you walked this morning?"

"Eleven. Three were only short walks before drop-offs at their groomers." She followed Trish across the white marble floor to a sitting area with a black leather sofa and two matching chairs. She lowered herself into one chair, careful not to spill her coffee.

Trish sat on the sofa and crossed long legs clad in beige linen slacks. "Have you heard anything more from your ex-husband?"

Whitney shook her head. "No, but he FedExed the papers to me. I don't see any reason I shouldn't sign—"

"Not without having a lawyer examine them."

"Right." Whitney had planned to contact an attorney, but she found Trish's attitude a little overbearing. "Miranda just married a lawyer. I think his firm might check my papers and—" She stopped herself before saying that she planned to ask to be billed later. Trish must have guessed she didn't have much money, but Whitney's pride kept her from letting the woman know just how broke she was.

Trish put down her cup of coffee on the Lucite cube-style coffee table next to the sofa. "Miranda married a local attorney?"

Whitney hesitated a moment, remembering the well-known lawyer didn't want his clients to know he was away on his honeymoon. "It's very hush-hush."

Trish's brow creased into a frown. Whitney didn't see any reason for not telling her. Miranda would be returning soon and would have a splashy reception. Then the whole town would know.

"Miranda married Broderick Babcock."

Trish blinked hard as if trying to clear her vision. "You're kidding."

Whitney shifted in her seat, more than a little uncomfortable discussing Miranda's business. If her cousin had wanted Trish to know, Miranda had had plenty of opportunities to tell her. She shouldn't have told, but something had urged her to confide in Trish.

"Promise me you won't mention this to anyone. Rick doesn't want his clients to know he's out of town."

"I won't say a thing."

Whitney waited for Trish to comment, but the older woman studied Whitney as if she were a painting by a child that had suddenly appeared on a wall in her gallery. Finally, Trish said, "I wanted to talk to you about your ex-husband. Did you file a police report?"

"No. I don't think that's necessary. I'm sure when I sign the papers, I won't ever hear from him again."

"Good. I thought it over and did some surfing on the Net. You know, to check the latest."

Whitney nodded, but she couldn't imagine why the woman was taking such an interest in her. Didn't Trish have a life?

"When I told you to file for a restraining order…" Trish let the unfinished sentence hang in a heavy silence. "Well, I was back in the past, when I was living in New York City. I was recalling my own problems."

Trish stood, absentmindedly shook the creases out of her linen pants, walked across the gallery and stared out the window at the passing traffic. Whitney silently cursed herself for wondering about Trish's motives. She'd guessed correctly. The woman related to her because of something that she had experienced.

Two beats of silence, then Trish turned, saying, "I had an abusive husband."

"I'm sorry." The trite words came out before she could think of something better to say. "What happened?"

Trish returned to her seat, and for a moment Whitney thought she wasn't going to answer. When Trish did respond, every word grew softer until she was almost whispering. "About a year after we were married, Carter slapped me during an argument. Of course, he was upset with himself immediately. He apologized all over the place and claimed to love me more than life itself."

Whitney had heard similar stories in interviews she'd seen on television, but this was different. She knew this abused woman personally. She couldn't help thinking about Ryan. This didn't fit the profile of their relationship at all. Now that she thought back, Ryan had been verbally abusive toward the end of their second year of marriage. But he'd never raised a hand to her until yesterday. He didn't need to; Ryan could devastate her with his sarcastic remarks.

"A few months went by, and we had another fight. This time

Carter shoved me into a wall. I had a bruise that ran the length of my back and four broken ribs."

"Oh my God! What did you do?"

"Left him." There was a pensive shimmer in the shadow of Trish's eyes. "I wanted to go home to my parents, but I had too much pride. You see, they hadn't wanted me to marry Carter, but I'd insisted."

Whitney wished her mother were still alive. She would love to know how her mom would feel about Whitney's divorce, but she'd died. The only person she had in this world was Miranda.

Again, she found herself wishing her cousin were here. They could talk—as adults—in a way they'd never been able to discuss things when they'd been in high school. Back then, they were too different—or so it had seemed. Now, Whitney wondered if Miranda's reckless attitude had been her way of dealing with the unexpected death of her parents.

"That's when the stalking began." A short, mirthless laugh followed, taking Whitney by surprise. "Of course, Carter didn't see it as stalking. He kept insisting he was checking on me."

Whitney couldn't imagine Ryan "checking on her." He had another woman in his life. Why would he bother?

"Carter scared off several men who tried to date me and got me fired from a job in a gallery. That's when I finally went to the police," Trish added sourly. "They were reluctant to even take a report."

"How terrible."

"Back then, less was known about stalking and abusive husbands." Trish was silent for a moment; the only sound came from the cars going by on Prospect Street. "Weeks went by and I didn't hear from Carter. I thought the police had told him about the report, and it made him stay away. Wrong. He was still spying on me, but he was getting sneakier. I didn't see him until a man—just an acquaintance—drove me home from work. He walked me to my door. Carter leaped out of the bushes and beat the guy senseless with a baseball bat."

Whitney shuddered at the image of a bloody, battered man sprawled across the cold concrete.

"Then Carter rounded on me. The only thing that saved me was a neighbor who'd heard the commotion and called the police. My jaw was broken as well as my arm."

"My God. What happened to your friend?"

"He survived, but he had to spend months in the hospital and needed three reconstructive surgeries." Trish sank deeper into to the sofa with a ragged sigh. "My father sent him money to pay his bills."

"You went home to your parents?"

"Of course, wouldn't you? At that point, I just wanted to get away from Carter before he killed me."

For a moment, Whitney remembered the night she'd thrown her things into the SUV and driven away from the home Ryan had insisted on buying. It had been the day she'd been served with divorce papers, and she'd realized all hope of salvaging her marriage had vanished. She'd spent the night with Lexi in a cheap motel. It would have been nice to chuck her pride and return to loving parents. Instead, she'd found a housesitting job in the newspaper.

"At least you got away from him."

Trish rested her head against the back of the sofa and gazed up at the stainless-steel ceiling fan silently spinning overhead, just barely stirring the air in the gallery. "Carter followed me to Miami."

"Y-you're kidding," Whitney stammered in bewilderment. "Wasn't he jailed for assault?"

"The man couldn't identify Carter. The first blow with the baseball bat hit him from behind. The guy didn't see who struck him, and neither did my neighbor who called the cops. Carter ran off when he heard the sirens coming up the street.

It was my word against his. The prosecutor was a man. He believed Carter's story that I was a rejected wife out to blame her husband for a mugging. Even the police report I'd filed earlier didn't sway him."

"I can't believe it. What a nightmare."

Trish's gaze met Whitney's. "About a month after I returned home, I drove out of my parents' home in Coral Gables. There was Carter, standing on the sidewalk, staring at our house."

"I'll bet you freaked."

"Of course. I had no way of defending myself. My jaw was wired shut and my arm was in a cast." The recollection seemed to weigh on her, choking the life out of her voice. "Besides, I was stunned that Carter would leave the law firm where he was on track to become a partner to chase me. It made no sense; that's when I knew he was unbalanced. I told my father and he finally convinced the police to issue a restraining order."

"That helped, right?"

"My father wouldn't take any chances. He sent me to Italy until the divorce was final."

Trish stopped there, but Whitney felt there was more to the story. She stood up and went over to the sofa and sat next to Trish. She looked into the older woman's eyes. "That wasn't the end, was it?"

"No. I came home and found Carter had moved to Miami and had taken a job with another law firm," she responded in a low, tormented voice. "He made no attempt to contact me for over six months. I thought, 'Okay, so he lives here. It's a big city. Forget him. Go on with life.'

"Then one evening when my parents were out, I came into the living room and there was Carter aiming a gun at me. He said if he couldn't have me—no one would."

Whitney put her hand on Trish's trembling knee and gave her a reassuring squeeze. "What did you do?"

Stains of scarlet appeared on Trish's cheeks. "Nothing. I

froze. All I could think was that I was alone in a huge house with a maniac. I honestly thought I was dead."

"What happened?"

Trish clicked her fingers twice and Brandy bounded over. She threaded her long nails through the soft fur on his ears. "My father's boxer raced into the room, snarling and barking like crazy. It distracted Carter just long enough for me to run out of the house."

"This sounds like a nightmare that just wouldn't end."

Trish nodded. "Exactly. The police came, but Carter was long gone. When they interviewed him, he had an alibi."

"No way."

"He found some guy that was willing to swear they'd spent the evening playing Texas Hold 'Em."

"What did you do?"

"I moved away. With my father's help, I changed my name and got a new start here." A tense silence enveloped the gallery. Trish stopped petting Brandy and the dog settled at her feet. "It worked. Carter's remarried and doesn't bother me anymore."

"You never married again?"

"No. Why put myself through all that? I'm happy, successful. If I need an escort, there are plenty of men available."

The man had ruined Trish's life and left her bitter, distrustful. How sad. Trish had suffered and continued to suffer. Whitney wondered if there was any way to help.

"I didn't mean to make this all about me." Trish paused, but her melancholy eyes prolonged the moment. "I rarely discuss my past, so please keep what I've said to yourself."

"I will," Whitney quickly assured her.

"I only told you so that you would realize I understand what you're going through."

Whitney wanted to protest that her situation was nothing like what Trish had experienced, but the woman had shared so many deeply personal things that she didn't want to discount those confidences.

"I put the past behind me until you came along, Whitney. I instantly knew I had to help you, and I'm afraid I may have given you bad advice."

"What do you mean?"

"Sometimes a restraining order can be a death warrant. You've heard about women who are killed by their husbands or boyfriends *after* they've obtained a restraining order."

"I've seen it a lot on television. I can't understand why—"

"They say—shrinks say—when the man realizes he's lost power over the woman, he goes nuts. The restraining order represents a higher power. My divorce showed Carter a higher power had taken over, and he couldn't accept it."

"Makes sense." Whitney hadn't given much thought to spousal abuse until the incident yesterday morning. She still doubted Ryan would resort to real physical violence.

Trish leaned closer. "Don't file a police report unless you have bruises they can photograph or a broken bone. Then—"

"I'm sure Ryan would never—"

"Never say never. This is the worst-case scenario. Here's what you do. Keep a journal." Trish rose and walked over to her desk. She took a leather folder the size of a paperback book out of the second drawer and handed it to Whitney. "Write down the time, date and place of each encounter. If there's a witness like there was yesterday, put down the complete name, address and any other contact information."

Whitney thought about Adam Hunter. How much of the argument had he seen and heard? Would he help her if necessary? Granted, she was attracted to Adam—but after hearing Trish's story about an abusive man, Whitney should keep in mind how physical Adam had become on the night they'd met.

CHAPTER NINE

ADAM RELAXED IN the dark living room of his uncle's home, his feet up on a leather ottoman that didn't appear to ever have been used. Now that he thought about it, the whole house seemed more like a model home than a place where anyone had actually lived. The only room here with a "lived-in" look was his uncle's office.

When he'd come in, he hadn't bothered to turn on a single lamp. The only light bled in from the nightscaping outside that artistically illuminated the plants and trees. There was no movement in the house other than the slight whoosh of his own breath and the barely audible hum of the refrigerator in the kitchen nearby.

The night had become his friend, a lesson he'd learned in Iraq. Their enemies avoided darkness, preferring to strike during the light of day. Darkness soothed, took the sharp edge off Iraq's blistering sun. The night welcomed him in a way that daylight did not. Night posed less threats, offered more possibilities.

Allowed him to think.

Daylight hurled distractions at him. In the dark, Adam could concentrate. He mentally reviewed the events of the day. He'd visited the forensic accountant who had been assigned his uncle's case. Adam had been expecting an older man in a staid office. Instead, a punk kid who lived and worked out of a loft in the Marina District had been hired to review his uncle's financial records. Despite Max Deaver's tattoos and gelled hair that shot up like a rooster's comb, Adam liked the accountant and could tell he knew his business.

Deaver had just gotten started on the case, but already described Calvin Hunter's finances as an elaborate shell game. According to Deaver, his uncle had switched his funds back and forth between various Swiss and offshore accounts to other secret accounts. Why? Deaver claimed it was too early to tell exactly what his uncle had hoped to accomplish with these maneuvers.

Click. The faint sound made Adam jerk upright. A key in the back door's lock. Whitney. He stood up and quickly switched on the lamp next to his chair. The amber light revealed Jasper huddling under the nearby coffee table.

"Jasper," Whitney called softly. "Here boy. Are you in there?"

Adam scooped up Jasper and headed toward the kitchen. "He's here. I've got him."

He rounded the corner and found Whitney standing by the oven, wearing shorts that emphasized her tanned, trim legs and a T-shirt that hugged her breasts in a way he found damn sexy. Her cheeks were pink and her mane of blond hair was tousled. Her SUV hadn't been in the carport when he'd arrived home a short time ago. He'd bet she was still out, rushing around, taking care of a pack of dogs.

He could have called to say he would feed Jasper, but he hadn't. His mind refused to turn off. He kept thinking about Whitney all day. He wanted an excuse to see her.

"I didn't realize you were here," Whitney said a little anxiously, as if she was still afraid of him. "Has Jasper eaten?"

Hearing his name, the Chinese crested licked Adam's hand and gazed up at him. *Swell. Get used to it.* For reasons Adam couldn't fathom, the little dog had a thing for him.

"No. I just got in. I haven't fed him. Why don't you go ahead since you're here? I'm not exactly sure how much to give him. Show me."

"Okay." She opened the walk-in pantry, where a large bag of kibble was kept. Adam noticed there wasn't much else on the shelves. Another sign of a house not really being used. "I didn't have time to walk him. I thought I would take him out after he ate."

"Good idea." He watched her scoop kibble into a silver bowl with Jasper's name engraved on it. She bent over, giving him the opportunity to check out the provocative curve of her cute butt.

"Have you noticed the red bump behind Jasper's ear?" Adam asked, just to keep the conversation going.

"No. Where is it?" She put down the bowl and Adam set the dog on the floor beside it.

Their gazes collided. He resisted the urge to reach out and touch her soft skin. *Take it slow and easy. Let her get to know you.*

He almost laughed at himself. When he'd left San Diego for duty in Iraq, he'd been a hard-charger. He would have come on hot and heavy if he'd been attracted to a woman. So much had changed. *Not really,* he thought. The world was pretty much the same. He was different.

He had more insight now than he'd had back then. He could sense Whitney's vulnerability. She'd been through a miserable divorce. She wasn't ready for a man to come on too fast.

Jasper sniffed the kibble but showed no signs of being hungry. Unlike the lovable mutts that Adam had been raised with, Jasper didn't seem to care much about food. He spent most of his time sleeping or hiding. He was so shy that it was difficult to imagine the dog prancing around a show ring. But what did he know? The only dog show he'd ever seen had been on television and he hadn't watched the entire program.

Adam reached down and held Jasper by his collar. On the right side beneath the little dog's ear was a red bump half the size of a dime. "See this?"

Whitney leaned over and her luxuriant hair tumbled forward. He caught a whiff of the rain-fresh scent he remem-

bered from when he'd tackled her. His pulse kicked up a notch.
Uh-oh. He did his damnedest to keep his eyes—and mind—
on the dog.

Whitney inspected the raised weltlike bump carefully, then
leaned back against the counter. "It looks like something irritated him a little. You know, since Chinese cresteds are almost
hairless, they are susceptible to skin irritations that don't bother
most dogs. I think we should keep an eye on the bump. If it
doesn't get better, we may want to take him to the vet."

"Right. Let's watch it."

She gazed at him steadily without—she hoped—giving
away her inner turmoil. She hadn't expected him to be at home
in the dark house. *Be careful,* warned an inner voice. *Don't
alienate him. Just get away from here.* He'd explained why he'd
mistaken her for a burglar, but she still couldn't bring herself
to trust him. Maybe it was instinct; maybe it was hearing
Trish's story.

"How are your cuts?"

"Not a problem. How's your head?"

She offered him a tentative smile. "I have a little bump.
No big deal."

Jasper finally deigned to munch a few bites of kibble. While
he was eating, Whitney tried to think of something to say.
"Looks like that's all he's going to eat right now. You should
see Lexi. She wolfs down everything in two seconds. She's in
the backyard now with three other dogs just waiting for
dinner."

Adam reached into the pantry and pulled Jasper's leash off
its hook. "Jasper's spoiled. Let's walk him."

Say no, Whitney told herself. *Don't be alone with this man
any longer than necessary.*

"Let me show you the route Miranda recommends," she heard
herself say. "You can let the dogs off the leash and they can run.
It goes along the bluff. When it's light you can see the ocean."

Adam followed her, noting that Whitney had taken a small flashlight out of her pocket. She stuffed blue plastic "poop" bags into the back pocket of her shorts.

"There's enough moonlight tonight to see the trail, but I keep the flashlight on and aimed at the ground so the dogs will come right back to me. Canines have an incredible sense of smell, but cats see much better at night."

The footpath started—or ended—at the edge of his uncle's rose garden, depending on how you viewed the trail. Neighbors had obviously hiked along it enough so that the trail was well worn. He wondered if this might have been the way the robbers had come. If so, it could account for why so little had been taken. There was only so much you could carry along this winding path and still get away in a hurry.

The trail was wide enough for two people, and Adam walked beside Whitney. "Have you seen many people up here?"

"A few, but remember, I haven't been here long." Whitney looked up at him, but it was too dark to tell much about her expression. "Miranda showed me the trail and we took Lexi along it for quite a distance. We stopped at the tennis court that you can see from the bottom of the hill. I think the trail goes another mile or so, but I'm not sure. We didn't walk very far. Why?"

"Remember I told you that a woman called 911 the night my uncle died. I don't think she saw or heard him from the street. They might have been walking on the trail."

Whitney remembered Adam asking if Miranda had called the authorities. She stopped and shined her flashlight on the path. "You can see it's well used. Someone might have been out for a walk and heard your uncle call for help or something. Have the police checked on it?"

After a slight pause, Adam told her, "I went to see the investigating officer today. I knew him. Not well, but I knew him from back when I'd been on the police force."

"Really?" She couldn't hide her surprise. "You're a policeman?"

"I was a detective. I worked homicide."

"Interesting" was all she could think to say. How wrong she'd been. She'd mentally categorized him as a hit man or worse. Something menacing about him still bothered her, but Whitney didn't have time to analyze it.

"The investigating officer didn't think it was unusual that the woman who called 911 disappeared. Apparently, it happens all the time. People just don't want to get involved. Since there were no signs of foul play, they didn't pursue it."

Something in his tone told Whitney that he was suspicious, or maybe just bitter. "Your uncle died of a heart attack?"

"That's what it appears to be. The coroner is running a few more tests. Then we should know for sure."

He seemed preoccupied, but Whitney ventured another question. "You're no longer on the police force?"

He walked a few steps in silence, then said, "No. Too many homicides were drug deals gone sour. I got sick of them. Half the time witnesses were too frightened to talk. When we could nail a suspect, he was back on the street in no time thanks to a screwed-up system and slick lawyers. I started a private security firm with a friend. Then my National Guard unit was called for duty in Iraq."

Iraq. How horrible. Images she's seen on newscasts and what she'd read of the horrors flashed through her mind. Small wonder the man was so edgy. No telling what Adam had been through.

"What was it like?"

"You don't want to know." The way he said it, Whitney could tell this was a closed subject. He bent down and let Jasper off the leash. The little dog bolted into the darkness beyond the path.

"Are you sure you should let Jasper loose? He doesn't come when I call. I let Lexi off all the time, but she always minds me. Jasper's another story. I won't risk having him disappear by letting him off the leash when I'm walking him."

Adam stopped, his gaze on Jasper's ghost of a shadow disappearing into the brush. "He comes when I call."

"It must be a male-bonding thing."

Adam chuckled, a deep, masculine sound. "When is Miranda returning from her honeymoon? Maybe she knows the names of some of the neighbors who use this trail. I'd like to ask if one of them called the authorities the night my uncle died."

"In about twelve days, I think. She said two weeks but didn't leave me an exact time or date."

"Where's she staying? I could call her. Two weeks is a long time to wait."

"I don't know." Her revelation was greeted by silence. In the darkness she couldn't read his expression to guess what he might be thinking. "My cousin and I aren't really all that close," she felt compelled to explain. "I married and lived out of state until last year when my ex came back to open his practice. He didn't get along that well with Miranda. We didn't see much of her."

That was an exaggeration, Whitney admitted to herself. She'd called her cousin to let her know she was back in town, but hadn't invited Miranda over or gone to see her. She'd behaved shamefully. She could blame it on Ryan, but in truth, it was her own fault that Miranda no longer had been part of her life.

"Like my uncle," Adam replied, his voice low. "I knew him but I had almost nothing to do with him until recently. Then suddenly he's gone."

She heard a heartfelt note of regret in his voice that mirrored her own feelings. She wouldn't have believed she had anything in common with the man who'd tackled her, but she was wrong. They both realized they'd missed an opportunity to develop a close relationship with a relative. She might have a second chance with Miranda, but Adam never would with his uncle.

"I regret not seeing more of my cousin. I should have made the effort. When I left my husband, Miranda took me in immediately. But now, I think she'll be busy with her own life. I doubt I'll see much of her."

"You never know," Adam replied, but he didn't sound convincing.

They walked a short distance in silence. Whitney couldn't see Jasper but she could hear him ferreting around in the underbrush.

"You know to be careful that coyotes don't get Jasper," she told him. "It's a big problem in these hills."

"You're right. I'll take better care of him. I always had large dogs that coyotes wouldn't bother." He whistled for Jasper and the little dog scampered out from the brush.

"Speaking of dogs. I'd better go feed my mine." She turned to head back toward the house.

"Why don't you feed them, then come up to the house? I'm ordering a pizza from Mama Gina's. The works. Everything on it, if that's okay."

Say no, cried an inner voice. *What's the harm,* she decided with her next breath. Adam had been a policeman and he'd served in Iraq. Just because they'd gotten off to a bad start didn't mean they couldn't be friends.

"Mama Gina's makes the best pizza. The works is great. I'm easy. I even like anchovies," she finally said.

"So do I."

It was too dark to see his face, but she could hear the smile in his voice.

CHAPTER TEN

ADAM HAD PHONED in the pizza order and was opening a bottle of Chianti he'd found in the sparsely stocked pantry when he heard Whitney calling to him.

"Adam! Adam! Have you seen Lexi?" She rushed through the door, a frantic look in her eyes.

"No. She wasn't in the yard?"

Whitney shook her head. "No. The gate was ajar. I'm sure I shut it, but she may have nudged open the latch."

"Are the other dogs there?"

"Yes. Just Lexi's gone. She may have come looking for me. We've only been here a few days. She really isn't used to the area."

"Let's turn on all the lights in the yard. She's probably sniffing around out there." He flipped the switches on the panel next to the door. Light flooded the back and side yards of his uncle's home.

"I don't see her," Whitney said as she stepped outside. "Here, Lexi. Here, girl."

Adam followed Whitney into the backyard, but the Golden retriever wasn't in the pool area, and there was no sign of her in the well-manicured bushes.

"I don't think she could get into the dog run along the side of the house," Adam told her. "It's only accessible from the dog door off the kitchen. That's how Jasper comes and goes, but let's check."

There was no sign of Lexi in the dog run. Whitney kept

calling and calling but the retriever didn't respond. Adam had a bad feeling about this. Lexi was a female, small for her breed. If she'd followed them out onto the trail, a pack of coyotes could have taken her down.

"I saw a Mag flashlight in one of the kitchen drawers. I'll get it, then let's check out the trail."

"Good idea," Whitney answered, a quaver in her voice. "She may have followed my scent in that direction."

It took Adam a few minutes to locate the flashlight and determine the battery was still working. He ran out of the house. Whitney was standing at the edge of the trail, calling for Lexi. The hollow tone of her voice told him that she didn't expect her dog to come.

"No sign of Lexi?"

"No. I'm just kicking myself for not double-checking the gate."

They hurried onto the trail. The wide beam of the Mag light illuminated the path and the brush alongside it. Ground squirrels skittered away from the bright light, but there wasn't any indication Whitney's dog was out here.

"Could she have gone the other way toward the street?" he asked.

"I guess, but I don't know why she would. I walk her along the trail or around my clients' homes. We haven't used the street."

Adam understood. This section of Torrey Pines was hilly and didn't have sidewalks. Cars traveled faster than they should. It would be dangerous to walk along the road. That's why whoever had called 911 for his uncle must have been walking along the trail or had driven up to the house in a car. They heard his uncle cry out for help…or something. They'd gone upstairs to the study, found the body sprawled across the floor and called 911.

That was one scenario. But if his uncle had been murdered, the killer could have been in the house. The first responders on the scene found the front door unlocked. That didn't sound like Uncle Calvin, but Adam didn't know him well enough to be positive. This was a safe, affluent area. The neighbors might not have been concerned about safety, but Calvin must have been, considering what he'd told Adam in Greece. Could Calvin have been expecting someone and left the front door unlocked for that person? It could have been a fatal mistake.

"Why don't I drive you through the neighborhood?" he asked. "Flash the light into the bushes and call to Lexi."

They searched the area for over an hour but couldn't find a trace of the dog. They drove back to his uncle's house in silence.

"Now what?" he asked. "Animal control doesn't pick up strays at night."

Whitney's lower lip trembled as she spoke. "Lexi's chipped so if she is picked up by animal control, they'll wand her and call the chip center. All the chip shows is an ID number. The center has my updated info. They'll call me right away."

"Let's leave on the yard lights and your porch lights. That way if she's out there somewhere, she can find her way back."

"I will," Whitney replied, her voice barely above a whisper.

"I don't suppose you want any pizza." He'd given Mama Gina's his credit card. He was sure they'd left the pizza while he and Whitney were out. "It's probably cold, but we could zap—"

"Thanks, but I'm going to keep looking for Lexi. Miranda didn't mention any dognapping problems around here, but L.A.'s had a lot of trouble. I've dropped off many dogs at groomers'. They're usually the first to know if there's a snatch-and-run scam operating in the area. Owners put up reward signs at groomers' on the off chance whoever took the dog will bring them in for a bath."

"You mean thieves snatch dogs, then ransom them?"

"Sometimes, but there are rings that grab dogs and pass

them to someone else who takes them out of the immediate area. That person often gives the dog to yet another person. The animal is sold quickly for less than market value."

"It wouldn't have papers."

"Not necessarily," she reflected with bitterness. "A computer can generate a document that looks amazingly like an AKC certificate. People don't ask questions because they're glad to get the dog at a bargain price."

Adam was amazed. "I thought people just wanted puppies."

"No. The thieves have great stories about owners who've been transferred or died or something to explain why they're selling a full-grown dog. This appeals to people who want to bypass the house training ordeal. The new owners get a pet that's housebroken and well trained."

"They must be selling them over the Internet."

"Exactly, but from what I understand, they post a picture of a dog that belongs to someone in the ring. Even if I surf the Web, I won't necessarily see Lexi's picture. People who respond to the ad are told to bring cash and meet the seller at a public place like the parking lot of a fast-food restaurant, where the exchange takes place."

Adam could understand why Whitney sounded so discouraged. If dognappers had stolen Lexi, the retriever would be long gone by morning. "I guess thieves remove a dog's collar, but what about Lexi's microchip? Won't that tell who she really belongs to?"

"Yes, if a vet has a reason to check the chip in her neck. It's routinely scanned by animal control, but that means a dog has to be picked up first. It happens, but people are usually careful with purebreds, so animal control doesn't have any reason to check them." She lowered her head and studied her hands, clutched together in her lap. "A chip's easy to remove. I could do it with a long needle, but they don't usually bother."

Adam had to admit finding Whitney's dog didn't sound

promising. If a pack of coyotes hadn't dragged off the retriever, thieves must have taken her. A thought occurred to him. "Why didn't they take any of the other dogs? Didn't you say they were smaller? Wouldn't they be easier to handle?"

"True, but certain breeds are more in demand. Golden retrievers, pugs and Labs rank right up there. It's also possible they had an order for a female retriever. From what I've been told, thieves target dogs they know they can sell instantly."

"You mean Chinese cresteds aren't at the top of the list?"

Whitney attempted a laugh. "Most people wouldn't recognize one. Until Kate Hudson starred in *How to Lose a Guy in Ten Days*, Chinese cresteds weren't on the radar screen."

"Hey! My uncle told me the same crested won the ugliest dog in the world contest two years in a row."

"That dog was pitiful. Most Chinese cresteds look more like Jasper."

That wasn't saying much, in Adam's opinion. It was hard to believe people actually bred dogs to look like Jasper. It was even more difficult to understand how shy little Jasper had become an international champion. Go figure. Still, he had to admit he was developing a soft spot for Jasper. It was hard not to like a dog who adored you.

"Do you think it's possible your ex took Lexi? He seemed really angry with you."

"I can't see Ryan taking her and leaving the gate ajar. The other dogs could have run off, and I would be in serious trouble." The words weren't out of her mouth one second before she gasped.

RYAN STARED AT HIS COMPUTER screen. He'd made a list of the bills he owed and ranked them by order of importance. The bank was already sending late notices on his home loan. He was behind on the second mortgage and home equity loan as well. He didn't have any hope of paying off his debts if his new partners realized his financial plight and dropped him from the new cosmetic surgery group.

Talk about hell on earth.

Maybe if he took what little cash he had, he could play the slots and parlay it into enough to hit the tables. With luck, he could run it into real money. Perhaps he could win enough to make all or part of the house payment.

Those problems paled when compared with the threat from Domenic Coriz. Being in debt was one thing; being dead was another. It wasn't an idle threat. The Indian tribes in San Diego County earned megabucks from their casinos. The operation had spawned a rough element that used mob tactics ruthlessly. They would kill Ryan without a second thought and dump his body on the rez where no one would ever find it.

Whitney had to sign those papers—immediately. He desperately needed a debt-consolidation loan. The interest rate would be stratospheric but it would just be temporary. When the cosmetic surgery group was up and running, he would pay off all his loans.

In the distance, the doorbell chimed. He glanced at his Rolex. Nearly eleven o'clock. Who would be at his door so late? *Domenic or his goon* flashed into his mind. They might hassle him at home. Sweat peppered the skin just under the hair on his forehead.

He heard Ashley answer the front door and voices drifted across the large living room to the back of the house, where he'd converted a rear bedroom into an office. It sounded like a woman.

"I don't know what you're talking about," he heard Ashley protest in a frantic voice.

"You have my dog! I know you do. Don't deny it." He recognized Whitney's voice. "How could you steal my dog right out of her yard? Isn't it enough that you have my husband, my house?"

Oh, shit! Just what he didn't need. Whitney going postal on

Ashley. The deeper rumble of a male voice sent him dashing through the living room where Ashley had been rearranging furniture again.

"We need to check the house and the yard," a stern male voice boomed through the large entry.

Ryan rushed into the foyer. "What's going on?"

He slammed to a stop, stunned to see Whitney and that jerk who'd ordered him off Whitney's driveway standing in the entry. Ashley was flushed and her lower lip was trembling. He raced to her side and put a protective arm around her.

"Lexi's missing!" Whitney pointed at him. "You took her, didn't you?"

"What? You've hit a new low."

"No, I haven't," she yelled in a strident voice he hadn't heard once during their marriage. "You stole Lexi to get back at me."

"I wouldn't take Lexi. You know that."

"I didn't think you'd hurt me, either," Whitney shrieked. "No telling what you'll do next."

Out of the corner of his eye, Ryan saw Ashley gaze up at him, a questioning look in her eyes. Shit! Why did she have to frighten Ashley? He'd momentarily lost his temper—that's all.

"I didn't hurt you. I just needed you to see reason and sign the papers."

"I want my dog back. You got this damn house and the furniture. All I asked for was Lexi. I want her back—now."

"I don't have her." He glanced at the powerfully built man with Whitney. He was frowning at Ryan like he wanted to deck him. "I swear I don't have the dog."

"Since this is legally still half Whitney's house, she has the right to look around and see if you have Lexi." The man spoke in a low, level voice, but his commanding presence reminded Ryan of Domenic Coriz.

"I don't appreciate your barging in here and scaring my

wife," Ryan told Adam, but Adam could see the wimpy doctor was shaken. "I didn't take Lexi. Why would I?"

Adam had been on homicide long enough and had interrogated enough lowlifes to realize Ryan Fordham was telling the truth. They weren't going to find the dog here.

"You took Lexi to get back at me for not signing the papers," Whitney insisted.

"Oh, for Christ's sake." Ryan ground out the words. "I'm not that childish. If you acted your age and signed the document you'd already agreed to, we could go our separate ways."

Adam didn't know exactly what was in the document or why Whitney had refused to sign it, but Fordham made Whitney sound peevish. Adam fought the impulse to turn and leave. He never became involved in family feuds—particularly divorces. Tempers flared and emotions ran deep. He didn't want to be in the middle of this.

"Look around." Ashley waved a manicured hand sporting a diamond the size of a golf ball. "You won't find her."

Adam nudged Whitney. "See if Lexi's here. I'll wait for you."

Whitney dashed to the right, heading toward the kitchen. From where Adam was standing he could see the wavering blue-white light reflected on the windows. Evidently there was a pool beyond the house, and Whitney had mentioned a dog run where Lexi once had a doghouse.

"What happened?" Ryan Fordham curtly asked him. Again, Adam had the distinct impression the doctor hadn't a clue about Lexi's whereabouts.

Adam told the doctor and his bombshell wife who he was and explained what had happened to Lexi. Fordham tried to frown but his brows barely moved. Must be injecting himself with Botox, Adam decided. It figured; cosmetic surgeons, even ones as young as Fordham, couldn't afford telltale wrinkles.

"That's strange. Lexi never wanders," Fordham told him in a puzzled tone. "We've had her since she was a puppy. Nearly five years. She never once ran off."

"Maybe the dog's confused," Ashley suggested in a breathy voice. "She thinks this is her home. She isn't used to her new place yet."

Fordham gave the sexy blonde an affectionate squeeze. "Good thinking, sweetheart. It's also possible thieves snatched Lexi and sold her to a test lab. There are several in the area. Golden retrievers are easy marks. They're trusting and anxious to please. Experimenter's favorites."

"Oh, no," Ashley moaned. It seemed a little put on, but who was Adam to say. "How terrible."

"I'll make some calls first thing in the morning," Ryan offered. "If she's at a local lab, I'll be able to track her down."

"Good idea," Adam said, and he meant it. He was positive Ryan Fordham was telling the truth. It would be so easy if Whitney's ex had taken the dog, but it was more likely the retriever would vanish into thin air. Whitney might never know what had happened to her pet.

"It would help if you could convince Whitney to sign those papers. She agreed to the settlement already, but the judge screwed up. He didn't notice the document hadn't been properly recorded." Ryan gave his wife a one-armed hug. "Then we can go our separate ways in peace."

Adam found himself nodding. He hadn't known her long, but he wanted Whitney to feel free, to want to start over. These papers—and the dog—seemed to be her last link to her ex. Was she playing it for all it was worth? he suddenly wondered. Could Whitney have the dog stashed somewhere, using this as an excuse to get back at her husband or something?

Why had he become involved? He was thinking with his dick. After nearly three years without sex, he'd gone bonkers over the first attractive woman to cross his path. Granted,

Whitney was sexy as hell—and interesting—but he didn't need to be involved in a domestic dispute like this.

"Look, Doc," he replied, aware he'd made "Doc" sound like a four-letter word. "This isn't any of my business. Take it up with Whitney."

CHAPTER ELEVEN

WHITNEY STUMBLED INTO the cottage. Da Vinci and Maddie greeted her with high-pitched yips. They ran in happy, excited circles around her feet. It was all she could do not to shout: Which one of you opened the gate? Who let Lexi out?

She collapsed onto the small well-worn sofa, admitting that it must have been Lexi who'd used her nose or paw to spring the latch on the gate. The other dogs were too little to reach the lever. Lexi had never done anything like that—ever. She'd never shown the slightest tendency to wander. But there was always a first time. Blaming the other dogs, yelling at them wouldn't bring Lexi back.

"Please, God," she whispered, "I'll do anything."

Then she remembered what her mother had always said. *You can't make deals with the universe. God has more important things to do.*

Still she prayed, because that was all she could do. Hot tears slowly seeped from her eyes and drizzled down her cheeks. Lexi's collar had a tag with her name and this phone number clearly engraved on it. Whitney had always taken precautions not to lose Lexi. When she'd first left the home she'd shared with Ryan to house-sit, she'd immediately gotten Lexi a new tag and called the chip center to update the information. She'd switched the tag for another one the first day she'd moved in with Miranda. She'd contacted the chip center again with the current information.

"It's too soon to give up hope," she told Da Vinci, who'd hopped up beside her and was trying his best to lick the tears dribbling off her chin.

A paralyzing depression gripped her. *How do we sense things before we know them?* she asked herself. When she'd left Adam to feed the dogs, something had alerted her. A sense of dread like a slow-moving fog had engulfed her on the stone path from the main house to the cottage.

The minute she'd opened the front door she'd…known. She'd raced to the back door to the small yard where she'd left the dogs. The gate was ajar. Lexi had vanished.

She'd rushed around like a crazy woman. Searching and calling. Searching and calling. Yet in her heart of hearts, she'd known she wouldn't find Lexi.

Even when she'd had the hissy fit at Ryan's, she'd known deep down that it was a vain hope. When he didn't get his way, Ryan did little vindictive things like "accidentally" throwing out cherished photographs of her mother. But she didn't believe he'd taken Lexi.

Another wave of tears brimmed in her eyes and streamed down her cheeks. What had her last words to Lexi been? "Go on, now. Do your business."

She tried not to think of what she'd read on the Golden retriever rescue Web site. Almost three-quarters of lost Goldens were never returned to their owners—despite having identification on them. They were intelligent, loving dogs. People who found them tended to keep them.

"Lexi belongs to me," she whispered to herself.

She remembered every day and every training session. Lexi had been so easy, caught on so fast. Still, Whitney had been the one—never Ryan—to put in the necessary time.

Why would a dog that was so well trained run away? It didn't make sense. She had to admit Ashley might have been correct. Lexi could have been confused by leaving the home where she'd been raised to move first to a house-sitting place and then here. She must have released the latch to go search for Whitney.

Because Lexi had simply vanished, Whitney realized she would always wonder about her dog. Was Lexi locked up somewhere, alone and afraid? Was she in pain? Did she need a vet?

And some part of Whitney would always hope that one day she would open the door and miracle of miracles—Lexi would be there. Sitting, of course. Waiting to be petted.

Whitney realized she would wonder and worry for years. Even when Lexi's natural lifespan was over, Whitney would continue to agonize over her loss. She would still know that no matter who'd kept Lexi, the Golden was hers. And no one else's.

"SHE'S A NUT CASE," Ashley said just after Adam and Whitney left.

Her voice was still shaky. How many overly emotional women could he handle in an hour? Ryan eased his arm away from his wife's shoulders.

"Whitney's crazy about that dog. Always has been."

It shocked Ryan to realize Whitney cared more about Lexi than she had about him. He hadn't known it until just now. Seeing how distraught and unreasonable Whitney was convinced him. Even when he'd walked out on her, Whitney hadn't been this upset.

"Let's get to bed," Ryan told Ashley. There wasn't anything he could do in the office tonight. Getting laid would take his mind off his problems for a few minutes.

On their way to the master suite, Ryan heard his cell phone ringing in the distance. It was still in the office, where he'd left it beside the computer. Who would be calling him at this time of night?

"A wrong number," Ashley suggested.

"Probably. I'll check and turn it off."

He hurried back to his office and grabbed the cell phone off the stack of bills on his desk, dreading answering it.

"Fordham," the man said before Ryan could utter a word.

"Yes." He tried to project confidence even though his balls ached at the sound of the voice.

"Dom wants to meet you tomorrow. He has a plan."

Ryan listened to the instructions, then hung up. He sank into his chair. He ran his tongue over his lips, but his mouth had gone bone dry.

A plan?

He wanted no part of any plan Domenic Coriz concocted. How was he going to get out of this mess? Now he knew why people committed suicide. If you had no way out, death might be your only choice.

You're stronger than that, he reminded himself. He'd grown up the youngest child in a working-class family. The youngest was supposed to be the baby, but it hadn't worked that way in his family. Youngest meant his older siblings raised him. They'd teased him mercilessly or ignored him. He'd never known what to expect, so he'd struck out on his own. He'd worked hard to put himself through college and medical school. True, he'd married Whitney and she'd been responsible for his medical education, but he had struggled to get ahead. And he'd made it. This was a temporary setback—nothing more.

Mentally reviewing his limited options, he meandered back to the master suite, taking time to turn off the backyard lights that Whitney had thrown on during her desperate search for Lexi.

"Are you really going to call the testing labs tomorrow?" Ashley asked when he wandered into their bedroom.

She was in bed, propped up against an armada of pillows and dressed in his favorite sheer black negligee that half exposed her perfect breasts. He'd performed more than his fair share of boob jobs and appreciated the real thing more than most men.

"Yes. I'll call around." He kept talking as he went into his large walk-in closet off the bedroom. He raised his voice so she could still hear him. "Lexi's my dog, too. I don't want anyone experimenting on her."

Ashley waited a second before responding, "Of course not."

For an extended moment, he stood there, one leg out of his trousers, the other still covered by the fabric. An unsettled feeling caused his shoulders to twitch. Something about Ashley's reaction to Lexi's disappearance bothered him.

He finished undressing and tossed his dirty clothes in the hamper he kept next to six long rows of shoes. Some, like his black patent leather tuxedo shoes, he rarely wore, but seeing them all lined up and polished made him smile. He had a shoe fixation for some reason, and he knew it. A shrink might ask if he'd lacked shoes as a kid or been forced to wear hand-me-downs. No. His family hadn't had much money, but he'd always had his own sneakers and church shoes.

Still, he never failed to notice people's shoes when he met them. Ashley had been wearing strappy high-heeled sandals when he'd seen her for the first time. Tonight, Adam Hunter had on new black Pumas. As usual, Whitney was wearing ratty cross-trainers she'd bought on sale. Dom Coriz's man had been wearing steel-toed boots most often seen on construction jobs.

He left his Nikes in their spot on the shoe rack and walked naked into the bedroom. Ashley was still sitting upright, her blond hair cascading over her shoulders. The thought niggling at the back of his mind resurfaced.

"Ashley, do you know anything about Lexi's disappearance?"

"Of course not," she replied a bit too quickly.

He stopped at the foot of the bed and asked himself how he knew she was lying. Nothing about the innocent expression on her face gave her away. Still, little red flags had been popping up since he joined her at the front door. Her tone of voice. Her flushed face.

"Don't lie to me."

The anger and frustration he harbored over his gambling losses and Dom's threats underscored each syllable. Ashley clutched the silk top sheet as if she expected him to backhand her. He held his temper and stared at the woman he loved. "Is there something you want to tell me?" he finally asked when the silence had lengthened.

Ashley blinked back tears with two sweeps of her long lashes. It was the first time he'd seen her cry. Ashley was his wife, the woman he loved in a way that he'd never loved anyone on this earth. At another time, tears might have moved him. Tonight his mind was numb from all the jackals after a piece of his hide.

"A—a friend swiped her dog," Ashley confessed.

"Aw, shit! Why?"

Ashley scrambled out from under the covers, dashed to his side and pressed her centerfold body against his. "We thought that if the dog went missing overnight, Whitney would be motivated to sign the documents."

"What? Of all the harebrained ideas! How was she supposed to link the dog to the papers?"

"In the morning my friend is going to call Whitney and tell her what to do if she wants her dog back."

Christ! Ashley *was* legally blond. "What if Whitney calls the police? They'll come after me."

A bitter-sounding laugh slipped out from between her pouty lips. "It would be her word against yours—and she wouldn't stand a chance of getting Lexi back. My friend will make that crystal clear."

Ryan had to admit the scheme might have worked, but it also would have told Whitney how desperate he was.

He backed away from Ashley. "Call your friend. Get Lexi

back to Whitney. Have her say she found the dog wandering. Do *not* let her say or do anything that would make Whitney suspect we were involved. Understand?"

He stomped into his closet and grabbed a pair of slacks off a hanger. Ashley followed him in and stood at the door. She didn't say a word but he could feel her watching him as he dressed.

Finally she asked, "Why are you getting dressed again?"

He shoved his bare feet into a pair of navy Topsiders he didn't remember ever wearing. "I need to get out of here and think. When I come back, I expect you'll have taken care of the problem."

"I will," she whispered. "Don't worry."

Ryan rushed out of the bedroom. He wasn't concerned. Ashley would do as she was told and her girlfriend would return Lexi. This gave him the excuse he needed to drive to the casino and see if Lady Luck would smile on him.

ASHLEY WAITED UNTIL SHE HEARD Ryan's Porsche roar out of the garage before she called Preston Block.

"Sorry it's so late," she apologized.

"Not a problem." Preston didn't bother to ask who it was. They spoke every day and instantly recognized each other's voices.

"Ryan's ex stomped in here tonight," she told him. "Whitney thought we had her dog."

"So? She couldn't have found a thing. The dog's right here beside me."

"Ryan's so smart. He figured out I was behind Lexi's disappearance. He went ballistic. He insisted I have—" Ashley paused "—my girlfriend bring back the dog right away."

Preston chuckled. "Your girlfriend? That's a joke."

"I didn't tell him about you. He's really upset and I didn't want to make him any angrier."

Preston didn't respond. Ashley knew he had a thing for her, but she tried her best to ignore it. She needed a friend, not another man with the hots for her.

"Do something for me." She hated the pleading tone in her voice, but what could she do? "Get that dog back right away."

"Tonight?"

"Yes. Please. Do it for me."

Ashley hung up, then turned off the light, but she couldn't sleep. She kept listening for the sound of Ryan's car. He was so jumpy and angry lately that she didn't know what to do. Something was bothering him. She tried to tell herself that it was the pressure of putting together a new practice, but now she wondered if that was all it was.

Ashley had to pull her hand away from the telephone. She was sorely tempted to try to reach her father. He lived in Bakersfield, not far north. Like Ryan, he was a man who worked for a living and owned his own business. He must know about stress. He might have some idea of how to handle Ryan.

But it had been years since she'd spoken to her father. He'd said he would always love her, but he'd left them. She was too proud to go sniveling to him. She could handle the situation.

THE TELEPHONE ON ADAM'S uncle's desk rang, startling him and waking up Jasper, who'd been asleep at his feet. A quick glance at his watch told him it was nearly three-thirty in the morning. Who would be calling at this hour? The caller ID screen read: Marshall.

Whitney.

What did she want? After her futile search for Lexi, they had driven home in silence. There was no need for words. Her eyes reflected a deep, inconsolable grief. It was impossible to gaze into those green eyes and not be touched.

As attracted as he was to Whitney, Adam refused to be drawn into this any more than he already had been. He'd convinced himself he possessed the good sense to realize Whitney was still emotionally attached to her ex-husband.

Adam did not want any more trouble. He'd spent the last hour sorting through his uncle's papers. He needed to keep his focus on investigating Calvin Hunter's death. Let Whitney attend to her own problems.

He was half tempted to let the machine pick up the call but he'd told Whitney to phone him immediately if anything happened. From the cottage she could see that his lights were on and would know he was still up.

"What's happening?" he asked as Jasper leaped up onto his lap.

"Good news," she cried, the sound of tears in her voice. "A jogger found Lexi."

"At this hour?"

"Yes. He's bringing her home right away."

"That's great. I'll be right down—"

"Don't bother. You've done enough." There was a slight pause. "I'm sorry for imposing on you. Thanks so much for all your help. Good night."

She hung up before Adam could respond. He stared at the receiver for a moment, relieved but still bothered by the late-night reappearance of the retriever. His police training made him question the situation even more. Kicking himself for not minding his own business, Adam trudged out of the house and down the path to the cottage that had once belonged to a full-time gardener. Jasper scampered along beside him.

Whitney must have heard his footsteps on the wooden porch. She flung open the door before he could knock. Her happy smile evaporated as soon as she saw who it was.

"Oh, I was hoping it was the guy who found Lexi."

Adam stepped inside with Jasper underfoot. He nearly stumbled over the little dog who'd become his constant companion. "I didn't want you meeting some strange man so late at night. There are all kinds of people around. It's good to be cautious."

The crunch of tires on the gravel driveway made Whitney charge by him. Adam followed a few steps behind her. A tall guy in a blue T-shirt and khaki pants got out of a Camry that had seen better days. He had sun-streaked blond hair and a bronze body. His biceps said he could snap a man's neck like a toothpick.

"Lexi!" Whitney raced toward the car as the man opened the back door and a Golden retriever jumped out.

The dog tugged on the leash and whirled in a circle, barking. Whitney dropped to her knees, arms outstretched, and the dog lathered her with kisses. Tears of happiness streamed down her face.

The guy flexed his powerful shoulders, his version of a shrug, and grinned at Adam. "I guess it's her dog, all right."

"Looks like." Adam stepped off the porch, still a little suspicious. He tried for his good-old-boy tone, the one he'd once used to put potential criminals at ease when questioning them. "Where'd you find her?"

"Down on Memorial Drive. I was out for a run and noticed her in the bushes."

"A little late to be running, isn't it?"

The buffed-out guy smiled, revealing California-white teeth. "I was helping out a buddy at Boomerang's, bouncing kids with phony IDs."

Adam remembered the place from his days on the police force. It was a punk hangout that had been busted numerous times for serving liquor to minors. As much drug dealing went on in the joint as it did over the border in Tijuana.

"I was kinda keyed up, so I went for a run on my way home. Spotted the dog, then she started following me. I checked her tags, then called the number."

Whitney wouldn't let go of the retriever. Her tears had stopped but her voice was still shaky. "Thanks so much. I've been out of my mind worried." She unhooked the leash attached to Lexi's collar. "I'm Whitney Fo—Marshall."

"Preston Block."

"Adam Hunter," he said. "I'm Whitney's friend. I live right there." He gestured toward the house on the rise behind them. For reasons he didn't have time to analyze, he wanted this guy to know he lived nearby.

Block pointed at Jasper. "Is that eyesore a dog?"

It took Adam a second to realize the jerk had insulted Jasper. He stepped forward, ready to cut loose with a smart comeback. He had to admit Jasper wasn't winning any beauty awards, but the little dog belonged to him now.

Whitney came to Jasper's defense. "Jasper's a Chinese crested. He happens to be the international champion."

Don't say he's worth a fortune, Adam silently cautioned. *We don't want another dog to disappear.*

"Really?" Block responded with a smile. "Coulda fooled me."

Adam battled the urge to whack him. Who was he to criticize Jasper?

"Let me give you a reward for returning my dog," Whitney offered, standing up. "You have no idea how grateful I am."

Good move, Adam thought. Block must have recognized the address on the tag as one of the more upscale neighborhoods and expected some money. That had to be the reason he was so anxious to return the dog in the middle of the night.

Block shook his head. "Nah. I don't want a reward. I'm just glad I could help. I know if my dog wandered off, I'd be outta my friggin' head."

There you go. What a sweetheart of a guy.

"What kind of dog do you have?" Whitney asked.

"I don't have one right now. I'm in an apartment, but I grew up with German shepherds. I'm getting one as soon as I can."

"German shepherds are great," Whitney said, stroking her own dog's head. "I'd better feed Lexi. She missed dinner."

"I'm outta here," Block said.

"Goodbye. Thanks again. I'm really grateful."

From the other side of the car, Adam watched as Whitney gave Block a grateful hug and thanked him yet again for returning her dog. Lexi followed Whitney up the steps toward the door of the cottage.

Adam kept his voice low, asking, "Do you always keep a leash in your car?"

Block had his body half in the door of his car—a tight wedge, considering his size. "Nah." He held up the leash. "I picked this up along with a Red Bull at the Stop 'N Go on Harborside. I thought I might have to walk her around for a while. There's an old biddy in our complex. Goes ballistic if she even sees a dog visiting."

"Gotcha. Some folks aren't dog friendly." Adam turned toward the cottage, Jasper at his feet. Whitney had already taken Lexi inside. "Thanks again for your help."

"No problem," the man said through the open window.

Adam watched Block back down the driveway. He had returned Lexi on a cheap nylon leash, the kind a minimart would sell, but something nagged at Adam. He wasn't sure what was bothering him. The guy seemed to be telling the truth. Adam noticed the Camry had a California plate and memorized the number.

CHAPTER TWELVE

WHITNEY WAS SO intently watching Lexi eat that she didn't realize Adam had come back into the cottage until she heard a soft sound behind her. She turned away from Lexi and smiled at him. "That gate needs a lock. Obviously, Lexi can figure out how to open it."

"I think a combination padlock would be easiest." He paused. "We have a storeroom at the office with all kinds of locks and security devices. I'll bring one home tonight."

"Thanks. I appreciate all you've done." She ruffled her hand through her hair, remembering how she'd flung accusations like hot coals. "Wow! I really overreacted. Much as I hate to admit it, I owe Ryan an apology. I'll call him first thing in the morning."

"Why don't you have an attorney look over those papers? If he says it's okay, sign them. You need to move forward."

"You're right," she assured him. "I'm ready to start over. I really am."

He studied her for a moment, then moved closer. "Are you?"

Electricity arced between them, so strong she could practically feel its heat. Her breath caught, then rushed out ragged and fast. His intense blue eyes dilated as he gazed at her and waited for a response.

"Absolutely." The word fell from her lips as a soft plea. "I want to get on with my life."

She wasn't sure how Adam felt, but she knew she wanted him. After that first scary encounter, she'd been afraid of him, but her impression had changed. He was an attractive man, but more than that, he was a kind person. She couldn't imagine Ryan running around in the middle of the night searching for a lost dog owned by a woman he hardly knew.

"Come here." There was a huskiness to his voice that spiked her pulse. When Adam reached for her, Whitney eased into his arms with a sigh that floated through the air.

He crushed his mouth to hers, muttering something that sounded like a low growl. Her lips instantly parted and she squeezed her eyes shut. She folded her arms around his neck and pressed her body to his as his tongue swirled into her mouth— hot, greedy. Her breasts molded against the hard planes of his chest and her nipples immediately began to throb. He tasted every bit as masculine and erotic as she'd imagined he would.

The warmth of his powerful body sent a heady sense of anticipation through her. What would it be like to make love to him? she wondered as he continued to kiss her. During the last year with Ryan, their lovemaking had been sporadic. She'd sensed his indifference and tried everything she could think of to please him. It had been so stressful that she couldn't remember what it was like to be desired. With a thrill, she realized this man wanted her as much as she wanted him.

Forget Ryan! He's so-o-o over.

Adam's hands wove through her hair, changing the angle of her head so he could kiss her more deeply. The feel of his fingers on her scalp sent languid heat radiating through the lower reaches of her body. Her toes curled. His tongue kept tangling with hers until she was nearly mindless with the need to have him inside her.

His hands left her hair and caressed the taut muscles of her back. Too many long, lonely nights seemed like something that had happened to a stranger. For an instant she wondered about Adam's past, about the haunted look in his eyes. But those thoughts vanished as his hands roved lower and squeezed her bottom, then pushed her flush against his erection. Senses reeling, she arched her back and moved invitingly against the turgid heat of his arousal.

He edged one hand between their bodies and captured her breast. The nipple was already a tight nubbin, but the heat of his hand made it ache with a need more intense than anything she'd ever experienced. She longed to feel his mouth on her breast, her nipple between his lips.

His thumb swept back and forth across her nipple, teasing the sensitive bead through the sheer fabric of her T-shirt. A primal moan rumbled from deep in her throat. She honestly couldn't get enough of him.

A chirping sound made her pull back. "W-what?"

Adam gave a snort of disgust. "My cell phone. I'm on call, but I don't know what could be going on at this hour." He yanked the tiny phone off his belt. "Hunter."

Whitney turned, noticed Lexi had finished eating and was standing at the back door. The retriever always went to the bathroom right after she ate. She let the dog out and stood watching her. The gate was closed, but she refused to take any chances.

She put a hand to her moist lips. Her heart was still pounding, her knees still jittery. What had she been thinking? She was acting like some wanton woman who'd been on a deserted island for the last year. Granted, few of her peers would fault her, but she had her own standards. Whitney had never been one to throw herself at a man. She heard Adam come up behind her and looked over her shoulder.

"I've gotta go. An emergency at one of our guard posts. Could you take care of Jasper?"

"Of course," she replied, resisting the urge to ask when she'd see him again.

He bent down and brushed a soft kiss across her lips. "I'll come back with the lock."

After he left, Whitney trudged into the bedroom, so exhausted she could hardly think. Jasper and Lexi followed her. They found Maddie and Da Vinci asleep on Whitney's bed. Creatures of habit, they'd put themselves to bed earlier in the evening. Surprisingly, the sound of a car and Lexi's return hadn't disturbed them. Common sense told her to take them outside—especially Da Vinci, who was prone to "slips," but she was too tired.

She nudged them aside so she could have a place on the queen-size bed, reminding herself that over forty percent of dog owners slept with their pets. She wasn't so strange. Jasper sprang onto the bed and joined the two other small dogs. She scooted sideways to make room for Lexi. She patted the mattress. Lexi stood there a moment, perplexed. She usually slept in her cushy dog bed on the floor. A second thump on the covers, and Lexi sprang up beside Whitney, then settled in.

Whitney stroked the soft fur on the retriever's head, her heart stutter-stepping when she thought how close she'd come to losing Lexi. Something hummed inside her chest. She wasn't sure if it was a cry of relief or despair. A post she'd read on Muttsblog.com sprang to mind.

When did Fido become Fred? The online question had been followed by a very thoughtful post about how the Fido of the fifties—a house pet—had become Fred—a bona fide member of the family. As society changed, the blogger claimed, pets assumed a new role. Dogs began to fill the emotional gaps in people's lives as the world became increasingly disconnected.

When Whitney met fellow walkers—dog owners often walked at the same time along the same route—they referred to her not by name but as "Lexi's mom." This implied her retriever had the status of a child. Few of those dog owners in the neighborhood where she'd lived with Ryan knew her name.

A soft snuffling sound told her Lexi was asleep but Whitney kept petting her. It was true, she conceded to herself. Lexi filled so many voids in her life. From the time they'd bought Lexi almost five years ago, the dog had begun to move into the place that Ryan had once occupied. It was the beginning of the end of their relationship. Looking back, she realized Ryan had begun to withdraw shortly before he brought home the puppy.

Without family or many friends, there was an empty space in Whitney's heart that she hadn't realized existed until now, when Lexi moved into it. She had been on the brink of utter despair when Lexi vanished. The depth of Whitney's vulnerability had been even worse than when Ryan had left her. She'd almost lost it—in front of Ryan and the bimbo he'd married. In front of Adam.

"You need a life," she whispered into the darkness.

Adam's face appeared on the screen in her mind. She could almost feel his lips against hers. If his phone hadn't disturbed them…well, they would have bounced Maddie and Da Vinci onto the floor.

She considered the situation for a minute, stopped stroking Lexi and rolled onto her other side. A person without friends or family shouldn't leap like a fool into…into what? A one-night stand? No, not with Adam. A new relationship should be entered into with more caution. After all, she'd already proven how poorly she chose men.

She needed family and friends. When Miranda returned, Whitney planned to make up for all the time they'd lost, but her cousin might be so absorbed in her marriage that she wouldn't need Whitney. All she could do was make the effort and see what happened.

As for friends, Trish Bowrather was the only person with whom she'd had much contact. She was friendly in a dominating sort of way. Still, they had a divorce and Golden retrievers in common.

In her mind's eye, Whitney saw Trish's impressive home and exclusive gallery. The woman might seem to have it all, but Whitney suspected Trish was lonely.

Whitney said out loud, "Tomorrow is the first day of the rest of your life." True, it was a trite saying, but it fit her situation. She refused to live a "disconnected" life with only a dog to care about her.

ADAM ASKED HIMSELF WHY IN hell he was in a guardhouse at the gated development of Ocean Heights. For some reason the guard had simply up and left without even calling the command post. A resident had returned and found the post deserted. Somehow he'd futzed with the computer until he'd contacted HiTech. Butch had attempted to contact Tyler at home and on his cell, but couldn't get a response. In desperation, he'd called Adam.

What Adam knew about running a guard post came down to opening the gate for residents, guests and service people. Over the phone, Butch had been able to walk him through the procedures. It was a little after four o'clock in the morning. He didn't expect much traffic until seven, when the next guard came on duty. If HiTech was making so much money, the least they could do was have a backup guard on call. Tomorrow, he'd take up this and a lot more with Tyler. If backup had been available, Adam would be snuggled in bed with Whitney.

Okay, *snuggled* might not have been it. Hot, sweaty sex was what sprang to mind. He could almost feel her beneath him, feel himself driving into her soft, sweet body.

He wanted a woman; he needed a woman—in the worst way. *Not just any woman,* he realized. Nearly dying had changed his outlook on life.

Once he'd believed he had years and years ahead of him to find a woman, have a family. His father's death—at a relatively early age—had been the harbinger of things to come. But he hadn't heeded the warning: Life is too short. It had taken his own near-death experience for him to appreciate just how fragile life was. Uncle Calvin's death sealed his impression.

"Get your mind off sex," he muttered under his breath. As

it was he was going to have blue balls for a week. He'd left Whitney's with an erection like an iron pike. He didn't need to sit at a guard post with another one.

He called Butch at the command post. "I need our pin number for Total Track."

"Anything going on?" Butch asked with a note of curiosity in his voice.

"Nah. I'm bored. I want to check out a guy I met."

Butch gave Adam the series of numbers and letters that would allow him to access the database of the private company used by many security firms and some of the smaller police departments. Total Track kept information from the DMV, utility companies, cable television services, as well as credit card reporting services. The system was used to determine an individual's current address, place of work, credit status and a lot of other supposedly confidential information.

Total Track was very expensive but worth it to security companies trying to locate people. Before Adam had been forced to leave for Iraq, HiTech had been poised to go into the security business. But now it seemed to be nothing more than a guard service. He wondered why they were still paying for Total Track.

Once he was in the system, Adam typed, "Preston Block." In the next breath up popped the standard information.

Address: 1297 Thurston Place Unit 4B
Place of Employment: Dr. Jox Fitness Center
Automobile: 1992 Camry (blue)
License: HWZ943

Adam scanned the guy's credit history. One credit card. Block made the minimum payment on time each month and carried a balance that was roughly half his limit. Typical. Most people in America carried a hefty balance and paid the minimum each month.

His Bank of America checking account showed a balance of just under five hundred dollars. Block didn't have a savings account. No surprise there. America had turned into a nation of debtors, not savers.

He scrolled down the screen. Holy shit! Preston Block had a sealed juvenile record. For what? In rare cases, a sealed juvenile record concealed a serious crime like rape or murder. Odds were against it. More likely Block had been convicted of petty theft or joyriding in a "borrowed" car.

He rocked back in the chair and stared at the screen. Block seemed to be a regular working stiff. Nothing unusual except he'd been jogging and came upon a lost Golden retriever.

So what was bothering Adam?

He logged out of Total Track and Googled "Preston Block." The guy had a Web site. Interesting. Adam clicked on the Web site. Up came a picture of Block, appearing even more buff than he had tonight. He'd oiled his muscles like weight lifters did so the guy looked very impressive on the screen.

Block advertised his services as a personal trainer. "I'll come to you or you come to me!"

What a guy. Adam clicked through a series of photographs showing Block working with clients at Dr. Jox Fitness Center. Most of Block's clients seemed to be women who were so toned and pretty that it was hard to believe they needed a trainer. But that was only his opinion.

Adam got tired of looking at all the babes that Block made his living training. It was just making him think about Whitney's sexy bod. He returned to the Ocean Heights screen and forced himself not to think about Whitney.

Like a chop to the back of his neck, it hit him. Now he knew what bothered him about Preston Block's story. Okay, okay, what freak went jogging at nearly three-thirty in the morning? That had been the first clue.

But it wasn't just that. There was a chink in Block's story.

Adam had spent enough time on the streets of greater San Diego as a homicide detective to remember many of the businesses—particularly on the main thoroughfares.

There wasn't any Stop 'N Go on Harborside. Why would Block lie about where he bought the leash?

CHAPTER THIRTEEN

WHITNEY CHECKED HER reflection in the towering plate-glass doors of the high-rise in the Marina District where Broderick Babcock had his offices. Her pale pink twinset and navy slacks didn't seem businesslike enough to visit a criminal defense attorney. Well, it was the best she could do.

Whitney had walked only the dogs that absolutely needed to be taken out before rushing downtown. She'd called Ryan to apologize and tell him Lexi had been found but he'd already left. She'd nearly choked on her apology to Ashley, but she'd managed to spit it out. Ashley had been "totally thrilled" to hear Lexi had been returned. Whitney told her to contact Ryan immediately. She didn't want her ex wasting his time calling test labs, searching for Lexi.

As she swung open the tall glass door and walked into the immense marble-floored lobby, she admitted to herself that a sense of relief had replaced the animosity she'd felt toward Ryan and his new wife. She wanted the divorce behind her. Last night, while she'd been in bed with the dogs, she'd realized how much she needed to begin all over. She told herself not to see Adam Hunter as part of this new life. *Put him out of your mind,* she kept thinking. But in the next minute, swear to God, his image would pop up unbidden.

She checked the directory on the wall and found Broderick Babcock's office was in the penthouse. Silently rehearsing what she would say to the attorney, Whitney rode the elevator to the lawyer's offices. Another glass door led into a large waiting room decorated with minimalistic furniture in muted shades of cocoa. It was empty except for an older woman behind a desk.

Whitney entered and the woman with blue-tinged hair and a gray suit looked up with a smile. "May I help you?"

"I'm Whitney Marshall." She expected "Marshall" to ring a bell. Apparently, it did not. The woman waited for her to continue. "I have a divorce agreement I'd like an attorney to look over." She stopped right in front of the desk.

"We're a criminal law firm," the woman responded pleasantly. "I can recommend—"

"I would really like to see someone here," Whitney replied. "You see, since my cousin—who's like my sister—is on her honeymoon with Mr. Babcock, I thought…"

"Your cousin?"

"They're honeymooning. You know, in Fiji." Was it possible the attorney hadn't told his office staff? The woman seemed perplexed, but she was smiling. The wedding was supposed to be a secret from his clients. She'd assumed his staff had been told, but she might have blown it by coming here and spilling the beans.

"Married?" the woman asked as if she'd never heard the word.

"Yes. I just thought maybe another attorney in the firm could take a quick look." She waggled the document she had brought with her.

"What did you say your name was?"

"Whitney. Whitney Marshall. My cousin is Miranda Marshall, now Miranda Babcock."

"I see." She rose, saying, "Wait here. Someone will be right with you."

The woman disappeared behind double doors that must lead into the inner offices. Whitney took a deep breath and gazed out the window at the amazing view of San Diego

Harbor. Looking at an aircraft carrier slowly moving toward the navy yard, she again rehearsed what she would tell the attorney. She needed to inquire about making payments on his fee. That was the important part; she had almost no money.

The door opened and the receptionist said, "Right this way."

Whitney followed her down a long corridor. She glimpsed several people diligently working at desks in various offices. At the end of the hall she saw a large office and beyond it the gleaming blue waters of the harbor. It had to belong to a senior partner, she decided. Her simple settlement agreement wasn't worth bothering someone so important. Why couldn't one of the other attorneys look at the document?

Before Whitney could suggest this, the receptionist stepped into the office and announced, "Whitney Marshall, sir."

From behind a glass desk the size of a pool table rose a tall man with black hair burnished at the temples with gray. His dark brown eyes warned her that he missed nothing in his field of vision. They also said he was a man who didn't know the meaning of the word *compromise*. What had she gotten herself into?

"Thanks, Karen," he said to the receptionist with a smile.

Whitney relaxed a little as the older woman closed the door. Men who were kind to their staff were kind in general. Right?

He extended his hand across the desk. "Broderick Babcock."

A whooshing sound like a shrill wind swept through her head. Whitney's lips parted and she croaked out the words "Whitney Marshall." She managed to extend her hand, but it felt limp in his.

"Sit, sit." He waved her to a chair in front of his desk.

She dropped into the seat, inhaling sharply, struggling to comprehend what she'd just heard. How could this be Broderick Babcock? What was going on?

His bold gaze assessed her with searching gravity, then he allowed himself to smile. "People have tried lots of tricks to get in to see me when they know I'm not taking any cases because I'm overbooked, but this beats all. That's why I told Karen I'd see you. I wanted to look eye to eye at the person who'd concoct such a story."

Beam me up, Scottie, was all she could think. Obviously, Miranda had played a trick on her or something. "I didn't concoct a story," she responded in a weak but high-pitched voice, sounding like Minnie Mouse's timid sister. "I actually thought... Never mind." She stood with as much dignity as she could muster. "My cousin must have played a practical joke on me. Obviously, I made a mistake. I'm sorry to have taken up your time."

"Sit down and tell me about it." He pointed to the stacks of papers littering his glass desk. "I need a good laugh."

Whitney had no trouble seeing how the attorney swayed juries. His words were spoken in a persuasive voice that permitted no argument. She dropped back into the chair. "My cousin convinced me that she was going on a honeymoon to Fiji. I hadn't seen Miranda much until very recently so I hadn't met the man she was supposedly marrying—Rick Babcock."

"That was her first mistake. I use Broderick professionally because big fancy names impress people, especially juries. But my friends call me Rod."

For the first time, it struck Whitney that Miranda might never have met the attorney. Strangers might think Broderick would be shortened to Rick, but his friends knew to call him Rod.

"Go on," he prompted.

"Miranda was very convincing. She moved everything out of her place and let me have it. You see, I'm going through a divorce. Ah, actually, I am divorced, but..."

"Either you are or you aren't. It's like being pregnant. You're pregnant or you're not." He said this in a joking tone that forced Whitney to smile, but she felt more like strangling someone—Miranda.

"I thought I was divorced." She held up the document she'd been clutching in her left hand. "I signed an arbitration agreement months ago, then my ex reappeared. He claims it isn't legal because it needs to be signed in front of a notary."

"That's correct."

"I'm a little—" she started to say *suspicious,* then amended it to "uneasy because the document seems longer than the original. That's why I decided to have an attorney review the papers. I came here because I fell for Miranda's prank."

He shook his head slowly, saying, "Arbitration. What a laugh. Arbitrators are usually law students who couldn't pass the bar. People think they're saving money. Most end up at an attorney like you."

She smiled weakly. "I'm sorry to have bothered you. I'll find another lawyer to review these papers."

"It's not a bother," he quickly assured her. "Leave the agreement with me. I'll have someone review it and get right back to you."

She hesitated. "I came here because I believed Miranda's story. I thought I could work out a payment plan because we were, you know…related."

He chuckled again, and she couldn't help smiling at him. She would bet he had most juries in the palm of his hand.

"I won't charge you. This probably isn't any big deal. Just leave the papers." He reached across the desk, and she handed him the document. It was slightly curled from her death grip. "I'm interested in your cousin and why she made up such a wild story. Tell me about her."

Whitney wasn't sure where to begin. Miranda's deception had been so unexpected. She hadn't had time to think.

"Miranda Marshall. Do I know her?"

"Maybe. She's my age, thirty-two going on thirty-three. We're first cousins and look a lot alike. Blond hair. Green eyes. We're the same size."

"I've never seen you before. Trust me, I have a good memory for faces."

She believed him. Broderick Babcock probably kept an entire law library in his head.

"Where does your cousin work?"

"She owns—owned—Marshall's Pet Concierge. That's a dog-walking and pet sitting service. Mostly dogs and a few cats."

He leaned back in his chair and frowned. "I don't have a dog. I can't imagine where we crossed paths."

"Maybe she just made it up. You're very well known. It—"

"It's still odd. I hope she didn't spread this all around town. I'm divorced—"

"I'm sure she didn't," Whitney quickly told him. "Miranda warned me not to tell anyone. She claimed you wanted to keep it secret so your clients wouldn't know you were out of town."

"Does your cousin have a history of mental problems?"

"No, of course not," Whitney assured him. But she realized how little she actually knew about Miranda.

RYAN CAME OUT OF Le Bistro, a fine sheen of sweat coating his entire body. Domenic Coriz had him by the balls and the prick knew it. There wasn't any way out of this mess except to let Coriz have his way.

He sat in his Porsche and checked the messages on his cell phone. He'd had it on vibrate and knew several calls had come in while he'd been with the Native American. Ashley had left three messages. Walter Nance, the head of the group of cosmetic surgeons he was joining, had called.

Shit!

What was he going to tell Walter? He didn't have his share of the money for the new building. He had little chance of getting it for a while.

Last night, Lady Luck had spit in his eye. He'd left Ashley

for the casino in hopes of accumulating enough money on the slot machines to have a run at the craps table. He'd bottomed out.

Ryan pressed speed dial and Ashley answered on the second ring. "What's up, babe?"

"Lexi's back with Whitney. She called to tell us and apologized for being so hysterical last night."

"I hope you were nice, considering…"

"Of course. I was very pleasant. She insisted I call you. She didn't want you contacting a bunch of testing labs when Lexi was already home."

"I appreciate that. Listen, sweetie. I've gotta go. I have a meeting with Walter."

He pressed End and heaved a sigh. Under normal circumstances, he would have ridden Ashley hard for having her girlfriend swipe Lexi, but he was nearly at the point where he was going to have to confess how broke they were.

Busted!

He couldn't imagine how Ashley would handle it if he confessed he had a gambling habit of this magnitude. She'd tried to be nonchalant but Ashley hadn't been able to conceal from him how happy she'd been to quit her job at the cosmetic surgery center. Money had been tight her entire life. She was counting on him to support her in a lifestyle that suited someone as beautiful as Ashley.

He stared beyond the steering wheel at the wall of the restaurant. He was positive Ashley loved him. But his financial situation and his status as a doctor meant a lot to her. She deserved the best and he was going to give it to her. No matter what it took.

IT WAS AFTER LUNCH BEFORE Preston Block appeared at the gym. According to the punk manning the reception desk, Block had spent the morning visiting clients at home.

"Block," Adam called as the buff guy slammed his car door shut.

He turned around and looked across the lot to see who had called his name. Block tried for a smile, but it didn't take a rocket scientist to realize the guy wasn't thrilled to see him. "Hey! How's the dog?"

Adam walked close enough to look into Block's eyes. "Lexi's home where she belongs."

Block switched the backpack he was carrying from one hand to the other. "I really don't want a reward. I—"

"I didn't come about a reward. I want to know the truth. You weren't jogging when you found Lexi, were you?"

"Of course I was."

"Bullshit. There isn't a Stop 'N Go on Harborside. You didn't buy the leash there. Why did you steal the dog?"

"Man, you've lost it. I found her, just like I said I did."

Adam glared at Preston Block and let his words hang like a noose in the air. Lies were like cockroaches. If you spotted one, others were nearby. A minute dragged by before Adam said, "I checked with Jake Conavey at Boomerang's. You didn't help out there last night."

If Block was surprised that Adam had contacted the owner of the punk bar, it didn't show in his face. He shrugged as if to say: So?

Adam was tempted to ram his fist down the cocky jerk's throat. Instead, he told him, "Before my unit was called up for duty in Iraq, I was a detective with the San Diego P.D."

That got Block's attention. His nostrils flared ever so slightly, a visceral sign of his anxiety. Adam didn't add that he was no longer affiliated with law enforcement. He allowed Block to assume he'd be going back to work on the police force.

"Now, this can go one of two ways," Adam said in a casual voice. "You can tell me the truth or you can expect a lot of nosing into your personal life. I'm sure you don't want to be looking in your rearview mirror every time you get in your car. I'm sure you don't want to smoke a joint and wonder if you're going to be busted. I'm sure you don't want to be late to your clients because you've been pulled over for something."

"That's harassment. I'll report you."

"You've got a sealed juvenile record. Maybe your clients wouldn't like you so much if they received copies of that report." Adam was bluffing with this. It was nearly impossible to access a sealed juvenile record.

"Oh, shit!" Block glanced toward the entrance to the gym as if he expected someone to come out and help him. He inhaled deeply, his nostrils flaring out even more this time. "I didn't mean any harm. I brought the dog back, didn't I?"

"Why did you take her?" Adam ground out the words.

Block ran his shovel-like hands through his hair. "It was my plan—all mine. It seemed like a good idea at the time. She didn't have anything to do with it."

"She? You mean Ashley Fordham?" Seeing the pretty women featured on Block's Web site had made Adam wonder about Ryan's new wife, but Dr. Jox was so far from where they lived that he hadn't been sure about the connection.

"Yeah. Look, man…Ashley wanted this new house. She was really upset. She's been on the road her whole life. One apartment after another; one city after another."

"A tragedy, sure, but what does this have to do with the dog?"

"I've been working with Ashley for three years, since she moved here to try out for Miss San Diego. We've become close friends. I was the only one at the funeral when her mother died. We celebrated together when the doc gave her that killer ring."

Adam just bet Preston Block was overcome with joy at Ashley's engagement. Any jerk could see the guy was bonkers over the bombshell Fordham had married. "Okay, pard, I get the picture. What does your friendship with Ashley have to do with the Golden retriever?"

"I thought we could use it as leverage to persuade the stubborn broad to sign some papers. Then the doc's credit history would be clear, and they could buy a new house. Ashley told me the ex had already agreed to this settlement, but she refused to sign it now."

Adam kicked himself for not figuring this out on his own. He'd run off Fordham while he'd been physically attempting to force Whitney to sign. "What made you return the dog in the middle of the night? Doesn't sound like part of the plan."

His gaze lowered, as did his voice. "The doc figured out Ashley was responsible for the dog's disappearance—"

"Fordham didn't know anything about it?"

"Christ, no. He went ballistic when he discovered what she'd done. He insisted Ashley have her girlfriend return the dog."

"Girlfriend? He doesn't know about you?"

"Nah, he wouldn't understand our friendship." His expression clouded. "Look, the dog's back. No harm, no foul. Right? Don't tell anyone what really happened. It'll only hurt Ashley's marriage."

"I think Whitney deserves to know the truth."

"What's the point?" Block shot back. "She should do what's right. Sign the agreement and move on. I'll bet you anything, Whitney won't believe her ex wasn't involved. She'll use it to stir things up even more. Ashley deserves a chance."

Adam wondered if Block didn't have a point. Whitney was seeing an attorney this morning. She expected him to okay the agreement, and then she'd sign it and return it to her ex-husband. What good could it possibly do for her to know Ashley's personal trainer had deliberately taken Lexi? She probably would think Ryan was involved.

All right, all right. *He* wanted Whitney to move on with her life. If he were honest with himself, he would admit that he wanted her to make a clean break now. He believed Preston was telling the truth. Whitney's ex hadn't taken Lexi. Whitney had her dog back. She didn't need to know all the details.

Leave well enough alone, he told himself.

CHAPTER FOURTEEN

"I CAN'T IMAGINE why Miranda would say she was going to marry Rod Babcock. What do you think?"

Whitney was sitting in Trish Bowrather's gallery and eating a salad. She'd come here directly after leaving the attorney's office. She'd walked Brandy again while Trish ordered lunch. Lexi and the other dogs were safely locked inside the cottage.

While she'd exercised Brandy, Whitney kept asking herself: Why? Why? Was Miranda in some kind of trouble? Could she be running from an abusive boyfriend? Debtors?

Whitney ruled out creditors. There hadn't been any dunning phone calls or collection agents hovering around. True, they could still appear, but Whitney doubted it.

What was so wrong that Miranda couldn't share it with Whitney? She'd poured her heart out to Miranda and told her the details of Ryan's betrayal. Miranda had never mentioned any problems and seemed really happy about her upcoming "wedding."

Of course, Whitney now knew why Miranda had never introduced her "fiancé" and why she wanted to keep the honeymoon secret. If Whitney hadn't been prompted by her encounter with Ryan and Lexi's disappearance, she never would have gone to see Broderick Babcock. She wouldn't have missed Miranda for at least another two weeks. Had Miranda been buying time?

Trish toyed with the romaine leaves in her chicken Caesar

salad for a moment before replying, "I can't even begin to guess why your cousin would make up such a bizarre story then disappear. You're sure she took *all* her clothes?"

"Yes. I helped her pack them. She put books and office stuff and—I don't know—junk in the garage." She thought a moment. "She took her laptop computer, too."

"If she took all her clothes and her computer, she planned to relocate somewhere. She left in her car, right?"

"Yes." Whitney remembered her cousin driving off at dusk in her Volvo.

"Miranda must have car payments and credit card bills. I think there are ways of checking on the Internet but I'm not sure how."

Whitney nodded slowly. She thought Adam would know how to track down her cousin. How could she impose on him yet again?

"Don't make Miranda's problems your problems," Trish cautioned.

"You'd think she would have told me something."

"Not necessarily. You said you two hadn't been close in some time. Maybe she didn't want to involve you."

"Anything's possible," Whitney admitted. She remembered how she'd felt in bed last night with the dogs. There wasn't much in her life except Lexi. She'd counted on reconnecting with Miranda, but now that seemed impossible.

"What's Rod Babcock like?" Trish asked, unexpectedly changing the subject.

"He's older. Mid-forties." As she said it, Whitney realized this was about Trish's age and hoped she hadn't insulted her. When Rod and Trish each smiled, little fanlike lines appeared at the corners of their eyes. She rushed on. "Attractive. Really smart. It was nice of him to agree to check over that document for me."

"It's been my experience that men—especially lawyers—don't do anything without expecting something in return."

Trish's horrendous experience with her ex-husband had clearly made her distrustful of all men. Perhaps that was why she'd never remarried. It certainly wasn't her looks; Trish was strikingly attractive.

Trish rose, went over to her desk and returned with several envelopes. "Here are some invitations to my next exhibition this Friday evening. You were admiring Vladimir's work. Come meet him at the opening."

"Great," Whitney said. The Russian artist who used just one name had painted the malevolent eye she'd once associated with Adam. The enormous eye was watching her even now.

Trish handed her the envelopes. "Bring a friend, and give one to Rod Babcock. I'd like to meet him. I'm sure he can afford Vladimir's work."

"I'll try," Whitney replied. "I'm not sure I'll see Rod again. Someone on his staff—"

"You'll see him. Mark my words."

IT WAS LATE AFTERNOON WHEN Tyler returned to the office. Sherry had told Adam that his partner had been out on "reviews" with several homeowner associations.

"Yo, Adam." Tyler stuck his head in Adam's office door. "You wanted to see me?"

Adam looked up from the computer analysis of security equipment that he'd been reviewing. "Come in and shut the door."

"Uh-oh. Sounds serious." Tyler closed the door, then sat in the chair beside Adam's desk. "What's up?"

"The guard at Ocean Heights walked off his post last night. I—"

"I know. Sorry about that. Doesn't happen often."

"Shouldn't we have guards on call?"

Tyler smiled sheepishly. "It's hard on that shift, but I think I've got it worked out."

"Good." Adam didn't ask any more questions. The guard

business was Tyler's baby. He'd developed it and worked with the accounts. "You were right about corporate security. We would need a lot more capital."

"It might be possible later," Tyler replied, but he didn't sound all that interested.

"I have another idea. We could go for it right now."

"Okay, shoot."

"Protecting buildings and offices has become a huge business since 9/11, right? I'm not talking about security personnel. I'm referring to security barrier systems like concrete barricades."

"Gotcha. We've had people call to see if we have things like that in stock." Tyler nodded slowly. "We might be able to move in that direction."

"I've located a company up north that makes swinging security arms like the ones we already have at guard kiosks and parking garages. Instead of being the lightweight type we use now, these are reinforced steel. They can stop a five-ton truck going seventy miles an hour. No one can just barrel in and blow up a building."

"That's really impressive." Tyler thought a moment. "If the arms are so much heavier, the motor that lifts them will have to be more powerful. It would mean changing our existing motors and buying new ones. I'm not sure homeowner associations—"

"I was thinking of businesses and the military installations around here, not gated communities."

"Doesn't the military have their own contractors?"

"Yes, but a lot of them have been diverted to Iraq. There's a serious shortage here," Adam replied. "I think we should start with bollards."

"What are they?"

"Knee-high cement posts that prevent cars or trucks from driving too close to buildings. There's a new type that can be temporarily removed if someone needs to access the building to move in or out or install large pieces of furniture or equipment."

"Okay. I know what you mean now."

"I'm going to start right away by getting us certified and arranging for security clearances. Could we use your father for a reference?"

Tyler cleared his throat, then replied, "I'm sure he'll agree. We actually had breakfast together, and he mentioned your uncle. I guess they met in Istanbul sometime last year. My father put some of his business info on your uncle's computer because his wasn't working. He'd like to retrieve it, but I told him the computer had been stolen. Any chance there's a backup disc somewhere?"

"I doubt it. I've been checking all the software the burglars left behind. There isn't much. What they did leave seems to be just discs for software installed on the computer like Quick-Books and Excel."

"Could you keep looking?"

Tyler sounded a little anxious. Adam knew his friend's relationship with his father wasn't very good. Obviously Quinten Foley must be upset about the theft and pressuring his son. "Sure. I should finish going through his office tonight—" he thought about Whitney "—or tomorrow. I'll let you know."

"Great. I'll—"

The buzzer on Adam's phone interrupted them. He picked up the receiver.

"There's a Max Deaver here to see you," Sherry told him. "He says it's important."

"Thanks. Send him in." Adam hung up. "I've got to talk to this guy. Let's touch base tomorrow."

Tyler nodded and left without another word. The forensic accountant hired by the attorney handling Calvin Hunter's estate entered Adam's office as soon as Tyler left.

"Hope you don't mind me dropping by. I have a client in the Halstrom Building next door."

"Not at all." Adam waved Deaver to the seat Tyler had just vacated. "What's up?"

Deaver sat down, his expression grave. "I'm still chasing your uncle's offshore accounts all over the place. It's a first-rate shell game. Best I've seen since I've been in the business. He might have had a pro help him."

"Really?"

"It's very likely. Most guys who show dogs wouldn't—"

"Remember, my uncle was in military intelligence before he retired. He might have learned these maneuvers in the service."

"It's possible." Deaver shifted in the chair. "That's not what's bothering me. Yesterday, twenty-five thousand dollars was withdrawn from one of his offshore accounts in the Cayman Islands that I did manage to locate."

"How could that happen? I thought you needed the account number and a password."

"You're right. That's exactly what's necessary. Someone knows about this account. Whoever it is has his special password, too." Deaver leaned forward slightly and his tone became even more serious. "As far as I can tell, that Cayman account is the end point of the shell game. It was harder than hell to find. Your uncle deliberately shifted all his money around and around so that it would be nearly impossible to discover where it was."

"Yet someone has found it."

Adam stared out his window at the ocean in the distance. The late-afternoon light reflected off of it like a mile-long mirror. "I can't find any of his account numbers. They don't seem to be listed on anything in the house. Of course, it was burglarized. The account numbers and passwords might be on his stolen computer."

"Could be, but it wouldn't be a very smart move for a man in the intelligence field. People tend to write down passwords and hide them. With an estate this large and complicated, the access numbers might be in code or something."

"Whoever withdrew the money knew exactly where it was."

"That's the only explanation, and if they were testing, as I suspect, they now realize the password is correct."

"Is there anything I can do to stop that person from withdrawing any more money?"

"You could contact the bank. As heir to his estate, they might put a hold on the account, but it's unlikely. Secret accounts often have partners who wish to remain anonymous. Banking establishments honor those relationships."

Adam thought for a moment. "It seems to me that I read somewhere that secret partners in Swiss accounts are often terrorist groups."

"Exactly. Legitimate organizations or individuals deposit money in Swiss accounts, then funds are withdrawn by God-only-knows-who. That's why the Swiss have come under such scrutiny. Going into this, I doubted your uncle's money would be in Switzerland. Too many prying eyes. He moved his cash from there to several other banks in the Maldives and Panama. They aren't as closely watched by the Feds looking for the sources of terrorists' funds."

Adam thanked Deaver for his time and the forensic accountant left. Uncle Calvin had been a very secretive man. Adam couldn't imagine him trusting anyone with such important information. The code *must* have been on his stolen computer. The thief or thieves had been after the code. It certainly explained why nothing else had been taken from the house.

Adam decided to talk to Quinten Foley. He might know something that would help. If not, whoever had the code could drain his uncle's remaining assets. Then Adam would be left with his uncle's bills and little money to pay them. He would run out of money in no time.

CHAPTER FIFTEEN

WHITNEY CHECKED HER cell phone, then put it back in her pocket. She told Adam, "I've never tried call forwarding before."

"Trust me. It works. I use it all the time."

They were on Adam's patio watching the sun set. Adam had phoned on his way home from work. He'd bought steaks to grill and ingredients for a salad.

"A prospective client called earlier to make sure I was going to be home this evening to discuss taking care of her dog. This will be the first client that I've gotten on my own."

Adam finished lighting the grill and turned back to her. "What kind of dog?"

"A poodle. I think the owner is a foreigner. She said Fiona was a *poo-dell*."

"Large or small?" Adam poured them each a glass of pinot noir.

"I didn't ask. I assume small because you see so many of them, but it could be a standard poodle. She must have gotten my name from a client, but she didn't say who."

"Did you see an attorney?"

Adam's tone sounded a little guarded. She wondered if he might be reluctant to pressure her. "Yes. Broderick Babcock is looking over the papers."

"You saw Babcock himself? What about the honeymoon?"

She sighed. "There wasn't one. Miranda made it all up."

His eyes flared in disbelief, then narrowed while Whitney explained exactly what had happened at the attorney's office.

"Babcock didn't even know your cousin?"

Whitney shook her head. "I guess Miranda read about him or saw him on television. He's a local celebrity."

"Yeah, probably," he replied, but he didn't sound convinced.

"I wonder where she's gone," Whitney said. "Maybe something happened to her. Miranda might be in danger—"

"When people disappear like that they're usually running from something or someone."

"I don't have a clue what was happening with her. I've only been here a few days. When I arrived, needing a place to stay, Miranda asked if I wanted to take over her business. She claimed to be leaving to get married."

"What about her other relatives? She might be with them."

"No. I'm her only relative except for some really distant cousins. Her parents were killed in an auto accident. If my mother hadn't taken Miranda in, she would have gone into foster care."

Adam touched her shoulder. His hand felt warm and reassuring. "It's damn hard to disappear without a trace. I suspect your cousin will be easy to track down." He stood up. "While the grill's heating, let's go upstairs to the office. I'll get on my computer and see what I can find out."

Whitney followed him up the wide curved stairway. Jasper scampered along beside him. She kept Lexi, Maddie and Da Vinci with her on leashes. After last night, she wasn't taking any chances. She had to wait at the top of each step for the smaller dogs to scramble up beside Lexi.

Inside the wood-paneled office, Adam went to a laptop computer that was already open on the desk with a screensaver of crashing waves on it. Jasper hopped up onto his lap. Whitney settled into a chair next to the desk and the dogs clustered around her feet.

"At work we use Total Track. It's a service that collects personal information like credit card activity, bank accounts, court records and DMV registrations. Let's see what it has on Miranda Marshall. Does she have a middle name?"

"Leighton." Whitney spelled the family name Miranda's mother had given her cousin. "Isn't a lot of this information private?"

"It's supposed to be, but in this computer age, there's virtually nothing that's totally confidential. The Total Track guys got into the business by going to courthouses every day and recording info that was public record. Court records like DUIs and even prison sentences aren't entered into a computer every day. Understaffing is common and it can be weeks before they input the info. Total Track immediately chases down those reports and sells their service. It's expensive but it became a hit right away. A lot of smaller police departments use them because they don't have the manpower to keep up with all the information that's out there."

"I see." Whitney wondered what info they had on her.

"Okay. Here's your cousin's screen." He glanced over at her. "She has two credit cards and they're paid off. No activity on either one in three weeks." He touched another key, then frowned at the screen.

"What is it?"

"She closed her Wells Fargo checking account a week ago and withdrew the three-hundred-and-twenty-seven dollar balance. Her car's paid for and her other two credit card accounts at Nordstrom's and Macy's have been closed."

"So all Miranda has is a little cash and two credit cards."

"Looks like that's it. But she hasn't used the cards. Existing anywhere for a period of time on less than three hundred dollars is difficult."

"She might have had more cash with her." Whitney tried to recall exactly what Miranda had told her. "Some of her clients paid in cash. She told me to offer new clients a discount for cash."

"If you receive cash," he said, "and don't report it, you keep those earnings off the IRS radar screen, but it's illegal."

"I know, but it means she might have more cash with her than it appears." Whitney replied with a shake of her head. Her cousin had always been one to play the angles. "The question is, where is Miranda? And why did she just disappear?"

"From what you've told me, I suspect she had this planned for some time. She knows enough not to use her credit cards."

"I think anyone would know that. Just watch television. The second someone goes missing, police look to see if their credit cards have been used."

"True. Probably the best way to track her is to focus on the car. You'd be surprised how many fugitives get parking tickets or are pulled over for a missing taillight or some minor violation. It goes into the system and bingo—we know where they are."

"If nothing happens, we may never find her."

Adam shook his head. "Possibly, but I doubt it. It's harder to disappear than you'd think." He tapped a few keys on the computer. "I'm checking the Highway Patrol database. They gather all the information from local authorities for Homeland Security. Since 9/11, law enforcement has become very interested in all sorts of vehicles that could be used by terrorists especially since San Diego sits on the border." He let out a low whistle. "I'll be damned. A hit!"

She jumped up and looked over his shoulder at the screen. She saw a license-plate number followed by: Location—metered parking at Lindbergh Field.

"Miranda's car is in the airport lot. She left it at a meter that's expired. Does she have friends she might have flown to visit?"

She slowly shook her head. "Friends? I don't know. Since she's lived here from the time she was fifteen, you would think all her friends would be local."

Adam picked up the telephone and dialed a number. "Gus?" he said after waiting several rings. "It's Adam Hunter."

She watched him while he listened to something Gus was saying. Then he said, "I need a favor. Could you check security lists at Lindbergh and see if a Miranda Leighton Marshall boarded a plane? If you find her name, let me know where she went."

Adam's voice was a low rumble that Whitney found very intriguing. Despite the seriousness of the situation, she couldn't help remembering last night. She wanted to be in his arms again, but she reminded herself not to rush things. Slow down. Her life was complicated enough with Miranda missing.

Adam listened a moment, then said, "Nah. I haven't lost a girlfriend." He winked at her and she couldn't help smiling back. "Miranda's family is worried about her. I told them I would check." He listened again. "Thanks, Gus." Adam gave him his telephone number then hung up.

"You think she left the country?" Whitney asked.

"That's a possibility, since she doesn't seem to have friends or relatives she could visit." He logged off his computer, put Jasper on the floor and stood up. "If she bought a ticket, she had to show ID or her passport. It'll be in the records. Gus will find it. He's SDPD's point man with Homeland Security."

"I can't imagine where she'd go," Whitney said, bewildered.

Adam slipped his arm around her shoulders and guided her out of the room. "The grill's ready. Those steaks are waiting. There's nothing we can do until Gus checks and calls back."

She maneuvered to avoid tripping over the three dogs on leashes hovering at her feet. "How long do you think that will be?"

"Gus said he has time tonight. He checks info that comes in from the border crossing with Mexico. It's a slow night because it's raining south of Tijuana."

Whitney stayed in the kitchen to assemble the salad. It didn't take much work. Adam had bought bagged lettuce, a tomato and a cucumber. He'd also bought blue cheese dressing. Not a fat-free choice but she guessed after his time in Iraq, he wasn't counting calories.

She thought about the way he kept looking at her while he'd been on the computer and talking to his friend. When she'd first met Adam, he'd been so…so stoic. It was almost as if he wouldn't allow anything to touch him. He didn't want to be bothered to think or feel. Now he seemed to be coming back to life by degrees.

Had something happened to him?

She suddenly wanted to know everything about him. Her emotions had been chafed raw by her experience with Ryan. She hadn't asked enough questions. She'd fallen for him and believed love could make up for the quirks in Ryan's personality.

Ryan had been great in bed but he'd always been emotionally unavailable. She smiled to herself as she sliced the cucumber. "Emotionally unavailable" was a term she'd heard on some self-help talk show. The minute she'd heard it, Whitney knew it fit her husband.

He never shared his thoughts or feelings. Other than saying he was exhausted after his shift at the hospital or when he'd been studying, Ryan hadn't expressed much about himself. She didn't bother to wonder if he was different with Ashley.

Ryan Fordham didn't matter to her any longer.

It was a relief to have him out of her life, she decided. As soon as Rod Babcock gave her the okay, she was signing those papers and closing that unhappy chapter of her life. She smiled inwardly and splashed a little dressing on the salad.

She brought the dogs outside and tethered them to the gatepost. That way they'd be nearby while they ate.

"I don't think you have to keep them tied up," Adam said from the grill, where he was tending the steaks. "We can keep our eyes on them."

She headed back into the kitchen for the salad. Over her shoulder, she replied, "I'm too nervous to take any chances."

Whitney returned with the salad and the plates. She set their places and served the salad. It was going to be a typical "guy" meal. A huge steak and a side of salad. She'd bet Adam wouldn't have bothered with the salad at all if she hadn't been there.

He brought over the sizzling steaks. The smell made her stomach growl and had all the dogs standing at attention, their tails wagging. "Medium rare, I think. Cut into yours and see if it's okay before I turn off the grill."

She tested her steak. It was a little rare, but she said, "Perfect. Let's eat."

Adam sat down and immediately cut into his steak and took a bite. She could almost hear him sigh with satisfaction.

"I guess the food in Iraq wasn't too good."

"Got that right." He took a sip of the pinot noir. "They try, but feeding hundreds of soldiers isn't easy. There's nothing like home cooking."

"Was your mother a good cook?"

He shook his head. "My mother died when I was about seven. She had breast cancer back when there wasn't much they could do. All I remember her making for me was cereal. After she passed away, my dad did his best, but home cooking was mostly macaroni and cheese or microwave dinners. What about your mother? Did she like to cook?"

"Yes," Whitney replied with a smile. "We cooked on the weekends. You see, Mom was a single parent. My father walked out on us when I was less than a year old."

"Do you ever hear from him?"

"No. Never."

"Have you tried to contact him?"

"No. I figure if he didn't care about us then, he won't now."

Adam was silent for a moment and they ate without talking for a few minutes. Finally he asked, "What about Miranda?"

Whitney hesitated. She didn't want to admit that she'd ignored her only relative for so long. "I went off to UCLA but Miranda didn't have the grades to get into the UC system. She went to San Diego Community College. I came back the first two years for Thanksgiving, Christmas and spring break. We saw each other then."

Whitney gazed into the distance for a moment. "You know, the older we became, the more alike we looked. People assumed we were sisters. They expected us to be as close as sisters, but we weren't."

"Did Miranda have friends or boyfriends that you met?"

"No. She had her own apartment. It was a small place near Mission Bay. I was really envious because I had to live in the dorm, where you couldn't think or study."

"How was she able to afford it?"

"Her parents had life insurance. Miranda received half a million dollars when she was eighteen."

Adam whistled. "That's a lot of money at that age."

"Mom wanted to handle it for her, but Miranda insisted she could do it."

Adam chewed his steak and gazed at her thoughtfully. "She doesn't seem to have any of it left."

Whitney shifted uncomfortably in her chair. "When my mother became ill with cancer, there were things the insurance didn't cover. Miranda took care of it. I tried to pay her back but she wouldn't let me. She insisted Mom deserved every cent for taking her in when no one else would." With a pang of guilt, she added, "That's why I have to help her now. If I'd spent more time with her when we moved here, she might not have disappeared without telling me what was wrong."

"How long have you been back?"

"A little over a year. I called Miranda right away. We said we'd get together but we never did. I tried—once. I invited her to dinner but she already had plans. I never called her again, and she didn't call me."

He cut up his last bit of steak into little pieces. Obviously, Jasper was in for a treat. "Wasn't that strange?"

"Not really. Miranda and Ryan didn't get along." The admission brought back so many memories—all of them troubling. "I guess Miranda saw things in Ryan that I didn't. I should have asked her—paid more attention to what she was thinking."

CHAPTER SIXTEEN

TYLER LEANED BACK, his feet propped up on the rail, and gazed out at the harbor lights from the balcony of his condo while he sipped his beer. A cat's paw of a breeze brought the briny scent of the ocean across his face. God, he loved this place.

He turned his head and intently watched Holly. She'd seemed preoccupied all evening. He wished she would be a little more open about what she was thinking.

"Should we eat, then hit one of the clubs?" he asked in case she was bored. The great thing about living here was being close to the best restaurants and a hot club scene.

She shook her head and sent her silky brown hair fluttering across her bare shoulders. "No. Let's catch a bite, come back and watch a movie."

"What do you feel like eating?"

"How about Wok 'N Roll?"

"Sounds great," he agreed, even though the Thai café with its aquarium walls and trendy sushi bar wasn't his favorite.

Holly stood up and pulled down the skirt of her dress with a smile that made eating Thai food worth it. "I'm going to grab my pashmina. I'm a little chilly in this dress."

While she went into the bedroom to get her shawl from the closet she used when she was here, Tyler closed the sliding glass door to the balcony. The cell phone on his hip jingled and he pulled it off his belt. It had better not be Butch at the command post. He didn't want to tell Holly that he had to fill in for a no-show again.

He'd told Butch to hire a few guys with minor violations on their background checks. He'd also authorized Sherry to pay them to stay on call during the graveyard shift. As he checked the caller ID, he saw "blocked" and knew it wasn't the command center.

"Did you talk to Adam about that backup disc?"

As usual, his father was all business. No inquiries about how he was or how things were going. No question about whether he was interrupting anything.

"I spoke with Adam." Tyler kept his tone low. He didn't want Holly to overhear him. Maybe it was just his imagination, but he wasn't as comfortable with her as he had been before Adam's return. He half expected her to say they were through. They'd been together for over two years. He had no reason to think she would leave but the idea kept popping into his mind. "He says the burglars took most everything, but he'll look—"

"I'm going to call him and tell him that I'm coming over to help search. Do you have his number? There's no listing for Calvin Hunter. Knowing Calvin, he must have had an unlisted telephone."

Holly walked out of the bedroom, a bright pink shawl draped over one arm. She'd put on fresh lipstick and sprayed on the perfume he'd given her for her birthday.

"I have his cell number back at my place," he fibbed. "I'm on my way to dinner with Holly. I'll call you with the number later."

"Later? I'd planned on going over there tonight."

Christ almighty. This missing info must be really important. Quinten Foley usually spent his evenings at the officers' club with his cronies when he was in town.

"I doubt he's home." Tyler deliberately did not use Adam's

name. Holly was standing next to him now, waiting to leave for a late dinner. "He has a girlfriend." This was a stretch. Adam had mentioned a woman who was living in the cottage behind his uncle's house. Something in the way Adam had said it had made Tyler wonder.

"All right. Call me with his number as soon as you get home." A faint click followed by a burst of static told Tyler that his father had hung up.

"Who's that?" Holly asked.

"My father. He's in town for a while." He hadn't mentioned his breakfast meeting with his father. Holly's parents lived north of San Diego in Newport Beach. They frequently invited Tyler and Holly for dinner or barbecues on the deck of their home on Linda Isle. Tyler was embarrassed at the way his father blew into town but never considered entertaining them, even though Tyler had made it clear he was serious about Holly.

"Who has a girlfriend?"

They were in the hall now and Tyler was locking the condo door. He considered lying, but not telling his father the truth was one thing. The bastard deserved it. Holly meant too much to him. Besides, it might be better if she thought Adam was seeing someone else.

"Adam."

The word detonated on impact. Tyler could see it in the spark of light that suddenly fired Holly's brown eyes. "Really? He just got back."

"You know Adam. He's a fast worker."

Holly didn't respond until they were in the elevator on their way to the street level. "Why don't we get together with Adam and his new girl? Let's have them for dinner. I'll make lasagna. He loves it."

"Okay," Tyler replied without any enthusiasm. The last thing he wanted was to have Adam around Holly.

RYAN SAT AT THE KITCHEN TABLE and watched Ashley rinse off their dinner dishes before putting them in the dishwasher. It was after nine, a little late to be eating, but Ryan had been with Walter Nance discussing new equipment for the cosmetic surgery facility they'd be opening soon. He'd sidestepped the money question, but Ryan wondered how much longer this would work.

"My mother made Swedish meatballs whenever we had a place with a kitchen," Ashley told him. "That's where I learned how to cook them."

The meatballs made of hamburger rolled around in his belly like golf balls. "We're going to need to eat home more," he told her. "For a little while."

Ashley looked over at him with wide blue eyes. "Okay. Whitney left several cookbooks in the cabinet over there. I'll try some new recipes. Mother didn't teach me much. We ate fast food mostly."

Ryan smiled and noticed Ashley didn't question his reason for eating at home, which made it more difficult to segue into a financial discussion. "We're a little tight for money until Whitney signs those papers."

She closed the dishwasher and started it. "I was thinking. Maybe we should sell this house and rent until we can afford to buy a place like the one we loved in Coronado."

He tried to keep his expression neutral. This was *exactly* what he'd been on the verge of proposing. Not that selling this place would net them much money after the loans were paid off, but at least he wouldn't have those huge payments clobbering him each month.

"You don't like this house much, do you?" he asked.

She sat down on his lap and stroked the back of his neck. "It's okay, but I'd rather take the pressure off you while you're getting the new practice up and running."

"Then I'll buy any place you want." Ryan kissed Ashley

and cradled her in his arms for a few minutes. "I'll call a Realtor tomorrow—"

"I'll do it. You're too busy."

He met her gaze dead-on and saw how much she loved him and wanted to help. "I need to cut a deal. I don't want to pay some dufus Realtor full commission. Once I've settled—"

"I'll take care of it. My mother and I had to make lots of deals for clothes and things so I could compete."

"Okay," he said slowly. She'd been a great saleswoman for the cosmetic surgery firm when he'd met her. That meant selling but in a way that clients never realized they'd been "sold" anything. She might be able to handle this.

Ryan let Ashley lead him off toward the bedroom. He was exhausted. He'd been at the casino until dawn. He'd intended to tell her about his gambling when he mentioned selling this house. Now wasn't the time. If Lady Luck smiled on him, Ryan's life would be back on track.

"Did your girlfriend have any trouble getting Lexi back to Whitney?" Ryan was in his closet now, undressing. For a moment he thought Ashley didn't hear him. She'd gone into her own closet opposite his.

"No. Whitney thinks the dog wandered off."

Ryan didn't give a shit what his ex thought. He wanted their marriage to evaporate as if it had never existed.

"I DON'T THINK THE NEW client is going to call."

It was nearly eleven-thirty. Adam and Whitney had been watching *Nuts for Mutts* on Animal Planet and talking since dinner. *Companion Carnivores* was on next. As attracted as he was to Whitney, Adam didn't think he could sit through another program about dogs.

"It's late for her to call, but she'll probably phone tomorrow."

Whitney nodded. She seemed distracted. She was probably

still worrying about her cousin. He had to admit disappearing after concocting such an elaborate story ranked right up there with the bizarre. He'd been in law enforcement since he'd graduated from college and he'd never encountered a disappearance as strange as this.

It wasn't as if Miranda had left suddenly. You heard about those cases all the time. A woman goes out for milk and vanishes. This wasn't one of those incidents. Miranda had planned her disappearance probably for some time.

Why?

As if on cue, his cell phone rang. Gus was finally getting back to him. "Find anything out?"

"Yeah. Miranda Marshall didn't get on any plane."

"She didn't board a plane," he repeated for Whitney's benefit. "But her car's at the airport."

"There's two, maybe three explanations," Gus told him. "She could have left the car there to make someone think she took a flight. It's possible she has ID showing another name, and she used it to board a plane."

"That's two possibilities. What's the third?"

A beat of silence. "Any chance there's another set of car keys around?"

The light dawned and Adam covered the phone. "Is there another set of keys to your cousin's car around the cottage?"

Whitney sat up straighter. "I think so. There are several sets of keys in the kitchen drawer. I'm pretty sure one of them is for her Volvo. Why?"

He didn't answer her. Instead, he told Gus, "We have keys. Thanks for your help. I—"

"Just a minute. There's something else."

It had been several years since Adam had worked with Gus, but he recognized the concern in his friend's voice. "What is it?"

"After I ran Marshall's name through the system and came up with zilch, I asked around the department."

Adam listened to what his friend had discovered about Whitney's cousin, made a mental note of several details, thanked him for his trouble, then hung up.

"What's going on?"

He regarded her with a speculative gaze, not knowing how to put this exactly. "Gus thinks I should check the trunk of Miranda's car. He gave me its location." He leaned a little closer to her. "You see, it's fairly common for homicide victims to be found in the trunks of their own cars."

She stared at him wordlessly for a moment. "Why do you think someone killed her?"

"It's just a possibility. Her name didn't come up on an ID check for flights. If she was in some kind of trouble, she could have been killed."

"Ohmygod," she whispered in a choked voice. "Why didn't she tell me? I would have done anything to help her."

Adam put his arm around her shoulders and drew Whitney to him. "Don't jump to conclusions. This is merely police procedure. We're eliminating things."

She pulled out of his embrace and jumped to her feet. "Let's check it out. I'll look for the keys right now."

"Okay," he agreed even though it was late. "There's one other thing."

Whitney must have picked up on the troubled note in his voice. "What? Tell me!"

"Guys on the vice squad told Gus that they knew your cousin. Miranda had never been arrested, but they'd seen her several times when they went out to Saffron Blue. It's a nightclub."

Whitney frowned, puzzled. "She never mentioned waitressing there."

"She wasn't waiting tables. Miranda worked as a stripper."

CHAPTER SEVENTEEN

WHITNEY STOOD NEXT to Adam and gazed at the trunk of Miranda's Volvo.

"I don't smell anything," Adam said, his voice almost a whisper.

They'd driven to San Diego's Lindbergh Field in Adam's Rava. It hadn't been difficult to find the metered parking space where her cousin had parked her car. They'd pulled up behind the vehicle and had gotten out, leaving all the dogs in the SUV.

"Smell?"

"A dead body—"

"Okay. I get it." Her stomach did a slow backflip as she imagined Miranda crammed into the trunk. *Please, God, don't let Miranda be in there,* she silently prayed. Whitney's neck muscles quivered as she watched Adam insert the key she'd found in the kitchen drawer of the cottage into the trunk.

The lid flew open.

Whitney braced herself and peered inside. "It's empty." *Thank you, God.* Miranda must be alive somewhere, she decided.

Adam asked, "Feel better?"

Whitney managed a nod and leaned toward him slightly. She suddenly felt light-headed. Relief or fear? Both. She was relieved that Miranda wasn't in the trunk of the car, but after finding out her cousin had worked as a stripper, Whitney's anxiety had increased. Had Miranda's job gotten her into so much trouble that she'd lied to her only living relative and fled?

Suddenly, Whitney recalled the way Miranda had acted the night she'd left. Miranda had hugged her fiercely...almost as if she had been saying goodbye forever. Something about Miranda's "wedding" story had bothered Whitney from the beginning. At the time, she'd attributed her misgivings to a boyfriend who didn't want to meet his fiancée's only relative. Now she wondered if she hadn't been picking up subtle clues that her cousin was lying.

"Are you okay?" Adam asked.

For an instant she wavered, her blue eyes flickering with uncertainty. Then she drew herself together and nodded. "I'm fine. Just worried about Miranda, is all."

He slipped his arm around her and brought her close. A little lurch skittered from her heart downward until she felt it in her toes. She was tempted to rest her head against his shoulder but didn't. *Be strong,* she told herself. *You've been through a lot. Don't get involved with another man so quickly.*

He placed a comforting hand on the back of her neck. Her body flushed with hot awareness. Despite all the problems she'd had with Ryan, despite common sense telling her to slow down, despite everything—she wanted Adam Hunter. It was as simple as that.

His mouth met hers, warm, sweet, and her lips parted. One large hand wove through the hair at the back of her neck while the other hand found its way to the lowest reaches of her back and urged her closer and closer until her whole body was flush against his.

Push him away, she ordered her body, but she was powerless to resist temptation. He teased her lips apart with the tip of his tongue. She returned the kiss, her tongue greeting his. The contact sent a bolt of pure pleasure through her entire body and her pulse went haywire, throbbing in intimate, sensitive places.

She ran her hands over the strong muscles of his back and

shoulders, enjoying the sensation. The woodsy scent of his shaving cream filled her lungs as she clung to him. She knew better than to keep kissing him, but she didn't have the will-power to stop.

How long had it been since she'd kissed a man with so much passion? She honestly couldn't remember the last time. *Don't think about Ryan,* she warned herself. *Live in the moment.*

At the sound of an engine, they reluctantly pulled apart. A security officer drove around the corner in a patrol car. Whitney stepped out of Adam's embrace, a little embarrassed.

"Something wrong?" the man asked.

The airport had closed for the night. Lindbergh Field was located near residential neighborhoods and flights were termi-nated before midnight to control noise. At this hour the parking lots were deserted. Whitney had no doubt they appeared to be very suspicious.

"No. We're just checking for Whitney's cell phone." He put his hand on her shoulder. "It isn't here. She must have left it somewhere else."

"I see," the man responded, but his tone said he had his doubts.

Whitney and Adam got into the SUV. Opening the door awakened the dogs. Lexi spotted the security patrolman. The retriever decided she was a watchdog. Lexi's barking incited the others, and a second later they joined in.

"No. Bad." The stern tone of Whitney's voice was enough to silence Lexi, but the others kept barking.

Adam turned around. "No!"

The dogs stopped barking. Jasper meekly lay down. Whitney doubted Adam had ever raised his voice to the little dog before this. He started the car and drove away slowly. The security car followed them until they arrived at the pay booth.

Whitney waited until they were on the freeway before suggesting, "Why don't we go to Saffron Blue? Maybe the other girls or the manager knows something about Miranda."

"No. The girls will be so busy right now that they won't take time to spit on you. Most people don't realize it, but strippers earn nothing but tips."

"Really? I had no idea. I assumed…" She'd never given strippers much thought until she discovered what Miranda had been doing. The screen in her mind played a sleazy bar filled with smoke and lecherous men. Cheap-looking women with teased hair and bobbling silicone breasts flaunted their bodies on a stage beneath a blaring spotlight.

"Forget your assumptions. This is an upscale club with a hundred-dollar cover charge. The police receive calls to Saffron Blue occasionally. Usually it's a fight in the parking lot. Jared Cabral doesn't put up with troublemakers. His bouncers kick them out at the first sign of trouble."

"Jared Cabral owns Saffron Blue?"

Adam turned off La Jolla Parkway onto Torrey Pines Road. "Yes. Cabral owns eight clubs—last I heard. Southern California, Arizona and Vegas. All cater to upscale clientele. Gambling's legal in his Vegas clubs. The others have illegal high-stakes games going most nights in a private room."

"Illegal gambling and fights. I suppose there are drugs around, too."

"Undoubtedly, but Cabral keeps illegal activities outside so he won't be busted."

A shudder passed through her. "I can't imagine why Miranda would be working there. She had plenty of money from the insurance policy."

"Don't be too sure. If it was in a bank or a brokerage house in the U.S., the money would have shown up on the Total Track report."

She moistened her dry lips and tried to think clearly. How could she have lost touch with Miranda like this?

"It's been, what? Almost fourteen years since Miranda received the money?" Adam didn't wait for a response. "She could have spent it on school, rent, vacations, jewelry, clothes and stuff."

"I don't think so. Miranda was working part-time to pay the rent when she was attending junior college. That's what she told me when she paid some of Mom's medical bills. She acted as if she still had most of the money." Whitney thought a moment. "What she gave Mom was less than five thousand dollars."

"Miranda certainly didn't spend it on a fancy car. That Volvo was new in the late eighties."

"She didn't buy a lot of clothes, either. I helped her pack. She had a few nice things, but nothing extravagant."

"Do you know how long she lived in my uncle's cottage?"

"About two years. We talked at Christmas and birthdays so I knew when she moved from her little apartment in Mission Bay. The cottage came rent-free if she took care of Jasper when your uncle was away." Whitney was silent for a moment, thinking. "You know, Miranda was always the frugal type. It wasn't like her to have squandered the insurance money."

Sirens behind them interrupted their conversation. Adam pulled to the curb, and the dogs who'd fallen asleep jumped up to see the fire engines whiz by.

After the last fire trucks passed, Adam asked, "Was Miranda the type to work as a stripper?"

"No way." Whitney released an audible sigh. "I guess I didn't know her as well as I thought. Anything's possible. She could have spent the insurance money."

Adam drove away from the curb. "Tomorrow I'll go to see Cabral. He may be able to shed light on Miranda's disappearance."

They rode toward their street in silence. Ahead, Whitney saw an orange glow above the trees, lighting the dark sky.

"Looks like there's a house on fire." Adam sounded concerned.

Whitney knew fire was a real danger in San Diego. In the last several years, fires that started in the brush-filled hillsides had rampaged out of control and destroyed many homes. It was early summer and the hills were still green. It seemed to be too soon for a brush fire, but anything was possible.

Adam braked suddenly as they rounded the corner. Fire engines and police cars blocked their way, red and blue lights flashing. Smoke filled the air and made it difficult to see exactly what was on fire. It was too close to be the hills. If it wasn't their place, it had to be a home nearby.

A police officer held up his hand to stop them. Adam rolled down the window. Warm smoke billowed into the car.

"Do you live on this street, sir?"

"Yes. We're at number 265."

"The small house behind yours is burning. Do you know if anyone was in there?"

Was? Her heart slammed against her rib cage in painful thuds. Suddenly it became difficult to breathe, and she could barely think. Thank heavens, they'd taken the dogs with them. Things could be replaced, she reminded herself, living beings could not.

"No one's in the cottage." Adam cocked his head toward Whitney. "She lives there alone."

"Park your car," the officer told him.

"I can't believe this," Whitney cried. "Thank God I have the dogs with me."

They parked, jumped out of the car and followed the officer up the street. Murky, acrid-smelling smoke curdled the air. Firefighters in neon-yellow suits blocked her line of vision. She couldn't see up the driveway to the small cottage. Adam's hand was on her arm, and he guided her forward.

"Hunter," called a man in slacks and a sports jacket. Apparently he was with the police and knew Adam.

"What's going on?"

The man in a sports jacket and a polo shirt walked up to them. "This is your place?"

"Yes," Adam replied. "Why are you here?"

Whitney registered the subtle change in Adam's voice. His expression was different, too. What was there about this man that disturbed him?

"Neighbors reported the blast."

"Blast?" Whitney choked out the word, her mind reeling at the scene before her.

"Who are you?" he asked.

"Wh—Whitney Marshall. I live in the cottage."

"I'm Dudley Romberg with homicide." He studied her for a moment, then asked, "Do you know anyone who would want to kill you?"

"No. Of course not," she managed to say, her stomach roiling.

"Someone threw a pipe bomb through the bedroom window. It caused the fire."

"Ohmygod! Why would they do that?" She caught Adam's eye. In a heartbeat the answer hit her. *Miranda.* The bomb had been intended for her cousin. This news, coupled with the earlier revelation that Miranda had been a stripper, crippled Whitney's ability to think clearly.

"What makes you say it was a pipe bomb?" Adam asked.

"The broken window. The first fire unit to respond called Reserve Officer Wells. He's with the Naval Explosive Ordnance Disposal Center at Miramar Air Station. He's right over there."

"Let's talk to him," Adam said to her.

Adam guided her up to a tall, gaunt man with pewter-gray hair in a military brush cut. He had his back to them, watching the fire. The flames weren't as high as they had been when they'd driven up, but the cottage was still burning.

"Officer Wells," Adam said, and the man turned to them. His face was ruddy from the heat of the fire. "I'm Adam Hunter. This is my home. I understand that you think a pipe bomb caused the fire."

"There'll have to be a post-blast investigation to confirm my analysis. The first responders took Polaroids of the scene." He handed three pictures to Adam.

Whitney looked over Adam's shoulder at them. When the photos had been taken, the fire was burning at the rear of the cottage. The front, now a smoldering ruin, hadn't been burning. The black-and-white photo clearly showed the shattered window.

"See—" Wells pointed to the picture "—no glass on the outside." He motioned for Adam to look at the next photograph. "Notice the mailbox?"

Whitney saw that the mailbox at the path leading up to the cottage was buckled in two.

"Pipe bombs are simple to make," explained Wells. "Instructions are all over the Internet. You just need a length of pipe, blasting powder, a power source—usually a nine-volt battery—and end caps for the pipe. The end caps fly off when the bomb detonates. They shoot out like they'd been fired from a rifle. A cap hit the mailbox. One of the firefighters was alert enough to spot it and notice there wasn't any glass on the ground the way there would have been if heat from the fire inside had caused the window to explode."

Dudley Romberg walked up to them again. The detective asked her, "Where were you when the fire started?"

"At the airport," she said.

He shook his head slowly. "Lucky you. If you'd been in the house, you'd be dead. Seems the pipe bomb was full of shrapnel. If the explosion didn't get you, flying shrapnel would have."

"Like the bombs in Iraq that kill so many people."

"Exactly." Adam's expression was more than grim.

"Don't go anywhere," Romberg said. "I'm going to need to talk to you."

He walked away. Adam waited a moment, then said, "Now we know why Miranda hightailed it out of town. She was mixed up in some serious shit. Someone wanted her dead."

"I can't imagine why." Fear sent hot blood pumping through her veins. "At least the dogs were with us. No life was lost. That's what really matters, isn't it?"

He slid his arm around her shoulders. "You bet. That's what matters, but we need to find out what's going on before anything else happens. Don't tell Romberg that Miranda was working at Saffron Blue."

"Why not?"

"I want to talk to Jared Cabral first."

"Won't Romberg know? All your friend had to do was ask around the station."

"True, but Romberg's a few beans shy of a full burrito. Around the station they call him Dudley 'the dud' Romberg. It'll take him a while to ask if the beat cops know your cousin. Meanwhile, I'll get first crack at Cabral."

CHAPTER EIGHTEEN

WHITNEY GAZED AT Adam from the armchair where she was sitting. He was walking Romberg to the door of his uncle's home. The detective had interviewed Whitney, asking her questions about Miranda. Since Whitney had lived in the cottage less than a week, the investigation was focused on Miranda. Whitney had not brought up Saffron Blue. She felt a little guilty about not disclosing this information, but Adam had helped her so much already and she trusted him.

She leaned down to give Lexi's head a quick pat. The cloying smell of smoke and the commotion of firefighters had spooked the dogs, especially Da Vinci. The Chihuahua was huddled against Jasper on the sofa with Maddie nearby. At least they were all safe.

Lexi's disappearance had prompted Whitney to keep all the dogs at her side. If she hadn't, they would have been in the cottage and died in the fire. She couldn't imagine a worse fate for a helpless animal than to be trapped in an inferno.

What about Miranda? she asked herself. Whoever had thrown the pipe bomb hadn't cared what kind of horrible death she suffered. *How could Miranda have gotten herself involved in something that would result in this?*

Adam closed the front door behind the detective and walked back into the living room.

"I'm sorry about the fire," she told him.

"Don't blame yourself. It's your cousin's fault—not yours."

He dropped down onto the sofa where he'd been sitting when Detective Romberg had questioned her. The motion caused Da Vinci to leap up on his short legs and look around anxiously. Seeing nothing troubling, he lay down again and snuggled up against Jasper.

"I would never have guessed Miranda was in this much trouble." Whitney twisted the hem of her shorts between her fingers. She'd been doing it since she'd sat down. She told herself to stop.

"I want you to be very careful," he told her. "You look a lot like your cousin, right? They could come after you by mistake."

She nodded. "When do you plan to visit Saffron Blue? I'll need to reschedule some of my walks to go with you."

Adam shook his head. "I'm going alone. Cabral isn't the easiest man to talk to. Cops make him antsy because he's sure they're looking for an excuse to bust him, which is true. He won't open up in front of a woman."

Whitney started to protest then the reality of her situation hit her. "I don't have anything but the clothes I'm wearing. I guess I'll have to go shopping first thing in the morning. Luckily all my client info was in my BlackBerry, and I always keep it in my purse." Another wave of reality crashed over her. "My Jeep—"

"The fire started in the bedroom where the pipe bomb was thrown, then leaped backward toward the carport and garage before the wind kicked up and sent it toward the front of the house. If the fire didn't destroy your SUV, then it suffered a lot of smoke and water damage. We'll know more in the morning when it's light enough to see."

She stared at him and blinked, her mind suddenly becoming focused. She'd been thinking about Miranda and who might want to kill her. She hadn't given much thought to her own plight. She had no place to live. No car.

Nothing.

Suddenly, the spacious living room seemed too tiny. The walls were closing in on her. She tried to breathe but her lungs refused to take in air. Throbbing started in her temples, then exploded through her head.

Her anxiety must have been reflected on her face. Adam rose to his feet and came up to her. Without a word, he pulled her into his arms. She tried to draw back but his arms tightened around her. After a moment, he took her face in one hand. One finger gently brushed her cheek. His other hand skimmed soothingly over her back.

"Don't worry about anything." He rested his cheek against the top of her head. "We'll work it out. I'll help you."

Adam seemed so strong, so supportive, and she felt so lost. She permitted herself to savor the moment, the comfort he offered.

But as tempting as it was to nestle in his arms and let him take over, Whitney asked, "Why? You hardly know me."

"I know all I need to know. When you saw your place was on fire, you weren't concerned about yourself. You cared more about the dogs."

Whitney didn't know what to say. She had always loved animals. When she'd seen the flames, her first thought had been relief. The dogs were safe. She didn't know how she could have faced their owners and told them their pets had been burned alive.

"You can stay here as long as you want," he told her. "The maid's quarters are off the kitchen. You'll have room for the dogs there and a lot of privacy."

She almost told him she couldn't stay here, then asked herself where she could possibly go. Who could she turn to? Not Ryan. Trish Bowrather was a possibility, but their friendship—if she could call it that—was new, untried. She wouldn't feel comfortable asking Trish for help.

"Thank you," she whispered, her voice choked.

He brought her over to the sofa and pulled her down beside him. "Escaping death does something to you," he told her. "It alters the way you see the world."

He was right, of course, but until he said it Whitney hadn't quite come to grips with her own close call. The bombing had been a devastating shock. All she could concentrate on was Miranda and the dogs. It was just now sinking in. She'd narrowly missed being killed by whoever was determined to murder her cousin.

If she hadn't come here for a barbecue, she would have been in the cottage, asleep in the bedroom where the pipe bomb had been thrown. She would have died. In a delayed reaction, her composure started to crack.

"Why didn't Miranda warn me?"

"She probably didn't realize what she was involved in would have such deadly consequences." His arm was around her, his tone comforting. A minute passed while she tried to calm herself. In the aftermath of her divorce, Whitney's emotions were unstable. Knowing her only relative had betrayed her made something inside Whitney shatter into a million jagged pieces.

There was no way to sugarcoat this, she decided. "Miranda must have known. No matter how happy she seemed, she vanished without a trace for a reason. She should have warned me."

Mind-numbing disbelief brought the sting of hot tears to her eyes. The tight rein she'd kept on her emotions collapsed. She refused to cry, but her body began to tremble so hard that she had to clutch her bare knees with both hands to keep the shaking under control.

"Try not to be upset," Adam said. "Things will get better. Time will help. I know." He squeezed her shoulders, but she didn't feel any better. "I know what you're going through."

"How could you? I don't mean to be ungrateful, but I just

lost everything I have on this earth. Not that things matter, but I almost died."

Adam didn't reply. She fought back the tears, then took a minute to let her painful breathing return to something near normal. "I'm sorry. I didn't mean to sound ungrateful. I don't know what I'd do without you."

He studied her a moment. His expression darkened with an unreadable emotion that revealed something she couldn't decipher. He'd shared almost nothing about himself and had shown little emotion. She had no idea what was going on in his mind.

"We have a lot more in common than you might think. My uncle was the last of my family. At least you have your cousin."

At this point Whitney couldn't honestly say that was a good thing. Family protected each other, didn't they? Miranda should have said something, done something so Whitney could protect herself.

"I had a brush with death that was even closer than yours."

His tone brought her up short. She'd never seen him this intense...this serious. She waited for him to continue but he didn't.

"You did?" she prompted. "When?"

She gazed into his eyes, but he didn't respond. His shuttered expression warned her that he might not want to talk about this.

Finally, he cleared his throat and spoke. "I was in Iraq with my National Guard unit. I'd known the guys for years. We were weekend warriors who never expected we'd find ourselves in a battle zone."

There was so much emotion in his words that she understood the Adam Hunter she'd known up to this point had been little more than an impression. From the moment he'd attacked her, Whitney had *assumed* things based solely upon her own conclusions—not facts. Adam had a power and depth to him that she hadn't realized existed.

"Our unit was in charge of the security checkpoints between Baghdad and the airport. It's five miles of hell. Every terrorist and every political faction wants to control the road or shut it down. I worked with Ed and Mike most of the time. We searched vehicles and checked identification at the first security post beyond the airport. After having our tours extended because we had special expertise, we were just ten days from coming home when we drove up to the Green Zone that morning."

"That's the safe area around U.S. headquarters, right?"

"Supposedly. We were in an armored vehicle, just the three of us, at the entry checkpoint. A woman came up with a baby in her arms. You could see the kid was sick. Its face was red and it was bawling. She held out the baby to us—"

Whitney waited for him to continue. She was almost afraid to hear what he was going to say.

He averted his eyes and directed his gaze across the living room to the landscape painting on the wall. "It happened all the time," he finally began, his voice pitched low. "Innocent civilians—kids and even babies—were injured in terrorist attacks. Their medical facilities sucked so they often came to us for help. Mike waved her off and just as he did I had this…feeling."

She waited in stricken silence, half knowing what he was going to tell her.

He turned back to her. "I knew. I don't know how, but in that instant I realized she was going to kill us."

Whitney tried to imagine how horrible that must have been, but couldn't. Until tonight her only experience with death had been her mother's battle with cancer. She had been warned. Death had been expected.

"I knew we were as good as dead. There was no way to get out of the vehicle in time. Hell, I didn't even have the chance to open my mouth and warn my buddies."

Anguish colored every syllable he uttered. She suddenly felt ashamed of herself. Her brush with death had been nothing compared to his.

"I still can't believe it. That mother had a bomb concealed under her clothes. She knew it was going to kill her and her baby."

Whitney couldn't imagine it either. How could any mother take the life of her own child?

"She detonated the bomb just as I yelled, 'Duck.' An explosion of light, a bang like nothing I'd ever heard, then the world went as black as hell itself."

Whitney didn't know what to say. Obviously, he'd survived. Had either of his friends?

"I woke up a week later in a field hospital. I had a massive concussion. I wasn't allowed to lift my head for another week. It hurt like a sonofabitch. There was a helluva ringing in my ears. The nurses had to shout for me to hear them." He shrugged dismissively. "My friends weren't so lucky. They were blown to bits."

The naked emotion in his voice told her how deeply he felt the loss. Nothing she could say would bring his friends back or make this situation easier. After a few seconds, she managed to whisper, "That must have been horrible."

"Not as horrible for me as it was for their families. You see, Mike had a pregnant wife. Ed had a wife and three kids."

She tried to imagine what their families must be going through but couldn't. True, she'd lost her mother, but there hadn't been young children involved. Her mother's cancer had slowly eaten her alive over the course of two miserable years. There'd been enough time to brace herself for the inevitable.

"I'm sorry I whined. My experience wasn't anything— not nearly—"

"Death is death. Like I said, knowing you almost died is a mind-altering experience."

"Yes, but you were wounded. You physically felt it."

"Small difference."

She waited a moment before telling him, "When Mom died I learned something very important. There are things in life that money can replace. Then there are the things in life that no amount of money can replace. I would have given all I had or ever hope to have to save my mother. But it didn't matter. She died anyway."

"I'm sorry, sweetheart." He reached over and took her hand.

"I'm sure you learned the same lesson. Money isn't everything. When I saw the fire, my first thought was the dogs hadn't died. It wasn't until a bit later that I realized someone wanted Miranda dead."

They sat in silence for a few minutes. Talking had calmed Whitney a little and made her realize others had been through much worse. Not just Adam, she decided, but thousands upon thousands of people she didn't know. Around the world others had faced death and had survived. She knew Adam was suffering from survivor's guilt, but she couldn't think of anything to say or do to ease his pain.

Adam rose to his feet and she let him help her up. "Let's find some bed linens and get you settled in the maid's quarters."

She followed him up the stairs to the linen closet in the hall. She noticed how neatly stacked the sheets and towels were. Military training, she decided, and wondered what his uncle had been like.

"How about one of my T-shirts to sleep in?" he asked.

It seemed a little personal but she had no choice. She was going to have to wear these clothes until she could buy new things. "Thanks."

She waited in the hall while he went into a bedroom. A cold nose on the back of her leg told her Lexi had followed her upstairs. The others were right behind her and Whitney couldn't help smiling.

Adam returned and handed her a blue T-shirt. "Get some sleep."

"Thanks, I'll…" Her voice trailed off as their fingers touched. She took a reflexive half step back.

What was wrong with her? She'd kissed this man—really kissed him. Why did this feel so much more intimate? Because she was alone with him in a big isolated house, she decided. Not only were they alone, she was going to be sleeping in a shirt he'd worn dozens of times. The fabric felt soft in her hand and she imagined it against his skin. Unexpectedly, her heart was racing.

His eyes gleamed at her, the pupils dilating as he spoke. "I wish I had something better, but—"

"No, no. It's fine, really." An anticipatory shiver tiptoed up her spine. She could feel the air between them almost sizzle. Heat unfurled deep inside her body, her heart now thudding against her rib cage.

He reached out with one hand and touched her cheek. It was a simple gesture, but his fingertips were warm and slightly callused—and unbelievably erotic. It was all she could do not to throw the T-shirt to the floor and fling herself into his powerful arms.

"Adam." His name came from between her lips in a whisper filled with longing.

He gazed down at her, his eyes dark, restless with the same desire she felt. Their bodies were just inches apart. She could feel the warmth seeping from his rock-hard body to hers. It wouldn't take much, she realized. All she would have to do was make a forward move.

She took a deep breath, intending to part her lips for a kiss. A trace of smoke lingered in the air and its smell reminded her of what had happened tonight. She awkwardly took a side step.

Adam got the message, saying, "The keys to the Rava are on the kitchen counter. You take it—"

"I couldn't. I—"

"It's okay. I'll drive my uncle's car. You have to work, don't you?"

She nodded. Right now she needed money and taking care of the dogs was her best way of making it. "Thanks."

"You can help me out by taking Jasper to the breeder. He's supposed to be there tomorrow morning. I'll put the address and phone number by the keys."

She turned to go. "Call me as soon as you talk to Jared Cabral. I want to know what he has to say about Miranda."

CHAPTER NINETEEN

ASHLEY TRIED TO concentrate on doing one more leg lift, but her mind wasn't on the workout. She told Preston, "Let's grab some juice and talk."

He shrugged, lifting impressive shoulders. "Okay."

He followed her into Dr. Jox's juice bar. She ordered her usual pomegranate juice and he asked for a Redline.

"What's that?"

"A new drink. Like Red Bull but with a bigger kick."

Red Bull made Ashley jittery but a major jolt of caffeine didn't seem to bother Preston. They took their drinks and went outside. Ashley hadn't had a chance to discuss the fiasco with the dog. The workout stations were too close to each other to risk someone overhearing their conversation.

She sat at the table under the tree with the shady canopy. "I'm sorry about the other night. Ryan somehow figured out I was involved."

"You told me that when you phoned me to return the mutt." His clipped tone told Ashley he was angry with her.

"You're upset with me. I'm sorry." Ashley didn't want him to hold this against her. She needed a friend now more than ever.

Preston chugged his Redline. "Don't blame yourself. It was my idea. I just didn't count on cops getting involved."

"Cops? What are you talking about?"

"Adam Hunter's a cop. He was here first thing yesterday morning."

Ashley listened while Preston explained about Adam's visit. "He agreed not to tell Whitney that you were behind her dog's disappearance. This way she won't blame your husband."

"Why didn't you call me?" Yesterday had been one of the two days each week that Ashley didn't train with Preston. When she'd been competing, she worked out for hours every day. Since her mother's death, Ashley allowed herself time to do things she enjoyed.

"I tried your cell but kept getting voice mail. I didn't want to leave a message in case…"

His words hung between them. She knew he intended to say: in case Ryan picked up her messages. She couldn't help being touched by the way Preston always tried to help her.

"Do you think Adam Hunter will keep his word?" She didn't want Ryan to find out her "girlfriend" was really a man. He had nothing to worry about, but Ryan was overly protective of her.

"I thought so. Then I saw the news this morning. I expect the police will be knocking on both our doors."

"What?" She stared at him slack-jawed, certain she'd misunderstood him.

"Didn't you catch the morning news?"

"No. I usually have the TV on while I'm dressing, but not today." When she'd awakened, Ryan had left already. It had been too early for him to go to the office where he was still practicing until the new clinic opened. She wasn't sure where he'd gone, but having him out of the house had given her the opportunity to look through the things on his desk.

In the bottom drawer she'd found a manila folder with DOMENIC CORIZ written across the top. Inside were names and telephone numbers. She couldn't decide what they meant.

Then Ashley had dressed and hadn't been able to find her ring. She thought she'd put it on top of her jewelry box last night, but it wasn't there. She might have left it on the windowsill when she'd prepared dinner. She'd been so nervous about cooking her mother's meatballs that she couldn't remember. She'd left the house without being able to locate the ring. She was going home to hunt through the trash.

"Someone firebombed the cottage where Ryan's ex lives."

It took a second for what he'd said to register. "How terrible! Was anyone hurt?"

"The reporter said no one was home even though it was late at night."

"Whitney was probably with Adam."

"What makes you say that?"

How could she explain women's intuition to a man? They didn't seem to have hunches the same way women did. "Trust me. Women know these things. When they came to the house, I could tell Adam has the hots for her."

"Whatever." Preston tinkered with his Redline can for a moment before tossing it all the way across the patio and into the trash can. "We can expect the police to contact both of us."

"Why? We had nothing to do with it."

"They'll question Whitney. She'll tell them about her divorce and Lexi's disappearance. The police will chase down all the leads."

"You're probably right," she replied. "What are we going to say?"

"Tell the truth. They'll find out anyway. I told Hunter. He's bound to—"

Ashley's cell phone erupted with the opening bars of "Proud Mary." She rummaged in her gym bag for a moment before locating it, thinking again about her father. Was he happy? Did he ever think about her?

"Hello?"

"Ashley? This is Whitney Marshall. Is Ryan there?"

It took her a second to remember she'd used call forwarding. Whitney thought she'd reached their house. "No. He's at his office."

Whitney didn't respond for a moment. "I called there, but he's not expected in today."

"Oh, yes, I forgot." Her quick comeback was a total lie. Why wasn't Ryan in the office? Could he be with Domenic Coriz?

"Would you give him a message for me? We had a fire here last night. The police questioned me. I had to tell them I'm finalizing a property settlement after a divorce. They may come to talk to Ryan. Tell him it's routine." Whitney paused before adding, "I'm not trying to make any more trouble."

"How's Lexi?" Ashley had been so shocked when Preston had told her about the bombing that she'd forgotten about the dog.

"She's fine. She was with me."

"Good, good." Ashley couldn't stop herself from asking, "Did the fire do much damage?"

"Yes. The cottage is completely destroyed."

"I'm sorry," Ashley said and she meant it. She couldn't imagine losing everything. Misplacing her wedding ring was no big deal compared to this. "Do you have someplace to stay?" The second she asked, Ashley regretted prying and quickly added, "In case Ryan wants to reach you?"

"I'm staying in the maid's quarters at the main house until I can make other arrangements. Have him call my cell if he needs me."

Ashley assured Whitney that she would tell Ryan, then snapped her cell phone shut. Preston was studying her, and Ashley explained why Whitney had called.

"We'll hear from the police for sure. There aren't many pipe bombings around here. The cops will be all over this one."

Preston sounded worried. She'd never seen him brood like this. He'd always been upbeat. It suddenly struck her that although she often told him about her problems, she'd rarely asked about his. "Is something wrong?"

"Not really. I just don't like cops messing in my business."

She sensed it was more than that. "What else has you upset? Talk to me. Maybe I can help."

He rocked back on the legs of his chair. "I was in some trouble when I was a kid. I took a neighbor's car for a joyride. I was arrested, and I've hated the police ever since."

Ashley had a feeling it was more than that. Men. Weren't they a trip?

ADAM WAITED IN SAFFRON BLUE'S parking lot. The so-called gentlemen's club opened at noon seven days a week and had for almost fifty years. Jared Cabral had made his money the old-fashioned way—he'd inherited it. His father, Simon Cabral, had started the strip club back in the fifties when bare breasts and naked women were taboo.

The wily old guy had managed to keep his club going even though he'd been busted at least once a month during those first years. A workaholic who didn't seem to have a life, Simon Cabral made money hand over fist and invested it in more clubs. No one knew he had a family until he dropped dead of a heart attack just after his fiftieth birthday.

Enter Jared Cabral. He'd been eighteen when his father died. The kid had no experience with nightclubs, let alone strip clubs and their special problems. Never mind. The apple certainly didn't fall too far from the tree. Jared stepped in and stepped up.

The kid took a year or so to acquaint himself with his inheritance. The dark, dank clubs that reeked of stale cigarette smoke and featured strippers well past their prime required major changes. He got rid of the "topless" signs and flashing neon lights. He remodeled the clubs, giving them a hip look, which included wallpapering the restrooms with Trojan Magnum XL wrappers. He also brought in younger "exotic dancers" who exuded a carnal energy that mesmerized men. The clubs boomed and you could almost hear the old man applauding from the grave.

The changes brought in a new, younger clientele who were willing to spend more money for call liquor and trendy drinks like Pimp Juice. They were also heavy tippers that kept the exotic dancers thrilled with their take home money. No doubt drugs thrived around Cabral's clubs, but all the drug deals seemed to be conducted in the parking lot. The police had never been able to implicate Jared Cabral.

Saffron Blue was known for its back room, where it was rumored a high-stakes poker game went on every night. Acting on tips, the police raided the room a few times and found the players were betting toothpicks. Adam didn't think it was worth the effort. There was enough crime in San Diego without trying to trap men gambling illegally, especially with all the legal gambling going on in the Indian casinos in the area.

From a homicide case he'd investigated years ago, Adam knew Jared Cabral arrived shortly after the club opened and stayed until it closed. According to his calculations, Cabral should be arriving shortly. Adam leaned back in the silver Lexus that had belonged to his uncle. He'd taken it from the garage even though it was part of the estate and still in probate.

His mind strayed to last night. Whitney came damn near being killed because of her cousin. Adam suspected the answer could be found here. Miranda had to have run through the insurance money and needed the cash stripping generated. She'd met someone or had seen something and become a liability.

Adam didn't want Whitney to suffer for her cousin's mistakes. She'd been through enough, he decided. A devastating divorce. Then the airhead second wife comes up with a crazy scheme to snatch the dog Whitney was crazy about.

A twinge of guilt hit him. He really should have told Whitney who had been responsible for Lexi's disappearance. Then he assured himself that Whitney had too much on her mind to bother her with one more thing. Anyway, it was in the past, and it was the least of her problems.

He remembered the way Whitney had acted last night. She'd willingly come into his arms and allowed him to comfort her. His entire body had been tense with the urge to take her to his bed, but he knew better. She'd been too shell-shocked by the fire to know what she was doing.

Did he know what *he* was doing?

Adam had to be honest with himself. He wasn't positive about anything the way he'd been before Iraq. He'd told himself to steer clear of Whitney until he was sure she was no longer entangled with her ex. Aw, hell. That was going to be damn near impossible with her living in the maid's quarters.

How did he plan to go to bed when she was sleeping so close? Last night, he'd lain awake, imagining her naked. Her warm body and soft breasts were in his favorite T-shirt.

He sucked in air between clenched teeth. *Admit it, buddy. You're in real trouble here. How can you live in the same house and not touch her?*

He ached to turn back the clock to last night. He would have hotfooted it down to the maid's room. Peeling his well-worn T-shirt off Whitney would have revealed creamy smooth skin and full breasts. Just the thought of her naked bod sent heat through his groin.

He could almost feel Whitney pressing against him. Her warm body molding itself to his. Almost. He stopped himself. He needed to be in detective mode right now. What was the first thing drilled into raw police recruits? Detach emotionally.

Cabral whirled into the nearly empty lot in a lipstick-red Ferrari with vanity plates that read: CABRAL1. He parked in a reserved space near the entrance, then opened the door of the sports car and unwound himself from behind the wheel. Adam had to look twice to make sure the guy was Jared Cabral.

Since Adam had last seen Cabral, the man had changed his hair. He was now wearing it in a spiked mullet that added four inches to his tall, lean frame. Gone were the jeans and polo shirt that Adam remembered, replaced by camouflage pants and jacket. The number wasn't a damn thing like what they'd worn in Iraq. This outfit was some idiot designer's idea of desert chic.

Adam gave Cabral time to walk inside and across the lounge area to his office at the rear of the club. It was too early for the bouncer to be guarding the entrance. Adam entered and paused for a moment to allow his eyes time to adjust. It was dark inside Saffron Blue, but it wasn't the kind of oppressive darkness Adam once associated with strip clubs. Saffron Blue was upscale all the way.

The leather banquettes surrounding the U-shaped bar were a shade lighter than the indigo-blue walls. Off to the sides of the room were alcoves with sofas and comfy chairs. Down lighting and lamps no bigger than his thumb cast a mellow glow across the room and reflected off the chrome trimming the bar and chair legs.

A waitress in a leopard-print thong and a matching something that might pass for a bra bounced up to him. Her boobs didn't look like original equipment, but hey, who was he to criticize?

"What can I get you, hon?"

"Nothing. I'm here to see Jared."

A mouth coated with lipstick applied with a painter's brush formed an O. "Who shall I—"

"Don't bother. I know my way to his office." Adam took off across the club and noticed a surprising number of men were there despite the early hour. An exotic dancer was strutting up and down the top of the bar, jiggling her melon-sized boobs and smiling as if she'd just won the lottery.

The door to Cabral's office was open. Adam paused, seeing Cabral seated inside, and knocked on the door.

"Wazzup?" Cabral asked. "Hunter. Adam Hunter, right?"

Adam nodded as he walked in. Cabral didn't look the least bit wary or even surprised. *Give the guy credit,* he thought. It had been over three years since he'd questioned Cabral about a man who'd visited his club and was later shot to death outside his home. Thousands of men had passed through Cabral's clubs during that time.

Adam stopped in front of Cabral's desk. "Good memory, Cabral. How are things going?"

"Can't complain." He gestured toward a tall bottle of liquor on his desk. "Trying to decide if my bars should stock 10 Cane Rum. It's made from the first press of virgin sugarcane from Trinidad."

"I never got the virgin bit. Virgin olive oil. Extra virgin olive oil. Now virgin sugarcane."

Cabral's laugh broke free as if it had been chained down for years. "That's what I liked about you. A sense of humor. Last I heard you were in Iraq and nearly bit the big weenie."

Again, Adam was surprised, but he shouldn't have been. With his wide blue eyes and ready smile, Jared Cabral seemed innocent. Far from it. He was a savvy businessman who played all the angles.

"Sit, sit." Cabral gestured to the chair in front of his desk. "I didn't mean to make a joke out of it. One of my buddies from high school bought it when an I.E.D. blew up the truck he was in."

Adam sat in the chair. He didn't want to discuss death, not after last night. "How's business?"

"Couldn't be better. We have our own Web site. We're CampTempTation on MySpace and other sites. Brings in more new customers than my father ever could have imagined. It's the Internet age, but nothing can replace real tits and ass."

Adam let him rattle on about New Age beverages and promotional opportunities on the information superhighway. Cabral liked to talk but he never really told you squat about himself.

"What brings you here?" Cabral asked when he'd finished with the lecture on how the Web had changed his clubs.

"A woman who used to…dance here is missing."

"What's it to you? Last I heard, you'd left the force."

"That's true. I'm in private security now. This is a personal matter."

Cabral steepled his fingers and gazed at Adam. "I don't get involved with the dancers. They're not employees. They just try out for spots in the Saturday-night show."

Adam nodded. Cabral was clever and managed to evade taxes as well as employment issues by letting women "try out" for places in his Saturday-night revue. The tips they could earn brought out more women than Cabral could use. Certain dancers kept "trying out" night after night.

"I don't even know most of their names. They use stage names like Candy Rapper and Sin Cerely."

"Do you remember Miranda Marshall?"

Cabral's face was totally expressionless. If he'd been playing poker, Cabral could have been holding a winning or losing hand and no one could have guessed which. He finally said, "Describe her."

Whitney had told him that Miranda looked a lot like her, so Adam rattled off a quick description.

"Could be half the cuties out there on any given evening."

Cabral sounded convincing, but Adam wasn't sure he believed him. "Last night someone tried to kill Miranda. They firebombed her place."

Cabral frowned. "No shit."

"Look, I didn't tell the investigating officer that Miranda worked here." Adam made it sound as if he actually knew the woman. "Level with me. Tell me what you know about her. I'll chase down the leads myself without involving the police."

Cabral stared at him a minute as if making up his mind, then said, "She called herself Kat Nippe. Her shtick—they all have a shtick—was the little-girl bit. She would prance out dressed like a kid going to school in a convent. That gave her a lot of clothes to take off."

"Do you have any idea if she ran into someone around here who would want to kill her?"

The telephone on Cabral's desk rang and he picked it up. "Cabral."

Adam waited while the club owner listened.

"Fuck no!" Cabral stared at the picture on the wall next to his desk. It was a black-and-white photograph of his father outside the original Saffron Blue. "What don't you understand? The fuck or the no?" He slammed down the telephone and smiled at Adam.

Adam tried to return his smile but he was pretty sure he just twisted his lips. The outburst had reminded Adam of what he'd learned three years ago. Jared Cabral was a man no one in their right mind would want to cross.

"If Miranda has an enemy," Cabral said, as if the argument on the telephone had never occurred, "I sure as hell don't know about it. She was a pro all the way when she worked here."

"Has she been hanging out with anyone lately?"

Cabral's eyes narrowed as he stared at Adam. "Just how well do you know Miranda Marshall?"

Something in Cabral's tone told Adam to level with him or Cabral would stop talking. "I've never met the woman. My girlfriend is her cousin. Whitney was living in Miranda's place. She almost died last night when someone tried to kill Miranda with a firebomb loaded with shrapnel."

Cabral shook his head. "Wish I could help, but I don't know a damn thing. Miranda hasn't worked at Saffron Blue in a year and a half."

CHAPTER TWENTY

WHITNEY HELD JASPER as she watched Kris Simpson bring out the teaser bitch. Jasper squirmed in her arms, anxious to be put down. Whitney didn't have much experience breeding dogs. When she'd been in high school, she'd worked part-time at a kennel. She'd seen two breeding sessions between the owner's Wheaten terrier bitch and a male who'd been brought in by his owner. No teaser bitch had been required.

"Ever seen an A.I.?" asked Kris.

Whitney shook her head. She supposed that if she'd thought about it, she would have realized champion dogs, like many champion racehorses, wouldn't be allowed to breed on their own. The risk of injury was too great. The sperm was collected, then the bitch was artificially inseminated.

"Mandy is in heat and so is my crested, Princess Arianna. She was best in her class at Westminster last year." Kris held up a small device that looked like a large syringe with a balloon-like sack on one end. "The teaser bitch gets the male excited, then I collect the sperm."

"You'll inseminate Princess Arianna yourself?"

"Yes. I'll freeze the leftover sperm for use on my other bitches when they come into season. That's why I paid so much money." She patted Jasper on the head. "I'll get three, maybe four litters out of this guy."

Whitney had no idea what this woman had spent for Jasper's services. Considering Jasper was an international champion, his offspring would be worth a lot. "Will we get the pick of the litter?"

Kris glared at Whitney. "Didn't you read the contract? I'll keep all of the puppies."

"I didn't see the contract," Whitney muttered. "I just help Mr. Hunter with Jasper."

Things must work differently when breeding champions, she decided. The owner of the male usually had pick of the litter.

"Put Jasper down and let him get a good sniff before I bag him."

She set Jasper on the concrete floor. He looked up at her and whimpered. "Go on now," she said encouragingly. Jasper pawed her shins, begging to be picked up again. Physically, he showed no sign of being interested in the teaser bitch.

Kris tapped her on the shoulder. "Let's leave them alone. We can watch it on the television in my office. I can get back out here before he ejaculates."

Whitney used her leg to scoot Jasper aside. She hurried out of the enclosure. Jasper scratched at the gate and yipped as if his paw had been caught in a trap.

Kris led Whitney down a short corridor to an office. The walls were lined with framed pictures of Chinese crested dogs and the ribbons they'd won. The photographs and ribbons were encased in Lucite boxes. A black satin ribbon was draped over one box and Whitney assumed that dog had died.

Kris sat behind a glass-top desk and carefully put down the collection device. Whitney took the chair opposite her. The breeder picked up the remote control and flicked on the wall-mounted flat-screen television. Jasper's plaintive yips filled the room. The TV showed the little dog still pawing the gate while the teaser bitch kept circling behind him.

Kris frowned. "That's what comes from holding a dog too much. I told Cal not to coddle his crested, but he wouldn't listen. He took him everywhere with him."

Whitney didn't interrupt to tell her that Miranda had cared for Jasper some of the time. She must have been partly responsible for spoiling him.

"Now look, the dog can't concentrate on his business."

The cell phone clipped to Whitney's shorts vibrated. Caller ID told her it was Adam. "I have a call I need to take."

"Go ahead. I'll monitor the dogs."

Whitney could hear Jasper's yelps still coming from the television as she walked outside into a blast of radiant sunshine. "What's happening?"

"I'm just leaving Saffron Blue. Jared Cabral says Miranda hasn't worked there in about eighteen months."

"What?" Whitney stared out at the white picket fence that encircled the sprawling ranch house where the breeder lived with what appeared to be at least two dozen Chinese crested dogs.

She gazed up and down the road, mindful of Adam's warning to keep her eye out for anyone suspicious. Nothing unusual was in sight.

"I was surprised, too. I assumed she'd been working there recently, but she hasn't. Cabral didn't seem to know much. I told him about the firebombing. He couldn't think of anyone or anything your cousin had been involved in that would make someone want to kill her."

"Saffron Blue's a dead end."

"Looks that way," he agreed. "We could try going through the stuff she stored in the garage."

This morning they'd inspected the charred remains of her Jeep. The garage attached to the carport had been partially burned. The contents of the garage had appeared to be a soggy mess.

"I guess we could, but I doubt she left anything important behind."

There was a burst of static and Whitney thought Adam had driven into a dead zone, but then she heard him say, "It's our only option. The police will go through her phone records and credit card charges. They may come up with something."

"I hope so." She was still jittery after last night. Not knowing what was going on or why her cousin hadn't warned her was making Whitney even more nervous.

"Are you okay?" he asked.

"I've been careful. I'm not being followed. No one suspicious is around."

"How's Jasper doing?"

"He doesn't seem to be all that interested in mating."

"He could be a gaynine."

"What?" Whitney wasn't sure she'd heard him correctly.

"You know, a gay dog. Maybe he prefers boy dogs."

"Be serious."

"I am. Who's to say homosexuality is strictly a human phenomenon?" He chuckled and she thought about the things he'd told her last night. He was opening up, revealing a sense of humor.

"I think Jasper is just nervous," she explained. "And I don't think the nodule you noticed behind Jasper's ear is any better. Shouldn't I take him to his vet?"

"Yes. There's a file on Jasper in the office. I'm sure it has his vet's—"

"I have the number. Miranda has the telephone number for the vet of every dog she walked. Emergency numbers of the owners, too. She was very thorough. I have it all in my BlackBerry."

A burst of static followed. "My phone's cutting out. See you later, sweetheart."

Whitney said goodbye and snapped her phone shut. *Sweetheart?* Adam was full of surprises. The way he'd kissed her— well, nothing had felt so *right* in a long, long time. After her ordeal with Ryan, she hadn't expected any man to interest her. Just the thought of her ex-husband sent up red flags. She cautioned herself to take time before becoming involved again. Make better, more responsible decisions about men.

She slowly walked back into the office, her mind on Miranda. Maybe she would never see her cousin again. It was possible she would never know who wanted to kill Miranda. Whitney needed to stay out of harm's way until the police came up with some answers.

Last night she hadn't been able to sleep. Adam was right. Nearly dying made her look at life differently. After her divorce, she'd become a fugitive from life by deciding to take over her cousin's business.

Whitney was realizing more and more that what she really wanted to do was become a veterinarian. She'd put her dream on hold to send Ryan to medical school. She'd passed up her chance. After all this time, she would need to take a few refresher courses in biology and anatomy before she reapplied.

She could do it, Whitney assured herself. She would have to go to school at night and scrounge to make ends meet, but she could do it. With hard work, she would be ready to take the entrance tests next spring.

If she was accepted—it was a really big *if*—she would have to leave the area. The nearest veterinary school was at University of California at Davis in the northern part of the state. It would mean leaving Adam behind.

Don't go there, she warned herself.

Her relationship with Adam was too new to factor him into her future. She had to chart her own course. She'd learned the hard way that setting your dreams aside for a man was a huge mistake.

As soon as Adam finished talking to Whitney, his cell phone rang. It was Tyler.

"Where are you, Adam?"

He heard the tense note in Tyler's voice and knew he was upset. "I was taking care of a little business. What's going on?"

"My father's been trying to reach you. Didn't you get his messages?"

"No. I've been really busy."

"Too busy to pick up voicemail?" Tyler's tone was hostile now. Anything to do with his old man made Tyler edgy, to say the least.

"I guess you didn't see the news." Adam went on to explain about the bombing and subsequent fire.

"Holy shit! You'll be tied up with insurance claims from here to eternity."

Leave it to Tyler to think about the financial ramifications of the fire. Adam hadn't even taken time to report it to the attorney. No doubt this would impact the probate.

"My father's on the way over to your place. He thinks there's a disc with a copy of the info somewhere in your uncle's house."

Missing financial records and now a missing disc. Things were not adding up. Adam was now more sure than ever that his uncle had been murdered.

"Adam, are you there? Can you hear me?"

"I'm here. I was on my way to the office but I can go home again."

"I'd appreciate it." There was no mistaking the relief in Tyler's voice. "Father's going postal over this missing disc."

Adam almost told him that Quinten Foley could drop dead. Searching the house was a waste of time. Adam had already gone over every inch. Then he recalled all the e-mails Tyler had sent him when he'd been in Iraq. He'd kept in touch, tried to lift Adam's spirits. Most of all, he'd worked hard and protected Adam's investment in the security company.

It wouldn't kill him to indulge Quinten Foley. He was the kind of guy who wouldn't take Adam's word about not finding the disc. He would have to see for himself. Adam tried to imagine what it must have been like for Tyler to grow up with such a demanding father—and couldn't.

When they'd first met as cadets at the police academy,

Adam had learned he and Tyler had a lot in common. Both had lost their mothers at a young age. He'd assumed Tyler had a great dad like Adam's own father. Then he'd met the man.

From then on, Adam had befriended Tyler. It wasn't hard. Tyler was easygoing—the opposite of his father. They'd become closer as they moved through the ranks and became homicide detectives. They both had become disillusioned with detective work at the same time. It was only natural that the two friends go into business together.

Adam assured Tyler that he'd go through all the discs with Quinten Foley. He'd rather be tarred and feathered, but there you go. Some things you did for friends—like it or not. Adam hung up and drove back to Torrey Pines.

A hulking black Hummer was parked in his driveway. Adam pulled in behind Tyler's father. Quinten Foley jumped out of the Hummer. Splotches of red mottled his face, and Adam knew the jerk would attempt to ream him a new one for not returning his messages.

"Don't you pick up your messages?" Foley bellowed at him the instant Adam opened the car door.

"Fuck off."

That got him. Foley stopped dead in his tracks. Adam was certain no one dared to curse Foley. The older man frowned and the red blotches deepened in color.

"I've been trying to reach you since late last night," Foley said as if nothing had happened, but his tone was conciliatory.

Adam headed up the walk to the front door and Foley fell in step with him. "We had some trouble here. My cell was shut off."

"What kind of trouble?"

"A pipe bombing."

"Christ! Why?"

Adam was at the front door now. He stopped, the key in his hand. "Apparently the woman who was living in the cottage behind the house got into some trouble."

"I see," Foley replied as if he had his doubts. "Did Tyler tell you what I wanted?"

Adam unlocked the front door and held it open for Tyler's father. "Yes. Something about information on my uncle's computer." Adam headed up the stairs toward the office. "It was stolen along with some other computer stuff during my uncle's funeral."

"Yes, Tyler told me. I think Calvin made a copy of the file."

Adam reached the office and flicked on the light. "What makes you think he'd copy your file?"

A beat of silence. "It's the way we were trained. You know, military stuff."

Yeah, right. Something else was going on, and it might be the link to his uncle's death. Adam dropped into the chair behind the desk and turned on his computer. "I've run the discs the burglars didn't take. What are you looking for *exactly?*"

Foley pulled up a chair beside the desk. "It would be lists of names with numbers."

Bank account numbers? Adam silently wondered. "I didn't find anything like that."

Foley craned his neck to glance around the office at the bookshelves. "It could be hidden somewhere. Mind if I check?"

Foley hadn't bothered to ask any questions about the fire or express concern. His attitude already had Adam pissed. "Yeah, I do mind. I've been through everything in this room. Nothing's hidden in any of the books or—"

"Did you check discs that seem to be something else like PhotoShop or QuickBooks?"

"Believe me, I read every disc."

"Why?"

There you go. Quinten Foley was an arrogant SOB but he hadn't been made with a finger. "Some of my uncle's financial records are missing. I checked to see if he'd hidden them for some reason."

Foley studied him for a moment. "Look, I'm going to level with you. No one knows about this—not even Tyler."

Well, hell. This wasn't exactly news. Tyler's father didn't tell him squat.

"Your uncle was working with me on a weapons deal."

I'll be a son of a bitch! Adam had never suspected his uncle might be involved in something that was, if not illegal, damn close to it. When Uncle Calvin told Adam he was afraid, the older man hadn't mentioned this.

Why would he sell arms? Money, of course. There were countries and groups of people all over the world who would pay vast sums to get the latest equipment. But he never thought his uncle would be involved with them.

How well did you know him? Adam asked himself. Not well. The man blew in and out of his life. Adam had assumed his uncle shared the same principles that Adam's father had instilled in him. Evidently, this was a serious misconception.

An arms deal gone sour could mean a bunch of pissed-off men who would stop at nothing. Maybe that was why his uncle had been so afraid someone planned to kill him.

"You see, there are times when our government doesn't want it to be known that they are supplying other governments with arms," Quinten continued. "They conduct business through a third party."

"That would be you and my uncle."

"Exactly. Information concerning a recent deal was on your uncle's computer. I can't tell you more—it's classified top secret. But I can tell you there are people who would stop at nothing to get the information."

"Would they kill Uncle Calvin?"

"No. Why would they?"

"A little over two months ago, I visited my uncle at his villa on Siros. He was worried about being killed. He wouldn't tell me who was after him or what it was about. He wanted to protect me."

Foley gazed at Adam with a stricken expression. "He didn't send me any message or try to warn me."

"Would you have warned him?"

Quinten Foley didn't respond. He didn't need to; Adam knew the answer. This was a man who didn't love his own son. How could anyone expect him to protect a business partner?

CHAPTER TWENTY-ONE

WHITNEY HUNG UP and walked down the breeder's driveway to check on the dogs. She'd left Lexi along with Maddie and Da Vinci in the back of Adam's Rava. They were far enough inland that the breeze from the ocean didn't keep the air as cool as it was in the La Jolla area. If Jasper didn't perform soon she would ask Kris if the dogs could be put in one of the dog runs.

Whitney stuck her head inside the window. "Are you guys okay?"

Lexi responded by licking her chin and Maddie hopped up and down, but Da Vinci merely opened one eye and gazed at her for a second before going back to sleep.

"I'll hurry," she promised, then walked back up the driveway toward the office. Her cell phone rang again. Rod Babcock's secretary was on the line.

"Mr. Babcock is in La Jolla for a deposition. He has a noon reservation at Starz and would like you to join him. He needs to talk to you."

"Okay," she reluctantly agreed and hung up. She had rushed into Wal-Mart on the way out here. She'd bought a few changes of clothes and some toiletry items, but she didn't have anything nice enough to wear to a trendy restaurant. What she had on would have to do.

Whitney walked back into the office and found Kris had left. The television showed the breeder in the pen with the two dogs. Apparently Jasper had finally become interested in the teaser bitch while Whitney had been outside.

She watched Jasper attempt to mount the female. She kept bucking off Jasper again and again. He finally managed to corner the female and climb up on her. Jasper was going at it when Kris knelt down, grabbed him, and quickly covered his penis with the collection device. The breeder began milking Jasper and Whitney turned away.

She couldn't watch. Instead she checked her voicemail. One was a client canceling a walk and the other was Trish Bowrather.

"Call me right away. I'm *so* worried about you."

Evidently Trish had seen news of the fire on the morning television broadcasts. There was no mistaking the concern in her voice. Whitney couldn't help being touched. Other than Adam, she didn't have anyone who cared about her.

"From the looks of it, you don't have a place to stay, or clothes…or anything. Why didn't you come in and tell me about it when you walked Brandy this morning?"

Whitney had been in a hurry when she'd taken Brandy for his walk. Trish must have been in the shower when Whitney came by for the retriever. She'd walked him then left. She'd needed to squeeze in another dog and a trip to Wal-Mart before driving out here to deliver Jasper. Whitney called Trish at the gallery but her voicemail picked up.

"Trish, it's Whitney. I'm okay. I'll tell you all about it this afternoon. I'm meeting Broderick Babcock for lunch at Starz. Afterward, I'll drop by the gallery."

By the time Whitney retrieved a very dejected Jasper and drove south, she barely had time to park the car in an underground garage, so the dogs wouldn't get too hot, and still make it to the restaurant in time. She rushed up to Starz, her hair flying behind her like a banner. Broderick Babcock was waiting at a table in the rear.

The lawyer rose and extended his hand. *He's dressed for a*

GQ *photo shoot,* Whitney thought, *and I'm a walking advertisement for the homeless.*

"Are you all right?" he asked, his brows knit. "I heard about the pipe bombing and fire on the radio while I was driving here."

"I'm fine." She lowered herself into the chair opposite his.

The waitress bounced over and took her order for iced tea. Rod must have arrived early. He already had a glass of white wine and had buttered a roll from the basket on the table.

"I wasn't home when it happened," explained Whitney. She thought she sounded a little breathless and told herself to calm down. Rod was adept at reading people. She didn't want him to know how frightened she was. He was doing her a favor by reviewing the document. She didn't need to drag him into her personal affairs. "Apparently someone has a grudge against Miranda. She lived in the cottage until a few days ago. I guess they didn't know she'd moved out."

Rod studied her a moment. "Did you find out where she is?"

Whitney shook her head and let the waitress deposit a tall glass of iced tea with a wedge of lemon in front of her before continuing. "We found her car at the airport. She must have taken a flight somewhere."

The attorney nodded thoughtfully. Whitney didn't tell him that Miranda's ID hadn't shown up on security checks. She didn't want him asking how she'd obtained the information.

"You needed to see me?" she asked.

"Yes. I want to clear up a few details. Let's order first. I'm starving. I had to be out here early for a deposition and missed breakfast."

Whitney picked up the menu beside her napkin and quickly selected an ahi tuna salad. She wondered why the attorney couldn't have cleared up a few details over the phone. Rod signaled and the waitress came over. They both ordered salads.

"I had my investigator go over the titles to both properties. Did you realize your former husband has taken out a second mortgage as well as a home equity line of credit?"

"No, I didn't," she replied slowly. "But I'm not surprised. We were tight for money when we split. He's starting a new practice. That requires a big financial commitment."

The lawyer didn't respond. He looked at her with an expression that said he expected her to continue.

"I'm not responsible for these loans, am I? We are divorced, right?"

He gave her an encouraging smile. "We double-checked the court records. You are divorced. It's not uncommon for couples to divorce then settle property matters later."

"Will I be responsible for loans he took out after—"

"What counts is the day the divorce papers were filed. Subsequent loans are his problem."

Whitney smiled to herself. Ryan had never been good at managing money. Let him sweat this one out with his Miss America wannabe.

"Did you realize your ex had a gambling problem?"

She bit back a startled gasp. "No," she managed to say after a moment. "I had no idea. Are you sure?"

"My sources—always reliable—tell me he's into the casinos for half a mil."

"Half a million dollars." The second the words were out she knew she'd raised her voice. She added in a lower tone, "I don't believe it."

"I've represented the tribes on several matters. They're as computerized and businesslike as Vegas. If they say Ryan Fordham owes half a mil, he owes the money."

"I see," Whitney said, the light slowly dawning. How many times had Ryan gone out in the evening? He'd claimed to be checking on patients. Now she knew the truth. When he hadn't been cheating on her, the skank had been gambling.

"I guess I'm not responsible for his gambling debts, if they were incurred after we filed. Right?"

"Correct, but it explains why he's so anxious to settle the property dispute. I doubt if he can scare up another cent."

Whitney couldn't feel sorry for her ex. She'd walked away from the marriage without much more than her maiden name. She'd lost her job, but Ryan hadn't cared how she survived. She'd taken a house-sitting job, then she'd been forced to turn to Miranda.

"You said the property near Temecula has Environmental Protection Agency restrictions on it."

"Yes. Ryan insisted we buy the land because development is moving in that direction and it would be valuable one day. When we were finalizing our divorce, he discovered the property had been a landfill. It can't be sold without an expensive cleanup and decontamination."

"Our preliminary check didn't reveal any EPA restrictions, but I'm told that isn't too unusual. A lot of those reports are given to county agencies that don't have the manpower to disseminate the information to all appropriate agencies. Often the EPA reports don't turn up until a transaction is in escrow."

"Ryan went to a Realtor and found out about the problems."

"Realtors often know—"

"Whitney," Trish Bowrather called from a few feet away.

"This is my friend," Whitney managed to tell Rod, even though she was surprised to see Trish. "I left a message that I would be here. She has an art gallery nearby."

Trish stopped beside Whitney. Today the gallery owner was dressed in coffee-colored linen with gleaming black onyx accessories. "I heard about the fire and I was so upset."

"I'm okay. I was out with the dogs. They were safe. That's all that matters."

"That's why I trust my Brandy to her," Trish told Rod as she turned and offered him her hand. "I'm Trish Bowrather."

"Rod Babcock," the attorney replied, rising. "Join us. We've just ordered."

Trish shook her head. "I didn't mean to interrupt. I just wanted to see for myself that Whitney was okay."

Whitney had the impression that the lawyer was intrigued by Trish. "You're not interrupting. I think we're finished with business."

"Yes." Rod pulled out a chair for Trish while telling Whitney, "I'll need to check a few more things before I'll allow you to sign the papers."

Whitney hid her disappointment. She wanted to put the past where it belonged—behind her.

"Do you have a place to stay?" Trish asked as soon as she was seated.

"In the maid's quarters at the main house." Whitney knew she didn't blush, but she hoped her face didn't give away how she felt about Adam.

"Sounds small," Trish said. "I have a client who's going to be in the south of France for at least six months. He's looking for someone to take care of his place."

"Thanks," Whitney replied with as much enthusiasm as she could muster. Adam cared about her, and Whitney liked knowing he was close by. She didn't want to move, but it might be for the best.

Rod waved over their server and Trish quickly ordered a salad. "I hope you're still coming to my opening Friday night."

Whitney nodded without enthusiasm. She'd forgotten all about the showing of the Russian's works.

Trish turned to Rod. "I own the Ravissant Gallery on Prospect Street. I'm showing Vladimir's works Friday night. He's the hottest artist on the local scene. Why don't you come?"

"Well, I…" Rod hesitated. Whitney had the distinct impression he was charmed by Trish but wanted to be persuaded.

"It'll be a lot of fun. Liquid Cowboy is catering the food." Trish produced an invitation from the elegant black bag she'd deposited beside her chair.

"How can I refuse?" Rod asked with a smile.

He was too sharp an attorney not to be able to slither out of this if he'd wanted, Whitney decided. She wondered if Trish had really dropped by to check on her or if she'd come because she knew it was an opportunity to meet a wealthy prospective client.

CHAPTER TWENTY-TWO

IT WAS LATE afternoon before Whitney could get an appointment with Jasper's vet. Dr. Robinson specialized in small breeds like Chinese cresteds.

The little guy squirmed as the vet ran her forefinger over the bump. "This is right where we implanted his ID chip. According to the records that was almost three years ago when Throckmorton—"

"He answers to Jasper. His ridiculous AKC name is Sir Throckmorton VonJasperhoven." Whitney realized the vet was about her age. She would be working with animals, too, if she hadn't set aside her aspirations for Ryan's career.

The vet consulted her chart. "Jasper was chipped at eight weeks. That was right after Mr. Hunter purchased him. I didn't insert the chip, but I'm sure our records are correct."

"It's odd that it would be infected now, isn't it?"

Dr. Robinson shook her head. "It isn't infected. It's just irritated."

"Do you think they rechipped him for some reason? He was flown internationally a lot. He recently won best in show at the Frankfurt International Dog Show."

"I'm not familiar with international regulations. It's possible he received a new chip, but I think it's more likely that this is a skin irritation typical of Chinese crested dogs."

Whitney nodded, thinking she'd overreacted by bringing in Jasper. "This breed is prone to skin problems, right?"

"You're right."

"Aren't many of them on special diets because of allergies?"

"Yes." The vet consulted the chart.

"Jasper's on a lamb-based kibble diet," Whitney told her. "No herring meal or fish by-products, which might cause allergies."

The vet studied her for a moment. "It's good to hear you know all this since you're taking care of dogs. Most people don't realize a number of dogs are allergic to fish by-products."

"They're in most commercial dog foods."

"Absolutely." She smiled at Whitney.

"Chinese cresteds sunburn easily because they're not covered with fur like other dogs. I keep Jasper out of direct sunlight."

"You're doing all the right things," the vet responded. "You're a much better caretaker than most pet owners I meet."

"Thanks. I try."

The vet patted Jasper's head. "I'll give you some ointment to put on the lesion. If the redness doesn't go away, bring him back in a week."

"You know, I almost went to veterinary school," Whitney blurted out. "I was accepted at Davis—"

"Really? It's tough to get in there. Why didn't you go?"

"I was sidetracked. But I was thinking of reapplying next fall. I'd need to take a few courses first to brush up."

The vet touched Whitney's arm. "Do it. You seem to love working with animals. It's a great career."

"I'll go online as soon as I can and find out what classes I need," Whitney replied.

Dr. Robinson studied her a moment. "Next month one of our techs is leaving. You could take the job and see if you like working in a clinic before you go back to school."

"I'd love to, I really would, but I don't have any experience."

"You won't need any. Our head tech will train you."

She couldn't believe her luck. "When do I start?"

It was two hours later when Whitney finally left. She'd met the head tech and had been given a tour of the facility. Her life was moving in a new direction, she decided. If the house-sitting job Trish mentioned worked out, Whitney would have a rent-free place to stay. And a fresh start on a new career. She kissed the tip of Jasper's nose, then put him in the back of the SUV with the other dogs. It was funny, she mused. A little thing like a bump on a dog's neck could change the direction of her life.

ADAM PUT THE SHOPPING BAGS filled with women's clothes on the floor in the maid's room. Someone had left the bags on the front porch. The television coverage had gotten them a lot of attention. Evidently, one of Whitney's friends had seen a newscast about the fire and brought over the clothes.

He heard the telephone ring upstairs in his uncle's office. After the second ring the fax machine kicked in. He hoped it was copies of Miranda Marshall's telephone records and credit card purchases. He'd leaned on a detective he used to work with to sneak him the records when Dudley Romberg wasn't around. He had no history with "The Dud" and couldn't ask him to bend the rules.

He raced upstairs and scanned the cover sheet the machine spit out. Miranda's records were coming through. He sat at the desk and waited. He'd systematically put the office back together as Quinten Foley checked all the software discs Calvin Hunter had stored in the wall rack. Then Foley had gone through every book on the shelves lining the walls to see if the disc had been hidden in one of them. He'd even checked behind the pictures on the wall.

Nothing.

Adam could have told Quinten Foley that he wouldn't find a damn thing. But Foley needed to see for himself.

Adam gazed at the framed awards and photographs on the

walls. Most were service commendations. Three were of Uncle
Calvin fishing. Several years back, Calvin Hunter had won
Bisbee's Black and Blue Marlin Fishing Tournament. The
photo showed a sunburned but smiling man proudly standing
beside a marlin twice his height.

Deep-sea fishing and dog shows had been his uncle's
passions. Interesting. You wouldn't think the two would appeal
to the same person. While he couldn't see his uncle being so
involved in those two different pursuits, Adam could believe his
uncle was involved in some black ops deal with Quinten Foley.
Uncle Calvin had spent his career in the naval intelligence
division. He knew secrets and had access to things others didn't.

This knowledge would be very lucrative on the black market.
Adam stared at another picture of Uncle Calvin on a fishing boat.
Radiant sunshine, crystal blue water, a smiling Calvin Hunter
standing on the swim step and wearing a baseball cap. The photo
was so sharp that Adam could almost read the printing on the hat.

The third photo was of his uncle on the sundeck of a home
somewhere. He was holding a platter with a large cooked fish.
By the smile on his uncle's face, Adam decided this was one
of his uncle's catches.

From what Adam knew about weapons deals, Foley and his
uncle were brokers. They were middlemen who arranged the
transactions and cut a huge profit out of each deal. They didn't
handle weapons themselves. But money, contracts, lists of
weapons and God-only-knew-what-else had to be exchanged.

The fax machine stopped churning out papers, and Adam left
the window. Noises came from downstairs. Whitney was home.

His pulse kicked into high gear. He'd been looking forward
to seeing Whitney since this morning when he'd discovered
she'd left early. He stuck his head out the door, calling,
"Whitney, please come up here."

Scampering, scratching sounds came from the stairway.
Jasper was on his way upstairs to find him. The dog bounded

up the last few stairs, spotted Adam and sprinted toward him. Adam hunkered down and Jasper took a flying leap into his arms and began licking his face.

"Hey, dude, how was your first hookup?"

"He rose to the occasion—finally," Whitney said as she reached the top of the stairs, the other dogs at her heels.

Adam stood up, Jasper in his arms. He wanted to pull Whitney flush against his chest, then drag her across the hall into his bedroom. He was reasonably sure the killer had been after Miranda, but you never knew. He warned himself that becoming distracted could cost Whitney her life.

"Did you spot anyone following you?" he asked. "Or notice anything suspicious."

"Nope, and I was careful."

"That's good. Don't let down your guard."

"The vet says the bump on Jasper's neck isn't infected. It just needs ointment put on it twice a day."

"Great." Adam held out the little guy to check. Jasper was still furiously licking but getting nothing but air. He was a goofy dog, yet Adam couldn't help being drawn to him. He remembered how Uncle Calvin had cradled the dog in his arms when they'd been in Greece. The dog craved affection.

"I have Miranda's phone records as well as her charge card bills. The police are going over them, but I thought we should take a look."

"How did you get them?"

"That's confidential. Don't mention to anyone that you've seen them. I don't want to get my source into trouble."

"Of course." She sat in the chair on the other side of his desk, Lexi and the two little dogs plopped down at her feet.

"Women are better at shopping than men. Go over the credit card bills and see if anything jumps out at you." He handed her a pencil and a pad. "Write down the purchase and date of anything suspicious so I can take a look."

Adam settled into the chair that had once belonged to his uncle. Jasper immediately hopped up into his lap. "Didn't Miranda put the utilities into your name?"

"No. We discussed it but decided to wait. I would have to come up with deposits. I didn't have the money. I had new business cards made up, and Miranda notified all her clients that I would be taking over. She gave them my cell phone number but her home number is still the one listed on the cards."

"I'm looking at her phone records for the last month. She made very few calls from home. I don't see any duplicates among them."

"You're thinking she would call a friend more than once, right?" When Adam nodded, she asked, "What about calls from her cell?"

"It takes longer to get cellular records than regular telephone records. We won't have those for a few days."

They worked in silence for almost an hour. By that time Jasper was snoozing on Adam's lap and the sun was dropping low.

"I'm not finding much on her charge accounts," Whitney told him. "Gasoline mostly, and a few department store charges. Nothing expensive. She paid the entire balance every month."

"I'm not finding anything either." Adam gently picked up Jasper and put him on the floor. "Let's see what she stored out in the garage before it gets dark. The fire destroyed the electrical wiring so we need to take advantage of what daylight is left. We can come back to this later."

Whitney rose and stretched provocatively. He longed to reach out and pull her into his arms, then kiss the sensitive spot he'd discovered at the nape of her neck. Don't start anything, he cautioned himself.

He reached out and brushed two fingers up the gentle rise of her cheek. He needed so much...*more* than this fleeting touch. But he refused to allow himself the pleasure. There was too much to do, too much danger.

His cell phone rang and he glanced down to where it was clipped to his belt. Max Deaver was calling. He hadn't mentioned the accountant or the missing money to Whitney.

"Why don't you get started?" he asked. "I need to take this call."

Whitney nodded as he pulled the telephone off his belt. She was walking out the door, the dogs at her heels, when he answered.

"Any luck in tracking down those cash withdrawals your uncle made every month?" Deaver immediately asked.

"No. It doesn't make sense." Adam had decided the money had been given to someone in the weapons deal. Cash payments kept that person's name off any records, but he wasn't comfortable sharing this theory.

"Are you sitting down?" Deaver asked.

"No. Should I be?"

The forensic accountant chuckled but couldn't manage to sound amused. "Your uncle's account in the Caymans. There's been more activity."

Now Adam was sitting down. He'd plopped into the office chair the second he'd heard "Caymans." If his uncle's accounts were drained, Adam would be on the hook for anything owed against properties he owned jointly with his uncle.

"Someone wire transferred seventy-five thousand dollars into the account."

"No shit."

"No shit. Seems bizarre, man. Totally bizarre."

"Where did the money come from?"

"A numbered account in the Bahamas."

"Why would they put money into a dead man's account?"

There was a moment of silence on the other end of the line, then, "I thought you might have some idea by now."

"Not really," Adam replied. He thought about what Quinten Foley had told him. It was possible the group purchasing weapons didn't realize Calvin Hunter had died and was still paying him.

"I'm going to keep working on this. We need to have a list of the assets for the probate, although I don't know what any attorney can do with numbered account information that he could obtain only by hacking into systems."

"I guess he'll have to leave it out unless I can find the code so I can withdraw the money."

"Someone else might beat you to it."

That was becoming more of a possibility by the minute.

"You know the old saying," Deaver said, irony in his tone. "Dead men tell no tales."

CHAPTER TWENTY-THREE

WHITNEY TETHERED THE three dogs to what was left of the back gate post in the small yard behind the cottage. The lingering smell of smoke and the sooty debris in the yard was a stark reminder of last night's fire. Nearby was the carport where she'd parked her SUV. Damaged by the fire, the structure's flimsy roof had collapsed onto what was left of her Jeep.

The firefighters had chopped holes in the garage walls and broken through the locked side door to fight the fire that had quickly spread from the cottage. Peering in, Whitney saw charred, water-soaked boxes. She wasn't looking forward to going through the sodden mess.

What choice did she have? She wasn't sure she could put into words the feelings she had about her cousin. Miranda wasn't going to miraculously reappear. They would have to find her, and it wasn't going to be easy.

With a quick glance to make sure the dogs were secure, Whitney edged her way into the old garage. Huge holes had been hacked in the roof and light streamed into the darkness. All she found as she rummaged through the things strewn across the floor was clothing. She sorted through the stuff to see if any of it could be salvaged—or provide a clue.

Several minutes later a scuttling noise made her jump. She stared into the corner where the sunlight didn't penetrate. In the dark shadows something moved. She released a pent-up breath of air. Rats or mice.

She needed to lighten up and soothe her raw nerves. Whoever was after Miranda was long gone. They weren't lurking in the shadows or following her every move as she walked dogs or went to the breeder's. Adam was merely being cautious.

"Find anything?"

Even though she immediately recognized Adam's voice, Whitney flinched.

"Hey." He slid his arm around her shoulders and lowered his head until his brow touched hers so gently that something caught inside her chest. "I didn't mean to startle you."

"It's okay," she replied as she pulled away. "I'm just a little spooked. That's all." She waved her hand at the mess on the floor. "I've checked out this stuff."

Adam pointed to several cardboard boxes. They'd been hosed down but still held their shape. "Have you checked those?"

"I looked in them. Nothing but books. I didn't see any reason to go through them."

Adam walked over to the boxes. "Things that seem to be un-related often provide important clues or links to other evidence."

Whitney supposed he was right. Adam had been a detective. No telling where he'd found clues. Later, when the timing was better, she planned to ask him about his career. Right now she needed to concentrate on finding her cousin.

"These seem to be cookbooks mostly," commented Adam.

"They're definitely something you would leave behind if you were on the run."

"Right." Adam studied the flyleaf of a book. "This one's *The Internet For Dummies*. Do you know a Crystal Burkhart?"

"No. I don't." Whitney walked over to him and peered over his shoulder. An address label was attached to the book's flyleaf. "Textbooks are really expensive. Miranda could have bought it used at the campus store."

"I doubt it's used. Most used bookstores put a stamp inside

the book. She must have borrowed this one and neglected to return it."

"It happens," she replied, her mind on her own books. She'd left most of them with Ryan but the few she treasured had been with her. They'd inspected the cottage first thing this morning. The contents had been completely destroyed. The books she'd saved from her mother's collection were gone forever.

"Look at this." Adam showed her another book. It also had Crystal Burkhart's address label in it. He pulled his cell phone off his belt. "Let's see if information has a phone number for Crystal Burkhart."

While Adam talked to the information operator, Whitney made her way over to the back wall where a number of boxes were stacked. They'd been doused with water but hadn't been disturbed. Evidently the flames hadn't burned the rear few feet of the garage. The first box she opened was filled with office supplies. Miranda had left supplies in the nook for Whitney to use. These things must have come from her previous apartment and she hadn't had room for them in the cottage.

"Thanks." Adam snapped his phone shut and looked at Whitney, shaking his head. "There are thirty-two Burkharts in the metropolitan San Diego area. Nothing for a Crystal Burkhart or C. Burkhart."

"We could try going over to the address on the label."

"Right. Let's have dinner, then drive over there. If that doesn't work, we can call every Burkhart listed and see if they're related to Crystal."

They worked in silence for a few minutes. Adam finished with the boxes of books and joined her. "Finding anything?"

"Not really." She showed him the box she was working on now. "There are photographs in this one. It looks like Miranda just tossed them in. You know how people end up with dozens of photos. Most of the time you never look at them again."

He moved nearer. "True, but let's take a close look. Photos tell you where a person has been. Ever heard of ComStat?"

"No. It sounds like a computer program. What is it?"

"Hey…" He touched her arm. It was just a fleeting brush of his hand but she felt it everywhere. "You're smart. It is a computer program that analyzes crime statistics. It can tell you where in a city a certain crime is most likely to occur, right down to the time of day."

"Most people can figure that out by reading the newspaper."

He chuckled. "There's some truth in that, but ComStat goes further than simple stats. It can tell you a lot about victims and perps. Most people have what we call a Com-Z. That's a geographic comfort zone. Killers don't strike far from home—usually."

Whitney thought about the person who'd tried to kill Miranda last night. She'd believed someone from far away had been after her cousin, but now she realized the killer probably lived in the area.

"People who go missing usually return to someplace where they've already been. It's rare to find them in a totally new location."

"Then Miranda's in the state," Whitney replied. "My cousin only left California once. A boyfriend took her to Hawaii."

"Once that you know about. Isn't it possible Miranda went other places during the years you were apart?"

"Anything's possible," she admitted.

They went through the photographs one at a time. They put certain photos that Adam felt needed a closer look in better light in a pile to take up to the house.

"You know," Whitney said, unable to check the excitement in her voice, "this might be something." She showed him a series of photographs with dates in the lower right corner. "These shots were taken last December on the eleventh."

Adam took them from her and studied them closely. "She's sunning herself at the beach. Not surprising."

"I don't think she was anywhere around here. I might be wrong but I believe it rained that week. I remember because Lexi's birthday is December seventh—Pearl Harbor day. I was house-sitting at the time. I'd planned to take her to the Bark Park but we couldn't go out for days because of the rain."

"Really? All we have to do is check the National Weather Service Web site. It'll tell us for sure." He pointed to something in the background of one photograph. "See that?"

Whitney squinted. "An umbrella, right?"

"Yeah, but I'm wondering if it's the kind we'd see around here. There's a magnifying glass up in my uncle's office. Let's take a closer look."

They set those aside and inspected the rest of the photographs. "Those pictures seem to be the only ones with the date on them," Adam said. "That makes me think they were taken with someone else's camera and given to Miranda."

"I saw her pack a camera. It wasn't a new digital model." She closed her eyes and tried to see Miranda sticking the small camera into the side of a bag. She didn't recall anything more about the camera and opened her eyes.

"Look at this." Adam showed her another photograph. A beautiful dark-haired girl was tilting a large cake toward the camera. Rows of lighted candles lined the top. Garish blue icing proclaimed: *Happy Birthday, Crystal.*

"Ohmygod." Whitney gazed up into Adam's eyes. "We're going to *have* to talk to Crystal Burkhart."

RYAN CAREFULLY PLACED ASHLEY'S ring just under the bottom rim of the chest of drawers built into her enormous closet. She usually put her ring on top of it, near a photograph of them taken on their honeymoon. Last night, she'd left it in the kitchen. He'd noticed the ring when he'd been watching her rinse off dishes.

Right then a germ of an idea had begun to form. The huge ring had cost him a bloody fortune. He'd willingly spent it, not just because he loved Ashley, but because back then he'd been winning big-time. He'd wanted the ring to be really large so Ashley could flaunt it.

He knew if he took the ring and had the diamond replaced by a cubic zirconia, he could raise a lot of money. He'd been right. The jeweler grumbled but gave him a nice check. True, it wasn't nearly as much as Ryan had paid, but he knew better than to expect to receive what he'd spent. Jewels were like cars—the minute they left the shop, their price dropped.

Ryan had taken the money and had gone straight to the casino. It was the middle of the day and only blue-hairs and the pros were playing. He'd won and won and won. Shit! Nothing could have stopped him except his love for Ashley. He left—in the middle of a winning streak—to pick up the ring refitted with the CZ.

He knew Ashley would have tried to put on the ring after she'd dressed. Hiding it under the bottom edge of the dresser as if it had fallen was the only plausible way to return the ring without arousing Ashley's suspicious. He faced the CZ away from the light and dug the ring into the carpet a little bit.

He heard a noise and bolted out of her closet and flew into his. He yanked off his tie and unbuttoned his shirt so quickly that he almost ripped off the buttons.

"Ryan, what are you doing home?" Ashley called.

"I'm not allowed in my own home?" he joked as she appeared in the door of his closet. She still had on her workout clothes and looked rumpled, which was unusual.

"Of course." She kissed his cheek. "I'm just surprised to see you. I thought you were in the office."

"Not today. I was looking into something for Aesthetic Improvements. That's the name we've chosen for the new group." He noticed her brow crimp into a frown. She might have called Walter Nance, trying to locate him. "I didn't mention it to anyone, but there's a guy in Newport Beach who's developed a cream to apply after laser treatments to prevent ghosting."

"Really?" Ashley perked up.

She knew better than anyone that some laser treatments resulted in pink skin that took days to return to normal. When it did, the lasering often left a line of demarcation called "ghosting." A light application of makeup concealed the ghosting, but some women resented having to use makeup, especially when working out or participating in athletic activities.

Ryan "feathered" his lasering to make the line less noticeable and blend it in, but it was still there. If anyone found a way to prevent "ghosting" it would be priceless.

"Does it work?"

"I'm iffy," he responded. "I would want to test it on a few patients first. But the guy wants a fortune for a three-ounce tube. I don't know if we want to ask our patients to buy it."

"But if it's so good I'm sure—"

"Let's not worry about it." He put his slacks in the wall-mounted ValetMaster to press the creases back into them. He usually sent his suits to the cleaners after he wore them once, but he needed to cut back expenses. "Let's go out to dinner. How about Pomodoro?"

"I thought—"

"You're right. We're saving money. Let's go to Sea Catch and buy some swordfish to grill." He'd said this impulsively. After the mess she'd served last night for dinner, who could blame him for wanting to eat out? But she was right; they did need to economize. He couldn't tell her about the money he'd won. He had it in his pocket. Tomorrow, he would pay down the loans on the house. The loans reminded him that she'd promised to contact a broker. "Did the broker agree to a reduced listing fee on the house?"

"I didn't have a chance. You see…" She hesitated, tears glittering like diamonds in her blue eyes. "I misplaced my ring. I've been looking for it all day."

Ryan had known she was going to tell him about the ring. He snapped back, "You lost it at the gym?"

Ashley slowly shook her head. "No, I tried to work out to get my mind off things, but I kept thinking about the ring."

"I saw it on the counter last night when you were cleaning up." He tried to sound helpful yet slightly aggravated, the way he normally would.

"I guess I must have picked it up, but I don't remember. You know how you do things automatically." She sucked in a sharp breath, then slowly released it. "I looked everywhere—even in the trash. It was picked up today. I went to the garbage collection center but they said finding anything as small as a ring would be next to impossible."

He couldn't stand to see Ashley in pain. He tossed her a lifeline. "Let's take a really good look, starting in the kitchen. Your ring could have fallen on the floor and rolled off where you can't see it."

"I looked," she protested.

"Let me get into my jeans and we'll both check again."

Of course, nothing turned up in the kitchen, but Ryan had them down on their hands and knees, peering under everything. He insisted on opening every drawer in case the ring had fallen in and gone unnoticed. From the kitchen, they went into the dining room and living room, crawling around and inspecting every inch of the house.

"It wouldn't be in my office," he said when they finished checking the entry hall.

"No," she assured him. "I never go in there."

He had cautioned her several times about his office. He'd told her that he had documents on his computer and research information on new surgical techniques that he didn't want disturbed. Whitney would have questioned him, but Ashley left his office alone.

"Let's try the master bedroom. You're in there most often."

Of course, a search around and under the bed yielded nothing. They removed the covers and shook out the spread and shams and every shitty toss pillow the decorator had insisted "made" the room. Nothing.

"The bathroom's next," he told her. "Or should we look in your closet? Isn't that where you keep it?"

"Yes, but I've already looked in the closet. It isn't there."

"Come on. Let's take another look. Two sets of eyes are better than one."

They went into the closet, and he started checking under the hanging clothes. He wanted Ashley to be the one to find the ring. *Come on, come on,* he kept thinking. His knees were killing him.

"Oh, gosh!" screamed Ashley. "Here it is!"

Ryan jumped up. "Are you sure? Where?"

Ashley held up the ring. Tears sprang into her eyes, making her look just like a little girl. He hated making her cry, but what choice did he have?

"It was under the dresser. I must have knocked it off." Ashley slipped it back on her finger and gazed down lovingly at the diamond. "I'm sure I checked under there. How could I have missed it?"

Ryan put his arm reassuringly around her and kissed her cheek. "The light changes during the day. You just didn't see it."

"I guess," she replied doubtfully.

"It doesn't matter. You have it now. Just be more careful. When you're cooking, take it off in here first."

He heard his cell phone ringing in his closet just steps away. "I've got to get that. It could be the office."

When he picked up the phone, Ryan didn't recognize the

number on the caller ID. It was Domenic Coriz. His bowels loosened and he swore his balls actually ached. He walked out of the closet and down the hall before answering. The last thing he wanted was Ashley overhearing him.

"Heard you won some money."

Unfuckingbelievable! Where did Dom get his information? Ryan had purposely gone to a casino owned by another Indian tribe. "A bit," Ryan conceded. "I need to make a house payment or I'll be out on the street."

"My heart bleeds. Now listen up, shithead."

He listened, his knees nearly buckling. "All right. I'll do what I can."

Money.

All his troubles came down to cold hard cash. Ryan put his hand on his back pocket. He had nearly ten thousand dollars. Once it would have sounded like a lot, but now he knew it wouldn't go far. All it could do was buy him a little time with the bank.

Or he could turn it into *real* money at the craps table.

He told himself to resist the urge to gamble. What had a few dollars gotten him? He needed megabucks. Plotting his next move was much more important. Taking your enemy by surprise was the key to victory. He was pretty sure someone famous had said this, but he couldn't remember who. It was the thought that counted. Do the unexpected. Take your enemy by surprise.

CHAPTER TWENTY-FOUR

"WHAT DID THEY say?" Adam asked Whitney.

After finishing dinner, Adam had gone upstairs and checked an Internet reverse directory for the address they'd seen on Crystal Burkhart's books. A man's name had been listed at that location. He'd asked Whitney to call because people were more likely to volunteer information to a woman than a strange man.

"Crystal Burkhart still lives there. Guess where she works?"

"Saffron Blue."

"Exactly. She'd just left for the club." Whitney thought a moment. "I wonder if Crystal met Miranda there."

Adam had his doubts. "It's more likely that the two met at college, considering the books we found. College girls often strip to earn money. People don't realize it, but most strippers are college girls or young housewives who need cash."

"Really? I had no idea."

Adam checked his watch. "It's early yet. The big tippers don't come in until after ten. Let's go out and talk with Crystal."

"Right," Whitney immediately agreed. "I'll lock the dogs inside my bedroom. That way I won't worry about them."

Followed by all the dogs, she trotted off in the direction of the maid's room. He mentally kicked himself for making her obsessive about the dogs' safety. He should have told her that Ashley had taken—

"Where did all those bags of clothes come from?" Whitney asked as she rushed back into the kitchen.

Adam had forgotten all about the shopping bags he'd put on her bed. "They were at the front door when I came home. A friend must have left them for you."

"I can't imagine who." She headed toward the back door and he followed. "I didn't get much of a chance to look at them, but the things on top were my size."

He led her to his uncle's Lexus. "Didn't you have friends where you used to work who might have brought by the clothes?"

"No, not really. I hardly knew anyone because I worked on a computer in my own space at a cube farm. I spent the day inputting sales data. I was the last to go when the entire department was outsourced to India. I haven't spoken to anyone there in months." She thought a moment. "I guess it could have been Trish, but I don't think so. I saw her at lunch. She would have mentioned it."

They drove toward Saffron Blue in silence. He'd considered going to the club alone, then decided having a woman would make it easier to get backstage and have a little talk with Crystal Burkhart. Besides, Whitney had a vested interest in this. She had every right to come along.

Over dinner, Whitney had told him about the house-sitting job that Trish Bowrather was trying to line up for her. He hated the thought of her moving out, but he didn't have the right to tell her what to do.

"Is something bothering you?" he asked when he realized she seemed to be staring out the window into the dark.

"I'm just thinking. I was offered a new job today. I'd like to take it, but I can't just give up Miranda's business. Clients are counting on me."

A warning bell sounded. "What job?"

He listened while she told him about the vet tech position. "Will you make more money than you do now?"

"No, and I'll have to work longer hours."

He was missing something here. "Then why would you be interested?"

Whitney angled herself sideways so she was facing him. An intense expression charged with excitement lit up her face. "I'd planned to attend veterinary school before I met Ryan. I'd been accepted at UC Davis."

Adam knew the University of California at Davis had a top-notch veterinary school. Being accepted to such a prestigious program was quite an honor.

"Instead of going, I married Ryan and helped put him through medical school. I'd like to give it another shot. If I take night classes I can reapply and I may have a chance of being accepted. Working with a veterinarian will give me practical experience."

"If they give you a good recommendation, that would help."

"It won't hurt. I have to give it a try. I don't want to wake up one day and find myself saying *I wish…* I want to know I gave it my best."

He had to admire her courage and sense of purpose. His life had once had direction and purpose, too, but that was before his stint in Iraq. He'd wanted to go into corporate security. Now he'd lost his moorings. He wasn't sure what he wanted to do. But sure as hell, sitting on his ass, guarding rich people's homes wasn't what he had in mind.

"What was being a detective like?" Whitney asked.

"Nothing like what I imagined. Nothing." He turned onto the highway. "You're probably smart to work at a vet's. I wish I'd had the opportunity to get a close-up view of detective work before I committed myself."

"You didn't like it."

"I enjoyed helping people, but too much time goes into paperwork and homicides linked to drug deals."

She didn't comment, but then, what could she say? The

average person had no idea what went on behind the scenes at the police station.

Whitney finally spoke. "My mother used to say that as long as there was a demand, drugs would be a problem."

"I couldn't agree more, but drug use is rampant in our society. It brings in big money and that corrupts even the most well-meaning people."

"Didn't you work on any interesting murder cases?"

"Not really. Most homicides are easy to solve. The perp is usually someone the victim knows. Killers rarely strike victims at random."

"There's a reason behind every crime, I guess," Whitney said. "Like the firebomb. Someone didn't just drive down the street and pick out the cottage because it was cute. Someone deliberately went there to kill Miranda."

"True, and this case is more challenging than most of those I worked while I was still on the force."

What also made this more interesting was Whitney. He'd never been personally involved before. In one way it bothered him, because being too close meant you might miss an important clue. But in another way, it gave him a sense of control. He doubted Dudley "The Dud" Romberg had interviewed Jared Cabral yet. Hell, for all he knew, Romberg hadn't discovered Miranda had worked at Saffron Blue.

He realized Whitey had stopped talking and was gazing out the window again. "What do you plan to do with your business?"

She slowly turned to face him. "I know there are other pet concierges in the area. I'm going to ask at Dog Diva tomorrow. That's the groomer. Dan's the best in the area, and he really cares about his dogs. If he recommends someone, I'll interview them and see."

"Sounds like a good plan. What about Lexi?"

"They said I could bring her to work. She'll be a calming influence on the dogs, the way she is on walks. Many animals are terrified of the vet. Dr. Robinson brings in her Lab and there's a parrot in the waiting room to help the pets chill. I think Lexi will like it."

Adam had no doubt the dog would be fine, but he didn't care for this new turn of events. Long hours. Living far away from him. He wondered how much he would see of Whitney. Not nearly enough.

He knew he was falling for her. Hell, he might even be in love with her. It had all happened so quickly that he hadn't had time to evaluate the situation. Maybe he didn't need time. Hadn't his brush with death taught him anything? Life could end in a heartbeat. Couldn't you fall in love just as fast?

Still, it was best not to plunge headlong into anything. There was stress and pressure and even danger all around. *Give this relationship time and space,* he told himself.

They pulled into Saffron Blue's half-full parking lot. A hulking guy in a neon-yellow shirt guarded the entrance. Later there would be a line and the bouncer would keep order until there was space inside the club for the men waiting.

"Does the club really need a bouncer that mean-looking?" Whitney asked.

"If guys are thinking about fighting, the bouncer intimidates them. Staff wear bright yellow because it's easy to spot in the dark. But that's not why he's at the door." He parked at the far end of the lot to be near the back of the building. "When strip joints first opened, law enforcement was under big-time pressure to shut them down. An easy way is to enforce fire regulations that limit the number of people in the club. The bouncer keeps count—on a clicker or, if he's good like Cabral's bouncers, in his head."

"Clever idea. The bouncer serves a dual purpose."

"Right. Give the credit to Jared Cabral's father. He was the first club owner in SoCal to use a bouncer to regulate the count." He put the car in Park and swiveled in his seat to face

Whitney. "We're going around to the backstage entrance. With luck, Crystal Burkhart isn't performing yet. If she is, we'll have to wait until she takes a break."

They went around back where there were several doors. Adam led her up to the center one with a card-key slot above the knob. He rapped on the door.

"Yeah?" A burly guy in a bright yellow T-shirt stuck his head out the door.

"We need to see Crystal Burkhart," Adam told him.

"Go in the front and pay." He started to slam the door, but Adam held on to the knob.

"I'm her cousin," Whitney piped up, surprising Adam. "There's been a death in the family." The guy hesitated. "I really need to speak to her. It'll just take a few minutes."

He glared at Whitney but his stare crumpled when tears jumped into her eyes. Damn, she was good.

"Aah, okay. But make it quick. The rapper's bangin' the shoe—" he checked his watch "—in fifteen."

He led them down a brightly lit hall that smelled of burgers on the grill. Adam figured the vents from the kitchen leaked a bit. To his right were a series of doors. Each had a name slot on it. By simply writing a name on a piece of paper and sliding it into the holder, the name could be changed by each dancer.

"Bangin' the shoe?" Whitney whispered.

"The bar is horseshoe-shaped. They bang—dance—on it."

The guy halted in front of a door and knocked, calling, "Yo, Candy, your cousin's here."

Adam read the plate on the door: Candy Rapper. Instead of being hand-written, this one had been engraved on a brass nameplate. Evidently, she'd worked here long enough to have a permanent nameplate inscribed for herself. Someone down the long hall yelled at the guy who'd let them in, and he hustled away from them.

The door swung open. "Cousin? What—" The woman's

bright pink mouth gaped open when she spotted them. "Who in hell—"

"Please, we need to talk to you," Whitney said. "Are you Crystal Burkhart?"

The woman nodded and her eyes narrowed. She was dressed in baggy jeans big enough to house five women at once and a huge shirt underneath a XXXL denim vest. Obviously, her shtick was to pretend to be a street rapper. Layers of oversize, ugly gangsta clothing concealed a stripper's hot bod.

"I'm Miranda Marshall's cousin."

"So? That supposed to mean something?"

Crystal sounded tough but Adam decided it was just an act.

"You're her friend, aren't you?" Whitney asked.

The woman's lips curved into a smart-ass smirk. "No."

"This is important," Adam told her. "May we come in and speak with you for a moment?" He thought she was about to refuse, so he pushed on the door and stepped into the brightly lit dressing room.

The room wasn't much bigger than a phone booth. In the center was a dressing table with a mirror illuminated by dozens of small bulbs. Makeup was scattered across the small table and Crystal's street clothes were slung over the back of a small folding chair in front of the mirror.

Crystal put a finger up to her lips to silence them. She grabbed a pack of cigarettes then headed out the door. Adam and Whitney followed the stripper as she rushed down the hall. He expected her to stop outside the stage door, but she streaked to the back wall behind three blue Dumpsters.

"You're a cop," Crystal declared emphatically.

"Not for over two years," Adam responded. "This is a personal matter. I won't bring in the police unless I have no other choice."

Crystal cupped her hand to shield the match while she lit her cigarette. "I can always spot a cop."

"He's a friend who's helping me," Whitney said. "Something's happened to my cousin. Miranda's vanished."

"Really? Do tell."

Adam asked, "When was the last time you saw Miranda?"

Crystal sucked in a puff of smoke, then slowly blew it out in a thin ribbon that drifted away in the soft breeze. It was dark behind the Dumpsters, the only illumination coming from the security lights at the back of the building. The stripper was overly made up, with stage makeup, and in the dim light she appeared clownish.

"I haven't seen Miranda in—" she hitched one shoulder "—at least a year and a half."

"Do you know if she had other friends or a boyfriend?" asked Whitney.

"What's it to you?"

Adam almost interrupted but decided to let Whitney handle this. People responded to her more easily than they did to him. "Last night someone threw a pipe bomb into Miranda's house. She isn't living there any longer. I'm staying there with the dogs. Luckily, I was out—"

"I saw it on TV. Were the dogs killed?"

"No," Whitney assured her. "They were with us or they would have been burned alive."

Crystal considered this information and a cold smile played across her pink-pink lips. "Miranda started dogsitting because of me. I earned money for college by walking dogs. It's cash, it's easy, it leaves no paper trail for the IRS."

"When did you two turn to stripping?" Adam asked.

"Back when we were in college, a girl in my econ class told me about Saffron Blue." She waved her arm in an arc and the tip of the cigarette in her hand glowed brighter. "The rest—as they say—is history."

"You told Miranda about it?" Whitney asked.

Crystal inhaled another stream of smoke. "We came out

here together for the first interview. Neither of us knew what to expect."

The feistiness seemed to have gone out of her, replaced by a tone that was almost melancholy. Adam wondered about her life. What would keep someone stripping in front of lecherous men night after night? The money, sure, but this woman had a lot going for her. She must have other options.

"They looked us over and gave us an opportunity to 'try out.' Little did we know that 'trying out' was the same as dancing. You get tips and you fork over a 'tryout' fee to the house each night."

"Why did Miranda quit?" Whitney asked.

"Damned if I know." Crystal threw down her cigarette and ground it out with the heel of her hightop sneaker. "We used to be best buds—then…she went jiggy on me."

Jiggy was a doper's term, but he doubted Whitney knew it. He asked, "Was Miranda using?"

"No, but she was edgy, like she was on ice."

Ice. Methamphetamine. Use of the drug had exploded during the last few years. "How did you know for sure Miranda wasn't using?"

"I was around her too much. I would have known." She shrugged dismissively as if to say: Who cares? "She up and quit. I haven't seen her since. It's been sixteen, eighteen months. Something like that."

"What about boyfriends?" asked Whitney.

"When we were first at college, she went out with a guy. Lasted a year, then he transferred to some school in Texas. She dated but nothing serious. Then we started stripping." Crystal squared her shoulders and looked directly at Adam. "Would you want your girl working here?"

An image of Whitney strutting across the stage flitted through his mind. Before he could stop himself, he said, "Hell, no."

"Men are like that," she told Whitney. "Work here, make money and get out—if you want to have a boyfriend and a real life."

Crystal wasn't nearly as tough as she'd initially tried to make them think. She'd been friends with Miranda, and Whitney's cousin had hurt her feelings. If they handled her right, the stripper would tell them what she knew.

"Please, help us," pleaded Whitney in a soft voice. "Someone tried to kill Miranda and nearly killed innocent people and animals. Have you any idea if Miranda was in any sort of trouble or anything?"

Crystal shook her head. "No, but like I said, I haven't seen her in a long time."

Adam asked, "Could she have met someone here that might have gotten her into trouble? Who were her friends here?"

"This isn't the kind of place you come to make friends. We knew each other before working here or we might not have done more than say hello."

"What about the men who come here?"

"Jared follows standard strip club rules. Men can't touch you. There's no going into back rooms or anything like what you see on TV."

"Can't they buy you a drink?"

"Sure. But no one wants to take the time. You earn more in tips by stripping than by sitting around with one guy."

Adam tried another tack. "Were you surprised when Miranda quit?"

"Everyone was, especially Jared. You see, Miranda was good on the computer and she put Saffron Blue online. She was more than just another exotic dancer." Crystal lowered her voice and leaned toward them as if someone might be eavesdropping from inside the Dumpster. "She worked the back room. Megatips. Trust me. Megatips."

"I take it Jared runs a high stakes poker game back there."

Crystal jumped around hip-hop style as if the ground was in flames. "You didn't hear it from me."

"Why?" Whitney wanted to know. "There are a lot of casinos around here."

"True, but high rollers who know each other like to play together," Adam responded. "They don't want to be forced to mix with strangers. Between hands they talk business, as if they were on the golf course."

"You got it. Games go on weeknights," Crystal added. "Nothing on the weekend. The guys who play here are out socializing on Saturday and Sunday."

"Did Miranda mention meeting any of those men?" Whitney asked before he could.

Crystal hesitated, shook her head, then admitted, "I'm not supposed to know anything about it. You have no idea how bonkers Jared is about security. Why do you think I brought you back here?"

Adam had been wondering. Most smokers would have stood just outside the stage door.

"The dressing rooms are bugged. There are security cameras everywhere. They can't see us back here. We're out of range of the cameras at the back exit."

Adam wondered why Crystal had taken the trouble to find out the security cameras' range but didn't ask. He figured he might be pushing their luck.

"We won't mention a thing about this to Cabral," Adam assured her. "Do you know the names of any of the men who gambled here when Miranda was still working?"

Crystal rattled off a list of names, and it included many of the heavyweight leaders in town. A thought struck him. "Did Broderick Babcock gamble here?"

"Oh, yeah. He's here a lot."

"What about Ryan Fordham, a doctor," Whitney surprised him by asking.

"I don't recognize the name. What did he look like?"

Whitney described her ex and Adam waited, watching her. Why would Ryan be out here? Sure, doctors made money, but he wasn't in the same league as the other high rollers.

"I'm not certain, but he sounds like one of the regulars. But I haven't seen him around in months. Come to think of it, Broderick Babcock hasn't been here either."

With those words Crystal Burkhart stomped off toward the stage door. They watched her go in silence.

"Your ex is a gambler?" Adam asked when Crystal disappeared inside the building.

"Yes. I just found out. Rod Babcock told me at lunch." She sounded despondent. He put his arm around her and pulled her close. "Funny, my attorney didn't mention that he's also a big-time gambler."

Adam's brain scrambled to connect the dots. Gambling. Ryan Fordham. Rod Babcock. Saffron Blue. Somehow they were all connected.

"Miranda quit just about a year and a half ago," Whitney said. "Right around the time Crystal says Broderick stopped coming here. He claims not to know my cousin, but I think there might be a connection."

"You're right. We need to ask him what he knows."

CHAPTER TWENTY-FIVE

WHITNEY WAITED UNTIL they had driven away from Saffron Blue before adding, "In retrospect, I should have had some idea, but I didn't. When Ryan went out in the evening, I believed he'd gone to the hospital."

"At some point you must have wondered. What made you suspicious?"

She considered his question for a long moment. "I'm not sure exactly. It was just a vague feeling I had that something was wrong." She hesitated again, uncertain how much of her personal life to reveal. She hadn't even told Miranda much except the barest details. Somehow she felt Adam would understand. Or maybe she just needed to talk to him, to feel closer.

Doing her best to keep her voice steady, she continued, "To be honest, a lot had been wrong in our marriage for some time, but I'd chalked it up to the stress of a pressure-packed residency followed by the difficulties of setting up a new practice. Then I began to have the feeling it was some-thing…more. I was taking his suits to the cleaners and discov-ered a hotel receipt. Then I knew. I thought it was just another woman, which would have been bad enough. Now I know he was also gambling and I never knew it."

"Babcock told you today at lunch?"

She picked up something in his tone that she couldn't quite interpret. "Yes, Rod was in La Jolla taking a deposition. He asked me to meet him for lunch. His firm had begun to review my property agreement. He doesn't want me to sign until he has the details about the toxic-waste report."

They were on the freeway now, heading back toward the house. Adam was staring straight ahead and didn't respond for a long moment. "Babcock could easily have discussed this with you over the phone."

For a second, her heart forgot its rhythm. He couldn't be jealous, could he?

"I think it's more likely Babcock wanted to see you again. To learn if you'd found out anything more about Miranda."

She was a tiny bit disappointed, she confessed to herself. Adam wasn't jealous. He was merely being a detective and analyzing the situation critically. "Well...he did ask if I'd discovered where Miranda went. I told him about her Volvo being in the airport, but I didn't tell him how we knew."

"He didn't ask?"

"No. Do you think that's unusual?"

"I'm not sure what to make of the whole situation. Babcock claimed not to know your cousin, right? And you didn't look familiar to him even though you closely resemble Miranda."

"That's right. He really seemed to be telling the truth. If he wasn't, he sure fooled me." But Ryan had deceived her, too, and she knew him a lot more intimately. How could she be certain the lawyer had been telling the truth? Something stirred deep in her brain, but she couldn't quite bring it to the surface.

"Maybe I ought to talk to Babcock."

She recalled the attorney's parting words to Trish Bowrather. "Tomorrow night, Rod will be at a reception Trish is throwing for one of her artists. I promised to be there. You could come with me. We might catch him off guard that way."

He grinned at her and winked. "Good idea."

They rode in silence for a few minutes, then Adam asked,

"Did that woman who phoned to interview you about taking care of her dog ever call again?"

With all the excitement, Whitney had forgotten all about it. "No. I never heard from her, and she didn't leave any message on voice mail."

"I'll bet she's linked to whoever tried to kill your cousin. They wanted to be sure she was home."

The second he said it, Whitney realized Adam was right. "Of course. The call came to Miranda's telephone. It was the first time I've ever used call forwarding to my cell. Now that I think about it, the woman sounded funny. It wasn't just her accent—calling the dog a poo-dell. It might have been a man disguising his voice."

Adam turned onto Torrey Pines Road. "I keep going back to motive. It's the detective training."

"You told me crimes of passion and money were behind most murders."

"True, but at John Jay we learned to analyze carefully. Crimes of passion usually involve a weapon that's handy—a knife, or more likely, a gun."

"It calls for premeditation to construct a pipe bomb. It may be relatively easy to make but it takes planning. It's not something a rejected lover usually does. They like to make it more personal. Look you in the eye so you know who's killed you."

Her stomach flopped. As much as she'd come to despise Ryan, Whitney couldn't imagine killing him. She couldn't envision hurting anyone or anything.

"The more I think about this, the more I'm inclined to believe Miranda knew something, and someone wanted to silence her forever."

Again something niggled at the back of Whitney's brain. Then she realized what was troubling her. "You know, Miranda had keys to a lot of homes. She went in when the owners weren't there to feed or walk their dogs. She told me about an incident when she'd been accused of stealing a woman's ring." Whitney explained the insurance fraud scheme that had finally been uncovered, clearing Miranda's name.

"It's possible Miranda saw something or came across something," Adam said.

"I was around her for several days. She didn't seem jumpy or nervous. She didn't act like anyone was after her."

"Yet she was preparing to vanish. What could Miranda have seen or found that would make her run but wouldn't panic her into leaving instantly?"

Whitney slapped her thigh with the open palm of her hand. "I've got it! The owners weren't due back for some time. When they returned, they would discover…whatever. That gave her a chance to leave without rushing."

"Possibly, but if she stumbled on something illegal or life threatening, why didn't she go to the police?"

Whitney hesitated a moment, not wanting to verbalize her suspicions. "She stole something from one of the homes and knew they'd discover it when they returned. Otherwise, why wouldn't *they* go to the police? Why try to kill her instead?"

Adam considered this for a moment. "Because whatever she found was illegal. That's the only reason I can think of that would account for everyone dodging the police. Most likely it was drugs."

"I doubt it. What would Miranda do with a load of drugs? Don't you have to have a network—"

"Could have been drug money. If you report a theft of a lot of cash, you'd better have a good explanation for where you got it."

"That must be it," Whitney told him. "Miranda stole someone's cache of drug money. It doesn't have anything to do with the strip club."

Adam turned up their street. "I'm not sure. There's a missing link somewhere. Miranda goes to work at Saffron Blue because she needs money. Then she quits just when she's making the really big tips in the back room and continues to walk dogs. A year and a half later, she skips."

"I can't explain it entirely, but the list of her customers is in my BlackBerry."

"The list she gave you, right? Miranda is one smart cookie. If she stole something, she probably deleted that particular client. What we need is her cell phone records. She must have called those people to make arrangements to care for their pet."

"Shouldn't we tell Detective Romberg what we know? He'll have more manpower to chase down leads."

He slowly nodded. "As much as I hate to rely on The Dud, we need help."

They pulled into the driveway of Calvin's home. They'd left the house and yard lights on. In the shadows, Whitney could make out the charred skeleton of the cottage.

When they stepped inside the back door, Adam punched in the alarm code. He checked the panel on the security system to make certain no one had entered, then reset the alarm.

"Should we take a closer look at the photos of Miranda at the beach?" Whitney asked as they got out of the car.

"Let's go for a swim first. It's a perfect night for it."

"Unless there's a swimsuit in those bags of clothes, I don't have anything to wear."

"I won't mind if you don't wear a stitch," Adam teased. "Or you could strip down to your undies. Won't that work?"

"I guess," she replied, attempting to keep the excitement out of her voice.

Adam unlocked the door. "Meet you in the pool. I'm going to call Romberg first."

Whitney knew better than to tempt fate by getting out of her clothes to take a swim in her underwear. But she decided to do it anyway. All the dogs were huddled inside the door to the maid's room. She nudged them aside, except for Jasper. As if launched from a cannon, the little dog bolted out of the room. No doubt he was streaking upstairs to find Adam.

Still puzzled by who'd left her the clothes, Whitney dumped the contents on the bed. Some items still had their price tags. She found shorts, capris, assorted tops and a few dresses. No swimsuit.

She changed into the black bra and thong she'd purchased at Wal-Mart. It wasn't any more revealing than a bikini—if she were in Rio. Covering up with a bathrobe she found among the clothes in the bag, Whitney grabbed a towel and left the room. Da Vinci, Maddie and Lexi followed her outside.

Adam hadn't come down to the pool yet so she took the opportunity to quickly get out of the robe and submerge herself. She released a pleasure-filled sigh as the warm water welcomed her. She looked down and decided the wavering water obscured the view of the demibra. If she kept her back away from Adam, the thong would just appear to be skimpy panties.

"That was fast," Adam called as he walked outside in swim trunks. "You found a bathing suit?"

"No. I couldn't get that lucky. I'm in my underwear."

"Want me to turn off the pool light?"

"Good idea." The light at the bottom of the pool went on automatically each evening, but it wasn't necessary for swimming.

He switched off the pool and yard lights, saying, "I spoke with Romberg. He contacted everyone on the client list. No one reported anything missing. He did the usual background check. Never can tell what you'll turn up that will lead to an arrest. Nothing much surfaced. A DUI. A guy behind on child support. A few unpaid parking tickets."

"Did Detective Romberg like our theory about drug money?"

Adam walked down the steps at the shallow end of the pool. Jasper parked himself next to the other dogs at the edge of the water. "Yeah. He'll look into it. The guy's under a lot of pressure to solve this. Pipe bombs are rare. Just say the word *bomb* and everyone thinks terrorists."

"Miranda couldn't have come across a terrorist plot, could she?"

Adam moved through the water and stopped a foot from her. "What do you say to letting the police handle it tonight? Tomorrow we can check and see what they found."

"Okay," she whispered.

The small waves his body generated lapped seductively against her skin. Above them a crescent moon gilded the water with beads of sparkling light. The moonlight played across the hard contours of his bare chest. There was something mesmerizing about his looks. His eyes were intense, but not that much different than other blue-eyed hunks. His lower lip was full, yet determined. She'd seen other lips that had been almost as intriguing. His angular face emphasized a strong jaw that sported a slight cleft in his chin. She'd studied other men's facial structure and found them equally as masculine. What set Adam Hunter apart, she realized, was her reaction to him.

Yes, other women found him attractive. She'd noticed them sneaking second looks, but she was captivated by him in a way she hadn't been drawn to another man. Not even Ryan. True, she had been taken with her ex-husband, but this was completely different, and it frightened her. Those feelings were too complex to analyze with him standing so close. She sucked in a breath that seemed to vibrate through her entire body.

Adam's eyes scanned her alluring figure. The caressing moonlight played across her soft skin and accentuated the sheer black bra lifting her full breasts. Her slim body nipped in at the waist where a thin band of black held up a small triangle of black satin. He'd seen bikinis that revealed more. None of the women wearing them had been this hot.

This sexy.

He extended his arms. "Come here."

She edged closer and her eyes glinted in the moonlight. The irises were wide and banded by a slim hoop of silver. He studied her mouth with its irresistibly full lower lip. He could feel her mouth against his, had been imagining it all day. Reliving those potent kisses.

Primitive desire coursed through him, hot and powerful. In a heartbeat he was dealing with a world-class hard-on. He reached out to pull her into his arms. She halted, a mischievous smile playing across her lips. She pivoted, jackknifed and dove away. With a few swift strokes and flutter kicks, she was across the pool.

Out of reach.

He was about to go after her when Whitney flipped over and backstroked toward him. The sexy bra lifted her breasts upward and emphasized the flatness of her tummy. The swatch of black silk between her thighs shimmered in the dim light.

Yeah, oh, yeah.

He was in real trouble here. *'S okay.* He'd been through hell and survived. He intended to live each day, each moment to the fullest. Right now every fiber of his being screamed for this woman.

CHAPTER TWENTY-SIX

WHITNEY STOPPED NEAR Adam and tossed her wet hair away from her face, flinging a shower of tiny water droplets into the warm night air. With her hair slicked back, the rise of her cheekbones was more prominent. Her expressive eyes seemed larger and exceptionally blue. He reached out and touched the soft curve of her shoulder.

The magnetic pull of desire surged through him, dismaying Adam. The throb in his swim trunks kicked up, his pulse accelerating. Hopefully, the darkness and the water concealed his erection. He forced himself to gaze up at the whirlpool of stars overhead.

Don't rush this, Adam.

"Come here," he repeated, a slight rasp to his voice.

Her matchless eyes surveyed him with mock suspicion. "Why? You aren't thinking about kissing me, are you?"

"It might have crossed my mind." He looked over his shoulder. "But the dogs are watching."

The dogs were standing at the edge of the pool and gazing at them expectantly, as if they would be receiving a doggie treat any second.

He chuckled and took her hand, pulling her close. "I think we should give them a show."

"You could butterfly across the pool. I'm sure they would love every second."

"Sweetheart, butterflying wasn't what I had in mind."

"Oh, what did you have in mind?" she questioned, all sass.

His eyes dropped to her bra straps and followed them down to the lush fullness of her breasts, bobbing slightly in the water. Her pert nipples were taut beneath the wet fabric. And incredibly erotic.

"You know what I have in mind."

He ran his fingers through the silky strands of wet hair pushed back from her face. The eyes staring up at him were charged with emotion. He knew she wanted him, could feel it, but he didn't expect her to admit a thing. Wounds from the past were still too fresh, and even though they were joking around, he knew she was unsure of herself.

Whitney turned her head to kiss the inside of his wrist. Her lips were as soft as the balmy air and just as tender. He drew her closer. She tilted her head upward to invite him to kiss her.

His mouth met hers and he reveled in the taste of her lips. He traced the moist interior, his tongue mating with hers. The water was warm but her body, flush against his, was hot. Its heat enthralled him, coiling around his thighs and sending a carnal charge through his lower body. Her nipples were thrust against his bare torso. An urge too powerful to deny filled him, the urge to mark every inch of her sexy bod with his mouth. Taste every inch. He didn't believe he could ever get enough of touching her, kissing her.

Don't rush it, he reminded himself.

His hands coasted over her back, slowly roaming lower and lower until he reached the gentle curve of her bottom. He eased his hand right, then left as he continued to kiss her. She was wearing a thong, a strand of butt floss forming the rear portion of her panties.

Works for me.

He used both hands to press her against his aching erection. With a startled gasp, she pulled back and stared up at him with wide, glistening eyes. Her lower lip trembled just slightly.

"I'm crazy about you," he heard himself confess.

"Adam, I—"

He had the feeling he wasn't going to like what she planned to say so he cut her off with another kiss. She didn't pull away—hardly—instead she wound her legs around his. Blood throbbed through his veins and breathing evenly became impossible.

Whitney moved against his jutting erection. His pulse skyrocketed; he groaned deep in his throat. He was tempted to take her standing up—right here in the water. But he knew better than to succumb to instant gratification.

When was the last time he'd desired a woman this much? He honestly couldn't remember and didn't have the willpower to give it more than a passing thought. She was special, and he'd known it from their first strange meeting on the floor of his uncle's living room.

Whitney shuddered, her fingers digging into his shoulders. He wedged one hand between their bodies and captured a breast. Some of its fullness escaped his fingers, but he savored the tightly spiraled nipple tickling the center of his palm. He pulled back a little so he could stroke the taut nubbin with his thumb.

"You were saying?" he managed to ask.

She gazed up at him with a dazed expression, her eyes smoldering with desire. "Saying?"

"I think we're waaay past talking, don't you?"

Her response was a moan of pleasure that made something catch inside him. *Do this right,* he warned himself. He allowed the moment to lengthen. The slow undulation of the water around them lulled him. Accompanying it, the sultry embrace of the night.

This was a special time, a special moment. Whatever the future held—he'd learned not to think about it—they would never be the same. He wanted them to be closer and… And?

He didn't have the inclination to go beyond that thought. For now this moment, this woman were all he needed from the world.

One of her hands dropped from his shoulders and wiggled its way between them. In a heartbeat, her hand was under the waistband of his swim trunks, nudging through the springy hair and coiling around him. *I'll be a sonofabitch,* he thought. He was close to losing it.

Already.

Aw, hell. What did he expect? He'd spent nearly three years in hell without a woman. Why wouldn't he go off when he was with someone so special?

"Hey, watch it," he warned, the words coming from deep in his throat.

Her hand clutched him tighter, then moved back and forth. A debilitating heat invaded every pore of his body. Christ almighty. What she could do to him without half trying. The sensation was so arousing he couldn't keep from moaning out loud.

"I need you," she half whispered, half moaned into his ear.

Adam lifted her into his arms, her head nestling between his head and shoulders. He plowed through the pool to the steps. The dogs jumped to their feet, tails wagging. He emerged and water cascaded off them. He walked toward one of the cushy chaise lounges nearby. Water sluiced off them now in small streams.

He lowered Whitney to the chaise. The dogs circled his feet and he nearly stumbled. "Sit! Stay!" He didn't spare the time to check to see if they all obeyed.

He carefully angled himself across her body to spare her the full impact of his weight. Stretched out, the full length of his body against hers, Adam didn't move for a second. He permitted himself a moment to enjoy the exquisite sensation of her warm, soft skin against his. In the dim light, her pupils were dilated and her long lashes dewy with water.

Sexy as hell.

The fragrant scent of her shampoo wafted up from her damp hair. One bra strap had slipped off her shoulder, and he pulled it down. With the black silk strap came the sheer fabric that almost concealed her full breast. Exposed to the soft moonlight, her skin took on a pearly sheen. He lowered his head and gently kissed her soft skin.

Whitney's hands found his butt and urged him closer and closer as she moved provocatively beneath him. "Yes, oh, yes."

He bit back the impulse to rip off the flimsy thong and bury himself to the hilt inside her sexy body. "Hold on," he told her, his voice rough with pent-up desire. "Let's make this special."

She ran the tip of her tongue across the skin along the curve of his neck, promising delights he could only imagine—if his brain could focus. A bolt of primitive heat lanced his groin. He'd told her to hold on, but it was all he could do to keep himself in check.

He lifted his head from the one breast he'd already exposed. He found the hook in the center of the bra and unfastened it. "Nothing like a front-loader."

Whitney might have tried to laugh. He couldn't be sure as he gazed down on her breasts, bared to the starlit sky. With a flick of his wrist, he tossed the garment over his shoulder. He was vaguely aware of the dogs scuffling for the bra as if it were some chew toy.

She arched under him, and the searing pressure of her body against his erection nearly sent him over the top. Every muscle in his body taut with need, he forced himself to concentrate on the breast he'd just uncovered. His lips circled the erect nipple, and he sucked hard, drawing it deep into his mouth.

"You're really good at this." She emitted a breathless sigh, her nails digging into his bare buttocks.

"I'm out of practice."

"Could have fooled me."

When had she shoved down his swim trunks? He managed to find the strength to stand up. His butt was half-exposed while the front of his suit looked like a tepee. He yanked down his trunks and kicked them aside. Then he bent over and eased off the barely-there thong Whitney was still wearing.

For a moment, he stood there admiring her. Her glorious body fairly glowed in the light of the most amazing moon he'd ever seen. A lover's moon.

Adam lowered himself to the chaise and settled over her, his throbbing erection finding the apex between her thighs. With a deep growl, he nuzzled her with the hot tip of his shaft. He slowly parted the moist folds and eased inside her by degrees. She was small, a tight fit, but he found the stamina to hold back until her body gradually accepted his.

She raked her nails across his bare back, murmuring, "Hurry, hurry."

With one swift movement, he surged forward and buried himself inside her hot, welcoming body. She responded instantly, moving up and down with each of his thrusts. Hips pounding, he hammered against her.

He heard a groan rumble from his chest as white-hot heat speared through him. His mind-shattering climax ripped through his skull, then shot down his spine. Trembling, he managed to hold it together and keep on moving for another few minutes until he felt her inner body tremble with release.

She cried, "You're the best!"

He mustered the strength to mutter, "Not the best, but close enough for government work."

He collapsed on his forearms to keep the brunt of his weight off her. Huffing like a racehorse, sheathed with moisture, he struggled to get his breath while his heart slowed.

She stoked the damp hair at the base of his neck and whispered, "Be serious. I'm crazy about you, too."

ASHLEY WAS WAITING FOR Preston in Dr. Jox's parking lot when the personal trainer drove his Camry into a space as far from the building as possible. She knew his theory. People didn't take advantage of everyday exercise opportunities. Use the stairs, not the elevator. Walk fast, not slow. Park as far as possible from your destination.

"Hey, you're early," Preston called as he eased his large body out of his car, his backpack slung over one powerful shoulder.

Ashley had the top down on her metallic-blue Mercedes convertible. She'd been sitting in the parking lot for over twenty minutes, thinking. "Let's go for a ride. I don't feel like working out."

Preston stood beside her car, a puzzled expression on his face. He dropped the backpack onto the small shelf behind the passenger side of her two-seater. "All right, but I need to watch the time. Arnold Wilcott has the slot after you. He's never late."

Preston climbed in and was fastening his seat belt when Ashley backed out and laid rubber on the asphalt. "Slow down unless you want a ticket."

Ashley didn't trust her voice enough to reply. She wanted to scream, to hit something, break something. But she hadn't a clue what would do any good. She hated losing control. It was like walking down the runway again, being in a beauty pageant and letting the judges decide your fate. When her mother died, Ashley had thought that life was behind her. Wrong.

"Upset about something?" Preston asked.

"Yeah, a little." She did her best not to sound as angry as she felt, but the weight of this was crushing her spirit.

"Wanna talk?"

She pulled into a parking space with a view of the harbor and turned off the engine. "I'm sorry. I'm always dumping my problems on you."

Preston shoved his sunglasses to the top of his head. "I don't mind."

Ashley could see Preston meant it. Sometimes she thought he cared more about her than Ryan did. Of course, Ryan had monumental problems while Preston led a stress-free life as a personal trainer.

She held up her hand. "Remember my ring?"

"You found it. Awesome! Be more care—"

"I never lost it. After I left you yesterday, I searched everywhere. I even went to the garbage collection agency that services our neighborhood. Nothing."

Preston's eyes narrowed, and she wondered if he guessed what she was going to tell him. Had she been a fool? Did other people see through Ryan?

"Know what happened to it?" she asked.

He waited for her to continue. When she didn't, he prompted, "What?"

"Guess. Tell me what you think."

He studied her a moment, and she saw the unwavering compassion in his eyes. "You found it…I don't know…somewhere you'd forgotten you'd put it. Like a different drawer or something."

Ashley shook her head, sending her hair across her shoulders in waves she could see out of the corner of her eye.

Preston shot her a questioning look. "Your husband found it and put it somewhere and forgot to tell you."

"You're closer now."

He leaned toward her. "Why are we playing games?"

Ashley stared at him a moment and asked herself the same question. This was no joking matter. Preston was her best—her only—friend. Why not come out and tell him?

He touched her shoulder in a tender way that nearly brought tears to her eyes. "Tell me what happened."

"Ryan took the ring," she said, bitterness echoing in every

word. "He sold the diamond—without telling me—and had a fake stone put in its place." She waved her hand under his nose.

"Is that so bad, if he really needs money?"

"I wouldn't mind—had he told me. But the bastard had me on my hands and knees double-checking the entire house for the 'lost' ring. Then it magically appeared under my dresser."

Ashley released a pent-up, exhausted sigh. "I couldn't sleep all night. I kept thinking about how thoroughly I'd searched the closet. The ring hadn't been there. Ryan conveniently found it when my back was turned."

"I get the picture."

"I started thinking about the unpaid bills and things I'd found in his office and I was sure he'd sold my diamond."

"Doesn't he have any other way to raise money?"

"No. He's taken loans out on everything."

Preston rolled his eyes heavenward. "But you were going to buy a new house."

"He said he planned to roll over the equity in the house and use it plus a piece of land to buy the property. After sifting through his records, I doubt the bank would have gone for it. I think Ryan was just humoring me."

Preston picked up her hand and studied the ring. "Are you sure this isn't the real deal? It looks great to me."

"This morning, I went to a pawnshop to see what I could get for it. I didn't want to pawn it but I thought that would be the fastest way to verify what I suspected."

"That's smart."

"They wouldn't give me a dime because it's a fake," she cried. "Why didn't Ryan just tell me?"

"He didn't think you would understand, and he was embarrassed."

"I know money's tight right now with the new practice and everything, but why couldn't he discuss it with me? That's what a relationship is all about."

Preston nodded his agreement. "Maybe he had a bad experience in his first marriage. That's why he doesn't feel comfortable talking over problems with you."

"Possibly. It's hard to know. He never mentions Whitney unless it's absolutely necessary."

"Why don't you just come out and ask Ryan about the ring?"

She hesitated, reluctant to confess the truth. "I'm afraid."

"Afraid of what? He won't hit you or anything, will he?"

"No, no. Of course not," she assured him, but in the back of her mind she remembered what Whitney had said the other night. Ryan did have an explosive temper. Apparently, he'd done something to Whitney.

"Okay, so, like, talk to him."

"I'm afraid of ruining our relationship. We never fight or argue. At least, we didn't until I took the dog. Then Ryan went postal on me."

Preston was silent for a moment before telling her, "The way I see it, if you don't talk to him, the relationship is ruined anyway."

There was more than a kernel of truth in what he said. Ashley hadn't been in a long-term relationship until now. She couldn't remember her parents talking about anything except her competing in endless beauty pageants. No wonder her father had walked out. As a teenager, she hadn't understood it, but now, she was an adult. A marriage couldn't be healthy without two-way communication.

Too late, she realized she should have called her father when her mother had suddenly died. Bakersfield was only a couple of hours north of here. He easily could have driven down. She hadn't called because she'd assumed he didn't care. Now she saw the situation from a different perspective. She knew her parents loved each other, but her mother had been obsessed with Ashley winning a beauty title. Her father had understood what a pipe dream it was and how little Ashley would gain from the title should she win.

She considered talking to Ryan tonight, but they were going out with Walter Nance and his wife. Ryan was determined to impress the head surgeon in his new practice. He'd told her to look spectacular. If things went well, Ryan might be in the mood to have a serious discussion afterward. She stopped herself. Why did so much of their life together have to depend on his moods?

"If only I could help Ryan in some way. You know, offer up a solution to the money problems when we talk."

"The solution is getting that woman—Whitney—out of your lives."

Preston was right, and she knew it. Ashley felt for Whitney. She'd lost Ryan, nearly lost her dog, then a fire destroyed everything. But that was no excuse for ruining Ashley's life.

On the spot, Ashley made a decision she hoped she wouldn't regret. Ryan had enough on his mind. She could take care of this on her own.

CHAPTER TWENTY-SEVEN

ADAM PARKED HIS car in the visitors' section of the lot behind the coroner's office. He looked around to see if anyone had followed him. When he'd left the house this morning, he'd carefully surveyed the street to see if any strange vehicles were parked close to the house.

Nothing.

Not that he expected anyone to be tailing him, but he couldn't stop worrying about Whitney. There wasn't any reason for concern, he assured himself. Whoever had thrown the pipe bomb had been after Miranda. Still, Whitney was constantly in his thoughts.

Since the night of the pipe bombing, he'd been worried someone might mistake Whitney for her cousin. He was even more troubled now, but he didn't know why. Okay, maybe he did. Making love to her had triggered a very masculine instinct. Protectiveness. When you cared about a woman, you wanted to protect her.

Whitney had come to mean a lot to him in a short period of time. Once he would have questioned this, but after facing death—and surviving—he knew how quickly life could change. Falling for a woman this soon no longer surprised him.

He walked into the building and down the stairs to the level where Samantha Waterson had her office. He'd received a text message this morning that the assistant coroner wanted to see him.

"Hey," Samantha greeted him when he appeared at her office door.

"Hey, yourself." Adam walked in with a smile for the redhead. "I received your message."

She waved him into the chair next to her desk. "I received the advanced tox report on your uncle. Nothing out of the ordinary."

Adam stared blankly at her for a moment. He couldn't believe this. He'd been so sure a toxicology screen would turn up something. "Nothing?"

"Nope. Traces of ibuprofen. That's all. Aspirin or Tylenol turns up in ninety-eight percent of all tox screens. It's the most common drug in America."

Adam recalled Quinten Foley's visit. They were dealing with sophisticated people who would stop at nothing to get what they wanted. He didn't know of any reason they would want to kill his uncle, but then, he didn't have all of the facts.

"Is there anything that wouldn't show up on a tox screen?" he asked.

"Sure. Lots of things. Rohypnol, for starters."

"The date-rape drug?"

"Yes. It's out of your system in twenty-four hours. If a victim isn't tested immediately, it's almost impossible to prove in court that a defendant slipped a woman the drug."

"How would Rohypnol figure in my uncle's death?"

"Victims go into a blackout state and don't remember anything. He could have been given the drug, then forced to exercise so vigorously that his heart gave out."

"I'm not sure…someone would have to have known heart trouble ran in the family. Even if they did, there's no guarantee it would work." He shook his head. "Anything else?"

"There are lots of designer drugs around. Remember the steroid substitutes invented to get around baseball's steroid ban?" she asked, and he nodded. "Like those designer steroids, there are a number of drugs that can elude toxicology panels. The one that comes to mind in this case is curare."

"That stuff that Indians in the Amazon used on their arrow tips?"

"Exactly. It's sold under a variety of names by drug companies. It's most commonly administered when a doctor is operating on someone's lungs. The drug causes paralysis so the lungs don't move during the operation. If your uncle was given an overdose, all his internal organs would have shut down. The process could have mimicked a heart attack."

Calvin Hunter had been involved in dangerous arms transactions. Considering those deals, the men wouldn't have wanted to find themselves involved in an investigation. They would have used something untraceable.

"I guess this is a dead end," he said with heartfelt regret in his voice.

"There's one other possibility," Samantha told him.

He refused to get his hopes up. "What's that?"

"Dr. Alfonse Taggart at Stanford is working on new tests specifically designed to detect drugs that current tox panels don't show. In this case, I would send him slides of the liver. Curare in any form impacts the liver. I didn't notice any inflammation and it didn't come up on the tox panel either, but maybe Dr. Taggart can find something. It's a long shot."

"Thanks. I owe you," he told her.

IT WAS NEARLY NOON BY the time Whitney arrived back at the house. She punched in the alarm code and entered the home followed by the dogs. During her rounds, she'd stopped in at Dog Diva. Daniel, the owner, had given her the names of two women who also worked as pet concierges in the area.

She'd spoken with one of them. Lyleen Foster sounded promising. She lived nearby and had an excellent reputation. She could take on several dogs, but not all of them. It was going to be necessary to split up Miranda's clients.

"Okay, guys, settle down," she told Lexi and Da Vinci. Maddie's owner, Debbie Sutton, had picked her up. Whitney was down to three dogs. Jasper came scampering into the kitchen at the sound of her voice. She assumed he'd been in his favorite hiding spot under the coffee table.

She went back into the maid's room and took a closer look at the clothes someone had left for her. Was there anything she could wear to Vladimir's exhibition tonight?

"You're queen of the clueless," she said under her breath. She had no idea what anyone wore to an opening. If she couldn't find something, she would have to spend money she didn't have on a dress.

Sorting through the clothing, she relived last night. Lord have mercy. Not only was Adam a hunk, he was an exceptional lover. She cautioned herself to keep this physical and not allow herself to fall for him.

She found a raspberry-colored sundress of sheer gauze. The fabric was held up on one shoulder by a lime-green butterfly while the other shoulder was bare. She smoothed out the dress and inspected it more closely. It wasn't very dressy, but it would work, she decided.

She tried to imagine what Adam would think. She'd tried so hard to be pretty for Ryan. He always found fault. She knew Adam wouldn't be hypercritical. He'd like whatever she wore. Still, she was determined to look her best.

Whitney hoped Trish's friend wouldn't need a house-sitter. She would just as soon live here with Adam. *That might not be such a good idea,* she reflected. Would she be able to study with him around? Wouldn't she just be jumping into another relationship too soon?

Well, she silently conceded, she *was* in a relationship. She never had casual sex. What had happened last night meant a commitment—to her. But after living with Ryan and having a marriage end in heartbreak, she wasn't sure she should be sharing a house with Adam. A little distance was probably a very good idea.

Becoming a vet would mean giving up a lot, and it would test a relationship. She'd buzzed by the animal hospital on her way home to see if they could suggest another person to help take over her cousin's business. They had a few suggestions. And while Whitney was there, she'd been drafted to help with a Jackahuahua.

The combination Jack Russell terrier and Chihuahua had been crossbred to create a unique dog. So-called "designer" dogs had become popular. Breeders mated two different types of purebreds like Labrador retrievers and poodles to create a Labradoodle. Golden retrievers had also been crossed with poodles to have Goldendoodle puppies. The positive characteristics of the Labs and Goldens combined with the fur of poodles appealed to people who were allergic to dogs but wanted a family-friendly pet that was easy to train. Jackahuahuas were new to her, and Whitney wasn't sure why they'd been crossbred.

The Jackahuahua had severely impacted anal glands. She'd nearly been bitten before they'd been able to bring the pet some relief, but she hadn't minded. Just being in the clinic and seeing the variety of things she'd need to learn excited her, even the gross procedures like expressing anal glands. The road wouldn't be easy, but becoming a vet was the career for her. She'd languished too long in a cube farm inputting data when she should have been doing something she loved.

"Don't set aside your dream because of a man," she said out loud. If Trish's friend needed a house-sitter, Whitney intended to take the job.

She was ironing the raspberry dress when she remembered the photos of Miranda taken last December. She and Adam had gone up to his bedroom immediately after they left the pool. They'd spent the night making love. Neither of them had given a second thought to the pictures.

She finished the dress and hung it in the maid's room. The photos were still on the kitchen counter and she took them up to the office, the dogs at her heels. She located the magnifying glass in the top drawer of what had once been Calvin Hunter's desk. She examined the photos closely, taking care to check the umbrella that Adam had noticed in the background.

It was a *talapa*-style umbrella made of dried palm fronds. Across the top, letters were stitched in blue. The words were a little grainy but she made out "Corona." The popular Mexican beer. Could the picture have been snapped in Mexico?

That would account for the dazzling sun in December when it had been raining here. Had it rained on that day? Adam had planned to consult the weather service Web site.

She spun around in the office chair and turned on Adam's computer. A quick check of the site confirmed what Whitney had remembered. It had been raining as far south as Ensenada, Mexico, which was an hour's drive beyond San Diego.

So Miranda hadn't gone there, even though it would have been an easy drive. But she could have caught a cheap flight to Cabo San Lucas at the tip of the Baja California peninsula. It hadn't been raining that far south. Or Miranda could have been in any number of places in Mexico. There were lots of inexpensive flights out of San Diego to destinations on the sun-drenched beaches in Mexico. Acapulco and Puerto Vallarta were among the most popular but other places were possibilities.

"Does it matter?" she wondered out loud. The other dogs were snoozing nearby, but at the sound of her voice, Lexi cocked her head. Whitney took the time to give her a loving pat.

Where Miranda had been last December could be very important. If Adam's theory was correct, Miranda might have returned to this sunny spot. But why hadn't her name appeared on the passport check? She gazed at the smiling picture of her cousin.

What had Miranda been thinking?

She studied the photo for several minutes. There was more writing on the *talapa*. The magnifying glass showed a smaller word after Corona. It looked like "de." No. There was another letter. An L. The second word was "del."

Maybe it wasn't the name of a beer after all. She'd taken three years of Spanish in high school. Corona meant crown. That accounted for the crown logo on each Corona beer bottle.

The third word was blurred. Evidently, the breeze had ruffled the dried fronds and they had concealed part of the letters. The magnifying glass had a small circular insert that magnified a bit more. She positioned it over the third word. "Mar," she finally decided.

Corona del Mar. Crown of the sea.

Okay, Crown of the Sea. Was it a resort or a restaurant? No, probably not a restaurant, she decided. The *talapa* was shading a beach chair. There wasn't any sign of food.

She went onto the computer again. Expedia didn't have any listing for a resort in Mexico called Corona del Mar. She tried Google and had over seventy hits. One was a beach in Southern California. Another was a swim suit manufacturer.

She diligently checked each one to see if there was any possible link. She was on fifty-three when she discovered Corona del Mar, an upscale development on the Mexican Riviera south of Cancún. The "villas" were in a tropical reserve called Mayakoba and started at a million dollars.

Miranda couldn't have been there. She didn't have that kind of money.

Whitney thought about it for a second as she leaned down

to pet Lexi again. "Doesn't work," she told Lexi. "Does it, girl? Not unless Miranda did come across a bundle of drug money."

ADAM STOOD BESIDE WHITNEY, a glass of champagne in his hand. He'd gotten home late, and he'd forgotten all about the opening. They'd rushed to make it to the gallery. Luck had been with them and they'd found a parking space down the street. They hadn't needed to waste time waiting for the parking valets who had been hired for the evening and were stationed in front of the gallery.

"That's Rod Babcock over there," Whitney told him in a low voice. "Next to the tall blonde. She's Trish Bowrather, owner of the gallery."

"Let's see if we can edge our way close enough to talk to them. Make it seem casual," he told her. "We want to catch Babcock off guard."

Adam had never been to a gallery opening. He'd expected a lot of dressed-up folks, but not this many. Either the Russian was a huge draw or the gallery owner had an impressive list of clients who were willing to turn out for free champagne and appetizers.

He put his hand on the back of Whitney's waist to guide her forward. He wasn't letting her out of his sight. When she'd waltzed out of the maid's room in a pink number that clung to her sexy bod like wet silk, he'd wanted to drag her upstairs and throw her on his bed.

"Dynamite," he'd told her. And he'd meant it.

Every guy in the place was gawking at her. Well, okay, not every guy. The gallery was so damn packed that only those close to them could see Whitney. Those men couldn't get enough. Sure as hell, he wasn't leaving her alone with some sleazebag lawyer.

"That must be Vladimir," Whitney said to him over her shoulder.

Adam assumed she meant the little guy with the grizzled goatee and wisps of white hair arranged on his bullet-shaped head in the comb-over from hell. His name had conjured up an image of a young, fit guy, but obviously Adam's imagination had taken flight in the wrong direction.

"I leave here five, all but six years," Vladimir was saying as they shouldered their way up to the attorney and the blonde.

Adam decided the Russian had been living here almost six years. His English was iffy, but who was Adam to judge. If he were living in Russia, he seriously doubted he could speak their language any better after five years.

"Whitney, there you are," exclaimed Trish Bowrather. The gallery owner's eyes surveyed Adam for a moment, then she smiled at the attorney.

Broderick Babcock was dressed in a black mock turtleneck and a beige linen sports jacket that hadn't come off the rack. His chocolate-brown trousers had creases sharper than most knife blades. He appeared fit with black hair burnished with gray at the temples. Adam had to admit that Babcock might have walked straight out of central casting to fill the role of a high-profile attorney.

"Whitney adores your work," Trish told the Russian. "Don't you, Whitney?"

"Very impressive." Whitney sounded convincing, but on the way over she'd confided in Adam that she found Vladimir's immense canvases strånge.

"You look great," Babcock commented, his eyes assessing Whitney in a way that made Adam want to punch out his lights.

Whitney introduced Adam to the attorney, and the guy blessed him with a brief glance. He couldn't keep his eyes off Whitney. Trish kept smiling, but her lips were crimped. Adam would bet his life the gallery owner wanted Babcock all to herself.

"Trish! Trish!" called an old battle-ax with garlands of pearls around her neck.

"Come on." Trish grabbed Vladimir by the arm. "Geraldine Devore already owns two of your paintings. She's dying to meet you."

Adam eyed Babcock while the lawyer and Whitney watched Trish tow Vladimir through the crowd. They were both smiling, on the verge of laughing. Babcock's eyes shifted left and checked out Whitney's cleavage.

"Let's go outside and get some air," Adam told Whitney.

The attorney took the bait. "Good idea."

It took the trio a few minutes to maneuver their way through the crowd. Along the way beach bunnies dressed as cowgirls offered them a variety of appetizers from Liquid Cowboy, the caterer. Adam noticed the opening was in full swing. Bored husbands quaffing martinis. Women checking out each other's jewelry. A few people looking at the art.

Prospect Avenue was on the bluff above the ocean. Outside the gallery a balmy breeze drifted in from the Pacific, bringing with it the briny scent of the ocean. There were a few guests on the sidewalk but it wasn't too crowded for a private conversation.

Whitney gave him an opening. "Rod's helping with my property settlement. I went to him because of Miranda."

Adam looked directly in the attorney's eyes. "They look a lot alike, don't they?"

"So I'm told." Babcock took a swig of scotch. "I never met the woman."

"Really?" Adam did his best to sound surprised. "Jared Cabral told me you were a regular at Saffron Blue."

Babcock's expression didn't change, but his eyes might have narrowed just slightly. "Jared didn't tell you anything. It's easier to persuade a dead man to talk."

True. So true. Adam had blown it intentionally to gauge Babcock's reaction. "Okay. Cabral didn't tell me. Let's just say someone mentioned you were a regular at Saffron Blue."

"That's right. I was—past tense. I haven't been to the club

in ages." Babcock turned to Whitney. "What's this got to do with your cousin?"

"You must have known Miranda. She worked there. You know, in the back room."

Babcock's expression never faltered. He casually sipped his scotch, then said, "You never mentioned that. You claimed your cousin walked dogs."

"She did. Miranda also danced at Saffron Blue. I didn't find out until after I went to your office."

"You could have told me at lunch."

Whitney gave him an apologetic smile. "It slipped my mind with the fire and everything, then Trish joined us. I forgot. Sorry."

"I went to Saffron Blue on occasion." Babcock didn't seem fazed. Adam gave the lawyer credit. The guy was damn good. "You said your cousin looks a lot like you. I don't remember—"

"Does the name Kat Nippe sound familiar?" asked Adam.

Babcock stared at Whitney. "Of course, now I see the resemblance. But Kat had jet-black hair. I never thought of her as a blonde."

Whitney turned to Adam. "She must have been wearing a wig."

"When was the last time you were out there?" Adam asked.

"It's been a year and twenty-three days," Babcock said matter-of-factly.

"How can you be so sure?" Adam wanted to know.

"I realized I was gambling too much. I mentioned it to a doctor friend while we were golfing. He told me a number of patients who took a certain medication to treat Parkinson's became chronic gamblers, even though they'd never had the problem before. He suggested I see a doctor at the Mayo Clinic who's been treating gambling addiction in Parkinson's patients. The treatment blocks the same part of the brain the Parkinson's medication affects. I tried it, and the pills work.

That's why I know how long it's been. I don't gamble any longer."

"That was the last time you saw Miranda…Kat?" Whitney asked.

"Yes. I used to tip her quite a bit, when I won. It's considered good luck to tip the back-room hostess." He finished off the dregs of his scotch. "Come to think of it, Kat wasn't around the last few months I was there. She quit or something."

Adam waited for Whitney to ask if Babcock had encountered Ryan Fordham in the back room. Just then a blue Bentley pulled to the curb, and the parking valet hustled to open the passenger door. Right on its bumper was a metallic-silver Porsche. Out of the sports car stepped a knockout blonde in a black sheath that fit like a tattoo.

CHAPTER TWENTY-EIGHT

WHITNEY NOTICED ADAM gazing over her shoulder, preoccupied by something. She didn't want to be rude and turn around to look. There were answers she needed from the lawyer that were more important. "Did you happen to meet Ryan Fordham while you were gambling in the back room?"

"Your ex?" Rod asked. "No. I would have recognized his name on the documents you gave me and mentioned it. Besides, the reason we play in a private room is to play with guys we know."

"I understand. I just wondered if he gambled there." Out of the corner of her eye, she noticed Adam was still watching something behind her. She wished he was paying better attention. She believed Rod was telling the truth, but she'd been fooled in the past.

"He could have started after I stopped gambling."

"Possibly." It didn't really matter, she decided. It appeared that Miranda had quit even before Rod Babcock stopped gambling. Her cousin wouldn't have run into Ryan.

"You see," Rod added, "gambling can be an addiction. Once you've quit, you can't go back. I haven't had much contact with those guys. Oh, I run into a few of them here and there. But for the most part I avoid gamblers. I was in danger of gambling away everything. Luckily, I got out on the downward slide but before I hit the skids."

Whitney wondered about Ryan. He'd been obsessed with

making money in the last year or so. At the time she believed he considered financial rewards to be his due after years of schooling. Now she understood gambling had motivated him. Was he near rock bottom? Was that why he'd been so threatening the other day?

Desperation did unbelievable things to people. Could Ryan—*Stop!* This man was no longer her problem. Ashley was welcome to deal with Ryan's gambling addiction.

"Walt, hey! Long time no see." Rod waved to a man behind Whitney.

"Rod, what are you doing here? I didn't know you were interested in art."

Whitney turned to the tall, slender man who'd come up beside them. He was shaking hands with the attorney when Whitney recognized an achingly familiar voice. The deep baritone she'd heard a thousand times was just behind her. She stared down at the bubbles floating to the top of her champagne glass, her stomach in an uncontrolled free fall.

Couldn't be.

Whitney edged closer to Adam as the hot flush of anger crept up her neck. She could feel Adam's hand on the back of her waist as Rod introduced them to Walter Nance and Emily, his wife. Whitney had never met the surgeon who'd convinced Ryan to join his practice, but she instantly recognized the name.

Ryan moved into their tight circle, his gorgeous wife on his arm. Whitney had only seen Ashley twice before this. Once she'd been in the car when they'd emerged from arbitration. The second time had been when Whitney had charged into the house demanding Lexi's return. She'd been so concerned about her dog that she'd barely noticed much about the woman Ryan had dumped her for.

Tonight, there was no ignoring the former beauty queen clad in a black silk sheath by some famous designer. The glamorous creature had an aura of poise and self-confidence that was exuded in every beautiful line of her face. A considerable amount of artfully applied makeup enhanced vivid blue eyes and made her lips appear soft and full. Whitney hadn't bothered with anything except lipstick. After the fire, she'd been left with nothing. She'd bought necessities but not makeup. It wouldn't have helped anyway.

Ryan spotted Whitney and blinked as if he'd seen a ghost. He usually wielded his charm as if it should be a controlled substance. Now he was smiling again, but Whitney knew him well enough to detect the fury simmering beneath the surface. Obviously, he didn't want to run into her any more than she wanted to see him.

"This is Ryan and Ashley Fordham," Walt told them.

"Meet Whitney Marshall and Adam Hunter," Rod replied as if he'd never heard of Ryan.

"Great dress," Walt told Whitney.

A strange, hollow feeling invaded Whitney's body, but before she could even smile a little at the compliment, Ryan told the group, "It should be a great dress. I bought it for Ashley."

Heaven forbid, Whitney thought, panic curdling her blood. Shock thrummed against her ribs. She had the insane urge to leap at Ashley and scratch her eyes out. The next second she wanted to run screaming into the night.

"R-really," stuttered Walt.

"Whitney is my ex-wife," explained Ryan with a chuckle that must have sounded false to everyone. They nervously looked around or sipped their drinks. "Her home burned down. Ashley tossed her a castoff. Right, honey?"

Save me, save me. Whitney prayed for deliverance, but nothing doing. How could she possibly be standing here in the beauty queen's dress? Wasn't there any justice in the world? Of all the people on the planet, Whitney would never have expected Ashley to give her clothes. What kind of karma did she have anyway? How could she run into Ryan and his stunningly beautiful new wife—and be wearing a dress the woman no longer wanted?

Her blue eyes wide, Ashley gazed at Whitney. "I wanted to help. It must be terrible having nothing. I—"

"Not as terrible as dying," Whitney cut her off. She deeply resented the woman's sanctimonious tone.

"We're late for dinner." Adam nudged Whitney. "Good to see everyone."

Whitney mustered the strength to mumble goodbye to Rod. She couldn't look at Ashley.

"Are you okay?" Adam asked as he hustled her down the sidewalk to his car.

"Never better." Tears burned the back of her eyes. She was thankful it was too dark for Adam to see.

He quickly unlocked the door and opened it for her. She scrambled inside as fast as she could, conscious of the noise from the gallery behind her. In despair, she slumped against the seat. Adam got in and turned to her.

"Oh, babe, what can I say?"

She told herself not to cry. Tears couldn't help anything. What had her mother always said? *Count your blessings.* The man next to her popped into her mind first. Then Lexi and the dogs whose lives had been spared because they'd been with her during the fire.

The fire.

Like a flashbulb going off in her brain, the fire flared on the screen in her mind. Lives could have been lost. But they'd all escaped the inferno. Now, *that* was a true blessing.

Pressure kept building in her chest and suddenly she heard herself giggling. It sounded a bit forced, maybe a little hysterical. She checked the burbling laughter. *Get a grip,* she told herself.

"What's so funny?" Adam demanded.

"Nothing. Nothing at all. Silly me. I could be dead right now. Just a charred crisp. Why let a stupid dress upset me?"

Adam cupped her chin in his warm hand. "Because the woman responsible for so much of the pain in your life owned the dress. Ashley should have left a note or something."

"True, but I'm going to be understanding. She wanted to help. Why I don't know, but she did. Maybe she felt sorry for me because Lexi had disappeared and she knew the dog was all I had."

Adam didn't respond for a moment. He dropped his hand and drew back. In the dark shadows of the car, she couldn't tell what he was thinking.

"Thanks for getting me out of there," she said softly. "It's not the worst thing that's ever happened to me. I'm sure one day, I'll look back and laugh, but tonight I wanted to run and hide."

He slid his arm around her shoulders and pulled her close. The look in his eyes was so galvanizing that it sent a tremor through her. The warm touch of his lips was a delicious sensation. She returned his kiss with reckless abandon.

He drew back a fraction of an inch and whispered in her ear, "That might have been Ashley's dress, but it was made for you. Let's not waste it. I'm taking you to dinner at Chive. We're celebrating."

"Celebrating what?"

His lips brushed her temple as he spoke. "Celebrating us."

ASHLEY WAS CAPTIVATED BY the enormous canvases and liked the little man who'd painted them even though he couldn't keep his eyes off her breasts. But Ryan was being a first-class jerk. Oh, he was chipper to everyone else but beneath the facade lurked a lethal coolness directed at Ashley.

So what if she'd given Whitney some clothes she no longer used? Ashley had stolen the most important thing in Whitney's life—Ryan. She felt sorry for the woman and embarrassed about her own behavior. True, Whitney seemed to have hooked up with that hunk Adam, but as gorgeous as he was, Adam Hunter couldn't be compared to a successful cosmetic surgeon.

Finally, Walter Nance decided it was time to leave. They had to wait in the valet parking line for their car. Emily kept prattling on and on about the new home they were building and how one of Vladimir's paintings was "so made for their living room." Ashley tried to listen politely but her mind was on what Ryan was going to say when they were alone.

"Ashley's not feeling well," Ryan told Walter Nance as the valet pulled up with the surgeon's Bentley. "We're going to pass on dinner."

"Are you okay?" Emily asked. "You didn't say anything."

"I—I'll be all right." Ashley glanced over her shoulder. Ryan couldn't have timed this announcement any better. There were too many people hovering in line behind him, anxious to get their cars, to discuss her health. The Nances hopped into their car, saying goodbye.

Ashley waited in silence. Ryan's Porsche was right behind the Bentley. They got in and Ryan drove off without tipping the valet. Ashley waited. She hadn't done anything *so* wrong. Why cancel their dinner plans?

"I bought that dress for you," Ryan finally said several tense minutes later. "I picked it out at a boutique with one-of-a-kind outfits. The butterfly pin cost extra."

"I'm sorry," she said. "I didn't know. I'd worn it and thought…" She didn't say how much she disliked the dress. She wouldn't have worn it at all if Ryan hadn't given it to her. She preferred black. It was a sophisticated color—a blonde's best color.

She could have added the dress wasn't chic enough for an evening like this, but didn't. She knew Whitney had nothing else to wear. And the raspberry-colored dress did look fabulous on her.

"I wonder why Whitney was there," Ashley said.

Ryan slapped his open palm so hard against the dashboard that she flinched. "Who gives a shit? That's not the point."

Ashley didn't ask what the point was. She was afraid to say another word. Ryan was moody at times, but he'd never been this angry with her. She recalled what Whitney had said when she'd come to the house looking for Lexi. Ryan wouldn't get physical, would he?

"That stinking bitch is holding my property for ransom, costing me an unfuckingbelievable fortune—and you give her the special dress I bought for you." Ryan was shouting now, and he gunned the engine. Like a rocket, the Porsche streaked down the freeway toward the home that always reminded her of Whitney.

"You don't get it, do you?" Ryan was yelling even louder now. "Whitney's the problem, yet you helped her. Do you have *any* idea how close we are to bankruptcy because of that bitch?"

Bankruptcy? Ashley had known their finances were shaky but things couldn't have degenerated this badly, could they? Like a robot she repeated, "Whitney is the problem. A big problem."

Ryan didn't say another word until he pulled into their driveway. "Get out! I'm going for a drive. I need to think."

Ashley had barely shut the car door when Ryan slammed into Reverse, then spun the car around and peeled off down the street. Ashley stood there for a second. Something told her to follow him.

She rushed into the house and grabbed her car keys off the hook by the door to the garage. She raced into the garage and jumped into her Jaguar. She flew down the street and took a hard right. She figured he would head for the freeway so he could floor the Porsche.

She sped up and caught sight of his car. Could he spot her? She doubted it. A quick look in her own rearview mirror told her how hard it was in the dark to tell what kind of car was behind her. As long as she wasn't on his bumper, Ryan wouldn't detect her presence.

He traveled north like a bullet, but she kept up with him. He slowed a bit, changed lanes, and she realized he was exiting the freeway. Maybe he was going to turn around and get back on the freeway to go home. Oh, boy. She would play hell explaining why she'd gone out.

Don't worry, Ashley told herself. She could go out if she wanted. She switched lanes and slowed down so that two cars moved in behind Ryan and her Jag. At the bottom of the ramp, he swung to the right; he wasn't getting back on the freeway to return home.

Where was he going?

For a second Ashley remembered the times Ryan had sneaked out at night to be with her. Just a tiny flare of guilt ignited deep in her chest. She'd ignored his cheating even though she knew it would be best to wait until he filed for a legal separation before dating him. She knew better, but she'd loved him so much. She hadn't been able to resist him.

The street was more brightly lit than the freeway. She was forced to drop back so Ryan wouldn't spot her. He went several blocks then turned into the Alvarda Casino.

She parked across the street and turned off her lights. Ryan got out of the car and locked it. He hurried toward the casino without even glancing in her direction.

If they were so close to bankruptcy, why was he gambling? Maybe he wasn't, she corrected herself. Casinos had wonderful food at cheap prices. Ryan had canceled dinner, but maybe he was hungry.

And needed to think.

Ashley wanted to think, too. She sat in the Jag, waiting for him to eat and come out. As much as she dreaded another fight, Ashley knew she couldn't put off talking to Ryan about their finances.

An hour dragged by seconds at a time. Ashley spent it thinking about her father.

Did he think about her? she wondered. Had someone told him about his former wife's untimely death? She doubted it. They'd moved around so much in search of an elusive beauty title that her mother had lost contact with the few friends she'd once possessed. There weren't any family members to tell her father, either.

Ashley let her head rest against the back of her seat. She kept thinking about her father and checking her watch. Had he remarried? Her mother had been beautiful; replacing her would have been difficult. But there was more to a person than looks. Surely, her father had discovered this.

Maybe he'd found someone who could make him happy in a way that her mother never could have. No. In a way that her mother never would have bothered with. As much as Ashley resented her father's refusal to stay with them as they roamed the country, she understood his reasons.

If they'd settled down and stopped pursuing a beauty title, Ashley could have finished school in one place. She would have had friends. She smiled bitterly in the darkness. Her only friend was a guy, her personal trainer. She paid him. How pathetic was that?

When an hour and twenty minutes passed, Ashley got out of the car. She was going after Ryan. If they had to sit at some café table at a casino to talk, so be it.

She went inside but didn't see him in the coffee shop. She ignored the men who stared at her; after years of males gawking, she was accustomed to the attention. A hostess directed her to the restaurant on the second level. It was nicer up there and the place was darker compared to the brightly lit casino. She could still hear the pinging of the slot machines and the buzz of the gamblers.

Ryan wasn't in the restaurant or the adjacent lounge. From

the second level she could gaze down on the gamblers below, but she didn't see Ryan. Where could he be? He wouldn't have left without his car.

Then she realized she must have crossed paths with him. He'd gone out one door while she'd been coming in another. No doubt he would be home waiting for her, more furious than ever.

She started to rush back to her Jag, then told herself to take her time. So what if he arrived home and she wasn't there? Taking a drive wasn't a crime.

Ashley went toward the spot where Ryan had parked. The distinctive silver Porsche was still there. How could she have missed him? True, it was a large casino, but she'd been able to look down at every table, every slot machine, and she hadn't see Ryan's dark blond head among the gamblers.

She walked back inside and strolled slowly through the casino. He wasn't anywhere in sight. Strange. Really strange. Then she saw a sign off to one side that advertised Texas Hold 'Em in a nearby room.

She walked around the corner and saw a small room with a lighted sign above the door. It flashed back and forth, back and forth, showing disembodied hands holding poker cards. Through the open double doors she saw a roomful of men seated at round tables. Ryan's back was to her but there was no mistaking her husband.

She started in, but a hostess dressed like a hula dancer stopped her. "Ma'am, these are thousand-dollar tables."

Ashley quickly backed away. A thousand dollars? What was Ryan thinking? No doubt he was gambling with the money he'd gotten for her ring. She slowly walked back to her car.

Whitney is the problem, she reminded herself.

CHAPTER TWENTY-NINE

"I ATE WAAAY TOO much," Whitney told Adam. "I should have skipped the chocolate soufflé."

"That's the first chocolate soufflé I've ever ordered. When I was trapped over in Iraq, I promised myself I would have one the first chance I had. I'd eaten one before and really liked it, but someone else ordered it."

She assumed he meant a woman but didn't ask. Dinner had been perfect. She'd never been to Chive. The sophisticated restaurant was in one of the Gaslamp's most historic buildings. The old Royal Pie Company had been transformed from a brick warehouse to a sleek minimalist restaurant with awesome food.

They'd enjoyed a leisurely dinner and talked about Rod Babcock. They decided the attorney couldn't help them solve Miranda's disappearance. Adam had complimented Whitney on discovering the Corona del Mar signs on the *talapa*. He doubted Miranda was hiding out at the upscale resort but believed there was a good chance her cousin was somewhere in the Cancún area. She must have gotten into Mexico with a phony passport. Or she might have hitched a ride over the border and taken a flight from a Mexican airport.

"At times like this, I wish they had sidewalks in these hills," Whitney told him. "I'd take Lexi for a long walk. I'd feel better after all I've eaten."

"We could walk along the trail." He pulled into the driveway of his uncle's home.

"It spooks me a little. I've been jumpy since the fire. Before I wouldn't have thought twice about hiking along the trail. With a flashlight, it's not hard to see where you're going."

Except for Jasper, the dogs were waiting for them inside the back door. He came scuttling out of the living room when he heard them greeting Lexi and Da Vinci. No doubt he'd been sleeping under the coffee table again.

Adam's cell phone buzzed. "Who can it be at this hour?"

They'd talked and lingered over coffee for so long that it was nearly eleven when they'd left the restaurant. It had taken them over half an hour to get the car and drive out to Torrey Pines. Whitney thought it was time well spent. They'd fallen for each other so quickly that they needed the opportunity to get to know each other better.

Whitney let the dogs out on the side yard and watched them closely. After Lexi's disappearance, she refused to take any chances. She could hear Adam talking and realized something was going on with his business.

"I hate to say this," he told her, snapping his cell phone shut. "I have to go into the command center."

"A problem?"

"I'm not sure what's going on. Tyler insists he needs me. He took care of everything all by himself while I was overseas. I need to help—"

"Of course you do. We're fine right here."

Adam started toward the door, then hesitated. "Don't go for a walk alone. Maybe it was just my imagination, but I thought I saw someone sitting in a car just down the street. It was a little far away to be watching the house, but you never know. I'm going to take another look when I drive out. I'll call you from the car to let you know what I see, but I want you to keep the alarm set until I return."

She went over and kissed him lightly on the cheek. He hauled her into his arms and his mouth closed over hers. What she'd intended as a little parting peck suddenly became wholly carnal. One hand cupped her bottom and squeezed gently. He kept kissing her, then his body stiffened and he pulled back.

"Hey, if I'm not careful, I'll just say to hell with Tyler."

"You can't do that. He must need you or he wouldn't have called so late."

"Right." Adam brushed her moist lower lip with the pad of his thumb. "I'll be back as soon as I can."

Adam left and Whitney set the alarm and stood in the kitchen for a moment. Should she go upstairs to his room? Or should she climb into bed in the maid's room? It seemed a little presumptuous to go upstairs so she walked into the maid's room.

She caught her reflection in the mirror over the dresser. Aaargh. The dress from hell. She yanked it over her head and dropped it onto the floor. She found the bags that Ashley had used to bring her castoffs to Whitney. She was packing all of them for Goodwill when the telephone rang.

"It's me," Adam told her. "Must have been my imagination. The parked car is empty."

"Great. I'll see you later."

She hung up and finished putting the clothes in the shopping bags. Her cell phone was on the nightstand next to her bed. She hadn't taken it with her because her only purse was too big and clunky looking for the outfit. The LCD display indicated she had voice mail.

"This is Betty Spirin," the voice said when she pressed the message button. "My daughter's been in an accident. I have to go to L.A. immediately. Grey's had his dinner. I need you to walk him tonight and again first thing in the morning. I'll call you tomorrow and let you know what's happening."

The woman sounded nearly hysterical. Whitney could only imagine how frantic she must be after learning her daughter had been in an accident. Whitney had never walked this particular pet but did recall Miranda telling her about a dachshund named Grey Poupon. The dog was a regular and Miranda had given Whitney the key to his home. It was on the key chain at the bottom of her purse.

She consulted her BlackBerry and found additional information. She'd remembered correctly. The dachshund lived in a condominium complex not too far away. A quick check of her watch told her it was just after midnight. The message had been left a little before five. The poor animal needed to go out immediately.

Whitney changed into jeans and threw on a T-shirt. She knew Adam wouldn't want her to leave, but she didn't have any choice. He would be gone at least an hour and by then Grey might have an accident. She thought about calling Adam but decided to leave a note instead. With any luck she would be home before he returned.

THE SECOND ADAM SNAPPED his cell phone shut, it buzzed. "Yeah?" he said, expecting it to be Whitney. Instead it was Max Deaver. "Working a little late, aren't you?"

Max chuckled. "Banks are just opening in Zurich. Diamond traders are busy in Antwerp. London's setting the price of gold. Paris—"

"Okay. I get the picture. It's morning somewhere just like it's always five o'clock somewhere."

"True, but I'm not kidding about banks opening in Zurich. There's been another transfer of funds."

Adam groaned. "You're kidding."

"Nope, but this should make you happy. The funds have been transferred to pay off debts against the property you and your uncle owned as joint tenants."

It took a second for Deaver's message to register. "What in hell?"

"Don't know. The money's coming from a numbered account."

"Is it one of my uncle's?"

"Not unless it's one I didn't come across when I was checking."

Adam pulled into HiTech's parking lot and stopped the car. "What do you make of this?"

"Haven't a clue, man, haven't a clue. I thought you might have some idea."

"Could it have been something my uncle set up before he died? You know, arrangements can be made with banks to transfer funds on certain dates. Hell, every credit card company in the world will be happy to zap money out of your checking account on a specified date."

"It's possible," conceded Deaver. "I just wanted to give you a heads-up."

Adam thanked him, hung up and sat in the car, thinking. He'd been stunned that his uncle had made him joint tenant of several properties. Then Calvin Hunter had saddled those properties with debt. He must have known Adam didn't have the capital to repay those loans. Before he died, Calvin had set up a payment schedule.

"What's up?" Adam asked Tyler when he walked into the command post adjacent to HiTech's offices.

Tyler was sitting beside Butch at the post's computer terminal. Red lights on the screen indicated the stations where guards were still working. Most closed at midnight while a few remained open until one-thirty.

Tyler stood up. "Let's go into my office."

Adam's sixth sense had kicked into gear the moment he'd heard Tyler's voice on the phone. He wasn't the least bit surprised to see Quinten Foley sitting in Tyler's office when they walked into the room.

"I trust I didn't take you away from anything too important," Quinten said in a general's imperious tone.

"Not unless you count my girl." It was obvious that Tyler's

father didn't give a damn about Whitney. He would have walked straight out the door except for all the hard work Tyler had done while Adam had been overseas.

"I needed to talk to you tonight."

Tyler shrugged and smiled apologetically at Adam. He couldn't be angry with his friend. What would it have been like to grow up with Quinten Foley? Adam had been lucky. His dad had always been there for him. It had been over three years since his death but Adam still missed him.

Adam pulled up a chair. "You couldn't discuss this on the phone?"

"You know how my father is," Tyler told him with a touch of sarcasm. "Phones can be tapped. Anyone with the right equipment can listen in on cell calls."

"Okay, I'm here. Shoot."

Quinten Foley frowned at his son. "I need to have a private conversation with Adam."

"Fine with me. My girl's waiting for me, too." He left, shutting the door behind them.

"I had a few thoughts about the disc I'm missing."

Adam was too pissed to ask a question. How could a man treat his own son like a scumbag? Why did Tyler take it?

"Calvin may have transferred it to another format," Foley said. "That's why we couldn't find the disc."

"Such as?"

"Another type of disc, or it may even be disguised as a book. It might even be in some unusual place like the freezer."

"There was nothing in the freezer except Rocky Road ice cream. I ate it."

"It's possible it's disguised as a music CD in his car."

Under his breath, Adam cursed himself. He'd neglected to inspect the CDs in his uncle's car. When Quinten had first come looking for the disc, Adam had told him some of his uncle's financial records were missing. He didn't say he believed it was a single line of information containing a bank code. For all Foley knew, Adam was after reams of paper. He didn't trust Foley enough to tell him the truth. He hadn't confided in anyone—not even Whitney.

"Did you search the discs in the sound system around the pool?"

Aw, hell. Screwed up again. He hadn't played the music outside and didn't even know where the CD player that serviced the barbecue and pool area was located.

"I'm positive the info is somewhere in the house or car. Those are the only places it could be."

Adam thought a second. "What about the plane he leased or the villa on Siros?"

"We've checked. It's not at either location." A cold smile played across his lips. "We'd like to thoroughly search your uncle's home."

Adam's thoughts whirled inside his head like the Milky Way. Who searched the plane and villa? "It's my home, too. Check the records. We owned it jointly."

"I have. That's why I'm asking your permission to allow experts to thoroughly go over the home first thing in the morning."

"Why the rush?"

"There's info on the disc that I need now," Foley replied, but there was something about the way he said it that made Adam suspicious.

He opened his mouth to tell Foley to go to hell. On the way over here, he'd decided to take Whitney to Cancún. There was a good chance they'd find Miranda there. If not, a little vacation couldn't hurt them. He decided not to shoot himself in the foot. He'd had absolutely no luck locating the bank code he needed. Why not let the pros give it a try?

"Okay," Adam replied slowly, as if he were reluctant to go along with this. "I'll need to be present."

"I don't think that's such a good idea. I—"

"Then I won't grant access."

"All right, all right. First thing in the morning. It won't take my boys more than an hour or two—tops."

FROM A ROOM DOWN THE HALL, Tyler listened to every word. He'd been testing a new gadget. It was a pricey Mont Blanc pen fitted with a microphone the size of a pinhead. It transmitted everything said within a ten-foot radius to a receiver concealed in a deck of playing cards. The receiver was so powerful that it could be located anywhere within a half mile of the pen.

What was on the disc that was so important to his father? Why did Adam insist on being present? Maybe Adam wanted to make certain his father's men didn't remove anything. That didn't make sense. The pros his father would use wouldn't be common thieves. He was missing something here.

Then the pieces of the jigsaw puzzle in his brain suddenly fell into place. His father must have been in business with Calvin Hunter. He thought a moment. It could only have been weapons. His father was supposed to be a consultant, but that must have been a cover story.

Tyler couldn't help wondering if money might be hidden somewhere in Calvin Hunter's home. That would account for Adam's interest. The disc provided an excuse to search. After all, his father worked with private militias as well as foreign governments on weapons deals. So had Calvin Hunter. They could have been paid "off the books" in gold or even diamonds.

He toyed with the idea of going in and looking himself. After all, he had been a detective. Nah, he decided. If Adam had searched the home, the disc—or whatever—wasn't easy to find.

He heard the men standing and shut off the receiver by pressing a microdot on the phony pack of cards. He sprinted out the side door and raced to his car. He was out of the lot before the men emerged from the building.

This crap with his father had made Tyler think about money. A lot of money. His father could live another twenty or even thirty years.

Granted, Tyler was making decent money, but Holly deserved the best. He smiled to himself, thinking about Adam's comment. He *did* have a woman he was interested in. Holly needed to know as soon as possible.

Tyler tried her cell number again but it immediately kicked into voice mail. He'd lied when he'd said Holly was waiting for him. They'd had an early dinner, then she'd claimed female problems were bothering her. She'd gone home. Tyler had picked up a bouquet of flowers and a box of chocolates. He'd taken them to her walkup flat in Coronado but she wasn't there.

Where the fuck could she be? Why would she lie? She couldn't possibly have another guy. No way. She spent too many nights with him.

He needed to present her with a whopper of a diamond. Once they set a date to be married, he would feel better. Not even his frustration with his father could bring him down then.

CHAPTER THIRTY

"HEY, CUTIE." The dachshund scurried up to Whitney, tail wagging. "Grey, right?" She dropped to her knees and held out her arms. The little dog leaped up and licked her chin.

She stood, Grey in her arms, and flipped on a few lights. "Let's see if you had an accident that I need to clean up."

"Good boy," she told the dog after she'd inspected the small, neat condo. "No accidents. Let's take you for a walk."

The dachshund lived in an upscale condominium complex not far from Scripps. If Whitney recalled correctly, Betty Spirin worked at the Scripps Institute of Oceanography. Whitney walked down a path illuminated only by low-voltage lights scattered among the plants bordering the walkway. Hadn't the moon been shining when they left the restaurant? She was positive it had, but in early summer a layer of marine clouds inched in at night, lingered, then became the morning fog that beachgoers called "June gloom."

The note she had on her BlackBerry said "back," which meant the best place to walk Grey was in the back of the complex. She headed in that direction, deciding there must be a common area behind the warren of condos. As soon as they were off the walkway Grey lifted his leg on a low-hanging bush.

"You really had to go, didn't you," she said, careful to keep her voice low. Very few lights were on in the complex at this late hour, and she didn't want to disturb the residents.

Grey finished and scratched the grass. Whitney led the dachshund toward the rear of the condominiums. The dog probably would do something more serious. She'd left her purse in the condo, so she double-checked the pockets in her shorts to make sure she had a plastic bag for a pickup.

Whitney slowed as she approached the rear of the complex. Security lights illuminated the building but five feet beyond was cloaked in deep shadows. She looked up again. Nothing but a black anvil of a sky.

Grey trotted forward. Obviously the dog had been here many times and knew his way. A sense of foreboding prickled at Whitney. Mercy, was she jumpy. She'd been nothing but raw nerves since the fire.

When she'd left the house, she'd checked for the car Adam had seen minutes earlier, but it had vanished. For some reason that bothered her when it shouldn't have. People came and went all the time. On the way over, she'd kept checking her rearview mirror. She'd spotted several cars but none of them appeared to be following her.

Near-death experiences caused anxiety, she decided. Adam had retreated into a shell after nearly being killed. He was just now emerging. It was no wonder she was upset. Someone wanted Miranda dead and that person was still out there.

"Grey, how are you, boy?" A tall man appeared out of the darkness.

Whitney nearly jumped, then managed to steady herself. It was only an elderly man walking his dog.

"Where's Betty?" he asked.

The neighbor had a Golden retriever that some people might have mistaken for Lexi. But this dog wasn't very well groomed. Tufts of fur grew out from between the toes of her paws. A definite no-no with Golden owners. The unwanted fur collected dirt that could be tracked into the house.

"Betty will be back soon," Whitney told him, even though

she had no clue when the woman planned to return. Miranda had cautioned her not to give out information. Pet owners didn't like anyone to know they were gone. Crime in the area wasn't a problem, but it paid to be careful.

"Good." He squinted at her. "You're not Miranda. For a moment, I thought you were."

"I'm her cousin, Whitney Marshall. I've taken over Miranda's clients."

"Really? I saw her just a week or so ago. We always talked. She didn't mention leaving."

You don't know the half of it, she wanted to scream. "It was sudden."

"Well, be careful back there." He pointed to the dark area that stretched behind them. "They're retiling the pool. Some workman accidentally severed the electric line. Can't see a dang-blamed thing."

"Thanks. I have my flashlight." Whitney pulled it from her pocket. "Good night."

He told her good-night and walked at a leisurely pace in the opposite direction, the Golden at his side. Whitney switched on her flashlight. It cast a narrow tunnel of light on the ground nearby. A row of parking places marked Guests was along the back of the building. She'd parked on the street but made note of it for future visits. She swung the flashlight around and spotted the fenced swimming pool and adjacent greenbelt.

Grey tugged on the leash. Obviously the animal had been here often enough to know where he wanted to go. The dachshund led Whitney down the asphalt drive toward the greenbelt.

Suddenly, high-beam headlights flared on, blinding her. The driver revved the engine and the car shot forward—an explosion of sound in the stillness—hurtling directly at her. Whitney had a split second to act. She lunged to the side, yanking the leash and hauling Grey with her.

Leaping from the pavement onto the soft surface threw her

off balance. She skidded on the wet grass, stumbled, lurched sideways, dropped the flashlight, then looked back. There wasn't enough light to make out more than a vague hulking shape. The car's tires squealed as the driver veered hard to the left. She heard herself scream as she realized he was changing course to aim directly at her.

If she didn't run like the wind, the car would mow her over in a heartbeat. Ahead and to her right was the flat greenbelt where she would be completely vulnerable. To her left was the large pool enclosed by a wrought-iron fence.

Blood pounding in her ears, Whitney realized she was as good as road kill. On the verge of utter panic, a galaxy of options swirled through her brain in a nanosecond. There was only one way to save herself. If she could make it to the pool fence before the car hit her—she had a prayer.

Just a prayer.

Dragging the dog, she charged forward, arms pumping, legs moving faster than pistons. Grey's piercing yelps of pain filled the night air. She tried to drop the leash, assuming the dachshund would be better off on his own, but Whitney had wound the leather strap around her palm and it was taut from pulling the dog.

All she could concentrate on was reaching the fence. *Had to get there. Had to. Had to. Had to.*

At her heels, she heard the ominous rumble of the car's engine. Even though she wasn't close enough to climb the fence, she launched herself at it, realizing this was her only chance. She smashed her knee against one of the fence's wrought-iron bars. Pain shot down her leg, and she screamed. Grabbing the vertical bars with both hands, she managed to vault several feet off the ground. She hung on, scrambling upward, using her tennis shoes for traction.

She grasped the top rail with both fists even though her arms were ripping out of their sockets. Poor little Grey was dangling from the leash, his weight tearing at Whitney's arm and wrenching one shoulder downward. The dog's terrified shrieks assured her that his neck hadn't snapped. Whitney was alive but in excruciating pain and she couldn't do a thing to help the little dog. Her heart lashed against her ribs like a caged beast.

Hang on. Hang on.

The car's lights shone from behind her and illuminated a drained pool with tiles stacked around the sides. Heart pummeling, she wondered how much longer she could hold on to the fence before her muscles gave out. She ventured a glance over her shoulder.

The glaring headlights blinded her, but she could tell the car wasn't moving. With each gasping breath, energy drained from her body. Already she'd lost the feeling in her fingers. She squeezed her eyes shut and willed herself to have the strength to hang on. She knew what would happen if she fell to the ground.

"What's going on?" shouted a male voice from a short distance.

"Help!" shrieked Whitney. "Help me!"

The car careened sideways and tore off across the greenbelt with a roar and a plume of exhaust. In the darkness its taillights appeared to be two evil eyes, reminding her of the malevolent eye in Vladimir's painting. The eyes glowed in the dark and vanished in less than a few seconds.

She released the bars and crashed backward.

ADAM SAW THE FLASH-FLASH-FLASH of the blue-white police car strobe lights as soon as he rounded the corner near the condominiums. He'd just walked in the door and read Whitney's note when the telephone rang. An older-sounding man told him there had been an accident, but Whitney wasn't seriously injured. The moment he learned this Adam had forgotten how furious he was with her for leaving the house.

He left his car at the first open spot he found, then stormed up to the cluster of people standing near two police cruisers and a paramedic van. Whitney was sitting on the curb, clutching a dachshund to her stomach as if holding herself together with the dog. An EMT was tending to a cut on her leg that didn't appear to be serious.

Adam elbowed aside a policeman he didn't recognize. "What happened?"

Whitney looked up at him, her expression blank, as if he were a total stranger. She finally opened her mouth to respond but no words came out. She averted her eyes. He dropped down onto the curb beside her and gently eased his arm around her shoulders.

"Are you all right?"

She slowly nodded and met his eyes. When he'd left Whitney, she'd been vibrant, happy—now she couldn't utter a coherent sentence.

An older man with a Golden retriever on a leash told Adam, "Someone was trying to scare her. They chased her with a car. A prank."

Adam's blood boiled. He wasn't buying this explanation. He asked the policeman, "What makes you think it was a prank?"

"We've had other incidents where cars have driven over our greenbelt," the older man responded before the cop could. "Ruins the grass. When the pool's finished, we're relandscaping and putting in big boulders to keep cars from driving on the grass."

"This is our second call to this location," confirmed the uniformed policeman, who was taking notes for a report.

"Did they chase anyone else?" he asked.

"No, but they might not have had the opportunity." The policeman flipped his notebook shut. "The other incident occurred just before dawn."

"That time rap music from their car's radio awakened one of the owners who lives close by," added the elderly man. "They called the police."

The EMT stood up. "I don't think you're going to need stitches," he told Whitney. "It's just a bad scrape. You'll probably have a doozy of a bruise, though."

"Th-thanks, th-thanks…so…" Whitney's voice quivered, then trailed off.

The EMT backed away and joined his partner. The policeman said to Adam, "She's badly shaken. You'd better get her home."

"Hot milk or tea might help," advised the man with the retriever. "Or bourbon."

"I wish I could say we're going to catch this jerk," the policeman told Whitney, "but I doubt it. Without a description of the car or…anything."

"I'm telling you, it was too dark for anyone to see a blasted thing." The old man pointed to the dark area behind them. "I've still got twenty-twenty and I couldn't tell you what kind of car it was. I heard screeching tires, then screaming. I came running. I'm not as fast as I used to be. All I saw was the outline of a car."

"He couldn't even tell us the color, except that it wasn't a light color," added the police officer. "Neither could she."

Adam bent close to Whitney. "Did you see anything? Was it big like an SUV or was it small?"

Her glassy eyes were wide, the pupils dilated. She hadn't been crying, but shock and a desperate need to control her emotions showed on her face. "I—It all happened so fast. M-my impression is mid-size. I don't think it was an SUV but I'm honestly not sure."

IT HAD SEEMED LIKE THE RIGHT idea at the time. The paramedics didn't think she needed to go to the emergency room. He'd been anxious to get her out of there, get her home. Now,

Whitney was sitting on the edge of his bed, and he wasn't so sure.

She'd insisted on bringing the dachshund with her, almost as if she was afraid to let the little dog go. She hadn't said a word on the short drive home. When he'd directed her upstairs, she obeyed in a robotlike way.

Shock.

Adam had seen it often enough in Iraq. He'd dealt with it himself after the suicide bomber killed his friends and almost took his life as well. There wasn't much he could do for her. Time and sleep helped. He'd learned that much from his own experience.

"Are you sure you're all right?" he asked. "Is something wrong with your shoulder? You seem to be favoring it."

She put down the dachshund and scooted between the sheets. Da Vinci and Jasper were already curled up on top of the bed and Grey joined them. Lexi was on the floor looking anxiously up at Whitney, mirroring what Adam was feeling.

Whitney leaned against the pillows he'd arranged for her while she'd been in the bathroom changing into his T-shirt. "I'm fine. My shoulder's a little sore because Grey was hanging from me."

"Do you feel up to telling me about it?" He didn't have any more information than what he'd learned at the scene.

She reached down to the end of the bed and stroked Grey. "You know what's amazing about dogs?" She didn't wait for him to respond. "They forgive you for anything."

Her answer seemed a little spacey and he wondered if she'd hit her head during the so-called prank.

"Even the most abused dog will lick his owner's hand—first chance the dog gets. You'd think they would bite or run away. They don't. Dogs are so forgiving." She petted Grey's head and the little dog nosed her with his snout. "I nearly killed this dog. He doesn't even know me, but the second we hit the ground, Grey licked my face to see if I was okay."

Hit the ground? Where had she been? Adam sat down on the bed beside her. He did his best to keep anger and fear out of his voice. "Tell me what happened."

He listened carefully as she described the car that appeared suddenly from out of nowhere. He envisioned it deliberately changing course and wheeling to the right and charging directly at her. Imagining her on the fence, the dachshund hanging from her arm, made him smile despite the situation.

"Good thinking," he told her. "Fast thinking. You might have been killed otherwise."

"If that's what was happening." She edged backward until she was propped up against the pillows again. "Mr. Fisher— he's the older man with the Golden—thought it was a prank. He may have been right."

"Why do you say that? It sounds intentional to me. If not, it was dangerous as hell."

"When I looked back, the car had stopped several feet behind me. It didn't ram the fence even though it could easily have crushed the back of my legs."

Adam had to admit that did seem a little odd. "Maybe he didn't want to damage his car."

"And maybe I overreacted. Even if it had been a prank, it was dangerous. I could have been accidentally killed. The driver needs to be found and stopped before someone gets hurt."

Adam wasn't sure what to think. His training as a detective warned him that two near misses on the same person's life wasn't just a random coincidence. "Maybe someone mistook you for Miranda," he said, thinking out loud.

"I doubt that. There's been enough publicity about the fire-bombing for anyone to realize Miranda isn't around."

"Criminals often seem clever, but most of them are stupid. I remember a case we had in Robbery—Homicide. There had been a series of bank robberies. The banks started booby-trapping money with vials of indelible ink that exploded when thieves removed the paper banding a stack of bills.

"We were pissed because the media found out about the trick and publicized it. Everyone and his mother knew about it. A few days later, another bank was robbed. We caught the guy because he was covered with ink. He hadn't seen the news reports."

"You think someone believes I'm Miranda?"

"It's the only thing that makes sense."

"It's possible, I guess. Mr. Fisher mistook me for Miranda at first."

Adam mulled over the facts for a few minutes but couldn't come up with a better explanation. Mistaken identity, or just a prank? "Listen, I'm going to hop in the shower. Why don't you get some sleep? We'll see what the police come up with tomorrow. They'll make plaster casts of the tire tracks in the lawn. That should tell us what type of car it was. With luck, that will help."

He leaned over and gently kissed her lips. He wanted to pull her into his arms and squeeze her tight—to reassure himself that she was all right. But she'd been through so much that he didn't want to risk hurting her.

She pulled the sheet up to her chin, and he turned out the light. He stood in the shower and let the water stream over his body. He felt helpless, the way he'd felt when he'd arrived at his uncle's villa in Siros. He hated not being in control, not being able to help Whitney.

As soon as Quinten Foley's men searched the house tomorrow, he was going to Cancún with Whitney. If Miranda wasn't working in a shop at Corona del Mar, he believed they would find her in Cancún. She had the answer to this—

"Holy shit!" he said out loud. He leaped out of the shower, wound the towel around his waist, left the bathroom and raced through the dark bedroom. He was down the hall and in his uncle's office before he saw Lexi had followed him.

"Go guard Whitney," he said, then realized Whitney was with the dog.

"What's the matter?" she asked, her eyes wide.

Adam grabbed the picture of his uncle fishing off the wall. "It just hit me. Something's written on my uncle's baseball cap." He flung open the middle drawer of the desk and found the magnifying glass.

"You think…?"

He examined the script on the cap. "I'll be damned. Corona del Mar." He gazed at her, thinking out loud. "How much do you want to bet Uncle Calvin took Miranda to Cancún last December?"

"But her passport—"

"Would have been examined by customs officials but not necessarily stamped. Airports for private planes operate differently."

"Do you think they were, you know, involved?"

He slapped his forehead with the palm of his hand. "Good thing I'm not on the force anymore. They'd bust me down to writing traffic tickets. I should have considered the romance angle before now."

'I didn't think of it, either. The age difference—"

"What? Twenty years—give or take. My uncle was a good-looking guy with a lot of money. It wouldn't be the first time a woman ignored a few years when a guy was rich."

CHAPTER THIRTY-ONE

RYAN SHAVED AND inspected his reflection in the mirror. Where in hell was Ashley? It had been almost dawn when he'd come home. He'd expected her to be asleep but it was evident that she hadn't even touched the bed. He'd lain awake—thinking, wondering.

He was willing to admit that he had been harder on Ashley than necessary. Poor baby couldn't help it if she had a heart of gold. She hadn't wanted Whitney to suffer. Ashley had no idea how much trouble Whitney was causing him.

"Wait!" he exclaimed to his reflection. "That's it."

Last night he had told Ashley they were on the verge of bankruptcy. Ashley must think she'd caused their troubles. She loved him so much that she might be trying to singlehandedly solve their problems. She might have gone to borrow money from someone she knew.

In the middle of the night?

Ryan splashed on the aftershave lotion Ashley had given him. "She's mad at me," he again said out loud. "She spent the night with a friend."

That made sense. He probably deserved it, but she had no idea what pressure he was under. Thanks to Whitney.

Ryan walked into his closet to get dressed. He halted and spun around. How long was Ashley planning to stay with her girlfriend? He went into her closet, but he couldn't tell what she'd taken. She had too damn many clothes.

Brooding, he wandered back into the bathroom and checked the vanity area where Ashley kept her cosmetics. "Oh, shit!" What did women do with all this crap? He couldn't tell if she'd removed a thing.

It didn't matter, he decided. He had to get dressed. A hell of a day was ahead of him. Tonight, Ashley would be here waiting for him. He wouldn't make it easy, but he would forgive her.

He loved Ashley so much that it hurt sometimes. It pained him not to be able to give her everything she wanted or be the successful doctor she believed him to be when they'd met. He needed her love in a way that he'd never needed anything else.

ADAM LOOKED OUT THE AIRPLANE window at the aquamarine water. It was so clear he could see the reefs below the surface. The ocean off California and the west coast of Mexico was deep blue. Here on Mexico's eastern shore the sea was the blue-green of the nearby Caribbean. Judging from the beaches below, Cancún enjoyed the same white sugar sand, too.

He glanced to his right and saw Whitney was still asleep. No wonder. They'd talked until almost dawn, then she'd been forced to get up and walk her clients' dogs, arrange care for her own dogs and buy some things for this trip. He'd arranged to have a security guard from HiTech go with her—just in case.

The timing couldn't have been better. While she was out, Quinten Foley's team had thoroughly searched the house.

Nothing.

They'd gone through every book, checked every CD and DVD, examined each photograph for hidden text, knocked on paneling to see if there was a secret hiding place and they'd used some special machine to inspect the stonework for loose places where the disc might have been hidden.

Nothing.

If Calvin Hunter had hidden the disc at the house, the

experts hadn't had any better luck than Adam. When they'd finished with the building—interior and exterior—they'd gone over Uncle Calvin's Lexus sedan.

Nothing.

While all this had been going on, another team had searched the charred, water-soaked contents of the garage where Miranda had stored her things.

Nothing.

Adam would have bet that they were coming up empty because the disc wasn't here. He was positive Miranda had it. Now that he thought about the situation, it made perfect sense. She'd faked the robbery and made off with the computer and the disc or discs.

The information on the disc was worth a lot of money. Not for the first time, he wondered if Miranda had killed his uncle. If they'd been involved, his uncle might have confided in her. She would have had access to the house, his car, his computer.

Beside him, Whitney stretched and yawned. "Are we almost there?"

"Yes. You can see the beaches below." He moved back so she could look out the window.

"Wow! Such white sand. It's nothing like Acapulco or Puerto Vallarta. Their beaches just have regular sand like California."

He nodded his agreement, thinking how special Whitney was. He needed to clear up this mess before something happened to her. He'd tried to piece the puzzle together but hadn't been able to make things fit. Miranda was the key.

Last night, after they'd discovered his uncle had also been to Corona del Mar, Adam went round and round in his head trying to decide how much to tell Whitney. He would have told her everything except she was still shell-shocked by the incident with the car.

In the end, he'd elected not to complicate matters by explaining his uncle's involvement with Quinten Foley in some clandestine government deal. What did he know for certain anyway? Not a damn thing, really.

He thought back to the last time he'd seen Calvin Hunter. His uncle had been worried, certain someone was going to kill him. He'd refused to reveal any details, but Adam felt his death had to be linked to the missing disc.

What other explanation could there be?

The plane had been slowly descending for some time. Now it dipped lower on final approach. The endless blue of the sea stretched out to the horizon.

"What's our first move?" Whitney asked.

He wanted to lure her to some cabana where sea breezes would cool their naked bodies while they made love. *Business first,* he reminded himself. There would be plenty of time for them later.

"Have a margarita and take a swim."

"Seriously," she replied with a laugh.

"Check into our hotel. Change clothes, then drive out to Corona del Mar for a drink. The cocktail hour should bring out residents who may have met your cousin."

"You think Miranda is out there?"

They'd discussed this last night, but Whitney had been a little groggy. "Hard to say. If she's not there, someone may recognize her picture. Cancún isn't that big. The thing to do is check Corona del Mar. Then we'll show the photos you had made around at *supermercados* and other places people who stay here long-term would shop. If she's living here, she's shopping somewhere. She can't be eating out all the time."

IT WAS NEARLY TEN WHEN Ryan checked the clock mounted on the wall beside the pool. The device gave the temperature and the time. He didn't need to check the temperature. He could tell it was still in the mid-seventies even though it was dark and the temperature had dropped the way it usually did on summer evenings.

Where in hell was Ashley?

He'd been ready to forgive her, but now he was pissed big-time. He'd come home to an empty house and a refrigerator with nothing but low-fat yogurt and cottage cheese in it. He'd gone for a swim to keep his body toned, expecting Ashley any minute. He'd been home for three freaking hours when he tried her cell. It immediately kicked into voice mail.

Ashley was in for it now. *Suggest a trial separation,* he told himself. That would upset her no end. Wouldn't it?

Ryan admitted to himself that he was no longer as sure of things as he once had been. His world had been on track. True, he'd had to make a midcourse correction and switch from general surgery to cosmetic surgery, but even then, things had gone his way.

The trouble had started with Whitney.

"Jesus H. Christ!" He cursed out loud and jumped to his feet. Would Ashley have gone to see his ex-wife? It was possible. After all, Ashley had given Whitney the dress that started this crappy argument.

He slung the towel over his bare shoulder and stomped inside. Ashley didn't have an office. What the fuck would she need one for? She used the nook area in the kitchen to keep a few things, like her checkbook and calendar.

He threw on the lights and searched the nook. Not much. Travel brochures for Hawaii. Nordstrom catalogs. An accordion folder with returned checks filed by date.

He rummaged through the stuff, searching for her telephone book. She kept phone numbers in a small leather booklet. It must be in her purse, Ryan decided. He didn't want to lower himself by calling the friend who'd helped her snatch Lexi, but if Ashley didn't show in another hour, he would.

The only friend Ashley had ever mentioned was her personal trainer. They'd been close when Ryan first met Ashley. He'd never met the woman because she lived across town and worked most of the time at a gym. Come to think of it, he didn't even know the woman's name.

What gym? He could call there and see if Ashley was around. Shit! She hadn't told him the name of the gym. Well, maybe she had and he'd forgotten it. He remembered Ashley saying she paid her friend in cash. The woman couldn't afford to pay taxes. Unfuckingbelievable! Who could? He'd been forced to instruct his accountant to file late this year.

He searched through her returned checks, for lack of anything better to do. Manicures. Pedicures. Boutiques. Nothing extravagant, but still—it was money they hadn't had. Ashley hadn't known this, he reminded himself.

Dr. Jox. The check stopped him. The memo line indicated Ashley had purchased vitamins. That must be the name of the gym where Ashley's personal trainer worked. He got the number from Information and called. He would have put it off, but most gyms closed at ten. He needed the number tonight.

"I'm a friend of Ashley Fordham's," he told the young-sounding guy who answered the telephone. "She recommended a trainer there. I was wondering if I could get her number."

Ryan didn't want word to go around the gym that he was looking for Ashley. He wasn't sure why he gave a shit. Personal pride, he guessed. Not just every guy married a beauty queen. No sense in seeming jealous when he wasn't.

"*Her* number?" the kid parroted back.

"Yes. Ashley really likes this trainer's workouts." Ryan heard a muffled sound as if the kid had put his hand over the mouthpiece.

"Just a minute," the kid told him. "I'll let you talk to my manager."

Ryan waited, getting more irritated by the second. What was the big deal? He would have driven over there but Dr. Jox was halfway across town.

"This is Al Schneider. What can I do for ya?"

Ryan repeated his spiel. Silence. "The trainer is still working there, isn't she?"

"You're Mr. Fordham, right?"

Ryan started to deny it, then realized the guy must have his name on the caller ID screen. "Yes. Ashley recom—"

"That trainer isn't accepting new clients."

The manager hung up before Ryan could ask another question. What the fuck? He almost hit Redial, then stopped himself. Something was going on.

Why wouldn't a trainer who needed money badly enough to risk trouble with the IRS not want new clients? He thought about it for a moment. He paid all their bills. He remembered commenting to Ashley about the number of calls made from their home phone. Not that it cost much; they had a wide-range dialing plan. But he knew he didn't make many calls.

Back in his office, Ryan pawed through the growing cluster of bills on his desk until he found last month's telephone bill. This would be the third month in a row that he'd neglected to pay it. He checked the local calls. Several were to the office he still had until the new group was up and running. Others he vaguely recognized. His service. Walter Nance.

One number came up several times. He thought he recognized it from previous bills but couldn't be sure. He'd trashed them or he would be able to check.

Ryan plopped down into his chair and booted up his computer. It was cool inside and he rearranged the damp towel over his shoulders to keep warm. It took several minutes to locate an Internet reverse directory for San Diego and look up the number. It was registered to a Preston Block with an address across town.

Block could be the trainer's father or a roommate. He studied the screen and memorized the address. He needed to speak to Ashley in person.

It took a little more than half an hour to drive to the address listed for Preston Block. It was a bunker-style two-story apartment building that wrapped around a pool with cloudy water. The place had been new in the seventies. From what Ryan could tell in the dark, that was the last time it had been painted. Exactly where he would expect a trainer subsisting hand to mouth to live.

He found the directory with Block/Swanson listed for apartment 2B. He stood there a moment to formulate the speech he'd mentally rehearsed on the way over. He didn't want to admit how much he missed Ashley. He planned to say her father had called.

Was that even possible? Now he wished he'd asked more questions. He knew Ashley had suffered through her mother's tragic death alone. Her father lived in some crummy town in the central part of the state, but he hadn't come to the funeral. Had she told her father about their marriage? He didn't remember Ashley mentioning it.

Unable to think of a better excuse, he climbed the stairs. A potted palm missing most of its fronds stood outside 2B's door. He mustered an assertive knock.

A television was playing inside, but a moment later the door swung open. A surfer built like a brick shithouse stared out at him.

"I'm looking for Ashley Fordham's trainer."

"Preston's out. He works nights now."

He? *He?* Ashley's personal trainer was a woman. Wasn't that what she had told him? Ryan blinked and tried to recall exactly what Ashley had said. The first time she'd mentioned the trainer had been when they were in bed and he'd been admiring how perfect every inch of her body was.

I work with a trainer five days a week.

The guy's smile evaporated. "Who are you?"

"Dr. Fordham. Ashley's husband." He couldn't keep from adding, "I'm looking for her."

"She's not here."

Ryan turned and trudged away without another word. Of all the scenarios he'd envisioned, he'd never imagined Ashley—his Ashley—being involved with another man. The knowledge made him dizzy, weak.

He ambled along, his mind unable to process any thought except: Ashley had betrayed him. He'd loved her so much—too much.

He'd given her everything she wanted, hadn't he?

No, he silently corrected himself. There were things Ashley had wanted, like the house in the Coronado Keys. He'd been too strapped for money to purchase it. Ashley had spent her life on the road. She deserved a home of her own. If Whitney hadn't been such a bitch, this never would have happened.

CHAPTER THIRTY-TWO

"IT'S BEAUTIFUL," Whitney said. "Even more spectacular than I expected."

"Why not? The homes around here start at a cool mil."

They were sitting in the Frio-Frio—cool, cool—bar at Corona del Mar. They'd checked into their hotel in Cancún, changed clothes and had driven out here in their rented Mazda.

It was so humid, the short skirt on Whitney's sundress was plastered to her legs by the time she walked from the air-conditioned hotel to the car. Mexico's beaches were popular tourist destinations in the winter, but by this time of year, the temperature skyrocketed and visitors tapered off. Their hotel was only half-full, as was the bar at this expensive development.

"This seems too...too sophisticated for Miranda," she told Adam.

"That doesn't mean she isn't working here. Tips must be great. Better than in Cancún. If she visited here last December, she could have lined up a job."

"Possibly. Should I ask our waitress?"

A woman wearing a wraparound skirt in the coral and azure tropical pattern of the resort was heading their way with double margaritas. Whitney had brought photographs of Miranda that she'd doctored on the computer at Speedy Press yesterday morning. It was the shot taken of Miranda on the beach last December. One picture showed her as a blonde while Whitney had altered the other to make her cousin have black hair.

"Give it a try. Use the blond photo first."

The waitress put down their drinks with a smile, and Whitney said, "I think my sister visited here." She showed the woman the photograph. "Does she look familiar?"

"Fam-lar?"

Whitney realized the waitress spoke some English but not enough to understand the question. "Do…you…know…her?" she said with deliberate slowness.

The waitress squinted at the photograph, then shook her head. Whitney was ready and whipped out the second photograph. "See…her?"

The woman's dark eyes studied the second photograph. *"No se."*

The waitress left the table, and Adam said, "Miranda might not come in here. We can't expect to find her at the first place we try."

"True." She hated to think this was a wild-goose chase, but it was a definite possibility. After the terrifying incident last night, it had seemed imperative that they find Miranda as soon as possible.

Whitney was still a little disturbed from the shock of the incident, and numbness had replaced the lingering questions. She couldn't decide if someone had mistaken her for Miranda—which meant they'd followed her from home—or if it had merely been a dangerous prank. She refused to dwell on it. If she did, a wave of fear broke over her.

They sipped the slushy margaritas and gazed out at the sea. The sun had slipped into the ocean, leaving shimmering streamers of crimson and gold on the water. It was a very romantic setting, she decided.

If the stress of the situation hadn't been so intense, she could have appreciated it. She really needed things to calm down so she could evaluate her true feelings for Adam. There was no denying he was a great guy. Last night and after the fire, he'd been the one to comfort her.

Despite cautioning herself to take this slow so she'd have the time and space to truly get over Ryan and his betrayal, events hadn't permitted Whitney that luxury. She'd been pressed into an intimate relationship. There was the obvious attraction factor, but if what seemed to be developing between herself and Adam was merely chemistry, she might have dealt with it more easily. What she was feeling went deeper, meant more.

Over Adam's shoulder she noticed their waitress was talking to the bartender. They kept looking in Whitney's direction. The young bartender came out from behind the bamboo bar and headed toward their table.

Whitney kept her voice low. "Looks like our waitress told the bartender we're searching for someone."

"Buenas noches," said the dark-haired man as he came up to their table.

They told him good-evening in Spanish, then complimented him on the excellent margaritas.

"Cuervo Gold," he replied, and Whitney decided he meant the expensive tequila gave the margaritas their smooth yet distinctive flavor.

"Looking for someone?" the man asked.

"Mi hermana," Whitney told him. *My sister.* It was a fib but it sounded better if Miranda was her sister.

The bartender pulled out a chair and sat down. Whitney tried to catch Adam's eye, but he was studying the younger man.

"You don't have to practice your tourist Spanish on me," he told them. "I'm Cuban. From Miami. My English is perfect. I just work here during the season. It's back to the States next week."

Whitney smiled and wondered how much to tell this guy. After the incident with the car and the fire, she wasn't in a very trusting mood these days. On the fly, she came up with a story.

"My mother is very ill." She leaned closer to the bartender as if divulging a secret. "Cancer. She and my sister haven't…"

Adam got the drift. "They haven't spoken in almost three years. We think she's down here but we don't know where."

"We'd like to find her and bring her home before it's too late." Whitney managed to add a touch of tears to her voice. She handed him the photo of the blond Miranda.

The bartender shrugged. "She looks like a lot of blondes whose parents have places here." He gazed at Whitney for a moment. "I can see you're sisters."

Whitney tried for a smile and pulled out the second photograph with dark hair. "She may have dyed her hair."

His eyes shifted from the photograph to Whitney. "I don't recognize her, but not everyone comes into the bar." He stood up. "Sorry I couldn't help."

They thanked him and the bartender hustled back to his station to serve a couple who'd just arrived. Whitney took another sip of her drink.

"What's our next move?"

"Tonight, I think we should check the shops nearby on the off chance someone will recognize her. Then let's get dinner and hit the sack early. Tomorrow we should come out here and speak to the sales office. They'll have records of people who visited the resort to consider a purchase, and they may recognize Miranda."

They chatted about Lyleen Foster, the pet concierge Whitney had asked to take care of her clients while she came here. Daniel had highly recommended the woman, but Whitney didn't like giving her charges to someone she'd just met. She supposed they would be fine for a few days, but Lexi had taken off once already.

"I hope Lexi doesn't try to run away again," she told Adam.

"I'm sure she won't."

"I wish I felt as positive as you sound."

"Look, I should—"

The bartender walked up and interrupted Adam. "You know, I've been thinking. This might be nothing, but..."

"But what?" Adam asked.

"Let me see the picture again. The one of the chick with black hair."

Whitney produced the photograph and told herself not to get her hopes up.

The bartender squinted at the picture, then said, "She looks a little like Courtney Hampton but it's hard to tell. Courtney's hair is red and really short."

Yes! Whitney silently screamed. Miranda's hair was a sandy blond. It would be easier to conceal her roots if she kept it in one of the short, sassy cuts that were so popular.

"Courtney lives at the far end of the road. She and her husband came here last Christmas to look over the place. They purchased a villa not too long ago."

Disappointment knotted inside her. It couldn't be Miranda. She wouldn't be with a husband.

"Her husband died. A sudden heart attack." The bartender shook his head. "Not surprising. The dude was a lot older than Courtney."

WHITNEY STOOD BESIDE ADAM at the door of the villa owned by the widow Courtney Hampton. It was located at the end of a cul-de-sac on a secluded cove. Apparently, the other owners had left for the season. The only lights in the area were on at this house.

Adam rang the bell and whispered in her ear, "Remember what I told you. Say as little as possible at first. Suspects often reveal much more if you just let them talk."

It was a full minute before they heard anything. Muffled footsteps came through the arched wood door.

"Who is it?"

Whitney instantly recognized Miranda's voice. She nodded enthusiastically at Adam, and he smiled.

"Miranda, it's me, Whitney."

Dead silence. For a moment, Whitney thought her cousin wasn't going to open the door. Then it swung open. The woman before them had copper hair in a spiked pixie cut, but there was no mistaking Miranda Marshall.

"Whitney, I—I a-a-ah…"

Whitney barged in, followed by Adam. Miranda's expression darkened with an unreadable emotion. A thousand questions pummeled Whitney's brain but she waited to see what her cousin would say.

"W-what are you doing here?" Miranda asked.

Instead of responding, Whitney looked around. The interior was furnished in Key West mode with comfy-looking woven wicker chairs and a chaise lounge-style sofa in the living area just beyond the entry. There were no paintings or anything on the walls or accessories on the end tables. The only homey touch was a hint of cinnamon in the air that must have come from the candles flickering on the coffee table.

Whitney turned back to Miranda and glared at her. And waited.

"Why are you here?" Miranda repeated. "It isn't even two weeks yet."

Whitney realized Miranda was referring to her two-week "honeymoon." Evidently, her cousin didn't think anyone would miss her for at least two weeks. "Some honeymoon."

Miranda reacted to the unbridled sarcasm in Whitney's voice by wincing just slightly. "I know you must be upset, but I can explain."

"Don't let me stop you."

"Maybe we'd better sit down," suggested Adam.

"Who are you?" asked Miranda.

"Adam Hunter."

The air emptied from Miranda's lungs in a rush. "Calvin's nephew. Of course."

She led them into a great room that faced the cove. The sun had set but there was still enough light to appreciate the fabulous view. Knowing Miranda was out here by herself, though, made it seem lonely and isolated. Whitney told herself not to feel sorry for her cousin until she knew more. Thanks to Miranda, she'd lost every possession she had—and was lucky to be alive.

Miranda took a chair while Adam and Whitney sat side by side on the sofa. Whitney let the silence lengthen.

Finally, Miranda spoke. "I didn't want to lie to you, but…I needed to protect you."

From what? Whitney wanted to scream, but Adam squeezed her hand to remind her to let Miranda talk.

"You see, I never expected you to appear on my doorstep, needing a place to stay. My plans were already in motion. I had to get out of town." She waved her hand, gesturing to her surroundings. "We'd planned to come here. Everything was all set. I was just taking care of the final details when you surfaced out of nowhere."

An uneasy hush followed her breathless explanation. Through the open doors that led outside, Whitney heard the soft purling of the surf on the sand.

"We?" prompted Adam.

Miranda studied Adam for a moment before saying, "Your uncle and I had been together for over two years. We planned to move here after—" she hesitated "—Cal stopped judging dog shows."

Whitney waited, expecting Miranda to say more, but the only sound in the room was the waves on the shore, bringing a trace of salt into the cinnamon-scented room. Out of the corner of her eye, Whitney glanced at Adam and saw he was studying Miranda.

Finally, Whitney couldn't stand the tension any longer. "Why would someone want you dead so badly that they would firebomb your house and nearly kill me?"

The thick lashes shadowing Miranda's cheeks flew up. "What? Someone…"

"You heard me. Someone firebombed the cottage. By the grace of God, I wasn't home at the time."

Miranda stared at Whitney, her face stricken with horror. "What? I can't imagine—" She jumped to her feet and rushed to the open doors that led out to the patio. Miranda faced the sea for a moment, then slowly returned to her chair. "I—I'm sorry—so sorry. I never thought it would come to this." She frowned. "So soon. I didn't expect anything to happen so soon."

"Why don't you explain it to us?" Adam asked, his voice sympathetic.

He must be playing the good cop, Whitney decided. He almost seemed like a stranger with no stake in these events. She was ready to scream at her cousin for not warning her about impending trouble.

"I-it's a long story. I don't know where to begin."

"We have all night." Adam glanced at Whitney. "Whitney nearly died. She's lost everything she has—"

"Was Lexi killed?"

Whitney shook her head. "No. The dogs were with me, but the pipe bomb thrown into the cottage caused a fire. I lost everything but what I was wearing."

"Oh my God." Miranda closed her eyes for a moment, then directed her response to Adam. "I'd been living in the cottage awhile before I really got to know your uncle. He was away judging dog shows overseas most of the time. Then we started seeing more and more of each other. We fell in love."

Whitney tried to imagine Miranda in love. Her cousin always had guys trailing after her, but she'd seemed older and more sophisticated than they were. Miranda had never been serious about any of them. Whitney could understand why an older, more worldly man would appeal to her cousin.

"Cal didn't want me to work so hard. He began giving me money."

"We know you were stripping at Saffron Blue," Adam told her.

Miranda's eyes flew in Whitney's direction. A hint of crimson seemed to flower beneath her tan. "I did some stripping," she replied apologetically.

"My uncle didn't like that. Did he?"

A flicker of a smile brightened Miranda's face. "No. Cal was old-fashioned in many ways. He insisted I quit."

"He gave you three thousand dollars in cash at the beginning of every month, right?"

How did Adam know this? Whitney wondered, an uneasy feeling creeping through her.

Miranda nodded. "Yes. It wasn't as much as I was making at Saffron Blue, but I didn't need more."

"What did you do with the insurance money you received from your parents' death?" Whitney asked.

"I invested most of it in the stock market. Tech stocks were hot back then and I thought I would make a killing. At first, I did—on paper. Then I lost every penny. Luckily I'd kept some to live on, so I was able to help your mother when she needed it. That was the last of my money."

A twinge of guilt passed through Whitney. She hadn't known Miranda at all. She'd never considered her cousin to be the type who would risk money in the market, but she was wrong. It touched her that Miranda had used what little she'd had left to help Whitney's mother.

"Last year Cal brought me down here," continued Miranda. "I thought it was just a trip so he could fish." She gazed wistfully out toward the ocean for a moment. "He adored fishing. He could spend hours bobbing up and down in a fishing boat waiting for a bite. I never saw the attraction. But what did it matter? I hung out on the beach, worked on my tan and read a book until sunset when the fishing boats came in."

"Your passport doesn't show any record of a visit here," Adam said.

"Cal leased a jet. We took off from a private airport and landed on a private strip constructed especially for this development. I had my passport with me, but no one bothered to stamp it."

Adam replied, "Private airfields are notoriously lax."

"Turns out Cal wasn't just interested in the fishing at Corona del Mar. He wanted to buy a place. He picked out this villa because of the view. He loved looking out at the ocean. You can see it from here, the kitchen and the master bedroom." She drew in a slow, deliberate breath and tears welled up in her eyes. "Too bad he didn't live to enjoy it."

Adam stared at Miranda, his gaze intense. "How did my uncle die?"

"Early in the evening, Cal complained of chest pain. He'd never had heartburn, but he claimed that's what it was." Miranda flung out her hands in simple despair. "If only I'd taken him to the hospital, but I believed him. Later, we were in the office, checking the computer for the Cancún weather report, and he gasped." She cast a pleading look at Adam, a lone tear dribbling down her cheek. "A loud gasp like nothing I've ever heard. It seemed as if Cal wanted to scream but couldn't, then he slumped over in his chair. I tried to get a pulse. Nothing. I immediately dialed 911."

"Why did you leave?" asked Adam. "No one was around when the paramedics arrived."

"Cal always insisted we be very careful. He didn't want anyone to know we were involved." Her eyes darkened with fear. "In the days before he died, Cal said his life was in danger. I was afraid I might be killed."

"Why didn't you tell me?" Whitney cried.

CHAPTER THIRTY-THREE

WHITNEY WAITED FOR Miranda to respond. "Why didn't you tell me?" she repeated.

Her cousin brushed the moisture off her cheeks with the back of her hand. "Whitney, I swear, I never thought you were in the least bit of danger."

"Why not? We look enough alike to be mistaken for each other."

Miranda huddled in her chair. "Our eyes maybe, but I don't think anyone would..." She turned to Adam. "Do you think we look alike?"

"Not to me. But then, I'm sitting very close to you. At a distance, you're both slim blondes with green eyes—"

"I'm two inches taller," interjected Miranda. "My face is longer."

"In the dark—all bets are off," said Adam. "Someone who didn't know you well could—"

"Why didn't you just warn me?" Frustration echoed in every syllable Whitney spoke.

"I didn't think it was necessary. They aren't due back until next week."

"Stop." Adam held up his hand. "Go back. Explain everything. Who are 'they'?"

Miranda was silent for a moment as if deciding just where to begin. "Cal and I fell in love. He said he wished he'd met me years ago. You see, Cal always wanted a son. Someone like you."

If this touched Adam, he didn't show it. His face remained attentive, yet strangely impassive. It reminded Whitney of the way he'd acted when they'd first met.

"Even though Cal was almost twenty years older, he wanted children. I can't tell you how excited he was when I told him I was pregnant."

"Ohmygod," cried Whitney. "You're pregnant."

Miranda lightly patted her tummy. "A little over three months along."

Whitney's eyes cut over to Adam. His detached expression hadn't changed. Was he made of stone? she wondered. The baby would be his cousin.

"If you're carrying his child, why didn't my uncle change his will?"

"He wanted you to inherit his real estate. The bulk of his money was in offshore accounts. He arranged it so all of his money would go to our child should anything happen to him."

"Something did happen to my uncle."

Unexpectedly there was a flare of biting sarcasm in Adam's voice. Miranda flinched as if he'd physically slapped her. What was Adam implying? That Miranda had something to do with his uncle's death? It was a simple heart attack, wasn't it?

"Your father…Cal's fa-father—" Miranda's voice faltered. "Both died at relatively young ages of heart problems. I tried to persuade him to eat better and exercise more but—"

"Did he take any medicine the night he died?"

"No. Why?"

Instead of answering, Adam asked, "Where did you eat?"

"We barbecued at home. Swordfish. It was the only fish he liked." Miranda forced a laugh. "He loved to fish but didn't like to eat it. Oh, he would prepare fish like a gourmet, but he just picked at what he'd cooked." Miranda hesitated a moment, looking out toward the cove where darkness had fallen. "I get it now. You think I killed him."

"Did you?" he shot back.

"Of course not! I loved him." Miranda gazed at Whitney. "I guess Cal reminded me of my father, but it was more than that. He was so smart, so well traveled. He was a man—nothing like those boys I used to date." She turned her attention to Adam again. "I didn't kill him. Who would want to go into hiding all alone?"

"Why *are* you hiding?" asked Whitney.

Miranda didn't respond. Whitney gazed at Adam. His stoic expression hadn't changed but she suddenly had the feeling he knew the answer. If not, he knew a lot more than he had told her. A slow burn began to creep through her.

"We came down here last December," replied Miranda. "I didn't know it at the time, but it was a test of sorts. Cal wanted to see if I liked it well enough to live here full-time.

"On New Year's Day, Cal told me he was going away—for good. You see, I'd gotten used to him disappearing overseas for weeks at a time for dog shows, but he explained this would be different. He wouldn't be returning for several years, and he wouldn't be able to contact me. In short, I might never see him again."

"Several years?"

"That's what I asked," Miranda replied in response to Whitney's question. "Cal said it might be two, three even five years before he returned. He wanted me to come with him, but he said I needed to think it over very carefully. Would I be comfortable not coming back for such an extended period? Would I be able to exist without contacting anyone?"

Adam asked, "Didn't his request seem strange?"

"Of course. I demanded to know why, but your uncle said he'd explain the details only if I decided to go with him."

"How could you agree? Your life, everything is in San Diego," Whitney insisted.

"Really? What life? Babysitting dogs? I went to junior

college, but I'm not like you. I hated it. I never found anything I really wanted to do...except be a mother."

Whitney understood. Miranda's family had been cruelly taken from her. She'd never gotten over it. Whitney decided she might have reacted the same way.

Miranda said to Whitney, "I knew you were back in town, but we never saw each other. I didn't have anyone or anything to keep me here. All I had was Cal. I truly loved him. I was willing to go anywhere with him."

Whitney couldn't help feeling ashamed of herself. She should have made more of an effort to see Miranda.

"I slept on it, but first thing the following morning, I told Cal I would come with him." She was silent for a moment, gazing out at the water as if recalling every detail of that conversation. "Cal explained a little bit about his business. He told me he'd been brokering arms and weapons."

"Using the dog shows as a front," interjected Adam.

Wow, thought Whitney. *What a scheme.* She'd been correct. Adam certainly did know a whole lot more than he had told her. Poor little Jasper had merely been a cover, a reason for traveling overseas.

"Exactly. I was shocked, of course. He'd always e-mailed me pictures of Jasper's shows. Other events he merely judged, but he always sent me messages, telling me about the places he'd stayed or eaten. Looking back, I guess I should have been suspicious because he never once asked me to come with him."

Whitney tried to imagine waiting at home for weeks on end. She couldn't, then she suddenly realized it wouldn't have been much different from her life during Ryan's two residencies. He'd been at the hospital six days a week. When he came home, he just wanted to eat, then sleep. He might as well have been on another planet.

"Cal's clients had been in Africa or South America for the most part, but he brokered the deals in Europe. He always made certain his travel was related to shows. You see, he made arrangements for arms transactions but didn't actually handle anything."

"Was it illegal?" Whitney asked.

"Depends upon what he was selling," responded Adam. "Most weapons the United States allows to be sold are highly restricted. Our government doesn't like encouraging rebels or supplying guerilla armies."

Miranda shrugged. "Cal claimed if he didn't broker the deals, someone else would. He told me the trouble began when he discovered that a shipment of armaments he'd sold to a group in the Sudan ended up in the Middle East."

"He should have seen it coming," Adam commented. "Bin Laden was in East Africa before relocating to Afghanistan."

"Maybe Cal did realize what was happening," Miranda said in a tone bordering on wistful. "Maybe he didn't want to tarnish the image I had of him. Anyway, I agreed to go with him."

"You accepted this without asking more?" Whitney couldn't help being astonished. A second later it occurred to her that she had often taken Ryan's word for things—without checking or asking questions. The revelation that Ryan had a severe gambling problem should have been something she'd sensed, but she hadn't. She'd been blissfully clueless.

"I wasn't sure I wanted to know more. Cal was leaving the business. We were going to be starting over." She hesitated for a beat. "He explained that the men he'd been dealing with would never allow him to just quit."

"Without giving them his contacts and access to his routing," Adam said.

The tension building inside Whitney kicked up another notch. She could tell none of this surprised Adam. He'd known all along, but never gave Whitney a hint. Why not? Miranda was her cousin. Didn't Whitney have a right to know?

"Exactly," Miranda said. "Cal didn't want Americans hurt

with weapons he'd arranged to be sold. Adam, when you were almost killed, Cal felt responsible. Alarming amounts of weapons were surfacing in terrorists' hands.

"Not only did he want out, Cal wanted to shut down the pipeline. He told me it would be just a matter of time before the terrorists made a dirty bomb or even a nuclear weapon. He didn't want anything to do with it."

It sounded very self-serving to Whitney, but she didn't voice her opinion. She knew only too well how women in love overlooked serious flaws in their men.

"Cal went about shifting his funds around so no one could find them, and he created new identities for both of us. I didn't actually take it seriously." She threw up her hands. "I mean, I did and I didn't. I believed everything Cal had told me, but I didn't realize how serious the threat was until one night about a week before Cal died."

Miranda stopped speaking, jumped up and rushed toward the kitchen. She returned a few seconds later with a tissue in her hand. She plopped down in her chair again, saying, "I'd bought this sinfully sexy red nightie. I put it on and hid in his office closet. I wanted him to be working hard—he always blacked out everything around him when he was on the computer—then I planned to jump out and we would have sex right there on his desk."

If the situation hadn't been so serious, Whitney would have giggled. She recalled the number of times she'd tried to entice Ryan with sexy lingerie. It had worked—temporarily—or so she'd thought.

"Cal came into the office with two men. I was stunned. He was supposed to be alone. They were talking business. I tried to be quiet, but I was hunched over, squeezed under a hanging shelf. A charley horse hit my calf. When I bent my leg a little to relieve the cramp, my foot hit something that made a scraping sound. Next thing I knew, this strange man threw open the door."

Whitney tried to imagine this but couldn't.

"I've never seen anyone look so positively evil. I thought they might shoot me on the spot. But Cal put his arm around me and explained we were about to be married—which was true. We were going to be married once we moved here. Cal told them I helped him with every deal. He insisted I had always been his silent partner."

Adam asked, "They bought it?"

"Yes. It took some convincing, but they finally accepted it. I was at his side when he arranged to give them what he called the support information."

"The routes he used. The ways he arranged for weapons to be shipped from the manufacturer to points overseas. People who helped," Adam said without hesitation. "Armaments must be carefully concealed, and you need a variety of routes. Too big a shipment is a risk because it attracts attention. If it's lost or confiscated, alternate routes become vital or the deal falls through."

"I guess." Miranda suddenly sounded tired and desperately unhappy. "It took some talking but Cal persuaded them to return in a month. He said 'we' would gather all the information and put it on a computer disc."

"That appealed to them because they could share it online with others in their group." Adam sounded so certain that Whitney became even angrier.

"That's right. They went for it because Cal demanded a million dollars for the disc."

CHAPTER THIRTY-FOUR

"A MILLION DOLLARS," Whitney blurted out. "Didn't they think that was outrageous?"

"No. Uncle Calvin was selling them connections and shipping routes that it would take years to build."

"That's right," agreed Miranda. "Later Cal told me the money angle saved us. These men think Americans do everything for money."

"Did my uncle make the disc?"

"Yes. I saw him working on it. He had info hidden in different places. He assembled it—"

"Why," Whitney asked, "if he wasn't going to give it to them?"

"He planned to take the disc to a friend he knew from his days in naval intelligence. Cal didn't trust many people but he trusted this man, who was now working at the Pentagon. He was going to take him the disc then disappear forever."

"Who was his contact?" asked Adam.

"I don't remember. Cal only mentioned his name once. It was an unusual name."

"Could it have been Quinten Foley?"

"Yes. That's it!"

Whitney was surprised Adam knew the man, but then Adam knew much more than he'd chosen to disclose to her. Like a corrosive acid, anger was eating away at her. Why hadn't he given her *some* indication about the extent of this situation?

Adam quietly asked, "Did he give you the disc?"

"No." Miranda shook her head. "When Cal died, I knew I had to carry out his last wishes. He wanted you to have his property. It was mortgaged because Cal said he needed to create confusion with his accounts. He moved funds all around so no one would think he had any money left. That way they wouldn't come looking for him."

"His money is nearby," Adam said, "in the Caymans. You withdrew twenty-five thousand dollars a few days ago."

Miranda's eyebrows rose in surprise. "Yes, I did."

"You also deposited money, or was that some kind of a wire-transfer payoff for one of Uncle Calvin's deals that he completed shortly before he died?"

"I closed out a smaller account and consolidated," she replied, her words measured. "I paid off the loans on the properties you owned jointly with Cal."

"Where is the disc?" asked Adam.

"Cal told me he hid it for safekeeping. I didn't even think about it until after he died."

"It must have been stolen on the day of the funeral," Adam said. "What I can't understand is why they would want to kill you with a pipe bomb if they had the disc?"

"Because I can identify them. They contacted Cal several months ago and threatened him. This time their leader came to 'persuade' him. That's why Cal wanted to make certain we were long gone when they returned to pick up the disc. He told me they would kill us both—even if he handed over the disc."

"My uncle warned me in Siros that someone would try to kill him. That must have been right after they contacted him the first time."

"What doesn't make sense is them wanting me dead before the pick-up date next week. You see, they can't possibly have the disc."

"Why not?" Adam asked. "Wasn't it with the computer they stole?"

Miranda tried for a laugh, then said, "No way. I stole Cal's laptop."

"You? Why?" Whitney and Adam asked almost in unison.

"I assumed the info was on his computer or on the software discs in his office. I didn't want those men to find it. I went to the funeral but didn't attend the reception at the officers' club. After all, no one knew about me...about us. I told the few people I met that I was Cal's renter. I came home, faked a break-in and swiped the computer."

"Smart move," Adam said, then glanced at Whitney. "Quick thinking runs in the family."

"It wasn't that smart. I've gone through all his files. It isn't there." Miranda sighed and sank lower in her chair. "If you don't believe me, you can check for yourself. The computer is in the guest bedroom."

RYAN'S CELL PHONE VIBRATED. He grabbed it, threw down a hundred-dollar chip on the craps table and walked away. Casinos had strict rules about cell phones. He usually shut his off completely but he didn't want to miss Ashley's call.

He flipped open his phone. He didn't recognize the number on the LCD screen. "Just a minute," he whispered.

Ryan shouldered his way through the double set of sweeping glass doors that led from the casino to a bar wrapped around a geyser of a fountain.

"Yes?" he said, louder now.

"Ryan Fordham?"

He didn't recognize the female voice. Shit! He'd walked away from the table with a hundred on the line to take what had to be a call from a bill collector.

"Who is this?" he demanded.

"Trish Bowrather."

The rich blonde who owned the swank gallery where Walter had taken him. That's where all the fucking trouble started. He could still see Whitney standing there in the sexy dress he'd bought for Ashley.

"Ravissant Gallery, right? Great show." He made an effort to flatter her. After all, Walter highly recommended the woman's taste in art. One day, he would again have enough money to indulge Ashley's desire to have a fabulous home filled with priceless art.

"That's right. I'm glad you enjoyed the show. We're looking for Whitney. We're wondering if you have any idea where she is."

"Who's we?"

"I'm with her attorney, Rod Babcock."

Babcock. Hadn't the guy married Miranda? Wasn't that what Whitney had told him? Now that he thought about it, he hadn't seen Miranda at the gallery. If that cocksucker was looking for Whitney, it was a very bad sign. "No," he made himself say calmly. "I'm remarried—"

"Yes, I know. I said this was a long shot." She covered the phone and all he could hear was muffled voices.

"How long's she been gone?" he asked, when the voices stopped, not liking the idea that had just cropped up in his mind.

It was bad enough that Whitney's attorney wanted to speak to her. It would be total disaster if Whitney and Ashley were together. Whitney would poison Ashley's mind and no telling what would happen.

"Do you know where Whitney is?" the woman shot back in a clipped tone that warned him to be careful.

"No, not really… Why?"

There was another long pause and more muffled voices he couldn't understand before Trish Bowrather replied, "I'm not sure how long Whitney's been gone or where she is. She had a total stranger walk my dog this morning."

Whitney must have gone somewhere last night. Ashley couldn't have left him to see Whitney, could she?

·· Ah, fuck, his life was unraveling like a cheap sweater.

Ryan snapped the cell phone shut without saying another word. Just as he slid it into his pocket, someone tapped him on the shoulder. He turned and found himself nose to nose with the shithead Dom used as a gofer.

"Dom's outside. He wants to see you."

"I've got a bet on the table." Ryan had been winning all night. When Lady Luck deserted his private life, the hussy rewarded him at the tables.

"Forgetaboutit."

The goon latched on to Ryan's arm and shoved him out the gate that led into the parking lot. Idling at the curb was Domenic Coriz's black limo. The cocky prick yanked open the rear door and shoved Ryan into the car.

It was dark inside except for the glow of the cigarette in Dom's hand. For a moment the burly Native American didn't say a word. When he spoke, his voice was low, guttural.

"Your wife called me."

The bottom dropped out of Ryan's stomach. How could Ashley know about Dom? She must realize he had a gambling problem. She had to be furious that he'd kept the truth from her. "Sorry, I—"

"We're through fucking around. Through. Understand?"

It was all Ryan could do to keep from wetting himself. "I understand."

IT WAS ALMOST MIDNIGHT WHEN Miranda and Whitney left Adam in the guest bedroom set up as a home office. He'd gone through the files on his uncle's computer and was checking the software discs. So far he hadn't located the information.

Miranda and Whitney decided to stretch their legs by walking on the beach instead of leaning over Adam's shoulder while he searched. The air was almost as warm as it had been during the day, but a light breeze drifted across the water. The ebony sky was strewn with brilliant stitches of stars. A bright crescent moon cast enough light for them to see. Like a glistening ribbon, the beach wound along a cove protected from the open water by a reef. Lazy waves pushed garlands of seaweed up on the sand.

"I'm sorry…" Whitney didn't know where to begin. "I've been a lousy relative. We're all that's left of our family. I never should have let Ryan—"

"He hated me from the minute he set eyes on me, didn't he?"

"*Hate* might be too strong a word." She didn't want to make excuses for her skank of an ex-husband, but she doubted Ryan expended the effort to "hate" Miranda. She wasn't important enough in his life.

"I think I know why Ryan hated me," said Miranda. "He's the type who needs to possess someone. He didn't want you to have friends or interests outside him. Basically, he's insecure."

Whitney started to deny this. Ryan was a handsome man that women fawned over. He was intelligent enough to win scholarships, be accepted to a top-flight medical school and be selected for the most prominent residency programs. Why would he be insecure?

She'd read enough to know sometimes the most unlikely people were insecure. It often had to do with their childhood. Ryan had siblings, but they weren't close. In fact, they rarely spoke. Ryan claimed they'd gone their separate ways. She'd suspected his siblings were blue collar and he was ashamed of them.

"Maybe you're right," she told Miranda. "Ryan is very possessive. It doesn't matter now, does it? He's out of my life."

"I'd say you've improved things considerably."

Whitney smiled, happy to feel close to Miranda again, but uneasy about Adam. Tonight proved how little he'd confided in her, how little she actually knew about the man. She'd met him just a week ago, as hard as that was to believe. In some ways she'd grown to feel as comfortable and as close to him as she'd ever been to any man. Obviously, he hadn't felt that close to her. She was angry and terribly upset with Adam but didn't want to burden her cousin with anything else. She changed the subject.

"Speaking of improving things. How did you come up with Broderick Babcock's name?"

Miranda gave her a smug smile. "I had to think hard, believe me. I needed to get away, but I didn't want to answer any questions. Why wouldn't I introduce you to my fiancé? Why would we go off on a secret honeymoon?

"Then it came to me. An attorney. They're slick. Secretive. No one would question their plans. You didn't. I'd met Mr. Babcock when I worked at Saffron Blue. His reputation said he was the kind of guy who might insist on a secret honeymoon."

"I bought your story." Whitney went on to explain how Ryan's sudden reappearance in her life with the property agreement led to her visiting the attorney.

"That's how I discovered you'd vanished."

"I'm sorry. I would have trusted you with my secret, but we hadn't been close. I thought—"

"Were you ever going to come back?" Whitney asked, raw emotion underscoring every word. "Were you going to tell me?"

Miranda stopped and slid one arm around Whitney's shoulders. "Of course. I was going to return and tell you everything."

"When?"

"I was going to call you—and not tell you where I was—next week. I thought the men might show up around that time. I was going to warn you, but I wasn't going to tell you enough to get you hurt." Miranda dropped her arm and gazed off across the wine-dark sea into the night. "I'm not sure when I was going to come home. Not for a year or more." She put her hand on her tummy. "I have to protect my—our—baby."

Whitney tried to see life through her cousin's eyes. The man she loved had died, ruthless killers were after her and she was pregnant. "Look, I can't change the past. But I can promise to be a better cousin."

"We should be like sisters," Miranda said, the threat of tears unexpectedly surfacing in her voice.

Whitney hugged Miranda. "You're right, we should be as close as sisters. I tried when you came to live with—"

"I know. You were so sweet. All I did was push you away. I didn't realize it at the time." She dug a bare toe into the wet sand. "I've been alone so much recently that I've had plenty of time to think. I'm sure I pulled into a shell of sorts after my parents were killed. I didn't want to risk getting close, then losing someone else. Still, I did feel close to you. Then you went off to college."

"And disappeared from your life."

"You visited when your mother was alive."

"I'm sorry," Whitney said. She meant it, but "sorry," like "love," was an overused word. But right now she couldn't think of any better way to express herself. "I'll do better. I want to be with you when the baby is born."

"No. If they haven't followed you down here already, those men are sure to find me if you keep visiting. The only way I'll be safe is if you leave me alone."

"But I don't want you to go through labor all by yourself in a strange country."

"There's an American hospital in Cancún. I'll go there. Don't worry."

"I am worried," Whitney protested. "I want to be with you. I—"

"They'll kill me if they find me." Miranda tried for a smile. "I'll come back when it's safe. Until then, the only way you can help is to leave. Don't call. Don't do anything that might lead them to me. I need you to promise me—for the baby."

CHAPTER THIRTY-FIVE

ADAM SAT IN THE crowded air terminal in Cancún. It was the off-season, but you wouldn't know it by the gaggles of tourists sporting lobster-red burns and toting bags filled with *Bye-Bye Cancún* T-shirts and other souvenirs.

"Miranda will be fine," he assured Whitney.

She was sitting beside him, her feet resting on the small over-night case he'd found in his uncle's closet and had given her for the trip. She'd been quiet, preoccupied since they'd left Miranda's villa. When he'd discovered nothing on his uncle's computer by morning, he insisted on taking the next flight home.

"I'm coming to stay with Miranda just as soon as those men are found. I don't want to put her in danger, but I don't want her to be alone when she delivers."

Adam patted the leather case that held his uncle's laptop and computer software. "The answer's here. None of us knows how to find it but Quinten Foley will have computer experts. Foley will bag those terrorists. Then Miranda can return home."

"Let's hope so."

Adam silently reminded himself to contact Samantha Waterson tomorrow and have her stop the special toxicology test on his uncle's liver tissues. At least now he had peace of mind. Calvin Hunter had not been murdered.

"I'm surprised that those men want to kill Miranda just because she can identify them. Most terrorists seem thrilled to get their pictures on the evening news. So what if she ID'd them?"

Adam glanced around quickly. No one seemed to be paying attention to them, but he kept his voice low. "These guys obviously plan to use my uncle's contacts and shipping routes. This is a no-brainer for them—if they keep quiet and don't call attention to themselves. Miranda's a weak link."

"That makes sense. But why kill her before they get the disc with the info?"

"Good question. I assumed they had gotten it when this baby—" he patted the laptop "—disappeared. But as I was searching through the files on my uncle's computer last night, I decided he may have given them a phony disc. He just didn't tell Miranda—or maybe he died before he had the chance to explain it to her."

"Why would he do that?"

"To fool them into thinking they had the info they needed. He could have been buying additional time. When they discovered the disc was a fake, he would have disappeared."

"Maybe," Whitney replied, but she didn't sound convinced.

They sat in silence for a few minutes. Whitney seemed withdrawn to Adam. Evidently finding her cousin and learning Miranda was pregnant had a profound impact on Whitney.

"I'm going to see if I can buy a magazine." He rose, hefted the laptop over his shoulder and headed toward the small gift shop.

A few minutes later, he stepped out of the shop with a *Time* magazine tucked into the side pocket of the laptop case. He scanned the room to see if anyone was following them, but he didn't spot anybody. Whitney was talking on her cell phone when he returned and sat down beside her. Cell service down here was iffy at best. Whitney had tried to call the woman who'd taken over her dogs but hadn't been able to get through.

"Anything happening?" he asked when she shut her cell phone and dropped it into her purse. "Are Jasper and Lexi okay?"

"They're fine," Whitney replied in a tight voice.

"What's the matter?"

"Nothing. Lyleen Foster seems to be doing a great job with the dogs. I had a message from Trish. Remember the friend of hers who needed a house-sitter?"

Adam recalled Whitney mentioning it. The fine hairs on the back of his neck prickled. "What about him?"

"He's left town. Trish told him I would house-sit."

He didn't like the thought of Whitney staying anywhere but with him. He could tell himself that he wanted her around until they settled this mess with her cousin and the disc—but that wasn't the reason. He cared about her. He wanted Whitney to become part of his life.

"I'm supposed to move in as soon as I get back."

A flare of anger hit him. "You decided all this without talking to me?"

She jerked sideways to face him squarely. "You haven't bothered to consult with me."

"What are you talking about?" he asked, although he had the sneaking suspicion he knew. He'd noticed the grim expression on her face at several points during the conversation with Miranda.

"Don't pretend you don't know! All that talk about Miranda and your uncle. Why didn't you tell me?"

He put his finger to his lips to indicate they should keep their voices low. "It didn't involve you, and I didn't want to worry you."

"I was already worried," she hissed at him, but lowered her voice. "I had the right to know but you didn't see fit to confide in me."

He couldn't deny it. There had been more going on than he'd permitted Whitney to learn. He hadn't wanted to upset her any more or he would have told her that night.

"I'm sorry," he said. "I should have told you. It won't happen again."

"Is there anything else I should know about?"

Aw hell, he cursed silently. Why had he listened to that overbuffed jock? He should have told her that Ashley had been responsible for Lexi's disappearance. "Lexi didn't wander off."

Whitney sat up straighter. "She didn't? What happened?"

"Ashley convinced her personal trainer—Preston Block, the guy who returned Lexi—to take her. They planned to hold her for ransom until—"

"Ransom? How could Ashley possibly think I had any money? Didn't Ryan tell her the truth about our divorce?"

"I assume he did. They wanted you to sign the property agreement immediately. There was a house Ashley really wanted, and your ex couldn't qualify for financing unless he could show he owned everything so he could arrange for a new loan."

"That bastard! How could he take Lexi and scare me like that?"

"Ryan had nothing to do with it. That's what Block told me, and I believe him. He claimed it was his idea. After our visit, Ryan guessed Ashley knew something and insisted she return the dog."

"Really?" She studied her hands for a moment. "I guess I underestimated Ryan." She shifted in her seat, thinking about Ashley and the clothes that had appeared after the fire. "No wonder Ashley brought me clothes. She isn't the sweet, innocent woman she pretends to be. She felt guilty for taking my dog. Why else would she have given me an expensive dress?"

Adam wasn't going there. He hadn't a clue what went on in women's minds. "I suppose that's the reason, but who knows?"

"Her reasons don't matter. Why didn't you tell me? I don't get it."

Again Adam cursed himself. "I should have, but Block was persuasive. He said you wouldn't believe Ryan wasn't involved. You'd cause more trouble and Ashley wouldn't get her house. I liked you a lot—more than a lot. I decided you had your dog and it would be better to close the book on the past."

Adam waited a few agonizingly long minutes before switching the subject and asking, "What did you tell Trish?"

"Nothing. I could pick up my messages yet I can't seem to call out. But I intend to take the job."

"Why? If it's money—"

"It's not. I'm starting over. This is the time and the place. I'm going to become a vet. I'll need to split my time between working at the vet's and taking classes."

"You're saying there's no time for us?"

"I'm not sure there is an us. You haven't shared things with me. You should have told me about Lexi. Every time she was out of my sight, I worried. There wasn't any need. She's not going to run away because she never did in the first place."

"Would you feel this way if I'd told you about Lexi and my uncle?"

"It doesn't matter. I've learned you can't change the past, but you can do things differently so the future isn't a replay of the past. I'm not going to have much spare time. When I do, I intend to spend it with Miranda."

Adam opened his mouth to argue, then decided against it. Maybe a little distance wasn't such a bad idea. It would give them both time to think. It would also get Whitney away from the house. He was pretty sure the media coverage had made it clear that Miranda had been the object of the firebombing—and she was no longer living there. But it didn't hurt to be careful.

WHITNEY PICKED UP WHAT few clothes she had and moved to the address that Trish had left on the machine. She and Adam had exchanged less than a dozen sentences—all of them necessary—between Cancún and San Diego. He'd dropped her off at the mansion overlooking the ocean in La Jolla. He'd waited for her to find the hidden key and let herself in before leaving.

Whitney wandered around the home, telling herself that Adam had his pride. He wasn't going to beg her to stay with him. Part of her wished things were different but another— wiser—part accepted the situation. She'd found her cousin and knew the truth about Lexi. Her life had a new direction now.

Time would tell if she and Adam had a future.

She heard the doorbell ring and knew it was Trish. She'd called her friend to say she was moving in, and Trish said she would meet her at the house to show her how everything worked.

Whitney opened the door and Trish breezed in, a happy smile lighting her face. "Where were you? I almost didn't tell Ian that you were going to take the house-sitting job. For all I knew you were gone forever."

Whitney followed her into the great room that overlooked the pool. In the distance the marine blue of the Pacific glittered in the midday sun. "Adam and I got away for a bit."

Trish arched one finely plucked eyebrow and smiled. Adam and Whitney had agreed not to reveal anything to anyone about their trip to Cancún. No one was to learn Miranda's where- abouts until this mess was straightened out.

"Sounds like fun," Trish said with a wink. Whitney half expected the older woman to warn her about treacherous men, but she didn't. "Ian Finsteter has an impressive collection of art."

Whitney had wandered through the new home and had noticed a number of paintings and fine sculptures on display. Knowing the owner of the home purchased art from Trish had told Whitney the collection was valuable.

"Ian usually has the alarm on with motion sensors. He left it off until you moved in and I gave you the code."

"What about Lexi? Won't she set off the motion sensors?"

Trish shook her head. "Not unless she moves one of the sculptures."

"Really? The motion sensors are under the pieces?" She glanced over to a postmodern sculpture of a ballerina gracefully pirouetting on one toe.

"Yes. It's state of the art. The alarm goes into a special security service that only takes extremely wealthy clients. They'll be here within three minutes if someone moves a piece of art and trips a motion sensor."

"Lexi won't touch a thing. I promise."

"Where is she?"

"With Lyleen, the woman taking over my pets. She's bringing Lexi here soon."

Trish opened the sliding glass door that led out to the pool. "I met her. She seems…okay. Brandy's happy, that's all that counts."

Whitney wanted to remind her that Golden retrievers were easy to please and thought everyone was their friend. That was why Lexi had gone off with Ashley's personal trainer. But she didn't open her mouth. Why alienate Trish when she'd gone out of her way to help her?

"Isn't this fabulous?" Trish waved her arm to indicate the pool. Off to the side was a large polished black rock precariously balanced on a much smaller rock. "Don't touch *Obsidian I*. It's a priceless sculpture by Diego Rameriz, the Spanish sculptor who died recently."

"Is it protected by a motion sensor?"

"Of course." Trish led her closer until Whitney could see her own distorted reflection on the glossy-black surface of the sculpture.

"I better keep Lexi away from this."

Trish patted the rock. "She'd have to jump on it to trigger the alarm. The sensors are designed to stop thieves from stealing the art. They're not so sensitive that a maid dusting them will cause a problem. You would need to knock this off its base to activate the alarm. Lexi doesn't strike me as the type of dog to cause problems. That's what I told Ian when I explained this fabulous house-sitter came with a dog."

"Thanks. We'll both be very careful."

They went through the magnificent home and Trish showed her what needed to be taken care of and how to do it. Whitney explained why she'd decided to work for the vet even though Trish hadn't inquired, which seemed odd.

"Smart move," Trish told her when Whitney finished. "I was in my later thirties before I opened my gallery and found my calling."

Whitney could have reminded Trish that she'd had a wealthy family backing her, but she didn't. Despite having money Trish had suffered a lot.

"What are you doing for a car?" Trish asked.

"Tomorrow I'm contacting the insurance company to see what they can do."

"You're welcome to use Ravissant's minivan. I won't need it for a few days."

"That's great. I really appreciate it."

They were standing in the opulent master bedroom—all white silk with sterling accent pieces—and admiring the ocean that stretched in an endless sweep of blue toward the distant horizon. Sometimes the beauty of nature overwhelmed Whitney, making her life, her troubles seem small.

"Hear anything from Miranda?" Trish unexpectedly asked.

How could Whitney lie to a friend who'd helped her so much? She evaded by saying, "I'm hoping she'll be back soon."

"Rod's really curious why she used his name."

The second the words were out of Trish's mouth, Whitney got the picture. Trish was interested in the attorney.

"I'm sure you and I are the only ones Miranda told. Rod won't have to explain all over town."

"Rod's not worried," Trish assured her. "Just curious."

Now Whitney had the complete picture. Trish wasn't just interested in the man from afar; they must be involved. Great, she decided. Trish had let the past haunt her for too long. It was nice to know her friend had found someone to care about.

"Rod's been trying to reach you," Trish added. "I tried to help him by calling your ex—"

"You didn't!"

"I did," Trish replied defensively. "Only because Rod needs to reach you. He's desperate to talk to you."

"About what?"

"He didn't tell me. You know how lawyers are. He flew to San Francisco this morning."

"It must be about the property agreement. I'm ready to sign it and have Ryan out of my life."

This was a new start, Whitney reminded herself. As soon as she signed those papers, her life would head in a new direction.

So why wasn't she happier?

CHAPTER THIRTY-SIX

IT WAS LATE AFTERNOON by the time Lyleen dropped off Lexi. Her dog was excited to see Whitney, but not nearly as excited as Jasper. The crested kept spinning in circles and yipping. Whitney realized she was going to miss Jasper. He had his quirks but he was a lovable dog. She would miss Adam, too, but she tamped that thought down.

The fiftyish woman had a nest of gray curls covering the crown of her head, but the rest was buzzed from ear to ear and along the back of her neck. Lyleen seemed a little intense to Whitney, but very competent. As Trish had said, the most important thing was the dogs liked her.

"I tried to reach Mr. Hunter but he's not home," the woman told her. "You said Jasper was skittish, and I knew Lexi had gotten out. Do you think I should leave such a valuable dog in the side yard?"

"No. Let him stay with me tonight. I'll have Adam set up an appointment with you. He needs to explain Jasper's schedule and show you the dog's special hiding places, like under the coffee table."

"All right. I'll ring him again."

They said goodbye and Whitney went over to the telephone in the media room just off the entry. Jasper and Lexi were at her heels. She remembered she didn't have food for either one of them. She needed to make a quick run to the supermarket, but first she wanted to call Ryan.

"Ryan, it's me."

"Where are you?" He sounded upset.

"I'm house-sitting for a friend of Trish Bowrather's."

"Where?"

She hesitated. Adam had warned her to keep her whereabouts secret if possible. The killers after Miranda probably realized her cousin no longer lived in the cottage, but it paid to be careful. Also, after the way Ryan had shaken her to bully her into signing the papers, Whitney wasn't sure she wanted him to pay her another visit.

"Where are you?" Ryan repeated.

"Why?"

"Trish Bowrather called here looking for you." Something new entered his voice. Harder, more judgmental. "I didn't know where you were."

She wanted to tell him, *There's no reason why you should.* Then she reminded herself that she was starting over. The past was behind her forever.

There was no reason not to tell her ex where she was living. After all, they'd been married. It would take some time before people stopped contacting Ryan when they wanted to find her.

"I'll be at 211 Ocean Vista for the next few months."

"That's a pretty swank neighborhood."

Trust Ryan to recognize a prestigious address. Whitney let the comment pass. "I want to thank you for making Ashley return Lexi. I realize her disappearance wasn't your fault." She waited but Ryan didn't respond. "My attorney's in San Francisco. He'll be back tomorrow. I'll sign the papers and get out of your life."

A grinding silence greeted her words. She finally asked, "Is Ashley there?"

"Why?" he snapped.

"I wanted to tell her that she's lucky I didn't file stolen-property charges against her. Lexi's a valuable dog. If Ashley comes near—"

"She's out." He slammed down the receiver.

Whitney hung up, a little annoyed with herself for being so peevish. Ashley had returned the dog. Why threaten her? She put the dogs in the minivan Ravissant Gallery used to deliver paintings. They had so much room that they started to play in the back.

"Settle down," she called over her shoulder.

She was on her way to the market when she decided to drop by the veterinarian's office and use the computer to update Lexi's chip. She wasn't due to start working until next week but maybe if she told them she was available she could start sooner. Heaven knew she could use the money. She was going to have to charge groceries and dog food.

"We're closing in ten minutes," the woman told Whitney when she walked through the door with both dogs on leashes.

Whitney explained she was going to be the new assistant, and the receptionist looked relieved not to have two sick dogs just before they closed at six.

"I don't have a computer at home." Whitney walked behind the counter to the computer. "I need to update Lexi's chip info."

"Go ahead, but did you know it can be done over the telephone?"

"Really?" Whitney responded as if she didn't know. She'd hoped to see one of the doctors and let them know she would like to work immediately. "Where is everyone?" Whitney casually asked as she logged onto the system and typed in the Web address for Pet Locate.

"They're at a Neuticles demo."

"What's that?" A small charge of excitement buzzed through her body. She hadn't had much sleep last night—just a short nap on Miranda's sofa and another quick nap on the plane. She was exhausted and looking forward to climbing into the white silk bed, but hearing about advances in veterinary medicine interested her.

"Testicular implants."

"No way!"

"I'm not kidding," the receptionist assured her. "Lots of people want their dogs—you know—unable to reproduce, but they don't like the look."

"Oh my gosh. It sounds painful and totally unnecessary."

The woman giggled. "I doubt if Dr. Robinson will be doing them, but she went to see what all the fuss was about."

Whitney changed Lexi's contact information to reflect the new address where Whitney was house-sitting and gave that phone number in addition to her cell. Lexi hadn't wandered off, but why take chances?

While she was at it she checked to be sure Adam had updated Jasper's information after his uncle's death. The pets were listed under the owner's name but nothing came up for Calvin Hunter. Pet Locate was the main chip database, but Whitney knew at least one other company was now providing the service.

"Isn't there another chip service?" she asked.

"Sure. PetFinders.com. It's bookmarked at the top of the screen."

Whitney quickly located the database. Calvin Hunter's name did not appear. "That's strange," she said, thinking out loud.

"Don't you remember what service you used?" asked the receptionist.

"I've updated my dog's information, but I wanted to change Jasper's." She pointed to her feet, where Jasper was wagging his tail at the sound of his name. "His owner died, so the info has to be changed. He's an international champion but I can't find his late owner's name in either chip database."

"A champion? Really?" The woman smiled at Jasper but shook her head.

"Yep. Best in show at Frankfurt."

"The breeder probably listed him. That's what usually happens."

"You're right. I'll have to check his file and get the breeder's name." Secretly she was thrilled to have another reason to talk to Adam. There was no excuse for what he'd done but something in her longed to forgive him.

"Good night," she told the receptionist. "I'll be starting next week, but if I'm needed sooner, I can come in. Would you tell—"

"Could you work for me?" The woman almost shouted the question. "My husband's company's sending him on a trip to Hawaii. I can't go unless I can find someone to work—"

"I'll do it."

"Oh, great. I owe you one. Come in tomorrow for an hour or so and I'll show you what to do." Whitney happily agreed and was halfway back to the minivan when it hit her.

The Chip.

Calvin Hunter had used dog shows as a cover for his arms deals. Could he have somehow transferred the information from a regular computer disc to a microchip? She knew the technology was there. Adam's uncle had once been in naval intelligence. Surely he knew how to do it. That would account for the skin irritation that appeared on Jasper's neck *after* he won at Frankfurt.

She rushed back inside. "Let me use the wand for a moment."

The receptionist was turning off lights, but she cheerily replied, "Go ahead. It's in the drawer in room two. Do you know how to use it?"

"Yes." With both dogs in tow, Whitney dashed into the room and found the wand. She had no idea why they called the electronic device the size of a pack of cigarettes a wand, but everyone did. It was a simple mechanism with an on/off switch and an LCD display where the number on the chip inserted behind the pet's ear came up.

She hoisted Jasper onto the examining table. Lexi wagged her tail as if expecting to be lifted up, too. Whitney switched on the wand and brushed it across the small bump on the back of Jasper's neck.

Letters flashed across the LCD screen. A name—not a number. The chip was supposed to show a number. That number, when put into the chip center's database, should yield owner information like the pet owner's address and phone number. She stared at the screen, not quite believing what she was seeing, although she'd suspected she might discover something like this.

She switched off the wand, replaced it in the drawer. Her insides jangled with excitement. She carefully lifted Jasper off the table. *How cruel,* she thought. Chipping a dog didn't hurt the pet, but imagining Jasper needlessly being jabbed with a needle upset her.

"You're not just worth thousands," she told Jasper. "You're worth millions."

The little dog licked her nose.

ADAM SAT ACROSS THE DESK from Quinten Foley in the older man's home. It had taken Adam the better part of the afternoon to locate Foley. He'd been on the golf course with his cell phone off. He'd told Foley that he had Calvin Hunter's laptop and software discs.

Foley leaned back in his chair and studied Adam. "So, Miranda Marshall is in Cancún. She had the computer all along."

Adam didn't respond, but he gave Foley credit. He must have had them followed. "She's long gone now," Adam said to protect Miranda. "She gave me his computer. It's going to take an expert to find the information."

"You tried?"

"Yes, but I'm just your average guy. No expert. I figure it's embedded somewhere. In Iraq the guys showed me how to access porn sites. Go to a seemingly innocent site and click on some part of the picture that comes up. Bam! A screen concealed behind the picture appears. Give your password—and if you've paid your money, you're into an orgy of porn."

"Exactly. Kiddie porn is often accessed by clicking on a chicken in a barnyard scene. Chicken-hawkers love the irony." Foley leaned forward and put both elbows on his desk. "You think Cal hid information like that?"

"Must be. I can't find any sign of it. Maybe if your guys—"

"I'll see if I can locate someone to—"

Adam shoved the laptop in the case with the software programs across the desk. "Don't bother to bullshit me. We haven't got the time. I know you work at the Pentagon. CIA?"

"No," Foley replied after an emotion-charged silence. "I'm with a special unit of Homeland Security."

Adam didn't have a whole lot of faith in Homeland Security but hey, maybe it was just him. Right now, he didn't have anyone else to turn to but Foley. Adam didn't even know if the terrorists had a phony disc and would return—mad as hell—for the real one. He assumed that was what would happen—but who knew.

"Operatives are expecting to pick up the disc with the info on it next week," he informed Foley. "We're not sure if they realize my uncle is dead or not. Even if they do, they're planning to wire transfer a shitload of money. I'm betting they'll show, expecting Miranda to deliver the disc."

"Why would they think she—"

"Miranda met them at my uncle's home. He convinced them that she was his partner."

Foley unzipped the computer case and ran his hand lovingly over the lid of the laptop. "This is a chance to catch them."

"Absolutely. But we'd better have something to give them. These aren't just couriers. They're high-ranking terrorists. I'm sure they'll have a laptop with them to scan the disc to make certain they have what they paid for."

"You're right. We're going to need Miranda here. Can you—"

A thunderous banging on the front door interrupted Foley. Adam instinctively grabbed the computer case, zipped it shut and hid it between the desk and the wall.

"I'll get rid of whoever it is. Probably Jehovah's Witnesses. They've been working the neighborhood."

Adam heard the front door open followed by the sound of Tyler's voice. "What's Adam doing here?" Tyler asked in a belligerent tone.

Quinten Foley responded, "We're discussing his uncle's estate."

The sound of footsteps meant they were coming toward the office. Adam stood up and tried for a welcoming smile. His brain kept insisting: *There's no time to waste.* "Hey, Tyler, how's it going?"

Beside his partner stood Holly. Adam hadn't seen her for nearly three years, but she was still as pretty as ever. Long shiny brown hair, sparkling amber eyes. "Holly, you're looking great."

"Hello, Adam," she replied with the warm smile he remembered so well. "It's good to see you."

"Trust me, I'm happy to be back in the States." He smiled at her but made sure he also smiled at Tyler. Adam didn't want his best friend to think he was hitting on his girl.

A troubling silence followed. Adam looked at Quinten Foley, who was now behind his desk again. The older man didn't seem inclined to say much.

"We didn't mean to interrupt," Tyler said, his voice tight. "But I have something to say to my father."

"I'll go in the other room," offered Adam. Normally, he would have left the house, but every minute counted.

"Don't bother. This isn't secret stuff." Tyler faced his father.

"Holly is very upset with me. She thinks I don't love her because I don't make any effort to have my family get to know her."

Adam shifted uncomfortably. This sounded a helluva lot more personal than he'd anticipated.

"Th-that's not true," Quinten Foley awkwardly replied.

"Holly's family is one of those close-knit groups. They spend time together and expect to get to know their daughter's boyfriend." Tyler gazed at Holly, and she smiled back. Adam could see they loved each other. He couldn't help thinking about Whitney. Aw, hell. Despite the short length of time he'd known Whitney, Adam realized he loved her. But he'd royally blown it.

"I EXPLAINED TO HOLLY that we aren't close," Tyler told his father, unable to conceal his bitterness. "I hardly know you. We never see each other even when you're in town. Isn't that right?"

His father responded without a trace of regret or concern. "I'm a busy—"

"He's always been too busy for me," Tyler said to Holly. "Even after my mother killed herself, he didn't have a second to spare for his only child. I was shuttled off to military school."

"That's not fair. I—"

"It doesn't matter. I've learned to live with it. I just wanted Holly to understand our family. Not asking her to spend time with you isn't a reflection on her. It's about us." Tyler was on the verge of shouting now, but he couldn't help himself. Years of pent-up anger exploded out of him. He felt Holly's restraining hand on his arm and lowered his voice. "Holly can't expect to get to know you when I don't."

In the bruising silence that followed Tyler stared at his father. Until this morning, when he'd confronted Holly, half expecting her to tell him that she wanted to end their relationship, Tyler had believed money was keeping them apart. She'd made him realize his mistake.

The old saying about money not buying you love was true. Holly cared about him and had since they began dating—when he'd had nothing but prospects. His father could take his money and rot in hell for all he cared. The company he had started with Adam was off to an awesome start. He wanted to look back and know he'd built it on his own. He wanted Holly to understand that he was a man she could be proud of.

"I don't need you," Tyler told his father as he slipped his arm around Holly and pulled her against his side. "But I need Holly. If she'll have me—" he turned his attention to Holly "—I want to marry her."

"Oh my gosh!" cried Holly. "You want to get married?"

"Of course." What did she think their discussion this morning had been about? True, he'd asked her where she'd been, and she said she'd gone to Newport Beach to visit her parents. But he'd asked what was wrong and she'd told him that she didn't think he was serious about her because he'd never allowed her to get to know his family.

"You never mentioned marriage," Holly said softly.

"Hey! That's great." Adam slapped him on the back. "Holly's a great gal. The best, and you're the best friend a guy could have. You deserve to be happy." He smiled at Holly. "Both of you."

"Maybe we ought to go somewhere and talk about this," Holly suggested in a high-pitched, excited voice.

"You're right. Let's get outta here." Tyler couldn't keep the excitement out of his own voice. As angry as he'd been a few minutes ago, now he was happier than he could ever remember being.

ADAM WATCHED THEM LEAVE, his mind on Whitney. He was thrilled for his friend and knew things would work out. What he needed to do was tell Whitney he loved her. Admit he'd made a huge mistake by not trusting her with more information about his uncle and an even worse mistake by not telling her the truth about Lexi. Then he'd tell her how much he loved her. True, they hadn't known each other long, but he was positive about his feelings.

"Where were we?" Quinten Foley asked, as if nothing important had happened.

Foley was a tough man focused on his career. A lot like his uncle, Adam guessed. Too late, Calvin Hunter had found someone to love and had realized he wanted a life.

"You know, I had a close relationship with my father. Not a day goes by that I don't miss him."

Foley nodded, but Adam had the feeling the man was just humoring him. He wouldn't have bothered except he could see how upset Tyler was by his father's attitude. Even with Holly's love there would be a void in Tyler's life unless his father had an attitude adjustment.

"My uncle found someone to love but he died before he could enjoy life with her. My own father died at an early age." Adam watched Foley's eyes narrow slightly. The man was listening, but it was impossible to tell if Adam's words were having any impact. "I was almost killed in Iraq. Both guys beside me died, but by some miracle I lived. I know what's important in life—and it isn't money."

"I have a job, duty—"

"Is that all you're living for?"

"Of course not," Foley assured him.

"You made a lot of money off the arms sales. Money must mean—"

"I was working undercover for the government the whole time. I never made a dime beyond my salary."

Shock thrummed through Adam's brain. From what Miranda had said, Adam had gathered Foley was a government agent and one trusted by his uncle. But Adam believed Quinten

Foley had made a ton of money dealing arms on the side. It was difficult to believe the man hadn't profited from selling contraband weapons.

"I did it all for my country," Foley said.

Kicking himself for assuming the worst, Adam asked, "What about Tyler?"

Foley's world-weary eyes were tempered by a face that revealed no emotion nor gave any hint of his inner thoughts. The older man seemed to consider the question for a long moment as if he had to come to grips with it. "I care about my son, sure. I loved his mother—" Foley turned away and walked to the window overlooking the swimming pool. In a very soft voice that bordered on a whisper, he added, "I didn't just love Claire. I worshipped her. When she killed herself, I couldn't bear to look at Tyler." He turned back to Adam. "He has her eyes, you know, her animated smile."

Adam felt a pang of sympathy. "My dad loved my mother. I look a lot like her, but he didn't give up on me." This was stretching the truth a bit. He did have his mother's hair but he looked more like his father. He was willing to fudge a little, if it could help his friend. "I am what I am—because he loved me."

"I never understood why Claire killed herself. She seemed a little depressed because we moved so often. I—"

"That was years ago. What about Tyler? Would your wife want you to treat him like this?"

"She loved Tyler. Her suicide note said, 'Love him for me.' I just couldn't—still can't—be around him without thinking of her."

"Get over it. Life goes on. I'm betting Tyler and Holly get married soon and have children. Don't you want to be part of their lives?"

"Yes, but I'm not sure I know how to act. I guess I could try. Invite them to dinner or something."

"That's a start." Adam reached over and picked up the telephone. He dialed Tyler's cell number, then handed Quinten Foley the receiver.

CHAPTER THIRTY-SEVEN

WHITNEY CLIMBED THE stairs to the white silk bedroom over-looking the ocean. The sun had dropped into the sea, leaving behind a faint glow of tangerine light that would quickly be consumed by darkness. She was dead tired but she didn't want to go to sleep until she'd spoken to Adam. As soon as she left the vet's, she'd tried to call him, but his cell phone's voice mail immediately picked up.

She'd swung by Calvin Hunter's home, thinking Adam might have shut off his phone and gone to bed early. He had to be even more tired than she was. He'd worked while she'd napped on Miranda's sofa.

Adam hadn't been there. She left him notes in several places so he couldn't miss the message. She'd been afraid to put in writing what she found. The notes said to call her—it was an emergency.

Whitney could have left Jasper there for Adam, but she told him in each note that she had the dog. She doubted anyone else knew the Chinese crested was carrying such valuable informa-tion, but she wasn't taking any chances. Jasper was safer with her.

Earlier she'd deposited two soft-sided suitcases containing her clothes just outside the double walk-in closets in the master bedroom. Jasper and Lexi followed her when she inspected the closets and found one was empty. She placed her suitcases on the floor inside the empty closet, but didn't have the energy to unpack what little she had.

Whitney thought a dip in the pool might refresh her and keep her awake until Adam called. She put on the swimsuit she'd hurriedly bought to go to Cancún and had never worn. She smiled inwardly, remembering the man from Adam's security company. Adam had insisted the man should go along to guard her. He'd been more than a little embarrassed to be hanging around Skinny Dip while she tried on suits.

Now that she looked back on it, Whitney decided she was stronger than she sometimes believed. Instinct had launched her at the fence. That quick action had saved her life. She shouldn't have allowed the incident to cause an emotional meltdown. After the way she'd freaked out, no wonder Adam hadn't wanted to tell her about his uncle. She could almost forgive him.

Almost.

If only he'd revealed Ashley's part in Lexi's disappearance, Whitney might have been more forgiving. But he hadn't. It said a lot about his character, she reminded herself. It told her even more about their relationship.

"Come on, gang," she said to Jasper and Lexi. "It's chow time."

They scampered behind her as she went down the sweeping staircase. After stopping to leave the notes for Adam, she'd swung by the supermarket and charged some necessities. While the dogs ate, she unpacked the groceries and put them away.

Inside the walk-in pantry, she froze. What was that? It sounded like a thump. The nearest house was too far for her to hear anything. She listened, attempting to detect something else over the crunching sounds of the dogs eating. Her hand shook when she eased the pantry door back so she could have a better look. She peeked out and saw the dogs with their noses in the fancy dishes that she was using for their bowls. Obviously, they hadn't heard a thing.

What a sniveling display of shredded nerves you are.

Every house had its own special sounds, she assured herself. She would just have to get used to this one. She could put on the alarm, but Adam might drop by without calling. She scribbled a note, saying she was in the pool, and taped it to the front door.

When she returned to the kitchen, the dogs had finished eating. "Come on," she told them, and they followed her out to the pool. Since the area was new to them, the dogs engaged in a sniff-fest. By the way they were hovering around the low-hanging bushes, Whitney guessed another dog had been out here recently.

"Stay away from the rock," Whitney told Lexi even though the dog wasn't anywhere near the obsidian sculpture.

It was dark now and the lights around the pool unexpect-edly snapped on. Her limbs locked in place. Fortunately for Whitney, her brain was still functioning. The lights must be on an automatic timer.

Dozens of low-voltage exterior lights now artfully high-lighted the plants and the house. Brighter lights on the rafters of the open-air overhang were aimed at the water. Like most pools, this one had a light at the bottom of the deep end. The rest of the yard was dark shadows.

When would she get over being so jumpy? she asked herself. A disturbing chill enveloped her. There was cause for concern. Calvin Hunter had gone to a lot of trouble to hide the information on a microchip and plant it under his dog's skin. But the people after the info didn't know Jasper had it—and couldn't possibly find her if they did.

What she was experiencing was the psychological after-shock of the fire followed by the scare with the car. *Get a grip!* Taking a deep, calming breath, she tamped down the wave of anxiety. If she didn't confront her fears, they would get the better of her.

She had a toe in the water when she remembered her cell

phone was on the counter in the kitchen. Adam had the number of this house, but he might call her on the cell. She went inside and retrieved it. Returning to the pool area where the dogs were waiting, tails wagging, she again had the eerie sensation someone was watching her.

Get over it.

She put the cell phone down on a small table near the middle of the pool where she could get to it easily no matter where she was in the water. Lexi barked excitedly. Whitney whirled around and saw a big dark shadow blocking the light. A man.

The hulking shape moved and the lights trained on the pool hit her in the eyes, blinding her for a moment. He walked closer and a scream almost ripped from her throat. In the next breath, she realized it was Ryan. Whitney released a pent-up sigh of relief.

Ryan was dressed in a polo shirt, pressed jeans and a light-weight bomber-style jacket. As always he wore loafers that could have passed for new. Lexi scampered up to him, but Jasper scooted under a chaise.

"Ryan, what are you doing here?"

He looked around the dark yard. "Have you seen Ashley?"

"N-no, of course not." His question surprised her. Why on earth would he think Ashley was here?

Ryan walked closer and Whitney instinctively backed up, but not too far. She was already near the edge of the pool.

"Have you heard from her?"

She'd lived with this man long enough to recognize stress and anxiety in his overwrought voice. "No. Why would she call me?"

"To explain about the clothes."

She didn't like what she saw in his eyes. Something had happened with Ashley and he clearly blamed her.

"She's not here, and I have no idea where she is." In her toughest voice, she added, "You'd better leave now."

"I will." He ground out the words. "But your nine lives are up."

His unanticipated anger directed at her was like a slap in the face. "What do you mean?"

"You'll see."

Now there was a deadly calm about him, in spite of the lethal tone of voice. Whitney suddenly became disturbingly aware of her situation. She was standing—as good as naked—at the edge of the pool without a weapon of any kind. She didn't need a weapon, Whitney told herself. She was panicking again for no good reason. She'd been married to this man. "Ryan, what's wrong?"

His eyes narrowed, bore into her. "Get in the pool. Start swimming."

"What? You're not making sense." Was he on something? she wondered.

Unexpectedly, both his hands slammed into her shoulders and shoved her backward. She hit the pool with a startled cry and sucked a mouthful of water into her lungs. She surfaced, gagging and struggling to get her breath in spastic gasps. Treading water and coughing, she looked up at her former husband looming above her.

She'd never seen Ryan this angry, this out of control. Suddenly all the years she'd put up with his antics infuriated her. What had she been thinking? This man was nothing but a self-centered egomaniac. Evidently, the beauty queen had seen the light and left him. It must have sent him over some psychological edge into lunacy.

"Start swimming, Whitney."

She sputtered, still unable to catch her breath, her throat burning from the chlorine in the pool. Finally she managed to ask, "Why? What's going on?"

He didn't answer and that sent a fresh surge of panic through her. She tried to touch bottom with the tips of her toes, but it was too deep. She took a few quick strokes to the edge of the pool near Ryan's feet. She grasped the rim of the pool with both hands.

"What's wrong with you?" she asked.

"Nothing you can't fix."

Whitney laughed—more of a cackle really. Once she would have walked on water to "fix" any of this man's problems. "I'm not interested in fixing a damn thing."

Whitney dipped under the water and swam to the shallow end where she could walk out. She surfaced, stood up, flung her head back and swept her wet hair out of her eyes. Ryan had beaten her to the shallow end. He stood there pointing a gun fitted with a silencer at her.

It took a second to absorb what she was seeing. Where had he gotten the gun? He'd never had one when they'd been together. He didn't know how to use it, did he? Doubts clouded her thoughts. The gambling. There was a lot about this man she'd never known. Often the craziest people appeared sane, she reminded herself.

"This can go one of two ways," Ryan said with unexpected savagery. "You can swim until you're too exhausted to take another stroke…and drown…or I can shoot you."

This had to be a sick prank, didn't it? That hope flared, then died when she assessed the hatred gleaming in Ryan's eyes and noted the deadly weapon in his hand. This was no joke. "Why?" she managed to ask. "I had no idea Ashley had left me those clothes. It was just an accident that I was wearing the dress—"

"Shut up. Leave Ashley out of this." He waved the gun and the blue metal caught the light. "Start swimming or I'll shoot."

"If I'm going to die, I have a right to know the reason."

For an instant, his eyes squeezed shut, then opened. He gazed at her as if seeing her for the very first time. "My, ah…friends tried to get rid of you. But you weren't home when you should have been. All the pipe bomb did was start a fire."

Her lower lip trembled as his words registered. Oh my God! They'd been after her—not Miranda. Whitney hadn't quite accepted Adam's explanation that Calvin Hunter had given the terrorists a fake disc. She assumed that believing they had the real one, they'd tried to kill Miranda. Now she knew why that scenario didn't make sense. And she realized why she'd been so panicky. Her sixth sense kept warning that she was in danger.

"Why would they want to kill me? I never harmed anyone."

"No, but you can be very clever when necessary. You climbed that fence in the nick of time, didn't you?"

His attempt at a laugh raised every hair on her body. A thousand thoughts whirlpooled through her brain as she realized that she'd come close to death twice already. This time might be the end—if she didn't keep her wits and turn the tables somehow. *Don't panic, don't freeze up. Not now.*

Adam's face appeared in her mind. Suddenly, she felt silly for putting up such a fuss over things he hadn't told her. He'd believed her, taken so much on faith even though he'd just met her. If she hadn't suffered through so many lies with Ryan, she might have been more understanding. Now she might never have the chance to tell Adam she loved him.

"I'll stay out of your life, Ryan. I swear I will."

"If you'd signed the property agreement, you would have been history and none of this would have happened."

Was this about the property settlement? He must owe a lot more money than Rod Babcock had told her. "I'll sign tomorrow when my lawyer returns. He has the papers."

"No, you won't. Babcock already called me. He knows the truth." Ryan shifted the gun from one hand to the other and back. "There's no toxic landfill. There never was. That land might as well have oil underneath it."

"What do you mean?" *Stay calm,* she reminded herself. *And think.*

"It's not far from the Indians' casino. They're expanding, putting in a bigger hotel and a second casino that will dwarf every other casino in the state. With you gone, the land belongs to me."

You're a fool, she silently raged at herself. Why hadn't she changed her will? How stupid could she be? "I'll sign it over to you."

"Too late. At the end of this week, the proposal comes up for approval by the county commission. The Indians need to have all the deeds in order. Your hotshot lawyer will talk you out of signing unless I promise you a bundle of money." He pointed the gun directly at her head. "This changes everything."

"You'll never get away with it. The police will know—"

"An accidental drowning? I don't think so."

"Then I'm not swimming. You'll have to shoot me."

"Suit yourself. It'll look like a burglar killed you."

"No, it won't." The soft voice cracked out of the darkness behind Ryan.

He spun around. "Ashley, what are you doing here?"

Well, this beats all, Whitney decided in frantic amazement. The situation could *not* become weirder. She watched the two of them stare at each other. Whitney couldn't just stand in waist-deep water. Already her legs were spongy, ready to give out.

Her first instinct was to bolt, to lunge through the water, legs splashing, arms flailing as she prayed for good luck. She'd read somewhere that even the most highly trained sharpshooter had less than a fifty-fifty chance of hitting someone who was running in an erratic zig-zag pattern. She bet guns were new to Ryan. Except at point-blank range, he probably couldn't hit her.

Ashley hadn't responded to Ryan's question. After a moment's silence, he asked, "Where have you been?"

There was a desperate note in his voice, Whitney decided, almost a pleading tone. She realized he loved this woman in a way that he'd never loved her. Not that she cared, but she might be able to exploit the situation to save herself. She edged closer to the steps out of the pool, taking care not to disturb the water and call attention to her movements.

"I went to Bakersfield to see my father." A look of pure anguish washed over Ashley's face, then vanished so quickly that Whitney wondered if she'd imagined it. "He agreed to give me every cent he had to help us get out of debt. I also personally went to Domenic Coriz, but he didn't want money. He wants the land."

"Ashley, honey, get back in your car," Ryan responded in the unemotional tone of a therapist. "I'll explain it to you later."

"Don't treat me like a child! I've been following you. I overheard you threaten Whitney. I know what you're up to."

"I just want the best for both of us." His calm tone unnerved Whitney even more. He'd gone ballistic before; now he was psycho.

"Killing an innocent woman won't end your problems. You're addicted to gambling."

Whitney sidled nearer to the steps. Ryan hadn't turned away from her, but his attention was focused on Ashley. If only she could get out of the pool.

Ryan cleared his throat, then gave Ashley a small, anxious grin. "I'll get help tomorrow. I promise I will. Just wait in the car for me. Okay?"

"No."

Ryan blinked and hesitated before saying, "Look, if you'll just wait in the car for me, I swear I won't hurt Whitney. We just need to have a little talk."

Whitney's toe bumped the first of two—or was it three? —steps out of the pool. Ryan's smile expired when Ashley didn't budge.

"Liar! I'm not letting you hurt Whitney."

Without warning, Ashley lunged for Ryan's arm in an

attempt to knock the gun out of his hand. Ohmygod! At this close range, Ryan might kill her. Not taking a second to think, Whitney hurtled out of the pool and flung herself at them as they struggled over the gun. She saw her own hand lash out in a desperate grab for the weapon.

Face contorted, Ryan fought them with manic savagery. He was taller than both of them and had them outweighed. He still had control of the gun.

Whitney pounced on him, clinging to him with both arms and legs the way a drowning person would. She had a split second to decide what to do so she bit the exposed part of his neck.

Pop!

Something sounded like a firecracker, she realized. Swirling colored stars burst behind her eyes. Then darkness obliterated the bright lights.

CHAPTER THIRTY-EIGHT

ADAM WAS READING the note on the front door when he heard a scream. Gathering all his strength, he charged into the door, shoulder first. It hadn't been properly closed and burst open. He crashed into the entry, off balance, and stumbled sideways. He regained his footing, then raced through the crypt-dark house. He rounded the corner into a large room. Beyond it he saw a pool area.

Another muffled shout echoed through the dark night. He charged out the open sliding glass door and saw Whitney sprawled beside the pool. He sprinted to where Ashley Fordham was standing over Ryan, a gun in her hand.

What in hell was going on here?

"I've killed him. I've killed him." Like a robot, Ashley jerkily turned to Adam and offered him the gun.

Adam tugged his shirt out of his pants. Careful not to leave fingerprints, he used the cloth to glove his hand and grabbed the gun. He dropped it on a nearby table. Had Ashley shot both Ryan and Whitney? He yanked off his belt and grabbed Ashley, binding both her wrists.

"No. Stop," she cried. "I was trying to save Whitney. Honest."

"Yeah, right." He shoved her aside. "You expect me to believe that? You stole her dog." He had a thousand questions for her, but right now all that mattered was Whitney.

She lay crumpled on the pool deck, bleeding. In Iraq his

closest friends' blood had been splattered all over him, and Adam had nearly died. That was nothing compared to the way his gut twisted at the sight of Whitney's blood.

Next to her, Ryan Fordham lay flat on his back, blood gushing from a wound in his chest. His flat, unseeing eyes told Adam the man was dead.

"Whitney, Whitney." He dropped to his knees and felt for a pulse. By some miracle she was still alive, but blood was seeping from a shot just above her waist. He prayed it hadn't hit any vital organs.

"Ryan shot her," cried Ashley. "I had to stop him before he fired again."

With trembling fingers, Adam pulled his cell phone out of his pocket and dialed 911. Somehow he managed to give them the address and order an ambulance on the double.

"Hang in there, sweetheart," he told Whitney as he examined the wound. He was afraid to move her in case it caused more bleeding. He applied pressure above the wound.

Jasper and Lexi circled the two bodies. One look told him the dogs had no clue how serious this was. "Get out of the way!" he yelled at them. Both dogs cowered. "Sit. Sit. Stay," he said in a calmer voice.

He barely heard Ashley babbling about what happened. The gambling debt. The supposedly toxic land that was so valuable. Something about her long-lost father and money.

Adam didn't give a rat's ass. All that mattered was saving Whitney. He heard the wails of an ambulance and police cars coming closer and closer.

"Hurry, hurry," he heard himself plead. He tried to think over the pulse thrumming in his temples, but there was nothing he could do except wait and pray. Her body was pathetically still, nearly lifeless, all color leached from her beautiful face.

"Aaah, aaahhh," Whitney moaned, her eyes still closed.

"I love you, Whitney," he said even though now was not the time to say it. He might never have another chance.

"A-a-ah-adam." Whitney's eyelids fluttered, then opened so slightly that he doubted she could see him.

"Shh. Don't try to talk."

"Ja-ja-jasper...ch-chip...neck." Suddenly her eyes snapped shut.

"WE HEARD ABOUT IT ON television," Holly told Adam. "We came right away. We knew you'd need us."

All Adam could do was nod at Tyler and Holly. He wouldn't need anybody or anything if Whitney didn't survive.

They were sitting in the surgery waiting room. It had been more than two hours since the ambulance had sped away with Whitney. She'd been rushed immediately into surgery. A nurse had come out with one update: Whitney was still alive. The seconds had ticked by like days.

"I'm here. I'm here," announced Trish Bowrather as she rushed into the waiting room with Rod Babcock. "Is she—"

"We don't know anything yet," Tyler told them when Adam couldn't speak.

"What happened?" asked the attorney.

There was a long silence, then Adam heard himself begin to talk. "According to Ashley Fordham, Ryan tried to kill Whitney."

"Lord have mercy. I warned her," cried Trish, turning to Rod. The lawyer put his arm around her and pulled Trish close. "I warned Whitney, but she wouldn't listen."

"On TV they said Ryan Fordham had been shot and killed," Tyler told everyone. "The police have arrested Ashley Fordham."

Adam slowly nodded. "I guess Ashley killed him. There was a scuffle or something. I don't know the details."

"Whitney wasn't able to tell you anything?" asked Holly.

"No. She only rallied for a moment." He turned to Trish.

"All she could think about was the dogs. She was worried about Jasper."

"Just like Whitney," Trish replied, then hesitated a moment. "She didn't mention Lexi? That's strange."

"She could barely utter a syllable," Adam told her. He lovingly recalled her last words. Jasper, chip, neck.

Holy shit!

She'd been trying to tell him something.

WHITNEY STRAINED TO LIFT HEAVY eyelids crusted with sand. Light. She finally glimpsed a single ray of light, but she seemed to be looking at the world through gauze.

"Whitney," someone called to her from very far away.

Adam hovered over her with his arm around…Miranda. Whitney tried to speak but her parched tongue could barely move. A white-hot bolt of pain lanced up her side, as if someone were twisting a shard of glass.

Where was she? What had happened? She struggled to remember. She saw the bank of frightening-looking machines with tubes attached to her body.

"Can you hear me, sweetheart?" Adam asked, his hand on her shoulder.

She parted her lips to respond. In a flash the room morphed into darkness and she was scrambling out of the pool again. Ryan was going to shoot Ashley if she didn't do something—fast. In freeze-frames her brain replayed the struggle over the gun.

"A-ash…ley?" she managed to say through a miasma of pain and confusion.

"She's all right," Adam assured her. "She got the gun away from Ryan and shot him." There was a change in the pressure of his hand on her shoulder. "He's dead."

Ryan—dead? Her muddled brain was too traumatized to process the information. The light slowly seeped away until she was all alone in the dark again.

"Whitney...Whitney."

The myriad machines twisted and garbled her name. She thought she heard it again but couldn't be sure. She seemed to be floating high above the earth on clouds like feather beds. She willed her eyes to open and they reluctantly obeyed. She sensed time had passed. It could have been minutes, hours or even days.

The room was dark now, the only light glowing from the armada of machines that gurgled and beeped. In the next breath, she realized the drip-drip-drip she heard was an IV pumping life-giving fluids into her body. Woozy, she struggled to remember what had happened to her.

A face emerged from the shadows. "Hey, are you awake?"

"Adam?" She realized her left side ached so much she could barely speak. "Don't leave me."

"I won't." He brushed his lips to her forehead. "I love you. I haven't left your side."

"You love me?" she found the strength to whisper.

"You bet I love you." He bent over and gently kissed her cheek. "I should have told you before—before I came damn close to losing you."

Those all important words—*I love you*—made her giddily happy despite the pain. The knowledge made her aware of the fracture deep in her soul. This man had touched her in a way no one else ever had. He made her accept how much she longed for love and trust.

When she'd been in the pool and realized Ryan had gone berserk, she'd fervently wished she'd told Adam how she felt. Now she had a second chance.

"I love you, too."

"You had me scared to death. I thought I was going to lose you."

She mustered the strength to give him a little smile. Memories eclipsed by drugs and pain slowly floated to the surface as the blurry watercolor softness of drugs lifted a little. "Ashley's all right? Did you tell me that or did I dream it?"

His warm hand cradled hers. "You didn't dream it. Ashley went home with her father to Bakersfield. At first, the police arrested her, thinking she'd shot both of you in some lovers' triangle."

"Oh, no. She—"

"I know, I know. She was trying to help you. The police corroborated Ashley's story very quickly. Forensics confirmed Ryan had fired the gun. After he shot you, Ashley grabbed the gun and killed him. The police know it was self-defense."

"Ryan was a very sick man. I never realized."

"Neither did Ashley."

"I...feel bad for her. She could have run away or something but she returned and tried to save me."

"Don't worry about her. I'm sure she'll be upset for a while but she's reunited with her father. And Preston Block cares about her—a lot. She won't be alone. I'm positive she's going to be fine."

"I hope so." Whitney tried to capture an elusive memory, but the drugs slowed her thought process. She stared at a framed travel poster of Venice on the wall. Adam offered her some water, and she took it. The thought resurfaced as she swallowed. "Ryan's friends threw the pipe bomb. The car—"

"We know. Ashley gave us Domenic Coriz's name. He's stonewalling but one of his men admits throwing the pipe bomb and driving the car. It was all about the land you and Ryan owned."

She listened, ignoring the persistent ache in her side. Another thought exploded in her brain. How could she have forgotten? "Jasper! His chip."

"I know. You told me."

"I did?" She couldn't recall telling him about her discovery.

"Yes. You came to for just long enough to tell me before

the ambulance arrived." He kissed her cheek, and she looked into those blue-blue eyes she loved so much. "I thought it might be the last thing you ever said. You've really had me worried."

"Sorry. I didn't mean to."

"You couldn't help it. You've been very sick."

"What's wrong with me?"

"The gunshot ruptured your spleen. You had massive internal bleeding that was hard to control. You've been here eight days."

"Eight days? How could I have lost track of so much time?" Another thought niggled at her brain. This one surfaced more easily. "What about those men and the disc?"

"Quinten Foley arranged to transfer the info from Jasper's chip and put enough of it on a disc to fool the terrorists."

"Miranda?" She had a muddled impression of seeing Miranda hovering over her with Adam. How many days ago had that been?

"I called Miranda while you were in surgery. She flew here immediately. She's just stepped out to get coffee. Your cousin is as brave as you are. Wearing a wire, she took the disc and met the terrorists. The wire caught enough on tape to keep them in prison for years."

"Is Miranda in trouble or anything for her part in the arms deals?"

Adam shook his head. "She cooperated fully with the authorities and has given them access to the offshore accounts. They waived any charges."

Whitney closed her eyes for a moment, trying to absorb it all.

"Get some rest," Adam told her.

She snapped open her eyes. "No way. I've been out too long. You solved the case without me."

"Be serious. If you hadn't discovered the chip, the terrorists would never have believed Miranda had the real deal."

"Then it's over, really over. I can begin a new life."

He lovingly studied her face for a moment. "Yes. It's time for act two. You're the star. I know you want to become a vet. I'm with you all the way."

"What about you? I might have to move up north."

"Don't worry about it. I love you. We'll work it out," he told her with a reassuring smile. "I've arranged to let Tyler buy me out over time. I'm not really interested in the business he's developed. I've always thought computer security is the wave of the future. After this chip thing, I'm sure I'm right."

All that truly registered in Whitney's brain was *I love you.* That was what really mattered to her. She'd taken a wrong turn, but now she was finally on the right path. "Adam, I couldn't love you more."

He squeezed her hand. "I think we should take some time for ourselves. To really get to know each other, Let's drive up North with the dogs and—"

"Oh my gosh. Is Lexi all right? How's Jasper?"

He kissed her cheek, his lips warm against her skin. "They're fine. Lexi sleeps curled around Jasper. They've taken over the bed. We're going to play hell getting any space for ourselves."

Whitney giggled, then smiled up at Adam. "It's okay. We'll figure something out." What really counted, she knew, was that they were together.

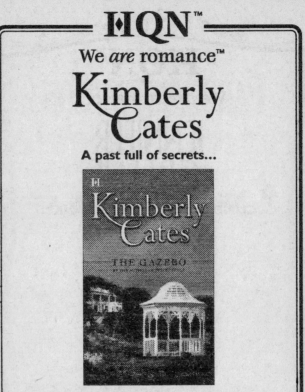

REQUEST YOUR FREE BOOKS!

2 FREE NOVELS FROM THE ROMANCE/SUSPENSE COLLECTION PLUS 2 FREE GIFTS!

YES! Please send me 2 FREE novels from the Romance/Suspense Collection and my 2 FREE gifts. After receiving them, if I don't wish to receive any more books, I can return the shipping statement marked "cancel." If I don't cancel, I will receive 4 brand-new novels every month and be billed just $5.49 per book in the U.S., or $5.99 per book in Canada, plus 25¢ shipping and handling per book plus applicable taxes, if any*. That's a savings of at least 20% off the cover price! I understand that accepting the 2 free books and gifts places me under no obligation to buy anything. I can always return a shipment and cancel at any time. Even if I never buy another book from the Reader Service, the two free books and gifts are mine to keep forever.

185 MDN EF5Y   385 MDN EF6C

Name _____ (PLEASE PRINT) _____

Address _____ Apt. # _____

City _____ State/Prov. _____ Zip/Postal Code _____

Signature (if under 18, a parent or guardian must sign)

Mail to **The Reader Service:**
IN U.S.A.: P.O. Box 1867, Buffalo, NY 14240-1867
IN CANADA: P.O. Box 609, Fort Erie, Ontario L2A 5X3

Not valid to current subscribers to the Romance Collection,
the Suspense Collection or the Romance/Suspense Collection.

Want to try two free books from another line?
Call 1-800-873-8635 or visit www.morefreebooks.com.

* Terms and prices subject to change without notice. NY residents add applicable sales tax. Canadian residents will be charged applicable provincial taxes and GST. This offer is limited to one order per household. All orders subject to approval. Credit or debit balances in a customer's account(s) may be offset by any other outstanding balance owed by or to the customer. Please allow 4 to 6 weeks for delivery.

Your Privacy: Harlequin is committed to protecting your privacy. Our Privacy Policy is available online at www.eHarlequin.com or upon request from the Reader Service. From time to time we make our lists of customers available to reputable firms who may have a product or service of interest to you. If you would prefer we not share your name and address, please check here. ☐

BOB07